COLLISION
C O U R S E

sequel to 'Course Correction'

DOUGLAS MORRISON

COLLISION
COURSE

sequel to 'Course Correction'

DOUGLAS MORRISON

Stonehouse Publishing
www.stonehousepublishing.ca
Alberta, Canada

Copyright © 2019, by Douglas Morrison
All rights reserved. No part of this publication may be used without prior written consent of the publisher.

Stonehouse Publishing Inc. is an independent publishing house, incorporated in 2014.

Cover design and layout by Janet King
Printed in Canada

National Library of Canada Cataloguing in Publication Data
Morrison, Doug
Collision Course
Novel

To all those who read *Course Correction* and asked me 'what happened next?', here is the answer. I want to thank all of you for your interest, support, and encouragement. You make all those hours spent writing and rewriting more than worth it!

PROLOGUE

Michael Barrett attempted, and failed, to stifle a yawn as he rolled down his car window to let in some of the cool, midnight air. As refreshing as the air was, he found himself missing the smell of the ocean; he'd become used to the smell of fresh salt air after the last two weeks. Breathing in the air helped to clear his head a bit, but his jet-lagged mind was too tired to notice that the car behind him had been following him since he'd left the airport.

The brief stop at the red light was a welcome reprieve from having to concentrate on driving. He really should have been more impatient to get home, but that would have required too much effort. They never did mention on travel agency websites just how exhausting international travel could be.

The light changed and he pulled into the intersection, relieved to know that he was now only minutes from home. Since last sleeping he'd flown close to a third of the way around the globe and despite his best intentions he had been unable to sleep on the way home. A quick calculation of the time zones told him it was already breakfast time in Greece, which is where he had spent the last two weeks.

The trip had been free, he thought with a half-smile, or at least it hadn't cost him anything this time. As a show of goodwill, the airline had covered the airfare, as well as providing some spending money, while the hotel had provided the room and all his meals in addition to local travel and attractions. In actual fact he had paid for it himself more than a year ago when he'd originally planned the trip, but it hadn't exactly worked out as he'd hoped the first time around. He had come to the realization that he would always think back on that first trip with mixed emotions; once again reliving the details in his mind as he approached his apartment building. The final leg of that first trip, the flight from Frankfurt to Athens, had taken a shocking turn when the flight had been hijacked to Kiev, Ukraine. That turned out to be just the beginning of an adventure that, rather ironically, saw him teaming up with the person responsible for causing the hijacking. The whole thing had been planned to bring about Dmitri's return to Ukraine. Dmitri had been attempting to flee the country with a large sum of money he had taken from his boss, Yuri Stepanovich, and Yuri had ordered the hijacking to get back both Dmitri and the missing funds.

As he manoeuvred into his parking space his thoughts turned to Dmitri who had somehow, through the whole misadventure, become a friend. Maybe it was simply that together they had survived the whole ordeal. Or maybe it was because Dmitri had passed up a perfect opportunity to flee the country and save himself when Michael had been captured by Yuri's men. He shivered involuntarily and rubbed his rib cage as he recalled the threats and the beatings he'd endured during his captivity. They'd pumped him viciously for information on Dmitri's plans and whereabouts. He'd often wondered if he would have told them Dmitri's plans in order to save himself. He couldn't have told them anything even if he'd wanted to because he really had known nothing at all about Dmitri's whereabouts or where he'd hidden the money. He couldn't pretend, not even to himself, that he'd been bravely refusing to give them any information. Dmitri had been willing to sacrifice himself for Michael, but would he have done the same for Dmitri?

In the end they had parted ways very abruptly. Dmitri and his girlfriend Youlya had dropped him off at the Canadian embassy in Bucharest, Romania, and driven off before they could be questioned about their involvement in his sudden reappearance and what had happened after the hijacking. They hadn't even had a chance to say a real goodbye. He'd watched the news carefully, and even done some internet searches, but he'd never been able to learn anything about what had become of them.

During his stay in Greece he'd often caught himself looking north, in the general direction of Ukraine, wondering how they were doing. He wondered what had become of Andrei and Katya, the couple who'd taken them into their home and sheltered them for a few days, and their pastor, and the young man who had planned to drive them to the border. Try as he might, he couldn't remember the man's name. He even found himself wondering about Vasili and the other Mafia enforcers who'd been chasing them. Were they still trying to find Dmitri? Had they found him and is that why he'd never heard anything of Dmitri? He sure hoped not.

His time there had been anything but a holiday, yet he still had a strange feeling whenever he thought about Ukraine. He had felt a warped sort of homesickness to find himself once again so close to where it had all happened. In its own twisted way, his time there had been one of the highlights of his life.

He'd found that he'd become a minor celebrity in Canada even before returning home. While that status had only lasted a few days, he often wondered if perhaps that was another reason he'd never heard from Dmitri. His mysterious disappearance in Ukraine, followed by his sudden reappearance in Bucharest, had been an international story; was it possible that Dmitri thought someone was watching him, hoping that Michael could lead them to Dmitri and the money? Even if he hadn't made such a splash in the news, the Ukrainian mafia still had his original passport which had been left on the hijacked plane upon his arrival. They would know where to find him if they wanted to badly enough, and if he knew where

Dmitri was they'd do their best to get it out of him. *Maybe it was better that he didn't know after all* he concluded with a sigh.

Perhaps Dmitri felt he was protecting Michael by remaining in hiding, but if Vasili and his men decided to track down Michael to find out what he knew, they weren't likely to believe him if he told them the truth: that he didn't know anything. They certainly hadn't believed him on that night last July in the basement of a house owned by another member of the Mafia, Anton. For months after returning home he'd found himself watching the crowds around him, wondering if someone was watching or following him. He'd found himself watching the mirrors in his car wherever he drove, his heart beating faster whenever the same car stayed behind him for more than a few blocks.

A year had passed since then, and he'd finally come to the conclusion that Anton and Vasili had no intention of using him to get to Dmitri after all. Surely they would have tried something by now. The whole affair was finally behind him.

* * *

The man in the passenger seat looked at the driver. "They watched him the whole time he was in Greece and he never made contact with Dmitri. We should let them know that he's arrived home now." It was already morning back in Ukraine, so despite the late hour in Canada, the driver pulled out his phone and made the call.

"This is pointless," the driver muttered. "If they didn't make contact in Greece, why would they make contact here? They should just forget it and let us go back home."

"You want to go home?" The passenger made a face as he waited for the call to connect. "I'd rather stay here."

It took a little longer than usual for the international call to go through, but finally he heard Vasili's greeting on the other end.

"Vasili, it's Tolia. He's home and he is still alone." He rolled his eyes at the driver as if to say, 'Vasili must think we are idiots.' "No, Vasili, no one met him at the airport, we watched him from the time he disembarked until now." The tone of his voice left no doubt as to how pointless he felt this whole operation was, and it was only partially from boredom. It was also his way of telling his boss they hadn't failed in their mission, that there really was nothing to learn from the Canadian. With Vasili, you always had to find a way to protect yourself whenever things didn't turn out the way he wanted them to.

"Very well, Tolia, continue to watch him. Let me know if anything else happens." Tolia blinked at the response and his face twisted into a puzzled look as he ended the call. He'd expected a mini-tirade when he'd had nothing solid to report, or at least some snide comments about how it was their fault that their surveillance had produced no results. Not that he should complain, of course, but it was a bit unnerving when the boss didn't act the way he was supposed to.

* * *

Vasili set his phone aside and turned back to his coffee. He'd developed a taste, and even a need for it, even though most of his fellow countrymen favoured tea. Despite the lack of results from Canada, he smiled to himself as he savoured the taste of the coffee and the effects of the caffeine. He had fully expected Michael to make contact with Dmitri while in Europe, and was still somewhat surprised that he hadn't. But even if that confused him somewhat, it didn't disappoint him. Perhaps that meant he knew more than Michael did, because he knew that Dmitri had attempted to contact Michael. Very recently.

* * *

As Vasili sipped his coffee and stared out the window while contemplating this new development, Michael was manhandling his suitcases through the door to his apartment. For now he satisfied himself with rolling them into the living room and then abandoning them there. He hadn't bothered to pick up the mail from the box in the lobby, though it was probably overflowing, and he wasn't going to bother checking for voicemail until tomorrow morning. Any messages could well be from as far back as the day he'd left, and if they were that old, a few more hours wouldn't make any difference. He didn't have to go to work the next day, so he'd use tomorrow to get caught up on messages and errands he promised himself, although he wasn't sure if he would bother keeping that promise.

That left the suitcases to deal with. What was inside them could be broken down into two categories: dirty laundry and souvenirs. Nothing that couldn't wait for morning he decided. For that matter, it could wait for tomorrow afternoon. He felt relieved at reaching that conclusion, and stumbled down the hallway to his bedroom. The only thing left to worry about tonight was whether or not he'd bother pulling back the covers before collapsing into bed. It was nice to have his life back.

* * *

Dmitri sighed into the silence of a room that had become much too quiet. He'd have to get used to that, wouldn't he? Though at that moment, he couldn't have said for sure whether the sigh was one of sadness, or relief.

It was several hours later in the day here than it was in Canada, but he still lay sleepless in bed, the open window allowing the cool night breeze to waft through his window. The moonlight silhouetted the swaying palm trees, and if he had sat up in bed, he could have watched the unceasing motion of the waves lapping against the beach. As peaceful as the night was, Dmitri was restless, and very worried. Why hadn't Mikhail responded to him? Was something seriously wrong? Was the Canadian mad at him, or was he simply trying to put their whole past behind him?

He didn't dare attempt direct contact, but he'd been certain that his message would have resulted in a reply of some sort. He sighed again and slid his laptop aside, deciding to make another effort at sleep. Hopefully a new day would bring news from Mikhail.

* * *

Youlya raised her seat to the upright position and looked down at the bag stowed beneath the seat in front of her. She'd kept one foot on it throughout the flight and had made sure to take it with her to the lavatory each time the trip had been necessary. Out the window she could see the once familiar, yet now somehow alien-looking fields and villages of her home country. It was as if she was seeing her own Ukraine through the eyes of a foreigner.

It felt strange yet comforting to be coming home; she'd never expected to be here ever again, and had once thought it too dangerous to even consider. She also felt torn and a bit guilty, even if she wouldn't admit it, not even to herself. She wondered if Ukraine would ever feel like home again; or for that matter, if anywhere could ever feel like home.

She had grown homesick, but that was only part of what made her risk returning home. The rest of it was Dmitri's fault. She kicked the bag softly, just to make sure it was still there, and pressed her face once more to the window. They were over Kiev now and she wanted very much to feel excited to be back, but she just couldn't quite muster that emotion. It had to be the jetlag, she told herself; she'd feel excited after a proper rest.

She looked down at the bag again. *Well, if being home again could not give her what she needed, she did have the contents of that bag.* She now had the resources to do whatever it took to find the happiness she deserved.

Chapter One

Michael didn't really wake up, he just gradually stopped sleeping. After a few blinks he decided the emptiness in his stomach was more irritating than the fatigue-induced headache, so he flipped the blankets back and rose reluctantly from the bed. He flicked on the television to catch up on some Canadian news as he foraged in his cupboards for something to eat. Everything perishable was long gone, but a loaf of bread in the freezer and some of his grandma's home-made jam would sustain him until he could get to the grocery store.

There wasn't anything earth-shattering on the news, so he gathered up a basket of dirty clothes and made his way down to the laundry room to get the first of several loads started. He checked the mail on the way back up to his apartment and decided to pay a few bills before tackling anything else. He switched on his laptop, opening and organizing the bills while waiting for it to boot and connect to the internet.

After logging into his bank, he grabbed the first bill, and glanced at his balance to make sure his cheque had been deposited. His heart skipped a beat and he dropped the bill to the floor. He tried to push the panic aside for a moment, and then double checked his name and account information at the top of the page. Surely he'd somehow logged into the wrong account? *If he logged out quickly it would be okay, no one would know.* It could hardly be his fault if someone else's log in information was so close to his.

He read the name on top of the page three times. *Could there be another Michael Barrett?* His fingers were shaking as he clicked to another page to check the contact information. It was his account, all right, but there had to be a mistake. A big one. He scrolled back in the account history until he saw a few transactions he recognized; some bills paid the night before he had left. Right after that was the source of the problem; a deposit in the amount of one million American dollars, converted to its Canadian equivalent.

It's a mistake, that's all. Funny that the bank had not caught and corrected it; someone, somewhere, was missing a lot of money and he had it. He had to laugh at that thought. Last summer he'd been in a lot of trouble because someone thought he had their money, and now he really did. A quick call to the bank would clear it all up.

A quick call to the bank was hard to make, however, and he had to fight his way through several levels of pre-recorded menus before the machine finally decided he wasn't going to be happy until he was speaking to a real live person. He was rewarded with a friendly greeting when that finally happened.

"Hi, this is Michael Barrett. I've been on holidays for the last couple of weeks and there seems to be a problem with my bank account."

"Oh, no! We'll need you to come down to the branch as soon as possible so that you can show us what transactions you think are fraudulent. It will all have to be confirmed, of course, but if we can prove you didn't make the withdrawals …"

"Everything is fine with the withdrawals. I'm looking at them now and they're all mine. The problem is someone put some money into my account by accident. A million dollars, would you believe it?" He had to laugh at the thought to keep from panicking.

The teller was laughing politely too. "Well, that's not a complaint we hear too often. It would be best if you could come down to the branch with some identification so we can confirm who you are. I'm sure we can get this all straightened out." Michael could imagine the smile on her face, as well as hear the relief in her voice at the realization that she wasn't going to get an earful from an angry customer. He'd be there right away, he assured her.

* * *

Getting paid to sit in a car sounds like easy money, until you try it. Fewer things could be more mind-numbing as far as the two Ukrainians were concerned; they couldn't even find a radio station broadcasting in their language. Only the passenger was really paying attention when Michael's car came out of the parking garage. He nudged the driver, who stowed his phone, and started the engine. Fortunately, traffic was light and they were able to pull onto the street a safe distance behind Michael, easily following him on his drive across town. They watched as he pulled into a parking lot beside a bank and managed to find a spot on the street from where they could watch both his car and the door to the bank through which he was now walking.

* * *

Elisabeth, or Liz as her name tag proclaimed, had worked at the bank for close to twenty years, long enough that she considered it *her* branch. Almost a year ago, when Michael's name had first made the news, he had been a complete non-entity to her; he was simply one of hundreds of customers at her bank, and not one of the important ones either. After his story had been splashed across the local papers, she'd come to know him somewhat, and in their few dealings had come to think of him as a pleasant young man. It had come as a shock to her when she'd been approached by a man with a foreign accent who presented documents indicating that Mr. Barrett was under investigation for illegal activities which included international money laundering; he'd been involved in planning the hijacking, and his mysterious disappearance had been orchestrated to cover his real activities.

The news stories were rather sketchy about what exactly Michael had done in the time he'd been missing, though there been some vague references to the Ukrainian Mafia, so it had all sounded very plausible when she'd been told by Igor that Michael had long-standing ties to organized crime both at home and in Europe. Not only that, but it was possible he was using *her* bank to funnel funds from illegal activities into Canada, with the knowledge and help of the branch manager himself.

That had made her very angry at first, but upon further reflection, it had given her a sense of satisfaction to know that the manager, with whom she'd never been on good terms, was a white-collar criminal. One involved with the Mafia, at that! As she'd reflected on these facts, she had glanced out into the parking lot, scowling as she spotted the manager's shiny, new car. No wonder he was always driving the latest model; he was financing his lifestyle with mob money. Something had to be done about him and that Michael Barrett character!

Thankfully she'd been able to set that ball in motion herself. Igor had told her to tell no one else since it was hard to know who else in the bank might be involved in the scheme. All she needed to do was to keep an eye on his account for any unusual activity. She was to do nothing but phone him if she noticed anything. After months of seeing nothing but regular paycheques and normal bills, she'd seen it! A seven-figure deposit from overseas! Michael had finally slipped up. Perhaps it was supposed to go into another account, but there it was. She'd felt almost dizzy with glee when she'd seen it, then had backed quickly out of the account before anyone could see what she was doing. She had, of course, informed Igor immediately and after being congratulated for her vigilance, she'd been told to let him know when Michael next came into the bank. No mention of the promised reward had been made, but maybe they were waiting until they could recover the funds? Of course, that must be it.

Today, as she served a never-ending line of customers, she finally spotted him. Michael Barrett. In the flesh! She felt a rush of anger and excitement as he spoke with the receptionist and then took a seat, waiting for an appointment with the manager, Mr. Simms, no doubt. What she wouldn't give to be able to listen in on that conversation. She put up the little sign advising the next customer in line that he was to please wait for the next available teller, then excused herself to make an important phone call. Liz's fingers were shaking with excitement as she placed the call from her cell phone in the break room. The phone rang several times before the lightly-accented voice answered.

"Hello?"

"He's here! Michael Barrett is in the bank. He has an appointment with the manager. They must be planning to move the funds I told you about!"

"Good. Make sure you do nothing and say nothing. We will take it from here. I'll be in touch soon." He broke the connection.

She might not have been surprised to learn that the man on the other end of the phone was sitting in a car outside the bank at that very minute, nor that he'd been following Michael since his arrival back in Canada the previous night. She would have been surprised, however, to learn that after all her months of diligent surveillance, that this was the last contact she'd ever have with Igor. None of her subsequent calls would ever be answered or returned.

For now, however, there was a spring in her step and a smile on her face as she returned to work. Just knowing that Michael and Mr. Simms would pay for their illegal activities was all the satisfaction she needed. Well, almost all. There was still the matter of the reward Igor had promised her. True, she'd broken some confidentiality rules in disclosing the details of the transfer to Igor, but he was a government official investigating organized crime. Yes, she'd almost have done it just for the satisfaction of knowing that she'd played a part in bringing international criminals to justice. Almost.

* * *

Michael found himself sitting at the bank's boardroom table waiting for the manager, more worried now than he had been when he'd first found the mistake in his account. First the receptionist, alerted to the reason for his visit ahead of time, then the head teller, had informed him that it really was his money. They'd offered no explanation as to its source, but said that the manager needed to talk with him. He'd been ushered into the board room, offered all manner of drinks and refreshments, and had then been left to await the manager's arrival.

As he sat there waiting, he tried to think of some rich relative that might have left him a large sum of money, but there was no one in his family like that. The description on the deposit had been rather vague; he'd been paying more attention to the amount than to its source since he knew that it wasn't his anyway. What had it said? Internet transfer? Online transfer? Wire transfer? Something like that. But no one moved money around on the internet in those amounts in real life, did they? The only person he knew who'd actually done anything like that was Dmitri.

Dmitri!

His thoughts were interrupted as the manager entered the room, smiling and offering him a friendly handshake, as if he were an old and dear friend. Well, maybe any of his clients that had a million dollars of cash on deposit was considered to be an old and dear friend.

"Mr. Barrett, I'm sorry to have kept you waiting. It's a pleasure to finally meet you. I'm Stephen Simms, the branch manager." He took his seat across the table from Michael and leaned back, trying to look casual. "I've been hoping you'd come in so that we can discuss what do to with your funds. It really is a waste to leave them in your chequing account, so let's look at some options." He pulled out a shiny folder emblazoned with the bank's logo, something he obviously had ready for just such an occasion. "Now, we have a wide variety of investment options, from the very conservative to others which carry a little more risk, but of course with the risk comes the opportunity for greater returns. You have enough that we can easily diversify your portfolio, which will allow us ..."

"Whoa! One minute! I don't even know if this is my money. I have no idea where it came from. Before I start spending … "

"Investing," the manager corrected him gently, with a wise, friendly smile that also came across as somewhat condescending.

"Whatever!" The irritation was obvious in his voice, more obvious than he'd meant it to be, but maybe he could blame that on the jetlag. "Before anything happens, I want to know who put that money in my account!"

The smile on his face was forced now. "Of course, Mr. Barrett. I assumed that you were aware of the source of the funds. One minute and I'll see if I can find that out for you." He picked up his phone, giving instructions to some unseen employee, then settled back into his chair. "Would you like something to drink while we wait?"

Feeling a bit foolish, not only for his outburst, but also for the fact that someone had put such a large sum of money into his account without his knowing about it, he declined as politely as possible and pretended to study his investment options until a timid knock at the door announced the arrival of the information.

The teller set several pieces of paper on the desk, and Mr. Simms smoothed them out, studying them as if reacquainting himself with the information they contained. Michael was sure he'd never seen them before. "Yes, well, I'm afraid there is not much I can tell you. The funds were transferred into your account from one of our own branches, in St. Thomas it appears, but that's all I can tell you from the paperwork. There was a message that came with the funds, but that is all. Maybe it means something to you?"

He slid the papers across to Michael, who spun them around so he could read them. Most of what he saw was simply the transfer information between the two branches which meant nothing to him. Then his eyes found the line that contained the message: 'I'm sorry I did not get this to you sooner. I was waiting for the right opportunity.'

"That doesn't mean anything ..." He interrupted himself as he re-read the message, and a single word leaped off the page at him. 'Opportunity'.

"Dmitri," he muttered under his breath.

"Pardon?" Mr. Simms smiled at him quizzically.

"Uh, nothing. Just trying to figure out what all this means." He already knew what it meant. He had a million dollars in his account that belonged to, or at least had been in the possession of, a Ukrainian Mafia boss. It might not be his fault that it was in his account, but how many years in prison was he looking at if he touched it? Wasn't there some law against living off the avails of crime?

He coughed and cleared his throat, giving himself time to form the words. "You need to send it back."

"Send it ...?" Mr. Simms lost his smile, seemingly unable to comprehend the phrase.

"It needs to go back. It's not mine."

"Well, you see, Mr. Barrett, it's not that simple. We know the branch it came from, but not the account. In fact, it may have just come through that branch. It could take some time to return it, assuming of course we can find where it came from in the first place. We can look into it, however. If you are certain it has to go back." The look on his face, and the tone of his voice, formed an unspoken plea to drop the matter and just keep the funds. He was mentally calculating and waving good bye to what he was about to lose in commissions if he didn't invest the funds through his bank.

Michael was only half listening to his words as he re-read the message. There was an email address at the end of the message, one he didn't recognize. He turned the paper around and pointed to the address. "Is this part of the transfer information?"

"No, it's part of the message to you from the sender. I assumed you'd recognize it."

"Can I keep this?" He was folding and pocketing the papers even as he spoke. "I really need to figure this all out before I do anything with the money, okay? I'll get back to you in the next few days. As soon as I know what's going on."

"Of course, happy to be of service, Mr. Barrett," the manager said to his back as he made his way through the door.

Michael didn't stop until he was outside the bank. Without even consciously knowing it, he lapsed back into his old habit of surveying the area around him, noting people and vehicles as he looked up and down the street. His mind was racing, trying to figure out what was going on, not wanting to admit to himself that he already knew. This was Dmitri's way of trying to make up to him for what he had gone through last summer. Maybe he should just keep the money.

Dmitri would never miss it and obviously wanted him to have it. But how illegal was this? Should he talk to a lawyer?

He glanced down at the email once more. He'd try the email address first and see if anything came of it. With one more glance at the vehicles parked around the lot and along the street, he climbed into his car and headed back home. He'd only driven a few blocks before he came up with a better plan. If he sent an email, it could possibly be traced back to him, his computer, and even his apartment. He needed to start thinking the way Dmitri had when they'd been on the run together. Tracks needed to be covered and confused as much as possible. He headed for the local library where an anonymous computer would get him online less conspicuously.

He glanced around as he entered the library, seeing everything around him, but not consciously. He still hadn't fully come to terms with what was going on, and his mind was occupied with trying to figure it all out. Maybe it was the fatigue. Within a minute he was online at a terminal in the back row where no one was likely to be looking over his shoulder. It took several minutes to create a new email account, then it was time to draft an email to the address on the folded piece of paper.

That took a lot longer. He didn't dare come out and say what was happening, or who he was. He needed something short and meaningless to anyone who didn't know exactly what was going on. Something like Dmitri's message. That proved much harder than he thought. Finally, he decided to settle for something simple and straightforward and hoped that Dmitri would know what it meant: 'I received your message. But I can't keep what you sent. I need to send it back to you. Tell me how.'

He hesitated for a moment, wondering if it really was Dmitri, then clicked the send button. He wouldn't feel comfortable checking this email address at home. He'd have to make regular trips to the library until this was all sorted out. It sounded paranoid, but beads of sweat appeared on his brow at the memory of what it had been like to be chased across Ukraine and, even worse, what had happened when they'd caught him. The physical bruises had long since healed, and even the fear had faded somewhat during the past year. But it all came flooding back as he realized that he'd only escaped temporarily. Michael's involvement in Dmitri's escape from his past life was not yet over. Now he would have to escape from his own past as well.

He might have noticed the car and its occupants when he left the library if a small plane hadn't been flying overhead. Watching it soaring overhead momentarily distracted him from his troubled thoughts and he smiled as he imagined what it would be like to be at the controls. As he did, his fingers curled unconsciously as if he were holding the control column himself. He hadn't had a flying lesson since before his trip, and he was almost to the point of doing his first solo cross-country flight. He made a mental note to book his next lesson as soon as he got home. Still peering up at the plane as he opened the door to his car, Michael was completely unaware of the two men watching his every move; and of a second car trailing them.

Chapter Two

Michael looked back over his left shoulder and decided that it wasn't quite time yet. Looking forward through the windshield he grinned into the clear, blue sky; it was a perfect mid-summer Saturday afternoon with just enough of a breeze to take the edge off the heat of the sun. After a couple of days back at work he still wasn't quite over the time change between Canada and Greece, but it was too nice a day to waste it napping or catching up on his laundry, so here he was.

He glanced back again and decided that it looked about right. The end of the runway was about forty-five degrees behind him. A few butterflies stirred in his stomach as he reduced the power to 1500 RPM, then reached for the lever to lower the flaps to 20 degrees. He nodded in satisfaction as the airspeed indicator slowed to indicate exactly 65 knots. He might not be as smooth as his instructor, the plane seemed to be riding a set of rails whenever he flew approaches, but his own flying was definitely improving.

Keeping an eye on the runway he began his turn onto the final approach, unconsciously sitting up a bit straighter, watching his alignment with the runway and making the necessary adjustments to keep the plane on course. The butterflies in his stomach were in full flight as he approached the threshold of the runway, pulled the throttle to idle, and began easing back on the wheel to raise the nose in preparation for landing, not relaxing until the wheels met the runway with a soft, satisfying chirp. When the plane had slowed enough, he let up on the brakes and cracked open the throttle as he taxied towards his parking spot.

With the plane shut down, he gathered up his flight bag and

began making his way across the ramp; but his pace slowed as he spotted a shiny Cessna 182 with retractable landing gear. His feet made a detour towards it. It could be his, he thought, as he peered through the window at the tall, somewhat intimidating control panel. It had all the same basic instruments that his trainer did, plus a whole lot of others that he recognized from his ground school classes. He really could buy it. The money was literally in the bank, and Dmitri was refusing to take it back.

It might be a bit premature to say that Dmitri was refusing, but the short email he'd sent back to Michael had made it clear that as far as he was concerned, the money was Michael's to do with as he pleased; it was the least Dmitri could do for all he'd put Michael through. He hadn't said so in so many words, but the message had been clear enough. He still hadn't decided what to do or what to say to Dmitri because, quite frankly the money, not to mention its source, scared him. Maybe he should keep it, invest some for an early retirement and buy himself a nice shiny airplane with retractable landing gear. That was a real airplane! He allowed himself to entertain that thought as he made his way to the dispatcher's desk. It was just a dream; it wasn't like he was really going to keep the money.

He signed the airplane back in and made the entry for the day's flight in his log book, bringing himself one step closer to being a real pilot. After booking another lesson for the following week, he made his way out to his car. The dashboard looked awfully simple, he mused while fastening his seat belt. As he drove back into town, visions of high-performance airplanes danced in his head.

Once again, he failed to notice the car behind him, but then, in his defence, the two men had swapped their rental car for a white one precisely so he wouldn't.

* * *

Two men were standing in the hallway of his apartment building. He slowed his pace, the hair on the back of his head rising when he saw that they were standing by his door. He stopped in mid-stride, his senses on full alert now, wondering if he should turn and run away, or turn and walk away. Before he could make up his mind, one of the men held up a badge. He couldn't quite see it from that distance, but it froze him in place.

"Mr. Barrett? Sergeant Chambers, RCMP. This is Sergeant Mitchell. Can we have a word with you please?" He nodded at Michael's door. "Inside?"

Time seemed to stand still as Michael considered this request. He didn't bother to ask how they'd got inside the building, wondering instead how they'd learned about the money and asking himself whether they were here to seize it, or to arrest him. He just nodded in response and opened the door, making his way inside with the two officers following. Once inside he hesitated again, before inviting them to have a seat in the small living room.

"Is there a problem of some kind?" *Play innocent* he told himself, *because you are innocent.*

"You are Michael Barrett?" Sargent Chambers asked drawing out a notebook. Michael nodded and he continued. "Are you aware that someone has been following you for the past few days?"

"What? Who's following me?" The colour drained from his face. If he was being followed, he knew exactly who it was, or at least who they worked for.

"Two men flew into Montreal from Munich two weeks ago, and then last week they flew here. We've been watching them because while in Montreal they were seen meeting with someone known to have ties to organized crime." This was all coming out in a very matter-of-fact tone, the officer ignoring the panic in Michael's eyes. "When they arrived here, we were assigned to keep an eye on them to ascertain the reason for their visit. So far all they've done is follow you." He paused and looked at his notes. "When we realized that they were following your car, we traced your plates to find out who they were following." He paused, seeming to notice Michael's expression for the first time. "Sir, do you have any idea who they are or why they might have an interest in you?"

"They are from Ukraine," Michael blurted out, more than a trace of panic in his voice, his fingers gripping the armrest of his chair tightly. "They are working for a guy named Yuri something-or-other; I can't remember the rest of his name."

Sargent Chambers was nodding as he began scribbling down notes. "Who is this Yuri and why is he interested in you?"

"He's with the Ukrainian Mafia, and they think I have a bunch of their money, or at least know where to find it."

The scribbling stopped, and the officer's eyebrows raised in surprise. "I see. Why do they think you can get them their money?" Was it Michael's imagination, or was there a hint of accusation in the tone of his voice?

Michael shook his head vehemently, honestly forgetting for the moment that he knew exactly where some of it was as his mind flashed back to the night in the basement of Anton's house when two Mafia thugs had tried to beat the location of the money out of him. He was back there again, heart racing, a cold sweat breaking out on his forehead as these two officers momentarily became his two assailants. He shook his head to clear his thoughts.

"I can't get the money for them," he finally managed to blurt out. "I mean, I know who has it, but I don't know where he is."

Both Mounties were now sitting up straight, their full attention on Michael's words. "How did you come to obtain this information, and why haven't you reported this to anyone before?" It was a simple question, the accusation of guilt was only implied, but it still hung heavily in the air.

"I did report it. First to the Canadian Embassy in Bucharest, and then I made another full report to the RCMP in Toronto after I got back to Canada last year." The officer's arched eyebrow spurred Michael on. "You can look it up in your files. Last summer, I was on that airliner that got hijacked to Kiev. I got tangled up with a guy named Dmitri; he was ex-Mafia and trying to get out of the country. This Yuri guy thought I was helping him to escape and things got really hairy for a while. Dmitri helped me get out of the country and then he left me at the Embassy in Bucharest and disappeared. I don't know where he is now." By now the officers were both nodding, recalling the news stories of a year ago and putting the pieces together.

They continued to grill Michael with questions, at least it felt that way, and piece by piece he told them most of the story. As he spoke, more and more details and memories of the experience came flooding back. He spoke until they ran out of questions and he had assured them several times over that he couldn't think of anything else that might help them. Only then did they finally rise to leave.

That's when Michael remembered that part of that money was now in his bank account, but as he was debating whether or not to tell that part of the story, Sergeant Chambers turned from the door to address him one last time. "Do you feel that these men pose any immediate danger to you?"

That question forced his thoughts in another direction. "Well, I really don't like the idea of them following me." He wondered if they'd take him into protective custody if he said that they did, and he didn't like that idea any more then he liked being followed by the Mafia. "They might have been watching me for the last year, for all I know. They're likely just waiting for me to make contact with Dmitri, so probably not."

"Do you think that you might be seeing Dmitri anytime soon?"

Another accusation? "I doubt it. His plan was to disappear and so far, it's working."

"If you do feel they are a threat, let us know. In the mean time, we'll be keeping an eye on them. We might even have to pick them up and question them. We will be in touch after we check out the reports you filed." He offered his hand and Michael shook it in silence.

Michael saw them out, made sure that the deadbolt on the door was locked, and then fired up his laptop. Dmitri got him into this mess and now a year later, he was still neck deep in it. Forget anonymous email accounts and public computers, Yuri's men knew where he lived; no sense in trying to keep it a secret any longer.

Angrily he logged into his email account, his fingers punching the keys viciously until Dmitri's latest email appeared on the screen. He clicked reply and started typing.

'Yuri's men are following me. They are probably watching my apartment right now. Call me as soon as possible.'

Adding his phone number to the message, he clicked send, not really sure what Dmitri could do from where ever he was, but he had no one else to turn to right now. Yuri's thugs were at his door and the police thought *he* was the criminal.

* * *

Dmitri sighed in satisfaction as he watched the waves washing the white, sandy beach in front of the hotel. He'd never had the chance to visit the Black Sea when he'd lived in Ukraine, he'd never seen anything bigger than a pond, and so the decision to buy a small hotel on a tropical island had been an easy one to make. A small staff ran it for him so he didn't have to have too much contact with the public. He still kept his guard up, and likely would for years to come, but as he was running the hotel with no debt, it was easy to be an absentee owner. The business didn't need to do much more than break even, and it gave him a beautiful place to live, and just enough work to fill a few hours of his time each day. It also gave him a reason to be living here, as opposed to suddenly appearing on the island as a mysterious, wealthy foreigner, living in a walled estate that would draw attention to itself. It was far better to be known as the new, if somewhat reclusive, owner of the resort.

Youlya had once filled much of his day, he recalled with a different kind of sigh, until she'd become resentful of the money he'd given away, and just as resentful of the money he'd refused to spend lavishly. He had more then he'd ever need, but she had imagined a flashy lifestyle in the west, one with shiny cars, big houses, and every conceivable luxury; everything she'd never had in Ukraine. He'd never been able to make her understand that those things weren't necessary, or that such a conspicuous lifestyle was sure to be noticed. Being noticed was one of the few things she had wanted that he would never be able to afford.

Just now he was returning from a walk along the beach, and after a short chat with the front desk clerk he took one last look at the beach before heading to his own room, which had an even better view of the ocean. Once inside he thought to check email, chuckling as he wondered to himself if Mikhail had emailed him again with another offer to return the money. Even with what Youlya had taken with her, a small fortune itself, he would not miss the sum he'd sent to the Canadian.

His chuckle turned to a laugh when a look at his inbox showed that he did indeed have an email from Canada, but the laughter died as he read the words. His fists balled in anger and for a moment he was once again the rage-filled Mafia enforcer he'd been known as in Ukraine, the man willing to destroy anyone that crossed him. *How dare they go after his friend? Didn't they have the courage to come for him?* Or course they didn't, they were cowards! He should have known they'd resort to this. He had the means to disappear, as well as the desire. Mikhail had wanted to go back to his old life, and that was a mistake. Yuri and Vasili and the others would use any means to get to him. With no plan, but knowing he had to do something, he dialed the number in the email, waiting impatiently for the call to go through. Finally, he heard the ringing on the other end of the line.

"Hello?"

He could not help but smile to hear that familiar voice again. Though Mikhail might not know it, he was the closest thing Dmitri had ever had to a real friend.

"Mikhail! How are you?" His voice was light and cheerful, not just to encourage his friend, but because it really was a good to hear his voice.

"Dmitri?" Any thoughts of friendly greeting or catching up were the last things on Michael's mind at that moment. "I'm just great! Two of your old friends have been following me for the last few days, and the police think I know where all the money is. Things couldn't be better!"

"I'm sorry, Mikhail. I should have known they would not give up. I'm going to help you, I promise."

"How?" The word came out with far more bitterness and sarcasm than Michael intended.

"I'm not sure yet. Give me time to figure something out. I will call you back. Soon."

"Okay, I won't do anything till I hear from you." Dmitri's accent was much lighter, Michael noticed as they spoke, and the Ukrainian's offer to help somewhat weakened his anger, if not his fear. "But hurry!"

"A few hours, Mikhail, I promise. I will call as soon as I can figure something out."

The line went dead and Michael settled back into his chair with a sigh. He felt vaguely guilty about being so abrupt with Dmitri, even if this whole mess was his fault. They had become friends, in a strange kind of way. He'd often wondered what had become of the big Ukrainian and he hadn't even asked how he was. Or where he was. Well, there was time for that later, he reflected bitterly, right now he had a couple of Ukrainian Mafia thugs to worry about.

* * *

It was late evening in Kiev, but there was still light in the western sky as Youlya made her way back to the apartment with an overstuffed shopping bag in each hand. The muggy heat of the day was rapidly disappearing with the setting sun, only to be replaced by a slight chill as the humidity began amplifying the cool of the evening. Reaching her building, she managed to tug the door open without setting down the groceries, and then began making her way up the well-worn concrete steps. The stairwell was poorly lit, but there was enough light to make out the steps and there was little else to see anyway. Her newly-rented flat was on the third story, which made it the second floor, according to the European numbering system, and while it seemed a long climb with a full load of groceries, there was still a spring in her step. She was home. She could read the signs along the streets and in the shop windows, or watch TV or listen to the radio without having to translate everything, and she could speak in her native tongue as well. Dmitri had insisted on speaking nothing but English to help them master the language and better fit into their new home.

There was no ocean view, no sandy beach with palm trees, but she was home. No more living like a pauper when she had access to a fortune. No more watching Dmitri squander their money on charities and people who he claimed needed it more than they did. If she felt a twinge of guilt at what she'd done she still wouldn't acknowledge it. True, Dmitri had masterminded the plan, only pulling her into it when he and Michael needed rescuing. She'd always wanted to believe his claim that he had planned to contact her when he was safely out of the country with the money. But had it not been for her, Michael would be dead and Dmitri might well have died trying to rescue him, so she deserved something. The 'something' was a little over two million dollars she had transferred into two different offshore accounts that only she had access to. She'd learned from Dmitri not to risk having all her wealth in one place. At least that was one thing he'd given her, a knowledge of how to move and hide money. It was her share of the windfall that would allow her to live like a queen in Ukraine.

Once inside her flat, with her new purchases stashed neatly into the small fridge and the cupboards, she turned on the TV and sat down with a cup of tea to catch up on the latest news. A small pang of loneliness gnawed at the edge of her mind. She had no living family that she knew of, and many of her old friends and acquaintances were employed in her former line of work. If she tried to contact any of them, word might get back to the wrong people, and she could not risk that. She changed the channel to a sit-com.

Well, there were millions of people in Kiev. She was sure to make some new friends among them. She could also consider a move somewhere else. Maybe even a vacation home in the Carpathian Mountains, or The Crimea. She had money enough for that. She'd have no trouble making some new friends, not with the kind of life she could now afford to live.

* * *

It was several hours later and Michael was playing a mindless game on his computer when the phone rang again. The call display read 'unknown number'. It had to be Dmitri again.

"Hello?"

"Mikhail!" Dmitri's voice sounded cheerful. "I have everything planned. You will be getting an email. I will see you soon."

"What do you mean? Are you coming here? That's just what they want! How is that …"

"Not over the phone!" His voice was suddenly stern, reminding Michael very much of the Dmitri that had once been an enforcer for the Ukrainian Mafia. It silenced him immediately. "The email will explain everything. Do what it says and it will be okay." The line went dead before Michael could ask anything else.

He logged into his email account only to see that there was nothing new, so he went back to his game of solitaire, but found himself refreshing his inbox every few seconds. He couldn't keep his mind on anything but the coming email and its instructions. Fortunately, it was only about ten more minutes before a new message popped up. He opened it to find there was no message from Dmitri, nor were there any instructions, just a link to a set of airline tickets. He read over the information on them before sending them to his printer. They were for an early, next morning departure to Miami.

Chapter Three

"Next?"

Michael, his carry-on bag in tow, approached the ticket counter where he wordlessly set the printouts and his passport on the counter. The ticket agent barely glanced at him as he began entering the information into his computer. Michael, trying to look as casual as possible, glanced about the tiny terminal building but he couldn't see anyone that looked out of place. The problem was, who would look out of place in an airport terminal? He was looking for two men together, but only saw families, a single woman, and a few men standing alone.

He'd left his apartment extra early, under cover of darkness, and had taken a taxi to the airport hoping that he might be able to slip away unnoticed. He might not know whether it had worked or not until it was too late, and at the moment he wasn't sure which would have been worse, being followed by the Mafia or by the police. Could he be arrested for fleeing the country?

"Is Miami your final destination, Sir?"

"Uh, yeah." The computer keys kept clicking as Michael continued to scan the room. Nope, no pairs of men anywhere, but what if the guy at the vending machine was with the guy leafing through the brochure rack? Or the guy studying the arrivals screen?

"How many bags to check, Sir?"

"Just my carry-on." He forced himself to watch the ticket agent, and when the man looked at him quizzically, he added, "I like to travel light."

A few more taps on the keyboard, a click of the mouse, and his boarding passes slid out of the printer. "You're boarding at Gate

Two in thirty minutes. You've got the boarding pass for this flight, and the one to Dallas, but you'll have to get a pass in Dallas for the Miami leg. Have a nice flight, Sir." The agent flashed him a tired smile and quickly turned his attention to the lineup behind Michael. "Next?"

The gate was all of forty feet from where he was standing, and was one of only two gates in the whole terminal building. He made his way slowly around the building studying the shoes of his fellow passengers, and those of the milling crowd that seemed a permanent fixture in every airport.

As he studied shoes, he tried to listen to snippets of the conversations taking place; he didn't hear any Ukrainian accents. The shoes ran the full gamut of running shoes to work-boots, but what he didn't see were the distinctive pointy-toed shoes so popular with men in Ukraine. Well, it was easy enough to buy a western-style pair of shoes, and the men standing alone weren't talking, so his reconnaissance wasn't sufficient to either justify or quell the gnawing fear that he was being watched. The hair on the back of his neck told him he was.

He walked over to Gate Two, which consisted of a sign over a door leading out to the tarmac, and a bank of uncomfortable airport benches that would maybe hold half of the passengers that would fit onto the twin-engine commuter which sat waiting on the ramp. Most people would consider it a small plane, but compared to the four-seater Michael had been training in, it seemed huge. He couldn't help but wonder what it would be like to fly something that big and heavy.

Behind the plane he would shortly board, he could see the hangar that housed his flight school, and for a moment felt a twinge of resentment that he was confined to the terminal building. He was a pilot! Well, a student pilot, but a pilot nevertheless. He didn't belong in the ranks of the passengers; he was one of the privileged. He took a seat and waited.

There was little chance that either of his tails would board his flight, but they'd know where he was going, and they probably had friends everywhere.

* * *

The first leg of the trip went without incident, although now that he'd piloted a plane by himself, he found that riding as a passenger just wasn't as exciting as it had once been, and he'd found himself envying the pilots much more than usual. He passed the first part of his layover by buying a Coke in the food court to give him an excuse to sit at a table in the observation area. The traffic wasn't as heavy here as it had been in Frankfurt, but there were enough take-offs and landings to keep him dreaming while he sipped at the Coke. This was the kind of place he belonged!

At one end of the food court was an area filled with interactive displays that he figured were designed for two purposes: to teach children the basics of aviation, and to keep them occupied so that their travel-weary parents could get a break. He walked through the displays in an attempt to pass the time until he could clear customs. He wandered back to where a real airplane was hanging from the ceiling, a set of stairs providing access to the cockpit. Since no one was watching him, he stepped into the cockpit and settled into the pilot's seat. For a few moments he was flying, his feet planted on the rudder pedals, right hand on the throttle, left gripping the stick. He scanned the instruments, adjusting the controls slowly, then glanced down through the left-hand window. In his imagination it wasn't the floor he saw a story below him, it was the ground, thousands of feet below.

"Mom, when do I get a turn?"

Michael's smile was a mixture of embarrassment and apology as he nodded first to the young boy, and then at his mother. "Sorry, I was just…" His voice trailed off and he climbed out of the cockpit to give the boy room to climb in. The boy was barely seated before he began doing his best imitation of an airplane engine and slamming the controls around wildly. Michael couldn't help but smile as he made his way down the stairs; that little boy could have been him a few years ago. Maybe someday that little tyke would get his pilot's licence too.

Glancing at his watch he saw that it was still a bit early to head to the gate, but customs might take a while, so he began making his way past the shops and stores to the customs area. The displays had, for a few minutes, distracted him enough that he'd almost forgotten the reason for this trip, but now he found himself checking to see who might be watching or following him. He picked out a few men here and there that might be showing a bit too much interest, but no one he could be sure about. That was the trouble with a big airport, there were just too many people headed every which way, and all of them had a seemingly legitimate reason to be there.

With time to spare before the departure of his next flight, he didn't mind the slow movement of the line as the U.S. customs officers studied passports and forms, trying to determine if any of the would-be travellers might pose a risk to national security. Though a few were diverted into secondary inspection, they seemed to be letting almost everyone through. Hopefully none of them belonged to the Ukrainian Mafia.

When it was finally Michael's turn, his lack of baggage and the one-way ticket raised an eyebrow and a few questions, but thankfully no red flags. He was finally allowed through after explaining that it was a quick, last-minute trip to visit a friend from Europe who was passing through the U.S. He felt a little more secure once he was, at least for legal purposes, in America. Only other U.S. bound passengers were allowed in this area. Still, after purchasing a paperback that he'd intended to read anyway, he purposely sat at the wrong gate, only pretending to read it until his flight was finally announced.

The flight was full, but he managed to find a spot in the overhead bin to stow his carry-on. After settling into his aisle seat, he closed his eyes and pretended to be asleep in order to avoid having to talk to any of the other passengers. Shortly after takeoff he reclined his seat and slept the rest of the way to Dallas.

* * *

The connection in Dallas was a tight one and by the time he'd walked from his arrival gate to the departure gate, he barely had time to get his boarding pass before the pre-boarding announcement was made for the Miami flight. With his passport tucked safely into his shirt pocket, he once again stowed his carry-on bag and settled into what was, thankfully, a window seat for the last leg of the journey. Even though he wouldn't need the passport again, he kept it in his shirt pocket. He'd learned that lesson last year when his bag, containing his original passport, had been left aboard the hijacked airliner that had deposited him in Ukraine. He would never let that happen again! It was a given, he'd concluded, that despite his precautions he'd been followed to the airport back home, and he had little doubt that they knew he was heading to Miami. Had there been someone watching him throughout the journey so far, or was there somebody already waiting for him in Miami?

Lowering his head, he rubbed his tired, red eyes and then, despite his resolve not to look again, he turned and glanced around the airplane, watching for anyone either looking back at him or looking away too quickly. With a loud sigh he turned his gaze out the window, trying to stir up the excitement that usually came when he was about to take off. He even tried to imagine the pilots going through their checklists, wondering how they differed from those of the small Cessna he flew.

"Are you okay, Sir?" He turned at the sound of the concerned voice and the light touch on his shoulder. It was the young lady who was seated next to him.

"Sir?" He couldn't help but echo the word, thinking that he must be looking old today if she was calling him 'sir'. She looked to be about his own age.

"Force of habit, I'm a flight attendant. Part of my training I guess." She laughed self-consciously, "I can't help watching the passengers before take-off. You know, flying is very safe, much safer than driving."

"Oh, I know," Michael replied. "I'm a pilot myself."

"Really? Who do you fly with?"

Michael felt the heat as his face reddened, realizing he'd been trying to impress her while she routinely flew all over the world with pilots that had tens of thousands of hours of flight time. "Well, I'm a student pilot, actually, I'm working on getting my licence."

"Oh, that's great! I guess you're not nervous about the flight then," She laughed again, this time at herself. "I thought maybe you were a nervous passenger."

Michael smiled back weakly, "No, I'm not nervous; guess I've just got a lot on my mind right now. I love flying!"

"Me too!" Her smile was contagious, though Michael couldn't help but wonder how much of the smile was real, and how much of it was her training. He'd rarely seen a surly-looking flight attendant.

"I'm Sandy, by the way."

"Michael," he responded, shaking her offered hand.

"Where are you going after Miami? I'm meeting some friends there and we're all taking a cruise together. We've been planning it for months."

Maybe she was still trying to distract him, or maybe she was just naturally friendly; or did she have another motive for getting him to talk about his plans? He hated being so suspicious of people, but Dmitri had taught him that lesson very well.

"I'm not sure." The answer came out much too abruptly.

She looked puzzled and he quickly continued, his words sounding awkward as he tried to cover up what he'd just let slip. "I mean, a friend sent me some tickets and – well – I don't really know what the plan is after I get there."

"Oh," Sandy shot him a knowing smile. "A girlfriend?"

He felt the flush return to his face, "No!" The word came out much too quickly again, and much too forcefully. He found himself wondering why. He hadn't had a date in months; work had kept him too busy, at least that was his excuse, and for some reason he wanted her to know that he wasn't meeting a girl. "I mean, um, well, it's a guy I did some, uh, travelling with in Europe last year. He emailed me the tickets and told me to come down and visit him and his girlfriend."

"Does he live in Miami?"

He almost said, 'I don't know' again, but caught himself in time. "Yes, well, he's staying there for now, I guess. He kind of travels around a lot on business. I lost track of him for a while."

"Wow, you do get around. Europe and Miami! I get to travel a lot too; I just never get to stay anywhere very long. That's why I'm looking forward to the cruise. I get to be a tourist myself for a change."

Her laugh lightened his mood somewhat, but he was starting to feel nervous about revealing anything else about his trip, especially since he didn't know anything other than that he was heading to Miami at the moment. For all he knew that wasn't even his final destination, so a smile was his only response.

As he struggled for something intelligent to say, he found himself wondering again if Sandy was the one following him, pumping him for information about his plans. Maybe it was a good thing he didn't know anything about the plan. Maybe Sandy wasn't her real name.

He cleared his throat, and abruptly changed the topic, "How long is the fight to Miami?"

* * *

"Da?" Anton turned from his computer to give his full attention to the phone call.

"Anton, he boarded a flight this morning. We could not follow him aboard the plane, but his final destination is Miami."

"Is it a direct flight?"

"No, there are several connections."

Anton frowned at his desk, knowing that it would be easy for the Canadian to jump the flight at any one of the connecting airports. He could remain at one of them, or catch a flight to anywhere else in the world. The destination on the original ticket might not mean very much at all.

"Very well, I will see what I can do from here. In the meantime, wait there and I'll have more instructions for you later."

Ivan acknowledged his instructions and slipped the phone back into his pocket. What a change it was working for Anton. So much easier and less stressful than it had been with Yuri, or even with Vasili. He was much more reasonable than either of them, and his realistic expectations meant that the men under him did a much better job, no matter what the task.

It was late evening in Kiev, where Anton was, but he was well aware of the time difference with North America, and quickly looked up the number of one of his contacts in Miami. Organized crime was global business, and he could find both vicious competition and willing help in almost every country in the world. Miami was an attractive business location for quite a few financial reasons, and he had several people there that could help him. For the right price, of course. As he placed the call, he made a mental note to have his men check up on Youlya again. She still didn't know they'd spotted her almost as soon as she had entered the country, but if this Canadian was on his way to meet Dmitri, then it might possibly be time to have a chat with her. It would be best to keep very close tabs on her.

* * *

By the time the airliner reached its cruising altitude, Michael had reclined his seat and was feigning sleep. He was exhausted, not having had a proper sleep since the visit from the two policemen. Was that really only yesterday? Sandy's questions were making him more and more uncomfortable. She seemed friendly enough, and was very attractive, but questions from anyone made him uncomfortable right now. Especially since he didn't have any real answers. The more he said, the more mysterious he and his trip sounded. She must have been one of those naturally chatty people though, because she'd quickly turned her attention to the person seated in the aisle seat. Maybe she was safe to talk to after all. Maybe.

When he felt the engines throttle back for the descent 'into the Miami area' he figured it was time to stop playing possum and stirred in his seat, glancing out the window and bringing his seat upright. In half an hour or so he should be on the ground and getting some answers from Dmitri.

"You must be a seasoned traveller; you sure had a good sleep!" Sandy's cheerful voice made it necessary to turn to face her.

"Yeah," he offered an embarrassed smile with his answer. "Well, it was a last-minute trip and I didn't get much sleep last night."

"You're going to have a great time in Miami with your friend; not as much as my friends and I will have on the cruise of course, but there's so much to do here as well. Does your friend know the city well? I can give you a list of things you just have to see!"

He considered turning down her offer, but then decided he'd been rude enough already and accepted her offer with a genuine smile. It helped to pass a few more minutes as she jotted down her list of sights and restaurants to visit on the back of an air sickness bag. It would also, he hoped, lend a little more credence to his cover story of visiting friends in Miami. If it mattered. He actually felt a little left out when, after handing him the list, she turned away to continue her conversation with the lady seated in the aisle seat. He looked back out the window.

As the landing preparations began, Sandy reacted like the trained flight attendant she was. Michael noticed she began scanning the cabin, ensuring that the cabin crew had performed all their proper duties, and confirming where the nearest emergency exit was located. At the same time, he was imagining the activity in the cockpit, the heightened tension of the flight crew as they drew closer to the ground and the congested airspace of the airport.

A flash of blue-green ocean caught his eye and he looked out the window again as the plane banked into a slow turn. Below them he could see crowded beaches and further out to sea, yachts and sailboats. The plane completed its turn back towards the west and they

CHAPTER THREE

flashed back over the shoreline.

The gear dropped and the ground was now rising quickly to meet them. Michael heard and felt the throttles close as the wheels gently kissed the runway. He braced himself slightly in anticipation of the sudden deceleration as reverse thrust was applied. The airplane slowed to a crawl as the pilot guided it onto the taxiway, and began lumbering towards the gate. After hours of flying at over 500 miles an hour, the rest of the journey would be completed at the speed of a car in a crowded parking lot.

One of the attendants made the standard 'welcome-to-Miami' announcement and he double checked to make sure his watch was set to the correct time zone. The trip east had shortened his day by several hours, and it was already early evening when the plane coasted to a stop at the gate.

He lingered behind as the other passengers began crowding their way off the plane. With no baggage to claim he was in no particular hurry, aside from the anxiety of seeing Dmitri again, and he felt the need to steel himself for their reunion. The big Ukrainian was in there somewhere, waiting to greet him. While he was anxious to learn the man's plans and to catch up on what he'd been up to since they'd last seen each other in Bucharest, he found himself a bit apprehensive at the thought of meeting him again.

He bid farewell to Sandy, wished her a good trip, and accepted her wishes for a good time with his friend, then waited until the plane was almost empty before rising and making his way off the plane. He paused for a few seconds at the door to steal a glimpse through the now open cockpit door, and smiled and nodded a *thank you* to the flight crew.

Once inside the terminal he followed the crowds of freshly arriving travellers out of the security area. As he passed the screening area on the way out, he began watching for Dmitri. There was the usual crowd of family and friends waiting the arrival of their loved ones, but no Dmitri. Ignoring the waving signs advertising various resorts and cruise lines he scanned the row of greeters again and again. There was still no sign of his host, so he made his way to the baggage claim area. It was an obvious place to meet a debarking passenger. As he descended the escalator to the carousels, he spotted several people he recognized from his flight, and held back until they had picked up their bags and made their way out. He even spotted Sandy, huddled with three other young ladies as they hugged and greeted each other, no doubt talking excitedly about their cruise. He wished, not for the first time, that he was here for a vacation too. That trip to Greece now seemed a lifetime ago.

Though there was little danger that anything would happen even if one of his fellow passengers did see him with Dmitri, he felt it would be better to remain as invisible as possible. Then again, if anyone was looking for him, they had likely identified him already.

Another ten minutes passed with no sign of Dmitri, and he was beginning to worry that somehow they had missed each other, or that something had happened before Dmitri could get to him. If that was the case, whoever was watching him would likely try something as soon as Michael was alone, so he just sat there trying to blend, as much as possible, into the crowd. It wasn't panic yet, but worry was starting to gnaw at the pit of his stomach. *Dmitri had a plan*, he reminded himself, and he always waited until the opportunity was right before making his move.

"Dmitri says to enjoy your trip." The words, spoken with a heavy Spanish accent, froze him in sudden panic. Then something was pressed into his hand and by the time he turned to see who had spoken, the man was already walking away from him. It took all his willpower not to rip open the thick envelope in his hand.

Gripping the handle of his carry-on tightly, he headed directly to the nearest washroom and into the relative solitude of the first available stall. With trembling fingers, he opened the envelope, careful not to damage the sheaf of papers inside. What kind of instructions could take this many pages? His anger towards Dmitri continued to rise as he pulled out the wad of paper.

A ticket for a Caribbean cruise?

* * *

Youlya busied herself in the kitchen of her new flat, getting everything arranged just so. As she worked, she hummed happily along with a song on the radio. The place was smaller than she would have liked, but it would do. For now. The interest her funds had earned had easily covered the first rent payment, as well as paying for the furnishings and decorations she had just purchased. Some people might be content to live off their investments, however, she considered this to be only a temporary state of affairs. Knowing she'd never have to work again gave her so many options that she needed to take some time to consider them. Once she decided where to settle, she'd buy something suitable for someone of her status.

Pausing to look out the window she couldn't help but furrow her brow. It was such a contrast to what she'd become used to; it was a bit depressing to look out over a comparatively drab row of flats when you were used to sun-drenched sandy beaches lined with waving palm trees. Then there was the unmistakable aroma of the city which contrasted just as sharply with the scent of fresh sea air mingled with bougainvillea. The country. She would have to live in the country.

Her thoughts were broken by a sharp knock on the door. For one, brief moment she smiled thinking that a friend was dropping by for a visit, but then the smile disappeared replaced by an icy feeling in her chest. She had no friends here. She started breathing again, trying to assure herself that it was someone trying to visit the previous tenant, that must be it. Before answering she picked up her mobile phone and placed it in the top cupboard, behind a neat row of brand-new teacups. She'd just used it to check her bank balances, and felt it best not to leave it laying around.

Struggling to control her trembling fingers she walked to the door and opened it just as whoever it was knocked a second time. She opened the door expecting to see Vasili, or perhaps Anton, or even Yuri Stepanovich, but the icy feeling still remained when she opened the door to two unfamiliar men, neither of whom she recognized. She didn't have to recognize them; she knew where they were from and who had sent them.

"Yes?" she asked, trying, and failing, to look calm and innocent.

"Good evening, Youlya." The smile worn by the stranger was anything but friendly. "We had a feeling you might be home." She swallowed hard. That was their way of telling her that she was being watched.

"What – what do you want?"

"Come now, you know why we are here." The smile became even broader. "You must come with us. You have an old friend who wants very much to speak with you. He wishes to find out where you have been and what you have been up to since you left."

Her knees almost buckled and she blurted out the word before she could stop herself. "Yuri!"

"You haven't heard? Yuri is dead. He died the night you left."

"What? I didn't kill him; I never laid a hand on him!"

The smile turned into an amused chuckle. "Oh, you are not responsible for his untimely death. At least not directly. That credit

CHAPTER THREE

must go to your boyfriend, Dmitri. Now, shall we go?"

Youlya could manage nothing more than a slow nod at his request, which wasn't really a request, but an order. She had to prepare herself for whatever might lie ahead. They wanted the money and to get that they needed Dmitri. To get Dmitri they needed her. Surely they had to know that she had not come home empty-handed. But the information she held would be worth something to them. She would work a deal of some sort with them, trade off some of what she had taken with her, and as little information as she could get away with. In exchange she'd retain as much cash as possible, and her life. Expensive unfortunately, but she had no choice.

She could do this. She had to.

* * *

A bus ride later, Michael found himself at the Port of Miami looking up at the biggest ship he'd ever seen. True, he'd never been to a port like this, but the cruise ship was much bigger than he imagined a ship could possibly be. He finally managed to tear his view from the massive ship and joined the line of passengers that led into the cruise terminal.

As he shuffled along with the line, dragging his bag behind him, he studied the sheaf of papers in the envelope that had been unceremoniously placed in his hand back at the airport. The line moved much faster than he expected and before he had any real idea of what he was supposed to do, he found himself at one of a couple of dozen check-in desks, handing the pile of papers and his passport to the smiling lady behind it.

She took the sheaf of papers, glanced at it, and then back up at him. "Welcome aboard, Mr. Barrett. I see this is your first time cruising with us. Have you cruised with any other lines?"

"No, this is my first cruise ever," Michael replied as her fingers flew over the keyboard.

"Well, you're going to have a great time. I see you haven't selected any shore excursions yet. You should book them as soon as you can because the best ones always fill up quickly. There's a list of them right here." She handed him a small booklet with lists of islands, times, and activities. "You can book them at the purser's office on board the ship. Your first stop will be St. Thomas so you can do some sight-seeing, or if you like the beach, then you absolutely have to see Magens Bay; it's one of the ten most beautiful beaches in the world. There's some great shopping too!"

Michael nodded as she spoke, not quite sure what a purser's office was or why he had to book shore excursions, but he thumbed through the brochure as she typed and spotted a few things that looked like they'd be fun to try.

"Okay, I have you all checked in now." She handed him a small folding map of the ship after circling his cabin on the deck plan. "Your cabin is on Deck 10, and this is where your dining room is. You have an 8 PM seating for supper but the ship is full of restaurants open 24 hours a day. All complimentary, of course, so you won't go hungry." He would understand that comment much better within the next few hours. "Now, if you have any questions at all, any of the crew will be happy to help you, and there will always be someone manning the purser's office on Deck Six. This card is your room key, and you can also use it to make any purchases aboard the ship. Have a wonderful cruise, Mr. Barrett."

With one sweeping motion, she pointed out the doorway leading to the ship and gestured the next person in line to her station.

As he had studied the list of shore excursions, he'd almost forgotten that he wasn't on a real holiday and for a few minutes he was debating between parasailing and a zip-line adventure. Now that he was back in another lineup, this one to board the ship, he remembered the real purpose of the trip. As far as he knew you couldn't just walk up and board a cruise ship, so he'd hopefully left the Ukrainian Mafia behind him, at least temporarily. But where was Dmitri? Was he aboard already? Were they sharing a cabin? That was the most likely scenario he could come up with, because the ship was going to make a big circle in the Atlantic Ocean and bring him right back here to Miami. So just what was Dmitri's plan?

He was made to pose for a picture as he boarded, then made his way to his cabin. Since he didn't have much to unpack, he tossed his bag onto the bed and went off to explore the ship. Nothing he'd experienced in his past prepared him for the splendour of the ship, especially the grand atrium. Eventually hunger won out over curiosity and he made his way up to the Lido Deck where a catered party was in full swing. He filled a plate, then found a spot on the Sun Deck, where he could watch the growing crowd below. Dmitri was not the kind of person to show up in a crowd like this, but he had to show up eventually.

Just as Michael was about to head back to his cabin in case Dmitri had tried to contact him there, he felt a hand on his shoulder. It was much too small and delicate to be Dmitri's, and the voice didn't sound the least bit masculine. For a just a moment he thought it might be Youlya, but there was no accent.

"Well, hey there! Why didn't you tell me you were going on a cruise? We could have invited you and your friends to join us!"

"Sandy!" His face broke into a smile. He took a breath to give himself a moment to think. He didn't want to lie to her, but he couldn't give her the whole truth either. At least his smile was real. "I didn't know this is what he had planned. I'm as surprised as you are. I got to the airport and he gave me a ticket for the cruise."

"Well that's sure a nice surprise, I wish someone had given me my ticket," she shot a playful scowl at her friend who made a face back at her. "This is Linda, my best friend. At least that's what I tell people when she's listening. Where are your friends? Why don't you want to introduce us?"

Michael felt a blush rise to his cheeks, pleasantly surprised that Sandy had actually made the effort to say hi to him. It wasn't possible that she liked him, was it? But then the suspicion returned. How much of a coincidence was it that she was on the same ship? She had told him about the cruise when they were still on the plane, and surely there was no way she could have known he'd be on this ship when he didn't even know that himself. Or was Yuri one step ahead of them? Could he have put all that effort into recruiting Sandy and her *friends* just to throw him off his guard? Dmitri would have his hide for revealing anything to her, and it would be even worse were he to actually introduce the two of them.

"Uh, I'm not sure, I lost track of him somewhere." *Somewhere like Bucharest*, he thought to himself. "He might have gone back to his cabin to unpack or something."

"You sure he's not an imaginary friend?" She poked his arm playfully.

"Oh no, he's anything but imaginary!" No imaginary friend could have put him through what Dmitri had. "I'm sure he'll turn up soon." He offered a weak, apologetic smile which was mixed in with a large dose of embarrassment, and even guilt. He really didn't want to lie to Sandy, even if he might never see her again. He was almost wishing he'd just stayed in his cabin and not bumped into her. Almost.

"Well, the lifeboat drill is coming up soon anyways, and then we sail! We'll catch up to you later. You and your imaginary friend."

They shared a laugh before Sandy and Linda wandered off, and Michael made his way back to his cabin.

* * *

Youlya locked the door, then collapsed against it. She would have felt relieved if there had been threats made or questions asked, but Anton had done neither. He had done nothing more than talk with her, which was far worse. The whole time it had been as if they were old friends talking over tea; but his message had come through very clearly. 'We are watching you, Youlya, and we will keep watching you until you give us what we want.'

Her first reaction had been to abandon everything but her mobile phone, take a taxi to the airport, and hop on the first flight to anywhere. She had the means to do that. But Anton had the means to follow her. She resisted the urge to look out the window. She may or may not pick them out, but they were watching. They had been since her return. She had to think of something, some way to shake Anton off her trail. Her options were to disappear, or to make a deal of some sort. But she couldn't disappear, she didn't have a head start like she'd had the last time. That left a deal; but could she trust Anton to keep his end of the bargain? Not likely.

Chapter Four

Michael was awakened early the next morning when the tropical sun won its battle with the thick curtains on the balcony door, sending its bright rays streaming into his room and onto his pillow. It might have been possible to have slept a bit later if he'd closed the curtains a bit more carefully the night before, after he'd come back in from the balcony after gazing at the tropical moon. He would have liked to run into Sandy again, but that wasn't the reason he was here, was it? Besides, he wasn't sure how to answer the questions she was likely to ask about his missing friend. Where was Dmitri and what was his plan? Enough of his waiting for an opportunity!

With a shake of his aching head, and an over-tired grunt, he rolled out of bed and slid the curtains open, blinking as the full force of early morning sun burst into the room. It was beautiful out there, and he wished that he had the luxury of enjoying it fully. Sliding open the door he took a deep breath of ocean air and stood watching the water slide by, until finally deciding that he needed to do something useful to start the day.

After a quick shower he dressed as appropriately as possible for the climate, certain that there weren't too many other people wearing jeans aboard the ship. He might have to visit one of the clothing stores after breakfast. Then what? Should he stay put in the room or wander the ship? All his old feelings of frustration with Dmitri began to return. Part of him knew that Dmitri must have his reasons for what he was doing, but couldn't he understand how nerve-wracking it was for Michael to be kept in the dark when his life might well be on the line? *Enough waiting for some golden opportunity*, it was time to take action. He kept repeating that to himself, but nothing came of it.

Michael all but slammed the door as he made his way from the room and down the hall to the elevator, his heavy, thudding footsteps somewhat muted by the carpeting. He forced himself to calm down a bit after two stewards stopped to ask him if something was wrong, and if they could help him in any way. Yes, something was very wrong, but there was nothing they could do about it. He forced himself to look as relaxed as possible, if for no other reason than to avoid drawing further attention to himself.

Breakfast outdoors on the Lido deck sounded tempting, but he reluctantly decided to find something on the lower decks in case he bumped into Sandy again. Not that he didn't want to of course, but it was the safer choice. Eventually he made his way to the formal dining room where he found a secluded corner in which to eat a slow, relaxed breakfast.

With most of his fellow cruisers enjoying the sun-drenched upper decks, he took his time scouting the stores where he found some suitable tropical attire before wandering to the purser's desk where he learned that they would be at sea for the next two days. He listened politely as the purser, who had a very proper British accent, gave him a long list of options for possible shore excursions. He said that he'd think about them and maybe book something later. To make it look good he took a brochure about places to go and things to see on St. Thomas, but for today, there seemed to be no alternative to sitting and waiting in his room.

* * *

"Well?" Vasili set his coffee cup down and waited for Anton to continue.

"She is scared." He considered his answer for a moment, then smiled as he corrected himself, "No, she's terrified. A little more pressure and she will tell us everything."

"We may not need her." Vasili waved his hand dismissively. "Michael Barrett is on a cruise ship out of Miami. He is sure to make contact with Dmitri now. He is running as scared as Youlya. We can get rid of her now; we will have the money back soon." He picked up his cup and took another sip before the look on his face could give away his feelings. Anton was soft and weak, too squeamish to get his hands dirty. He should have forced the information from Youlya the moment she arrived; after all, no one would ever miss her.

Anton read the hard gleam in Vasili's eyes and deduced what he was thinking. "Perhaps, but underestimating Dmitri would not be a good idea at this point." He managed not to smile as he saw the changed expression in the eyes looking at him over the coffee cup. Dmitri had managed to escape Ukraine not once, but twice, and the fault was Vasili's even if it had been nominally shifted to Yuri upon his very timely death.

The slow shake of Anton's head would be interpreted as disagreement, but was really an expression of his contempt for Vasili. Vasili was rash, rough, and violent, and while such action was often needed, it was rarely enough to properly handle things. Vasili thought with his muscles, and as useful as he was in his place, he had risen as far as he ever would. Much more could be gained from selective use of force; and often the hint of violence was all that was really needed. That took wisdom and understanding, a knowledge of one's opponent and where pressure could best be applied.

"She knows where he lives, and where he keeps the money. I'm certain that she has access to some of it herself. Surely you don't believe she returned empty-handed?" He let the question hang while swirling the tea in his cup; not at all surprised when Vasili offered no response.

"Vasili, I want you to fly to Miami and be ready when we find out where they are." It was stated as an order, not a suggestion, just to remind Vasili of his place. Of both their places. "In the meantime, we will keep an eye on our returned friend. Who knows, we may recover some of what Dmitri took from us right here at home. It was very thoughtful of her to bring it to us."

They shared a laugh at that thought.

* * *

Dmitri looked at his watch. It was too soon to be counting down in hours, but he couldn't help himself. Michael would be confused and scared. He had the luxury of being able to see things more objectively than the Canadian could. Yuri and his gang would not hinder or hurt Michael in any way; he was being used as a bloodhound, to lead the hunters to their real prey, and Dmitri was the real prey. It wasn't that Michael was not in danger, but he was in no immediate danger; they would not lay a hand on him until they had what they wanted.

Yet, at the same time, he could sympathize with Michael, and he wished he had a safe way to convey that information. He looked at his watch again. "Soon, my friend. Very soon."

* * *

Two full days of hiding out in his state-room had been tolerable only because he had been able to leave his balcony door open as he passed the hours watching movies on the closed-circuit TV system. The complimentary room service didn't hurt either. Thankfully, when he'd awakened this morning the ship was docked. According to the itinerary and the briefings broadcast on the TV, they were in Charlotte Amalie on the Island of St. Thomas, though he had no real idea of where that was. With the ship no longer in motion the breeze from the balcony had disappeared, only to be replaced by an oppressive early-morning heat that seemed to suggest that a lazy day on the beach would be the best and only way to spend it.

Since he had not booked a shore excursion, he decided to wait till most of the passengers had disembarked for theirs, and then wander ashore to stretch his legs in the relative safety of the crowd. With two other cruise ships also disgorging their passengers he was fairly certain he would not bump into the only other person he knew on the whole ship. While that should have been a relief, he felt a stab of disappointment at the thought that he likely wouldn't see Sandy again.

After a solitary breakfast on his private balcony, Michael showered and changed into his tropical gear. A look at the pier told him that the crowds weren't likely to dissipate any time soon. The whole place was a swirling mass of unorganized confusion filled with buses, taxis, and tour guides waving signs with large numbers on them. *Well, it must all work somehow,* he decided with a shrug of his shoulders. The steel drum band playing at the bottom of the gang plank lent an exiting and exotic air to the whole scene and unable to wait any longer, he exited his cabin and made for the stairs.

There was still a bit of a lineup to get off the ship, he discovered upon reaching the bottom deck. It moved quickly and he soon stepped off into the full force of the tropical sun. As nice as the ship was, it felt good to be back on dry land. What he failed to realize was that while descending the gangplank, he had been very easy to pick out before he had the chance to disappear into the crowd.

Once clear of the area immediately in front of the ship he wound his way past the lines of taxis and buses and followed a small knot of tourists heading for the nearby shops which carried everything from cheap trinkets to fine jewellery and watches. He peered into some of them, wondering how he'd explain to his family that he'd managed to bring them souvenirs from both Greece and the Caribbean if he did decided to buy anything, let alone how he'd explain a sudden second vacation to his boss. He'd been in such a hurry to rush off at Dmitri's orders that he hadn't let anyone know he wouldn't be coming into work for a few days. If he didn't call in soon, he might need to keep Dmitri's money because he wouldn't have a job!

He was looking for a payphone when he heard the voice behind him. "Mikhail! It is good to see you, my friend!" Before he could finish turning around, Dmitri had locked him in a tight bear hug. Not knowing whether to be happy to see him, or upset at having to see him, Michael gave him a half-hearted hug in return and then, upon being released, looked up at him expectantly, waiting to hear the plan. "I'm sorry you have to go through this, Mikhail, but it is very good to see you!" Dmitri's smile was huge and genuine as he clapped Michael's back a bit harder than necessary, and then began leading him through the milling crowd and across the street.

"Have you been on board the ship this whole time?" The question came out sounding harsh and abrupt.

Dmitri prefaced his reply with a soft laugh. "No, I live down here now. I've been waiting for you."

"Why didn't you have me fly here from Miami then?"

"I know you must have been wondering what was going on, but this made you a bit harder to follow." Dmitri crossed another street, seemingly oblivious to the creeping line of tourist-laden vehicles impatiently fighting the bottle neck of the docks as they waited their turn to fan out to the island's many attractions.

"Your English has improved."

"Lots of practice. Let's go inside."

Dmitri guided him into a small cafe, where they took a table in the back. Most of the passengers from the cruise ships had just finished breakfast aboard their respective ships, so it wasn't hard to find a table. He waved to the waitress and ordered each of them a tea.

"So, you live here on this island?"

"No," a shake of his head punctuated his terse reply and he glanced around to make sure no one else was within earshot. "I came here last night to meet you. We will go home once it is not so crowded. It will be noticed that you are missing once your boat sails tonight, but that happens to you tourists all the time." Another laugh. "They will expect you to meet them at the next port." A shrug this time. "But you won't be there."

"You mean I'm going to disappear again? This is getting to be a habit with me." Even Michael had to chuckle at that thought. Then he turned serious again. "But what's the plan? I mean, what are we going to do about Yuri and his gang?"

Dmitri glanced about the room again, almost wincing at the mention of his former boss. "I don't know yet. The important thing for now is to make sure you are safe."

"Then we're just waiting for an opportunity again?" The bitterness was returning to his voice.

"I need to get you somewhere safe, somewhere that I can protect you. Home turf, I think you call it."

"Okay, so you get me somewhere safe, but Yuri's not going to stop looking for me. Or for you. We need a plan!"

"Like what?" Dmitri was sounding defensive now. This reunion was not going the way he'd imagined it.

"Like ... I don't know, but we need a plan. I'm not spending the rest of my life running and hiding from your friends. No amount of money is worth that!" His voice was rising and Dmitri motioned from him to lower his voice.

"Do you think we should just kill them all?"

"If that's what it takes!" The harshness of his reply surprised him, and he wondered if he really meant it.

"How do you plan to carry out that many murders?" He waited a moment, knowing he'd stunned his friend into silence. "Mikhail, I did not mean for any of this to happen. I am sorry you became involved in all of this. All I wanted was a new life for myself." He sighed deeply. "If it had all gone as planned, I would have left the country and they would never have found me."

"But you needed to get Youlya out too. What if they'd tracked her instead of you? How is she anyway? Is she here?"

Dmitri shook his head, but showed no emotion as he spoke. "No, she is no longer with me."

"Oh," Michael was about to add 'I'm sorry to hear that,' but wasn't sure if he was expected to be sorry or not, so he simply stopped talking.

The waitress arrived and they sipped their tea in silence, waiting for the crowd on the docks to thin out before heading back out to where ever it was that Dmitri planned to take him. Michael wanted to bring the conversation back to forming a plan. He should, he supposed, have been thankful that Dmitri was offering him a safe, if somewhat temporary haven, but what he needed was a permanent solution to the problem of being wanted by the Mafia. They wouldn't rest until they had their money back. No, even that wouldn't satisfy them. They wanted Dmitri as well. Even if they got back every cent, they still needed to make an example of him. For a few heartbeats Michael actually contemplated turning him over to Yuri's henchmen just to end things, but he knew he could never really do that. He was just angry and frustrated. He blinked hard when he realized that they just might want to make an example of him too, once he'd led them to Dmitri.

"Don't worry, Mikhail, we will think of something." He was unaware that Dmitri had been studying his expression as he had sipped the tea thoughtfully, gazing absently out the window without really seeing anything.

Michael brought his gaze back inside and nodded wordlessly in response, setting his now empty cup on the table.

"When do we go?"

Dmitri looked out the window. From where they sat it appeared that the crowds had thinned considerably. There were still a lot of people milling among the shops and stores in the immediate area of the docks, but most of the crowd had headed out on tours, or to check out the beaches. They rose from the table and Dmitri left some cash to cover the tea, as well as a sizable tip, before they headed back out to the street.

They both blinked hard as they came back out into the tropical sun, and Dmitri pulled a pair of sunglasses out of his shirt pocket.

"Is there somewhere I can get a pair of those too?"

Dmitri nodded and they headed down the street, back towards the shoreline, pausing to look into the stores along the way until they found one with a selection of sunglasses prominently displayed near the door. With Dmitri's help he tried on pair after pair before deciding on one with suitable UV protection that more or less suited him. As he pulled out his credit card Dmitri motioned for him to put it away and pulled out a wad of cash, peeling off a few bills to pay for the glasses.

"Thanks, I'll pay you back."

"No need, we are both millionaires, right?" The cashier joined in

CHAPTER FOUR 65

their laughter, not realizing that they were laughing because it was true. As they turned to leave, Dmitri murmured just loud enough for him to hear. "Best not to leave a trace of where you've been. Credit cards will do that. I never use one."

The gesture of buying him sunglasses was a small thing, but to Michael it was a reminder of the person Dmitri really was. He was regretting how he'd treated his friend now that they were back together.

"Dmitri, I'm sorry if I was upset with you. It was just such a shock to find out that Yuri had me followed back to Canada, you know? I was hoping when I got here that you'd have already …"

They were looking at each other as they spoke, and didn't notice that a figure had suddenly appeared before them, blocking their path to the door. Michael was about to excuse himself and step aside, but when he realized who it was, he froze in place. It was the last person on earth he wanted to see right now.

"Hey there, mystery man, those shades look good on you!" Sandy smiled at him and turned to face Dmitri. "And you must be Michael's imaginary friend. Nice to finally meet you! The two of you must have been having a lot of fun. I haven't seen you since that first night at the party." Her smile was usually something he could feel right down to his toes, but at that moment, Michael felt a mild state of panic setting in. He felt a stab of guilt as he glanced sideways at Dmitri, who was no more pleased than Michael to discover that someone on the island recognized both of them. Dmitri's sunglasses hid his eyes, but Michael had a very good idea of what his expression was. He'd seen it before, back in Ukraine.

"Hi, Sandy, yeah, we've been keeping busy. This is, uh, this is …" He winced inwardly knowing he had already said far too much.

"Dmitri, I'm Dmitri," the big Ukrainian offered his hand

in greeting.

"Nice to meet you, Dmitri, Michael was saying the two of you met in Europe, and that you planned this trip for him."

"He told you all that, did he?" Dmitri shifted his gaze momentarily towards Michael who knew that despite the smile on his lips, his eyes were saying something else. "I've borrowed a boat for the day. Mikhail and I were going to go for a short ride and see the island from the sea."

Michael looked at his friend warily. There was something in the tone of his voice that sounded suspiciously like an invitation.

"That sounds great! I figured you'd get enough time on a boat this week though, Mikhail," Sandy grinned and gave Michael a teasing smile as she used Dmitri's pronunciation of his name. "But you really don't see much more than open ocean from the cruise ship. It might be kinda cool to see some real scenery."

Michael's panic was passing the state of mild and threatening to become massive, because now her voice suggested that she wanted to come along. He looked over at Dmitri, expecting him to put a kibosh on that idea.

"It is a very nice boat, come and take a look at it. You can come along if you want. There is lots of room."

As Sandy's smile widened, Michael realized it was time for him to take action. "But what about your friends?"

"Oh, that's okay," Sandy dismissed his objection with a laugh and a wave of her hand. "They'd much rather shop. I was going to meet them for lunch and then we were going to go to Magens Bay for the afternoon. I've had enough shopping already, so I'd love to come along."

"I think Dmitri was planning an all-day cruise," Michael offered through a forced smile.

Sandy was looking at Dmitri and didn't seem to hear his words, "As long as you two don't mind me tagging along that is."

"Not at all, and we will have you back in lots of time for lunch with your friends." With that Dmitri steered her towards the marina, with Michael following in tow and wondering why her mom hadn't done a better job of warning her to stay away from strangers. Especially strangers who were ex-Mafia enforcers. The problem was that they had become friends, sort of, or at least acquaintances, after the time on the plane and the chance encounter on the ship. He must have come across as innocent and harmless. After all he hadn't hit on her or stalked her. Or maybe she liked him? If that were the case, why hadn't he met her in another place and time?

Sandy and Dmitri made small talk as they wound their way to the docks, with Michael only half listening, growing angrier with each step. He still didn't know himself what Dmitri's plan was, and now he was helping to drag Sandy into it. Unless they really were just going for a boat ride. He tried to keep that hope alive, but somehow he just couldn't. Dmitri was seizing an opportunity here. One that served himself and no one else. He should warn Sandy to run before they took another step, but that would only draw attention to all three of them, and quite possibly from the wrong source. That might only serve to put all three of them in danger.

Then again, maybe his fear was unfounded; the three of them would take a short pleasure cruise and be back in time for Sandy to meet her friends for lunch.

Sure they would! He wasn't any better than Dmitri.

Before he could wrestle through his tangled thoughts, they'd reached the marina and Dmitri brought them all to a halt alongside a cabin cruiser. It was far from the largest of the boats moored here, but it was impressive enough. The lettering adorning her stern informed them that this was *Spirit of the Caribbean III*. Michael couldn't help but look at it a bit enviously. Not that he had ever wanted to own a boat, but if Dmitri could use his money on a boat like this, then maybe he could justify using the funds Dmitri had given him to buy his own Cessna. After all, it wasn't like he was considering a Learjet.

Dmitri helped them aboard then went into the cabin to begin his start up procedures, leaving Michael and Sandy alone on the open, rear deck of the boat. Michael cleared his throat, searching for some subtle way to get Sandy back ashore. "Look, I really hate to drag you away from your friends, and I'm not really sure how long a cruise Dmitri has planned, so if ..."

"Thanks, I was looking forward to a relaxing day and a bit of beach time, but a boat ride will be even nicer. Besides we all have to be back in time for the sailing this evening, right?" A sudden change in her expression gave Michael hope that she had decided not to come along. "Did the two of you want this to be a 'guy thing'. I'm not imposing on you, am I?"

"No, it's not that at all. I was hoping to see you again." That much, at least, was true. "I just don't want to ruin your plans. It's kind of like I'm imposing on you, really; so if you'd rather be on the beach with your friends, that's okay."

Sandy laughed and patted his arm, "Someone needs to teach you how to ask a girl out. You don't try to get rid of her after she's already agreed to go with you. I'm sure we'll have a great time. Mikhail."

Michael was pretty sure she couldn't be more wrong, but as he struggled to get the conversation back on track the engine roared to life, then settled down to a deep, steady purr. The opportunity to talk her off the boat had passed. What should he do now? Throw her overboard?

CHAPTER FOUR

Dmitri hollered down from the cabin, instructing them to cast off the bow and stern lines, to which Sandy offered a mock salute and hollered back, "Aye aye, Cap'n!" She studied the stern line for a moment and cast it off, while Michael made his way forward and cast off the bow line. As the boat slipped smoothly from the dock, Michael's heart began to sink. This was the bus trip in Ukraine all over again, only this time Michael was a willing participant and someone else was the innocent victim.

* * *

It was late afternoon in Ukraine and Anton was contemplating which restaurant he'd dine at that evening as he picked up his phone and called the number of one of the men he had watching Youlya's flat. "I want her picked up and brought to the warehouse. Tell her I have a few questions to ask her," he informed the voice that answered. "No, I will not be there tonight, I'll come by in the morning, but you don't need to tell her that."

Chapter Five

Dmitri guided the boat rather skilfully through the bobbing flotilla that filled the harbour, with Sandy waving cheerfully back at the passengers on the other boats and to their fellow cruisers who lined the railings of the big vessels. Michael could catch snatches of music coming from the open decks of the ships, which lent a festive atmosphere to the day. Somehow that only served to make him feel worse about what was happening. He waved along half-heartedly with Sandy, but felt as if he were waving goodbye to his life; it was the same feeling he'd had last summer when Dmitri had kidnapped him in Ukraine, only now it was for someone else.

After clearing the port, the traffic thinned out, and with no one left to wave to he plopped down onto one of the lounge chairs while Sandy stood at the bow of the ship, letting the wind blow her hair about and enjoying every minute of the sun and sea. He wanted desperately to confront Dmitri about his plan, and why he'd felt it necessary to make Sandy a part of it, but he didn't know where to begin. As Dmitri brought the boat around to the left to follow the shoreline, Sandy made her way back towards him.

"You're looking relaxed," she smiled down at him. He gave a nod, hoping the expression on his face wasn't giving anything away. "I thought I'd ask your friend if we could go past Magens Bay, maybe even cruise into it. They say it's one of the most beautiful beaches in the world, you know. It would be cool to get a look at it from the sea."

"I suppose we could," Michael shrugged, not having a clue where Magens Bay was located, "But I think Dmitri has his own agenda for this trip."

"Oh? Does he know the area well?"

"Apparently."

"Well, I'll see it this afternoon anyway, even if we don't sail past it now, but I think I'll ask him just in case."

With a sigh Michael rose to follow her up the ladder to where Dmitri was manning the helm. He turned and nodded to them, but made no effort to start a conversation. He was acting more and more like the old Dmitri, the one who trusted no one but himself.

"Hey, Dmitri, this is great! Isn't the ocean beautiful?" She got a nod in response, but nothing more. "I was wondering, could we have a look at Magens Bay if we're going that far? Do you know where it is? On the north shore of the island?"

"I know where it is. We will go by it, but I don't think we have enough time to go in there."

"Oh, okay, no problem, just thought I'd ask." Sandy's smile was unfazed by his curt answer. "So where are we going, just around the island?"

"Culebra."

"Where?" Sandy and Michael asked in chorus.

"Culebra," Dmitri repeated, "It means 'snake island.'"

"You mean it's another island?" Sandy asked, an uneasy tone creeping into her voice. "Will we be back in time for lunch?"

Dmitri shook his head.

"But we'll be back before we sail this evening, right?"

He shook his head again and Sandy shot Michael a worried glance.

Michael decided it was way past time to step in himself. "Dmitri, let's drop her off. We could even pull into that bay she wants to see, then you and I can keep going."

"Keep going where? Where's Culebra?" Sandy demanded.

Dmitri gestured over his shoulder, "It's that way. We will circle the island and then head that way. It's maybe twenty or thirty kilometres away."

"Dmitri!" Michael's voice rose, taking on a stern tone he rarely used with anyone, let alone Dmitri. "Drop Sandy off so her friends can pick her up. Then we can go wherever you want."

Dmitri removed his sunglasses and looked sharply at Michael. "Mikhail, we cannot do this," his accent was becoming thicker. "You know we cannot do this, and you know why. You brought her into this by telling her you were coming here to meet me."

"Brought me into what?" But both men ignored her.

"All I told her is I was meeting a friend! I didn't say where or why or even what your name was! You're the one that told her that; if you'd kept your mouth shut back on the St. Thomas, she'd never have known I was missing even after we sailed. I saw her on the plane and the first night of the cruise and that was it! I had to tell her something; it would have sounded even more suspicious if I couldn't explain why I was here or what I was doing! You're the one that invited her along on this mystery cruise of yours." Michael was breathing heavily as he finished his tirade, almost hyperventilating, and for a moment he thought he saw a look of regret on Dmitri's face; but it didn't last long.

"Somebody tell me what you guys are talking about!" Sandy was angry now, with much more than a hint of fear in her eyes as she glanced back and forth between the two angry men.

"It's done, Mikhail!" The discussion had ended as far as Dmitri was concerned.

"It's done when you drop her off at – what's that place called?"

"Magens Bay, it's on the north shore," Sandy gave Michael a thankful smile, then turned her attention to Dmitri. "I can get a taxi to the docks from there. I won't tell anyone what you two are up to, honest. I don't have a clue anyway."

"I tried that argument last summer," Michael muttered to himself. "Didn't do any good back then." Turning to Dmitri, he said, "Drop her off, Dmitri, she's got nothing to do with this and won't tell anyone. She promised." She nodded vigorously as Michael spoke. "I'll go anywhere you want me to, but she's not coming. This isn't her concern; don't drag her into it."

"She knows where we are going now."

"Only because you told her!" Michael spat the words out.

The logic of that argument was moot as far as Dmitri was concerned, and he cracked the throttle open even wider, the boat picking up speed and making it difficult for Michael and Sandy to keep their footing; they grabbed at each other for support. "Go sit down and enjoy scenery. We are finished." Then his tone softened a bit and he managed a smile towards Sandy. "I will not hurt you; I promise. I will even pay you back for your trip. But I cannot let you go right now. Mikhail will explain."

Michael gave a sigh of exasperation and motioned for Sandy to head back down to the lower deck. "He won't hurt you, Sandy, in fact he'll do everything in his power to keep you safe." Knowing he was telling the truth helped to give his voice a tone of genuine reassurance, "But he's not going to change his mind. I'm sorry you'll miss out on the rest of your cruise, but he will pay you back for the cruise, and if he doesn't I will. Look, I'll even pay for another cruise for all your friends." He was getting pretty generous with Dmitri's money.

"Pay for it with what? Drug money? Can I at least call them from this 'Snake Island' we're going to? I don't want them to worry."

Knowing the answer to that question already, Michael just nodded towards the aft deck. "Let's talk about that over there. Out of the wind." He couldn't read the look on her face, but she made her way aft and he followed her to the stern, where they found seats that sheltered them from the stiffening breeze.

"Okay, start talking, buddy!"

"Look, I'm on your side!" Michael responded, raising his hands in a show of innocence.

"Yeah, I know, you did tell him to drop me off." Sandy's tone softened for a moment, then the fire returned to her hazel eyes. "But why didn't you say something back there?" She stabbed her thumb angrily back towards Charlotte Amalie.

"I didn't know what was going to happen, honest. I thought he was on the ship when we left Miami." One look into her eyes and he knew that he was deceiving himself as much as he was Sandy. "Okay, I knew he might pull something like this." She glared at him, daring him to tell her more. "He did this to me last year."

"So I gathered. Some friend this guy is. He kidnaps you and then you let him kidnap me. If he has a habit of doing this kind of thing then you should have told me to run for it back in town."

"I should have," Michael nodded in full agreement. "I can't argue with you. But ... "

"But what? What did you get me involved in? Are you two running drugs or guns or what?"

"We're not running anything. We're running from something."

"What are you running from and why do I have to come along?"

Michael took a deep breath, wondering how he could make sense of all this. "Sandy, Dmitri did this to protect himself, and me too. Maybe more to protect me. In his own twisted way, he thinks he's protecting you too."

"By kidnapping me? Oh sure, that makes perfect sense."

"I'm trying to explain this!" He immediately regretted his tone of voice and held up a hand so that he could keep talking, "I'm sorry, I'm not mad at you, I'm mad at Dmitri, and myself. I'm really, really sorry you got mixed up in this, but you see, there's a good chance we were being watched back there in town. If someone had asked you about me, you might have told them something about where I went and who I was with." One look at her expression told him he had to explain that. "I'm not saying you'd have done it on purpose; you might have thought you were helping me by telling them who I was with when I didn't show up for tonight's sailing, and these guys don't usually ask nicely when they want to know something. I know that from personal experience." He rubbed his ribs thoughtfully as he recalled that night in Anton's basement with two goons who wouldn't believe he had no useful information.

Sandy noticed the way he gingerly rubbed his ribs, and her anger was replaced by fear as she repeated her earlier question. "What are you running from?"

"The Ukrainian Mafia."

"What? Why?"

"You're a flight attendant, you must keep up on aviation news?" A confused nod. "Remember that airliner that was hijacked last summer in Europe? It was on its way to Athens and ended up in Kiev." A slower nod, as if she was starting to put the pieces together. "I was on that plane and so was our friend there. He was on the run from the Mafia and, well, for some reason he figured that I was helping them to follow him, so he snatched me off the plane and dragged me along till he could figure out what to do with me."

"So you were the one that disappeared." Sandy's eyes were open wide in understanding now. "They never did give the full story on the news. I just remember you showed up somewhere about a week or so later."

"Bucharest," Michael finished the story for her, at least as much as had been revealed in the media. "I was finally able to convince Dmitri that I was just an innocent bystander, but by that time the Mafia figured I was helping him. "They –" he hesitated, recalling details he hadn't fully shared with anyone, "They caught me and tried to force some information out of me." He actually enjoyed the look of pity in her eyes and was briefly tempted to play up the horrors of that night, but decided it was best to move on. "Anyways, I didn't tell them anything and Dmitri actually came back and rescued me when he could have got away and left me behind. That's why I know he won't hurt you; he just doesn't want to leave any loose ends back on St. Thomas that might lead these guys to us."

"He doesn't think our disappearance will raise any suspicions? What do you think will happen when we don't show up on the ship tonight? My friends aren't going to assume I met up with some cute guy and ran off with him without telling them, you know."

Michael actually kind of liked that thought, but now wasn't the time to pursue that possibility.

"Well, Dmitri planned this disappearance even before I boarded the ship. I just didn't know it back then, honest. I guess he figures as long as no one knows where we disappeared to, that we'll have time to figure out what to do about it."

"But why do you have to disappear now? I mean, if this all happened a year ago, then why all this cloak and dagger stuff?"

"Because they still want Dmitri, and they figured I could lead them to him. I just found out they've been watching me back home. I was able to get word to Dmitri, hoping he could help me out, but all he did was send me a plane ticket to Miami and, well, you now know as much as I do."

"Not quite. What does he have that they want so bad? Does he have some information on them? Was he going to testify against them or something? I mean, why are they still following you a year after you got away?" Michael hesitated, not sure how to answer her question. "Well, what does he have?" Sandy persisted.

"Fifteen million dollars," he answered with a sigh.

* * *

Vasili and his translator, a young recruit named Bogdan, had arrived in Miami. Bogdan was very excited to be making his first trip to America, and had eagerly shown off his mastery of the English language with the U.S. Customs agent. Now that they had cleared customs, however, his only duty here in America appeared to be to drag around Vasili's carry-on bag. The way to the baggage claim area was clearly marked by pictures, and Vasili hardly needed help to translate those.

While Bogdan waited for their luggage to arrive, Vasili checked his email only to learn they had another flight ahead of them. Apparently the cruise ship's first port of call was in some place called St. Thomas, which was not even in the United States of America. According to the best information they had, Mr. Barrett had been seen leaving the ship but not reboarding it. Other pairs of eyes would check the ship at its next stop, while the two of them were to proceed to St. Thomas just in case that is where he was to make contact with Dmitri. If Dmitri and Michael did make an appearance on another island, then he and Bogdan would continue to follow them until they were located.

It made sense, Vasili thought. The Caribbean islands were flush with international banks and it would be a simple matter to hide money in one or several of them without creating a lot of attention. Too bad that they couldn't stay here in Florida though, he was sure that either Disney World or Disneyland was somewhere nearby. He'd always wanted to go there, and who knew when he might be this close again? Oh well. Perhaps when they had Dmitri and the money, he could stop back on the way home.

Bogdan reappeared with their luggage and he showed him the email. Together they went in search of an airline offering flights to the Caribbean.

* * *

Dmitri had very kindly, or so he had thought, pointed out the entrance to Magens Bay on their way past it, and then proceeded out into the open Caribbean Sea, making for Culebra. The sea was relatively calm, but a swell left the small craft rolling from side to side, something neither Michael nor Sandy were comfortable with. Even after a couple of days on the cruise ship, their sea legs weren't quite ready for the motion of a much smaller boat. They found that being outside in the breeze was much better than trying to rest in the confines of the cabin, and had settled themselves in the bow of the ship where they could get its full effect to help ward off the dangers of seasickness.

Michael had made a few attempts to start a conversation, but while some of the anger Sandy felt had worn off when she realized that Michael was almost as helpless as she was, she was still in no mood to talk. When the island of St. Thomas had disappeared from view, they heard the engines throttle back to idle, and the boat settled into the sea, rolling slowly with the swell. Under other circumstances it might have been very peaceful, but at that moment everyone on board was upset with everyone else.

They rose from their seats to ask Dmitri what had happened, but he was already making his way down the ladder from the helm and motioned for them to take their seats. They both obeyed, but were scowling at him.

"My friends are going to wonder where I am!" Sandy blurted out, before Dmitri could say anything. "They'll be very worried, and the cruise line will be looking for me too. For both of us," she pointed at Michael. "People are going to be asking questions and when they do, you're gonna have some explaining to do!"

"Passengers miss the ship all the time," Dmitri shrugged off her concerns. "They will expect you at the next island."

"What about my friends?"

"Call them when we reach shore then," another careless shrug from Dmitri. "Tell them that you had a family emergency and had to fly home."

"What if I tell them the truth, that I got kidnapped by some European madman?"

Dmitri removed his sunglasses again and gave her what Michael thought of as his 'Mafia-enforcer-glare'. It kept her quiet long enough for Dmitri to state, in an icy calm voice, "If you tell them that, and where we are, then some very bad things could happen to all of us."

She opened her mouth to reply, but no words came out.

"Mikhail, did you explain to her who is after us?"

"Yeah, and why they're after us too."

Dmitri turned back to address Sandy again. "These people are not after Mikhail. Or you. They are after me. But they will gladly use either of you to get to me." He paused, gathering his thoughts. "I am not a bad man, at least I'm not one now, no matter what I did in the past. I am trying to protect both of you; that is the most important thing. Then I will deal with these men." Michael sat up, hoping that maybe, just maybe, Dmitri had come up with a plan; Sandy just crossed her arms and listened as she glared at him.

"I am taking both of you to where I live; you will be safe there. At least for a little while."

"So what's the plan?" Michael blurted out impatiently.

"I keep you there until Yuri finds out."

Michael pondered that for a few seconds until the words sank in. "You mean he's going to find out? You want him to find out?"

"Yes. If he does not find out, if he is too stupid to figure it out, or someone else does not tell him, then I will."

"Why?" Sandy looked as shocked as Michael did. "What's the point in that?"

"Mikhail," Dmitri explained slowly, "Yuri will not give up. Even if I did not have a single dollar left, he would not give up looking for me. I knew that when I left, but I thought I could get away for good. I was wrong. I know that now. You want your life back, do you not?" He didn't wait for an answer. "Unless you want to hide for the rest of your life, we must give Yuri what he wants. Me."

Michael knew it was wrong to feel guilty for ruining Dmitri's plans for a clean get away. Still, he couldn't help but feel a twinge of regret. After all they still didn't know where Dmitri was, but now that Yuri's men had found Michael, Dmitri was going to purposely put himself in harm's way to save him. He couldn't let Dmitri do that alone, he had to stand by his friend, "I'm not going to let you face them alone, I'll ..."

"Mikhail, there is to be no argument about this. You and your friend," he nodded at Sandy, who didn't seem to appreciate being called his friend. "You will stay with me until I know what Yuri is planning. Then I will send you to a safe place so I can deal with him without worrying about you. Word will come to you when it is safe to return. You will both be well compensated for this. Do you understand?"

The question was directed at Michael who understood exactly what he meant by 'compensated', he also had a pretty good idea what Dmitri meant by 'dealing with Yuri'. Sandy nodded as well, recalling what Michael had said about the fifteen million dollars.

"I will not put you in danger again, Mikhail, or you, Sandy. You may not believe this but I really have done this for your protection. Someday you will understand this."

Michael understood his line of thinking, even if he didn't quite agree with it, or with his methods. Sandy continued to scowl at the big Ukrainian, undaunted by his size or his past. "When do we get to your secret hideout?"

Dmitri chuckled at her question, completely unaware of her sarcasm, which only made her angrier. "I do not want to arrive during daylight, so we will spend the day right here. There is food in the kitchen." Despite his ability to handle a boat, his improved English did not include the proper use of nautical terms. "Time to eat now. Then you can do some fishing. We will not arrive until after dark."

* * *

Youlya had spent a sleepless night in a drab little office in a run-down warehouse. She hadn't been kept awake by the man guarding her, but sleep would not come; her mind was too busy imagining all the things that Anton might do to her to get her money. Dmitri didn't enter her thoughts at all.

The guard had simply stood there, offering neither food nor water, nor did he offer even a hint of what was to happen. All he'd said was that Anton wanted her here and wished to speak with her. He had no idea when that might happen. He'd willingly let her use the lavatory several time during the night, but offered nothing else. By the time the sun had risen she was a nervous wreck. It was almost a relief when Anton finally entered the office.

He was neatly dressed in a well-tailored suit and looked ready for a very swanky formal affair, which only made her feel even more uncomfortable and unkempt for having spent the night in this filthy office. Anton brushed some dust from the corner of the desktop to make sure his suit stayed clean. After perching on the clean corner, he nodded to the guard who wordlessly left the office, but doubtless remained just outside the door.

"You have something that belongs to me, Youlya. I want it back."

"It's not yours!" The vehemence of her indignant reply surprised both of them, but left Anton chuckling.

"It belongs to our organization, Youlya, you know that as well as I do. If you want to keep what is yours, then you must give me what is mine." The icy calm tone of his voice robbed Youlya of whatever strength she had left.

He paused to let the meaning of his words sink in. She made no reply, so he continued. "You will also tell me where Dmitri is." He paused again and lit a cigarette, taking a long, slow puff to savour the sensation. "That is the deal I am offering you, and it is the only one I will offer you." He took another puff and blew the smoke in her direction. The expression on his face seemed to suggest that he was completely indifferent as to whether she accepted it or not.

"But what will I do? Where will I go? I have no friends, no family. Nothing!"

She was pleading now, but Anton was careful not to let his satisfaction show. "Youlya!" he said in a tone that showed both condescension and surprise at the same time. "Did you not think this through before you left us? You had a good job with Yuri and could have continued to work with me, had you only chosen to stay. You had the money Dmitri stole from us when you were with him. Was life not good then? You were the one that chose to leave him and come back to us. Surely you must understand that you cannot come back empty handed?"

Shaking his head in mock sadness he looked about for an ash tray. Not finding one he flicked the cigarette butt to the floor, watching it slowly for a moment before lifting his eyes to Youlya's as he crushed what was left of it under his heel. "When something is no longer of any use to me, Youlya, well, there is just no use keeping it around, is there?" He gave his foot one last twist, then turned towards the door. Without facing her he repeated his offer. "If you tell me where Dmitri is, and give me what is mine, I will let you keep what is yours. That is my offer, and my promise."

Opening the door, he addressed the nameless guard, the door left open so that Youlya could hear him speak. "I will be back later." The guard stepped back into the room, closed the door, and absorbed himself in a magazine, leaving Youlya with nothing to do but to consider Anton's offer. If she gave him the money he thought was his, she would get to keep what was hers, which could only mean her life. She had to find a way to strike a different deal.

Chapter Six

If Dmitri noticed that he was the only one that seemed pleased at their arrival on Culebra, he didn't let on. They tied up at a private dock and he led them up to his residence. A beautiful tropical moon hanging over the sea was wasted on both Michael and Sandy, who followed him grudgingly inside and mumbled what may have been *thank you's* when room service had been ordered for them from the resort's kitchen

Michael knew that he would have to see this whole adventure through if he were to get his life back, and as little as he liked it, he was a willing participant, he had been since he'd boarded the plane that morning. Sandy was another story. He really could empathize with her, even if she didn't understand or believe that. Should he be working on a way to get her out of Dmitri's clutches and on her way back home? He trusted her to keep quiet even if Dmitri didn't.

After she'd finished her meal, Dmitri offered to order seconds, an offer which she curtly refused before storming off to the bedroom. As she'd been about to close the door, Dmitri casually mentioned that this was known as snake island for a reason, and that some of his employees would be patrolling the grounds just in case some dangerous, slithering reptiles should attack them in the night.

"So I AM a prisoner here, am I?" After she'd slammed the door they'd heard nothing further from her.

Dmitri had made up spare beds in the living room, one on the couch for Michael, and one on the floor for himself. Before going to bed he called the cruise line to inform them that two of their passengers had stayed too long on the beach and would make arrangements to fly to the next port. They would meet the ship the day after tomorrow. In turn, they'd promised Dmitri that they would advise Sandy's roommate so that she wouldn't worry needlessly. The look Dmitri had given Michael afterwards told him that the call was not to be mentioned to Sandy. It would buy them a couple of days to see what might develop in the meantime.

* * *

"Good morning, Youlya, how did you sleep?" The voice brought her abruptly from a fitful sleep to sudden alertness, her head rising with a start from the desk to look around for the source of the voice that had roused her. For several moments she wondered where she was, why she'd fallen asleep on a chair at the desk, and why a feeling of dread seemed to be hanging over her, but then it all came flooding back to her conscious thought.

Anton's voice was bright and cheerful, as if he actually did care how she'd slept. Her lack of response seemed not to matter to him as he pulled back two chairs, sat down on one and then propped his feet up on the other. Without so much as a glance at her, he lit a cigarette and enjoyed a long puff, seemingly lost in thought. Youlya watched him suspiciously, as if at any moment he might pull a knife or a gun from his suit pocket, but after that first, long drag on his cigarette, he said nothing, merely looking at her expectantly. She had no idea what time it was, but felt certain it was definitely not morning.

Anton leaned back in his chair as if he had nothing to do all day long but to sit there and smoke. Youlya, who'd had nothing but fitful naps in the last few days, found his attitude to be anything but relaxing, and finally felt the urge to break the silence.

"If I tell you where he is, what will you give me?"

Anton took another long pull of his cigarette. "I told you already, Youlya, you will keep what is yours."

"And what exactly is that?" Her tone was a mix of fear and agitation. She already knew the answer.

"What is yours? Your life is yours."

"But I told you, I have nothing, I need something. Some way to start a new life. You must leave me something. I deserve a reward."

He sat upright in his chair, his voice sharp as he slammed his fist down on the desktop causing Youlya to jump and pull back. "And I told you that what you have is mine! You helped Dmitri to steal it from Yuri and now you will both pay for that. If you tell me where he is I will let you live, nothing more. That is more of a reward than you deserve. If you don't tell me what I want to know then you will be left with nothing at all. Do you understand me? Nothing!"

Her mind was racing now. She had two accounts and all the plans she had made required the full balance of each. On the other hand, one of those accounts alone could help her to at least start over somewhere else. Somewhere that would now have to be a country other than Ukraine. Could she succeed where Dmitri had failed? Could she get out with anything at all and truly leave her past life behind? It looked like that was her only choice now. She cleared her throat, seeking a way to gain some form of control in this failed negotiation.

"How do I know you will let me go?"

"You don't. But then, you have no choice really, do you?"

"So if I give you the money and tell you where Dmitri is I can go? Anywhere I want?"

"You will give me the money and tell me where he is. Then, when I have Dmitri, you are free to go anywhere you wish."

She realized there was no way to get an honest guarantee from Anton; he was smarter than Yuri, and much less hot-headed than Vasili; and as determined and cold-blooded as both of them combined. He was in control, so she had no choice but to let him think she was giving him what he wanted. Of the two accounts she had, one was much larger than the other. Hopefully Anton would never figure that out.

"A piece of paper, please," she said with a sigh of resignation that was only half feigned.

Anton pulled a Mont Blanc pen from his suit pocket and handed it to her along with a receipt for last night's meal. The rather exorbitant total was plainly visible and she knew he'd planned it that way. He was taunting her, showing her what he already had in order to make her own loss that much more painful. Youlya turned it over and scribbled out the account number and access code for the smaller of her two accounts. Barely had she finished when Anton swept both pen and paper from her hands, tucking the receipt back into his pocket without looking at it.

Youlya was neither comforted nor fooled by the friendly smile that came to his face as his eyes met hers. "Now, where is Dmitri?"

* * *

Vasili smiled to himself as he reclined on the pool-side lounger. He'd enjoyed an outdoor breakfast buffet under the rising sun, and had concluded that there was no better way to spend the day than outside, enjoying the hotel's courtyard. He'd never seen a real palm tree before, yet now he was surrounded by them as he sipped a drink in front of the pool. He'd take a swim, later, after he'd enjoyed the sun a bit longer. This was the life. Perhaps Dmitri had the right idea, even if he'd gone about it all wrong. Maybe after he'd made enough money, he'd move somewhere like this himself. Come to think of it, if he got enough of a cut from recovering Dmitri's money, he might be able to make that dream a reality very soon. This was living!

He was about to have Bogdan order him another drink when his mobile phone sounded. With a grunt of irritation, he picked up the offending device and saw that it was Anton. Well, who else would be calling him?

"Da, Anton."

"Youlya has very graciously returned some of what Dmitri took, and has also told me where we can find him. You need to go to the island of Culebra; it is near a place called Puerto Rico. You need to get there as soon as possible."

"I will have Bogdan book us some tickets right away. Hopefully we can get there by tomorrow." With a wave he caught Bogdan's attention and then, with another impatient wave, motioned him over to receive his new assignment. He had no idea where these places were, Culebra and Puerto Rico, but hopefully they were just as warm and exotic as St. Thomas.

"Do you think she is telling the truth?"

"I believe she is telling the truth about where he is. She knows we will not let her go until we have him. She may very well have access to more of the money than she is letting on, but there will be time to find that out later. I'm sure she is keeping a little something for herself."

"What if you can't get anything more out of her? Dmitri may have taught her to hide it well."

"It won't matter. Getting Dmitri is the important thing. Even if she does have more stashed somewhere – well – she will never have the chance to enjoy it, will she?"

* * *

Michael awoke with the guilty knowledge that he'd slept in much later than usual, forgetting that it was a good three hours earlier here than it was at home. The guilt deepened when he remembered that he had helped to kidnap Sandy the previous day.

He had slept in his clothes, everything else he had was still on the ship, wherever that might be now. Kicking the light blanket aside he sat up and rubbed his eyes sleepily.

Though a large window that offered a view of a very inviting-looking beach, he caught sight of Dmitri pacing back and forth in the sand while speaking on his cell phone. The bedroom door was still closed and he assumed that Sandy was either still sleeping, or still sulking. He couldn't help but think back to the first morning he'd awoken in Ukraine, trying to plot some way of escaping from Dmitri. With a sigh he wondered how he could be sympathizing with both Sandy and Dmitri right now. He half-hoped that she'd somehow found a way to slip away during the night. Dmitri finished his call and turned to make his way back towards the patio door.

"Good morning, Mikhail, are you ready for some breakfast? Find out what your friend wants and I will call the kitchen."

"Maybe we should let her sleep a bit longer."

Even has he spoke the door was swinging open. "No, she doesn't want to sleep any longer." Sandy sounded no less upset this morning than she had last night, and even though she did pause for a moment to take in the view, the scowl didn't leave her face. Both men watched as she took a seat at the kitchen table. "All she wants is to know when she's going home."

"As soon as it's safe you can both leave, but for now, what would you like for breakfast?"

"I guess I'll have to keep my strength up if I want to make a run for it," she muttered, fighting a bit to stay grumpy as Dmitri honestly tried to be the best host possible under the circumstances. "What's on the menu?"

"Almost anything you want."

"Scrambled eggs, ham, toast, yogurt, and fresh fruit?" The words came out sounding more like a challenge than a request.

Dmitri nodded and then glanced at Michael, waiting for his order.

"The same. Except I want bacon instead of ham."

Dmitri picked up his phone again, and they heard him repeating their orders to whomever had answered, adding his own request into the mix.

Turning to Sandy, Michael opened his mouth then closed it again, trying to find the right words in a situation that didn't seem to have any right words. She seemed to be enjoying his discomfort, a satisfied smirk coming to her lips as she arched a brow, challenging him to come up with something that might make their situation any better.

"Look, Sandy I know how you feel ... "

"Oh, really!"

"Yes, really!" he snapped back, then took a deep breath. "I'm sorry, I really am, but I really do know how you feel." He waited for a moment for any further objections, but all he got was a cold, challenging glare. "When Dmitri kidnapped me last year, I ended up in a bus accident, and then spent the first night sleeping in the backseat of a stolen car."

Beginning from that first night he gave her a recap of his entire ordeal, filling in details he'd left out the previous day, and making sure to emphasize the dramatic parts, especially his capture and the beatings he'd received from Yuri's men. She looked suitably shocked as he related the death threats he'd received when he couldn't give them the information they wanted. Then he gave a dramatic recount of how Dmitri had stormed the house, overcome two guards and Yuri himself, before rescuing him. Dmitri busied himself at his computer, pretending not to listen as Michael spoke. It felt good to be telling the full story to someone; even his friends and family had never heard the full account. He was pretty sure his parents wouldn't be able to handle how much danger he'd really been in. When it came right down to it, there wasn't anyone with whom he could share the full story.

"Look, I'm no happier than you are to be here, Sandy, but I think Dmitri really does know what he's doing. He'll do his best to look after us and get us home safely."

He managed not to smile as he finished his recitation, thinking to himself that he'd done a pretty good job of it, and hoping that Sandy was suitably impressed. Of course, the real point was to show her he really was on her side, but impressing her with the details wouldn't hurt any, would it?

Sandy sat back in her chair, processing everything she'd just been told and trying to arrive at her own conclusion. Just as she was about to speak there was a discrete knock at the door and the three of them exchanged glances, agreeing wordlessly not to say anything further until their breakfast had been delivered.

A waiter entered when Dmitri opened the door and exchanged good mornings with each of them as he served their orders. As he left, Dmitri carried a pot of hot water to the table and offered his guests a box of assorted tea bags. The thought of drinking coffee at any time of the day simply never occurred to him.

They ate in silence, none of them having realized how hungry they were until they started eating. Too much had happened in too short a time for them to have thought much about food. The distant hum of the air conditioner filled the silent gaps between the clink of silverware against plates as they polished off the generous portions sent to the boss's special guests. Dmitri poured each of them a fresh cup of hot water, then they pushed back from the table and looked at each other in silence; each waiting for someone else to resume the conversation.

"Okay," Sandy finally said, figuring another shot at it might convince Dmitri to let her go. "So in your own twisted way, you're trying to protect us." Michael shot a worried look at Dmitri at her choice of words, but Dmitri only chuckled, rather enjoying her attitude. "You want to wait till you know what this Yuri guy is going to do, then you send us to safety? Why not just let us go home now?" Her tone was somewhat softer than before, but not much.

Dmitri shook his head in disagreement. "Because they know where Mikhail lives. Until I deal with them, he is not safe at home."

"But they don't know where I live."

"Don't they?"

Sandy blinked at his reply, first in surprise, then in shock. Dmitri waited till he could see the spark of understanding in her eyes before continuing. "Are you sure no one on the plane or on the boat saw you talking with Mikhail? Are you sure they have no way of tracking you down? For the last year they have believed that he could lead them to me. What if they think that you can lead them to me now, that they can use you because you know Mikhail? You heard from him what they will do to get what they want. Do you want to take the chance you will be safe at home?" She was trying to look defiant, but her lack of response told Dmitri that his words were beginning to have the desired effect. He took a sip of tea and looked back and forth between the two of them.

"If you really want to go home, go ahead." Reverse psychology might be an English term, but it was an old and effective trick in many cultures.

CHAPTER SIX

Michael cleared his throat. "I know I'm not safe at home, so I've got no other choice. I have to trust you, Dmitri. I do trust you. You came back for me in Ukraine, and I won't ever forget that." He smiled at Dmitri for the first time since their reunion before returning his attention to Sandy. "I really think you should listen to him. I mean, neither of us will stop you if you really want to go, okay? But give Dmitri a chance. He knows these guys and how they work. We really are better off sticking with him."

His voice hadn't sounded as strong and certain as he'd hoped it would, but Sandy could see the sincerity in his eyes and nodded as he spoke. She took a sip of her tea, then studied the cup's contents as she swirled it slowly. After another slow sip she set it down on the table and shot yet another defiant look at Dmitri.

"Okay, Dmitri, I'll do what you say. For now. But you owe me and my friends another cruise."

"If that's what you really want," he responded. "I could also give all of your friends two weeks at an all-inclusive resort."

Sandy stuck out her hand and smiled for the first time that day. "Deal!"

The mood in the room lightened for a few moments, and Michael sighed with relief as the two shook hands. Maybe now they could start concentrating on what to actually do about Yuri, Vasili, and the rest of them.

Dmitri grinned as he shook Sandy's hand and let her enjoy the mood for a minute, but then, as if reading Michael's thoughts, he turned serious again. "We need to take a drive now." Michael and Sandy looked at him quizzically as he rose to grab a set of keys from the kitchen counter and motioned them towards the door.

He didn't say anything else as he led them out to a small pick-up truck parked behind the hotel. Sandy crawled into the middle while

Michael slid in beside her and Dmitri claimed the driver's seat. He put the truck in gear and backed down the driveway and onto the road before he spoke again.

"We are going to stay somewhere else for a few days," he finally said.

Michael noticed that Dmitri was paying a lot of attention to the mirrors and tried to use the mirror on his side to keep an eye on the traffic behind them, but the angle was wrong. Not wanting to needlessly alert Sandy to the possibility of immediate danger, he refrained from turning to look through the back window. He'd trust Dmitri to keep watch for all of them.

"Why?" Sandy finally asked. "Why somewhere else?"

"Because I think there will soon be some unwelcome guests at my place."

Michael looked sharply at Dmitri. "You said that you'd keep us until you knew what Yuri was up to. How will you know? Or do you know something already?" He felt a wave of suspicion break over his chest, leaving a heavy feeling in the pit of his stomach. Was Dmitri up to his old trick of only telling him what he thought he needed to know? As far as Michael was concerned, he and Sandy needed to know everything. Now.

"I told you that Youlya was no longer with me."

"Yeah, you did, but she'd never tell anyone."

"No, but she won't have a choice when they find her."

"Why do you think they'll find her?"

"Because she went back to Ukraine. It is only be a matter of time before they find her. They probably already have." He gave a helpless shrug as he spoke, and took yet another look in the mirror. Neither of his passengers said anything, figuring this was a personal matter between Dmitri and Youlya. "She was mad at me because I would not spend all the money. Plus, I gave a lot of it away. I think that she was homesick too. I would never go back there, but Youlya, well, she thought she couldn't be happy anywhere else."

Michael looked out the window, catching glimpses of the beach through the trees and brush that lined the road. He couldn't understand how anyone would want to leave what he considered to be paradise if they didn't have to. As he watched the scenery slide by, he felt a twinge of regret that they had to hide themselves here in the Caribbean. There was no time to try parasailing, or ziplining. It had been the same in Ukraine the previous summer when they'd rushed across the countryside from Kiev to Bucharest; there had been no time to enjoy and experience the country. Already his trip to Greece seemed ages ago and he would love to be able to explore and enjoy this island the way he had Greece. Maybe he should keep all that money from Dmitri and use it to see the world. Well, all the world except maybe Ukraine, as much as he'd like the opportunity to see it properly as well.

He let out a sigh, pondering the scenery until his thoughts were broken by Sandy.

"Why won't she have a choice?" she asked, a soft tremble in her voice. Even she knew it was a rhetorical question. She was still finding it hard to believe that there were men in the world that would actually torture information from a woman.

Dmitri gave her a quick, meaningful look before turning his attention back to the road. "Because these men will do anything to get what they want, and they want me very badly."

Michael felt a stab of guilt; he should have thought of what was happening to Youlya instead of just thinking of himself. After all, she had risked an awful lot for Dmitri last year, and he was alive because of those risks. What was she going through right now? Was she even alive? A glance at his friend's eyes told him that Dmitri had been wondering the same thing ever since she'd left him.

Sandy looked sick as Dmitri's words sank in, "But surely you don't mean they'd ..."

"I said they would do anything."

His words hung heavily in the cab of the truck and they rode in silence for a few minutes before Michael broke the silence. "If we're going to stay somewhere else for a while, how do you know we'll be any safer there?" He could see the same question in Sandy's eyes.

The look on Dmitri's face was almost condescending, and he actually smiled as he responded to Michael. "I knew there was always the risk they would find me, so I made some preparations. I have a safe house ready for us." He turned serious again, "I just hoped I'd never have to use it."

"But what if she tells them where the safe house is too?" Sandy wanted to know.

"It's not a safe house if anyone besides me knows about it."

"Okay," Michael countered, "But if Yuri's men are looking for you at your place, and we're at the safe house, how will we know if they show up?"

"Because I have some very loyal employees."

The truth was he paid rather handsomely for that loyalty, even though he really didn't have to. It was just the way he was used to doing things. Almost anyone would give him up under the right, or wrong, circumstances, of that he was certain. So, he really was the only one that knew where the safe house was. His manager could quite honestly plead ignorance as to his whereabouts and would provide a cover story to explain his absence, but he would also let the boss know if and when that happened.

"When someone shows up looking for me, we will hear about it.

Then I will send you two somewhere safe while I deal with them. If they think they have found me they will stop looking for you."

"You'll send us somewhere besides the safe house?" Sandy asked.

"What do you mean somewhere 'safe'?" Michael demanded at the same time.

"Somewhere off this island," Dmitri replied in a tone of voice that suggested he expected Michael to object, but wasn't going to listen. "I can deal with them best by myself." He kept his eyes fixed straight ahead as he spoke.

Sandy looked at Michael, arched a brow and gave a nod as if to say, 'sounds like a good idea to me.'

Michael, didn't agree with her; with words that sounded braver then he felt he leaned around Sandy and looked at Dmitri, whose gaze was still fixed straight ahead.

"No! We can send Sandy somewhere safe but I'm staying here to help you!"

"You are going with her." His voice was calm, but very firm.

"No, you need some help. Just tell me what to do and I'll do it."

"Can you kill someone if you need to?"

Sandy gasped audibly and Dmitri patiently waited for an answer he was sure would not come. It didn't.

"Are you really going to kill someone?" Sandy was thinking she needed to get as far away from this man as possible, no matter what reasons he might have.

"Not unless I need to, but if there is no other way, if they are going to kill me, or you, I might have to." His answer was devoid of emotion, it was merely a statement of fact.

"You left the Mafia so you wouldn't have to do that anymore. If you hadn't taken the money ..."

"Sandy, if I had not taken the money, they would still be coming for me," his accent was back, as thick as ever, as if he were reverting back to the person he'd once been. "I will do what I have to do to save my life. You would prefer I let them kill me?"

"No, of course not!" Michael objected. "Maybe together we can figure something out. Sandy can hide out until we deal with this and then we can let her know it's safe to go home."

"What if you two don't survive? Do I have to hide out forever?" Both men ignored her question, though it was a good one.

"You will both go!" repeated Dmitri.

"But you came back for me last year; I owe it to you. It's the least I can do."

"I came back for you because you would have died if I hadn't. I was protecting you then, and I'm protecting you now. You cannot handle this, Mikhail, that is why I will do this alone. It will be safer for both of us if you go."

"Then why did you bring me here in the first place?" Michael sat back and crossed his arms, glaring out the window.

"So that I can get all of Yuri's men in one place and know that you are safe."

Sandy gave Michael a subtle poke with her knee and when he turned to look at her, she shot him a reproving glare which suggested that he should be thankful for what Dmitri was doing. Michael made a face, knowing she was right, that he should be thankful. If he was honest with himself, he was secretly relieved that he didn't have to face these guys again; one experience like that in a lifetime was more than enough. Hadn't he just been wishing for time to enjoy the place? He certainly wouldn't object to being able to spend some time with Sandy. Still, it didn't sit well with him that Dmitri had played the hero in Ukraine, and now he was going to do it again. Michael seemed to be destined to play the part of the helpless man in distress. Okay, so this whole mess was Dmitri's fault, but shouldn't he play some part in resolving it this time?

"Isn't there something I can do?"

"Yes. Stay out of sight so I can deal with Yuri and Vasili without having to worry about you and your friend." His answer was softer this time, as if he were pleading with Michael to listen to reason.

Chapter Seven

Vasili and Bogdan stepped out of the small commuter plane that had carried them to Culebra, and into the oppressive late-morning heat. Descending the stairs, they stepped onto the paved tarmac, which further magnified the temperature. They both adjusted their sunglasses and looked around, trying to appear casual as they searched the area for any indication that they were being watched. They were travelling light, with only a small carry-on bag each. Most of their baggage had been left on St. Thomas.

Vasili spent a long moment surveying the countryside, the lush green hills rising against the horizon were in sharp contrast to the flat vistas of Florida, and much different from what he was used to in Ukraine. This would be a wonderful place to live; it was warm, tropical, exotic. Not to mention the fact that it was likely ripe for the picking. He had no doubt that someone was profiting from this setting, and even less doubt that he could do a better job of it than whoever that might be. With his experience he could soon be running all kinds of schemes on this island.

He watched as his fellow passengers deplaned and made their way across the tarmac, imagining the types of 'entertainment' each of them might desire and what he might be able to pocket by providing it for them. Depending upon what they wanted he might be able to double his profits with a little blackmail as well. Not to mention gambling and protection money. The possibilities were endless. Yes, he'd definitely have to think about that once he was finished with Dmitri. His associates would get a share of the profits of course, he didn't dare dream of trying to go solo knowing the fate that was awaiting Dmitri, but he would be able to keep a generous portion for himself, and live in a tropical paradise while doing so. A dream come true indeed!

He took one last look at the scenery before motioning Bogdan to follow him. They'd reserved a rental car before leaving St. Thomas to make their arrival here as smooth as possible. Bogdan did the talking and signing, so it was a simple enough matter to pick it up and get on the road. Armed with a map of the island, thoughtfully provided by the rental agency, they made the short drive to a Bed and Breakfast where they'd booked a room. The internet really was a great way to make discrete reservations.

Once they had checked in, they sat at the small kitchen table and spread out the map to get a better feel for the lay of the land. Vasili marked the map with the location of Dmitri's property. They studied the map for a while and decided it didn't show enough detail, so Bogdan pulled out a tablet and called up an online map. This one was much more detailed, especially when they zoomed in, and they were quickly able to figure out the best ways to and from the resort.

When Bogdan pulled up an online advertisement for Dmitri's place, Vasili felt a twinge of envy. He'd been so intent for so long on tracking down his 'enemy' and former friend, that all he'd felt was betrayal and the need to avenge what Dmitri had done. Now as he looked at the buildings nestled among the palm trees, and the white sandy stretch of beach, he realized that he wanted the life Dmitri now had. Such a place was wasted on scum like Dmitri. He was the one who really deserved it!

"I think we should drive by his place," Vasili said, not looking for any input or agreement from Bogdan, merely stating his opinion. Bogdan wasn't paid to think, just to obey. "We can get a first-hand look at it, and then get some lunch."

Since both men were already dressed as typical tourists, they sauntered out to the car and, with Vasili giving directions, Bogdan navigated his way to the resort. At Vasili's instruction he slowed down as they drove by so that they could confirm that they were at the right place. That is, if Youlya had told them the truth. If they hadn't been told the truth, then Youlya would have a lot of explaining to do. Nothing permanent would be done to her, of course. At least not yet. They had to find Dmitri first.

The name of the resort was correct, and it matched the general description that Anton had passed on to them. Either Youlya really had been living here and was being honest, or she'd seen pictures of it online too. Though he didn't admit it to Bogdan, Vasili was hoping to catch a brief glimpse of Dmitri, but that was not only too much to hope for, it might also be dangerous if Dmitri recognized him. For now, he would content himself with the knowledge that they'd found the right place. Perhaps he could send Bogdan in under the pretense of looking for a place to stay. Once they'd confirmed that Dmitri was indeed here, they'd call in some reinforcements and formulate a plan.

"Okay, let's get something to eat. We'll come back later this afternoon," Vasili rolled up his window and cranked the air conditioning back up to its highest setting. "Dmitri has never met you, and you speak English, so I'll send you in to see what you can learn."

He picked up his mobile phone and checked the time, did a mental calculation of the time difference between here and home, and made a call. Time to remind Anton that he was on the job and doing the real work in this operation.

* * *

Youlya had now been moved into a room even smaller than the one she'd previously been held in, but at least this one did have a cot on which she could sleep. There was nothing else to keep her amused, no books or magazines, no TV, not even a window to enable her to watch and gauge the passage of time. She couldn't do much more than lay on the bed and wish she'd gone anywhere but Ukraine after leaving Dmitri. She'd been so sure that being back home would make her truly happy. Perhaps she should have flown to Germany or Poland and taken a train back to Kiev. Or settled in another city. Why had she been so foolish as to believe that they would not be looking for her?

With a sigh she rolled to her side and swept her eyes across the bare, drab room that had now become her whole world. She was longing for a break in the routine, yet at the same time dreading the next time the door might open. As if in response to her fear there came the soft noise of the door handle turning and the creak of hinges as the door swung open. Feeling guilty, or perhaps vulnerable, as she lay there, she quickly swung her legs over the edge of the cot and sat up, smoothing her dishevelled hair with her hand. She had no idea what had become of her hairbrush which had disappeared along with her purse and the rest of its contents.

"Good evening, Youlya," Anton's voice was cheerful, but he didn't bother to look at her, seemingly intent on a text message as he sat down on the edge of an old, dusty desk that had been pushed against one of the walls. He took an inordinate amount of time to respond to the text and even though Youlya knew he was doing it purposely to make her uncomfortable, she couldn't help but respond exactly how he hoped she would.

He smiled at the phone then looked up at her, the smile still in place. "Vasili has been to the place you told us about on Culebra. He says it is pretty much as you described it, but he saw no sign of Dmitri." She gave an uncomfortable shrug as if to say 'so what?' Vasili paused to let the accusation hang over her before continuing. "He feels you might have just picked a place at random and are lying to us." Another long pause. "Or maybe Dmitri just stays out of sight." Vasili had said no such thing, of course, but he needed to keep her off balance.

"He does try to stay out of sight as much as possible," her words came out quickly, nervously. "He was always afraid that someone might recognize him and report back to Yuri."

"You didn't mention that when you told us where to look, did you?"

"You asked me where he was and I told you! I also gave you the money back. When can I go?"

He smiled and shook his head, almost sadly. "Not yet. First we have to get our hands on Dmitri."

She felt a twinge of regret, knowing full well what would happen when they found him. So far, she'd done her best not to think about it, but it was too late for second thoughts now, wasn't it? All she could do was look out for herself. If she had refused to talk – well – things would have gone a lot differently and they'd have got the information out of her anyway.

"We will continue to watch for him. I'll let you know what happens when I hear something from Vasili. In the meantime, perhaps there is something else you'd like to tell me? Something you've forgotten until now maybe?"

She felt her heart skip a beat, and then start to race. To buy some time she moved her gaze up into the corner of the room, concentrating on a spider web and pretending to search her memory for something that might help them find Dmitri. What she was really pondering was whether or not it would be worth the rest of the money to gain her freedom. She glanced at Anton and then quickly back up at the web. There were two problems with that plan. First, there was simply no way she was getting out of here until they really did have Dmitri no matter what else she gave them. The second problem was that if she suddenly came up with more money, then they would suspect that she had even more. They'd let her go when they had Dmitri. They had to.

She shook her head slowly, as if still searching for some forgotten tidbit of information. "No, Anton, I don't think there is anything else at all. I told you where he is living and that's all I can think of. He is there, or at least he was when I left." She forced herself to look him straight in the eye. "But if I think of anything else, I promise I will tell you."

Anton's attention was once more fixed on his phone as he rose from the table and walked from the room without so much as a glance in her direction. There was an audible click as the door was locked from the outside.

* * *

Michael had completely lost track of where he was but for once in his life he didn't really care. There were too many other thoughts vying for his attention, not to mention his desire to be as far from Yuri's men as possible. After more than an hour of driving, and possibly some doubling back for all he knew, Dmitri turned from the main road and followed a winding driveway to a single-storey house that sat well back from the road. It was almost completely hidden from view on the ocean side by a grove of palm trees and other assorted tropical growth. He pulled the little truck into a small shed that would conceal it from view should anyone take a casual look at the property.

Michael slid out of the truck and held the door for Sandy, who rewarded him with a smile. With no luggage to worry about they followed Dmitri as he made his way to the house, fishing in his pocket for the key to the back door. Once inside they each headed for a window to get a breeze blowing into the building, which felt oppressively humid and stale.

"There's food in the pantry," Dmitri informed them. "Nothing fresh but we will not starve. There are also some extra clothes in the bedroom closet." He sized up Sandy for a few seconds, "I think you will find some things that fit you in the closet. You can take whatever you want to that room over there," he said, indicating a spare room. "Mikhail, you and I can share the other room, or I can sleep on the couch. Most of the clothes will be too big for you, I think, but there should be something."

Despite their reservations, and the fervent wish that they'd never become mixed up in Dmitri's problems, both Michael and Sandy figured that they could be faring a lot worse. Aside from needing a good airing out, and a bit of house cleaning, the place wasn't all that bad. It was secluded and quiet, and located on a beautiful stretch of beach.

Sandy was already rummaging through the closet, eager to change out of the clothes she'd been wearing since leaving the ship. She figured Dmitri was right, that some of it would fit her just fine. "Hey, can we at least go to the beach, or does that violate our terms of incarceration?" she called down the hallway.

Dmitri looked at Michael with a puzzled expression. "She wants to know if we're under house arrest, or can she go to the beach," Michael explained.

"You can go to the beach. There are no other houses nearby, but if you see anyone else, come back to the house right away. We might have to leave again in a hurry, so don't go too far."

"Okay, but hold the bad guys off at least long enough for me to get some sun. I missed out on my beach time yesterday. You owe me that much!" She selected a few items she thought might be appropriate for a bit of time on the beach, and made her way to the spare room.

Michael waited until she closed her door, then went to rummage through the clothes himself. "Guess you never intended to have anyone smaller than you stay here," he grumbled. He too felt the need to change, but the best he could do was a much-too-large t-shirt and an extra baggy pair of swim trunks. They'd have to do, so with a shrug he went to change as well.

By cinching the drawstring as tight as possible he managed to satisfy himself that the trunks were likely to stay up; the t-shirt was almost long enough that it wouldn't matter even if they didn't. Dmitri was busy tiding up and taking stock of what was in the house. Whatever plans he might be making to deal with his old associates he was keeping to himself. Michael offered to help with the housework, but Dmitri insisted he could manage it himself and all but forced him out the patio doors.

He wandered self-consciously towards the beach where Sandy was standing beneath a palm tree, looking up and down the deserted beach. She caught sight of him and laughed aloud at his appearance. "Most people gain weight on a cruise. You do know the food is free, right?"

He was searching for a smart comeback, but recalling how he'd looked in the mirror he couldn't help but laugh at himself. "Yeah, well, it turns out the clothes are free too, but there isn't much of a selection. You look pretty good though." Suddenly realizing how that might sound he tried to back-peddle. "I mean, the clothes look pretty good on you. You must be about the same size as Youlya. Not that you don't look good!" He was getting more flustered with each word and finally gave up as she burst into laughter.

"Well, thank you, Mikhail, I'll assume that was a compliment. Wanna go for a swim? I brought some towels along."

Michael tugged off the baggy t-shirt and double checked that the waistband was tied as tightly as possible, then the two of them ran into the surf. The water was warm and for twenty or thirty minutes they enjoyed themselves enough that they both forgot that they weren't really there on a holiday. As they towelled off on the beach, and Michael tugged the shirt back on, reality came flooding back.

"Look, I really am sorry about how all this turned out," he said as he plopped down in the sand in the shade of a clump of trees. "I didn't plan any of it. Honest!"

"You keep saying that, and I'm to starting to believe you," Sandy replied with a sigh. "I just hope whatever your friend has planned doesn't take too long. I've got a job to get back to and a bunch of friends who are going to start worrying about me if I don't show up soon."

"I almost forgot about my job," he winced as he spoke. "I just got back from a holiday and I already used up all my time off for the next year. I didn't even tell anyone I was going; it all happened too fast."

They sat in silence for some time, both of them gazing out at the constant line of waves washing onto the beach, and each lost in their own thoughts.

"Maybe if I can talk Dmitri into letting me help him, we can get this whole mess cleaned up sooner," Michael said at last.

"Look, I want to go back to my real life as soon as possible too, but do you think that's a good idea? These guys sound pretty dangerous." Michael gave a shrug, not to boast of his courage, but rather to show how desperate he was to put this part of his life behind him. Sandy thought a few minutes and then added, "Do you really think you could kill someone if it came to that?"

Now it was Michael's turn to sigh. "No, I guess not. They would have killed me, I think, if Dmitri hadn't come back for me. They couldn't very well let me go, and I wasn't any use to them. But, no, I guess I couldn't. But you know, I'm not sure Dmitri could either. Maybe at one time he could have, maybe he even did for all I know. He really has changed, even since last summer. I think he was just trying to scare me off to make sure I wouldn't get tangled up in things again and get hurt." He saw the look on her face and gave a wry laugh. "Guess it's a little too late for that, huh?"

"Yeah, I'd say it is."

"Sandy, I know you don't know him like I do, but he told me about his past, how he started stealing when he was a kid and got recruited into the Mafia. He knew he was taking his life in his hands when he left Ukraine, and I believe him when he tells me that he only took the money to start a new life. From what I can tell he's given a lot of it away to people that really needed it."

"A real Robin Hood, huh?" The sarcasm in her voice was impossible to miss. "How do you know he really gave it away?"

"Well, I do know for a fact he gave some to me, that's how things started up again." Her raised eyebrow told him he needed to explain further. "From what I can tell, the Ukrainian Mafia's been watching me since I got home and somehow they found out that Dmitri deposited a bunch of money into my bank account. I didn't even know he'd done it, but they seem to know I've got it and that's why Dmitri brought me down here; to make sure I was safe while he deals with them."

She didn't ask for any further information, but he could tell she was curious. He looked back out to sea as he continued to speak. "When I got back home there was an extra million dollars in my bank account, and the police told me that I was being followed by two men that they thought had ties to organized crime."

"Oh," was all she said in response, as if she heard stories like that all the time.

Michael's confession about the cash seemed to make both of them too uncomfortable to discuss the matter further. They continued to sit in silence for a while, until Michael rose to his feet.

"I'm hungry. Want to see what Dmitri has for us for lunch?"

"Yes!" Her response was more relief than agreement, but she rose and followed him back to the house.

* * *

Bogdan strolled casually into the hotel lobby, looking slowly around as if sizing the place up for a possible stay. He nodded to the desk clerk and took another look out the window at the ocean before approaching the desk, it really was beautiful. Like many people who've learned a second language, he didn't realize that he spoke with a heavy accent.

"Hello, I'm visiting your island for the first time, but I'm thinking of coming back with some friends later this year and I'm looking for a place for all of us to stay."

"What size group would be staying here, sir?" Yes, Juan thought to himself, he sounded just like the boss did. Maybe it was just a coincidence, but how likely was that? This must certainly be the man he had been told to watch for.

"Oh, I suppose that there might be about ten of us."

"Well, I'm sure we could work out a deal for a group that large." He pulled a brochure from beneath the desk and they spent a few minutes going over seasonal rates and discounts, as well as possible dates.

"Thank you," Bogdan said after studying the brochure and the notes the clerk had made on it. "I will talk it over with my ... my friends, and we will let you know if we decide to stay here."

"Of course, sir, and if you have any more questions please feel free to email us. We will do all we can to make your stay here on our island a pleasant one."

"Thank you. Are you the owner?" The question was supposed to be casual, but there was an edge, an eagerness, in the words.

"No, sir, I'm not. He's not here right now. He is dealing with some personal matters right now, but he should be back in the next day or so." Juan gave the answer Dmitri had instructed him to give should the question arise. Hopefully that would keep them close by until Dmitri actually did return. "Would you like to leave a message for him?"

"No!" Bogdan's answer was a little too emphatic, confirming Juan's suspicions. "I will talk to my friends and we will be in touch with you."

"Very well, sir. Enjoy your stay and I hope you come back to Culebra."

Juan waited until Bogdan had walked back out to his rental car and watched him drive off before picking up the phone and dialing Dmitri's number.

* * *

Dmitri's phone was ringing as Michael and Sandy entered the kitchen. He motioned them to sit at the table where a plate of sandwiches was waiting for them, and took a seat himself as they listened to his end of the conversation. They couldn't tell much from what Dmitri was saying; all he did was to acknowledge whatever the person on the other end was saying.

Each of them had polished off one sandwich and started in on a second by the time Dmitri hung up. The look on his face was hard to read, but Michael thought he saw an eagerness in the Ukrainian's eyes, which left him feeling uneasy. He set down his sandwich in anticipation of the news.

"That was Juan. A man with a Ukrainian accent was asking about me. He has to be one of Yuri's men. They are here."

The last sentence seemed to have been spoken to himself, not to his guests, as if a decision had just been made for him. Or perhaps as if a plan was to be put into motion.

"Okay, what do we do now?" Sandy shot a look at Michael as if to warn him into silence, to stay out of it and let Dmitri handle things.

"First, we do the most important thing," Dmitri responded, waiting till he had the full attention of both Sandy and Michael. "We eat!"

Despite himself Michael grinned and picked up his sandwich, taking a big bite and forgetting his manners as he asked, with a full mouth, "What do we do after we finish eating?"

"After we finish eating, we make a phone call and you and Sandy," he nodded at each of them in turn, "Go somewhere safe." He raised a hand before Michael could finish swallowing, anticipating an argument, "We will not discuss this anymore, Mikhail. You two will go somewhere safe and I will send word when it is time for you to come back. That is all that 'we' will do. I will see to the rest."

Chapter Eight

Michael finished the rest of his meal in silence, resigning himself to the fact that it was useless to argue with Dmitri. Sandy, sensing the tension between the two of them, thought it best to remain quiet herself. She had already decided that the safest thing for both of them was to get as far away as possible and to let Dmitri handle his own problems. Despite what Michael seemed to think she had come to the conclusion that neither of them owed him anything. If he was going to send them away, so much the better! They might even find an opportunity to sneak off and get away all together, although she did have some reservations about that. If Dmitri was right, and she wasn't saying he was, but if he was right in his assumptions that they were in danger until he'd 'dealt' with these guys, then it wouldn't hurt to play it safe. She glanced over at Michael as she sipped the cup of the hot tea that Dmitri seemed to think made every meal complete. Aside from helping to kidnap her, Michael seemed like a nice guy. It really would be terrible if anything bad happened to him. She could understand his desire to help Dmitri, she just didn't think it was a good idea.

After cleaning up the dishes, Dmitri handed each of them a shapeless, floppy beach hat and a pair of overly-large sunglasses, the purpose of which was to disguise them as much as possible. Michael managed a laugh as he saw Sandy decked out in her new apparel, and another after looking at himself in a mirror. Even some of his friends might not recognize him at first glance, especially since the baggy shirt and pants went a long way towards disguising his slender frame.

"Jake!" Michael turned to see Dmitri speaking into his phone. "I need that favour I told you about. Yes, exactly. But there will be two of them, okay? Good, how soon can you leave?" He glanced at his watch. "We will be there, and thank you, my friend."

"Time to go," Dmitri announced after hanging up. "Mikhail, take those two suitcases," he nodded towards two small carry-on bags sitting beside the door. "I've packed a few things you will need for the next few days. There is some money in there as well if you need anything else. I've arranged for someone to meet you when you arrive. They have been told that you are on your honeymoon and that I've given you a room at their resort for a wedding present."

He and Sandy avoided eye contact when Dmitri mentioned a honeymoon, and Michael felt himself blush, but he recovered enough to change the subject.

"Where are we going and how are we getting there if you're not coming? Is this Jake guy driving us somewhere?"

"Get the suitcases," he repeated. "You will see."

After stowing the bags in the back of Dmitri's truck he squeezed into the passenger seat beside Sandy and rolled down the window before closing the door. He preferred the wind to air conditioning, and it gave him an excuse to look out the window as they headed back for the main road. That way he didn't have to look at Dmitri or Sandy.

It was a quiet drive as no one seemed to want to break the silence, but Michael perked up when he saw a sign indicating an airport and Dmitri turned up the road indicated by the sign. He looked expectantly at Dmitri.

"We're flying somewhere?"

"You are flying somewhere," Dmitri corrected.

"Yeah, I get that," he retorted, trying not to sound too bitter and succeeding only because there were few things in life he enjoyed more than flying. Dmitri parked the truck near a small terminal building with a sign over the door announcing that they had arrived at the Aeropuerto Benjamin Rivera Noriega.

"Wait a minute, Mikhail," Dmitri ordered in a soft voice that still carried a tone of authority. By now Dmitri had also adopted a bit of a disguise. The same kind of large, shapeless hat that Michael and Sandy wore, covered his head almost down to his eyeballs. Given his usual tropical attire, and lack of pointy shoes, he didn't look very Ukrainian at first glance, but given his size and bulk, Michael wasn't too sure that he could fool any of Yuri's men.

As Michael gently pulled the door closed again, Dmitri checked the truck's mirrors and studied the people standing around the terminal building's exterior. Satisfying himself as completely as possible that there were no immediate threats, he nodded to his two passengers, signalling them to get out of the truck. Michael gallantly took both bags himself and they followed Dmitri as he led them not into the terminal building, but to a small van parked a few spaces over.

He walked up to the driver's door and stuck his hand through the window to give the hand that met his a firm, solemn shake. "This is Mikhail and Sandy," he informed the man, pointing to each of them in turn. As they each shook his hand Dmitri continued the introduction. "Jake is a trusted friend of mine. He will look after you."

Before either of them could respond he turned on his heel and strode purposely back to his truck. Without so much as a wave or a glance at them he started the truck, put it in gear, and drove off.

Michael raised an eyebrow as he looked at Sandy.

"Well, I guess he'll be in touch."

"Yeah, I guess so," she responded, managing not to add 'good riddance'. She supposed he might possibly make a good host under the right circumstances. He did run a seemingly successful resort after all; but that was for guests that arrived of their own free will. If she ever did take him up on his offer of a free stay, she'd see for herself.

"So, into the terminal building?" Michael asked, but he was surprised when Jake shook his head.

"Nope. Throw your bags into the back of the van and climb in," he replied in a friendly enough tone.

Surprised, and a little disappointed that they would not be flying as he'd hoped, Michael opened up the back door of the van and added the bags to an eclectic collection of tools and other personal effects. From all appearances they may very well have taken up residence in the van when its current owner had first taken possession of it, and remained there undisturbed ever since. He held the passenger door open for Sandy, who gave him a weak, nervous smile. His own smile seemed to be trying to say that if Dmitri trusted Jake then he must be okay, but either Sandy didn't get the message, or didn't quite believe it.

Neither of them had anything to say, and Jake seemed content to drive in silence as he pulled back out of the parking lot and headed left, towards the beach. They made a hard left turn, almost reversing direction, and then followed the road as it circled to the south of the airport. Michael couldn't help but look back at the airport where he noticed a large hill right off the far end of the runway. A single engine Cessna was approaching to land from that end and he sat up to watch as when he noticed that the pilot wasn't lined up with the runway. The hills made it impossible. Instead he was making an approach that had swerved back and forth along a valley between two hills, only lining up with the runway at the last moment. He had enough trouble landing on a straight-in approach himself, and wondered if he'd ever have the skill to make that kind of landing. How did you gauge your altitude when you weren't even looking straight at the runway? Whoever was flying seemed to know what he was doing though, appearing to straighten out and line up with the runway at the same moment that he raised the nose to touch down. Well, maybe someday he would be able to handle a plane that well himself. He was so intent on watching the plane as it completed its landing roll that he didn't notice what Sandy did: that Jake was constantly checking his mirrors to make sure that no one was following them.

The road was now running more or less parallel with the runway, but on the side opposite the terminal building. They drove past a road that led left, back towards the airport, and continued up the road until, when there was no traffic visible in either direction, Jake suddenly swung over as far to the right as he could, and made a U-turn, heading back towards the beach. His two passengers looked at each other, wondering what was going on. Neither felt comfortable enough to ask where they were going, though. Michael's only solace was that if Dmitri said he was a trusted friend, then he must have earned that trust.

Still eyeing his mirrors, Jake made the right turn down the side road they'd just passed and soon parked beside a ramp that sat across the runway from the terminal building.

"Ok, grab your bags and follow me," he instructed, climbing out of the van. Waiting until Michael had collected both of the bags, he guided them onto the ramp towards a white and red Cessna, the same make and model that Michael had been dreaming about ever since he'd seen it on the ramp back home; a Cessna 182 Skylane. It was a single engine plane, a bigger, faster brother to the trainer he flew, and it had retractable landing gear.

"Dmitri tells me that you're a student pilot," Jake commented as he took one of the bags from Michael and held it as if to weigh it. Satisfied that it was well within acceptable weight limits, he slid it through the cargo door behind the rear seats and took the second bag. "What are you flying?"

Sandy gave a sigh, having heard all too many conversations between pilots already, but both men ignored her. This was important stuff they were discussing!

"Cessna 172's, but I can't wait to fly something bigger. I'm ready for my cross-country solo now."

"That's almost as big a step as your first solo," Jake said, shutting the cargo door and beginning his pre-flight inspection. Sandy knew how important this was and stood back, watching with a detached curiosity; she had her own pre-flight duties when she was flying.

Michael was about to comment on how he'd do the flight when he got home, if he got home, but he wasn't sure how much Jake knew about what was going on and decided to err on the side of caution.

"Is this your plane?"

"Yeah, one of them. I run a small air service. A couple of float planes and a Cheyenne that I do some charter with. I use this one to run around in when I don't need something bigger." Michael was impressed, just owning a plane like this was all he'd ever dreamed of. "Tell you what, if your lady friend doesn't mind the back seat you can sit up front and I'll let you fly her for a while."

Michael looked at Sandy with a hopeful grin, at which she rolled her eyes in mock exasperation. "Well, if I have to, I guess. Not like I've never ridden in the back of an airplane before!"

"She's a flight attendant," Michael explained to Jake.

"Just don't expect a beverage service on this flight, unless one of you brought a pot of coffee along."

Jake chuckled as he finished the walk around.

"Maybe I can hire you for my charter runs, though I'm sure you're used to much bigger equipment than what I fly. But if you're a flight attendant then you must know how important pre-flight briefings are."

He spent a couple of minutes explaining the operation of the doors, seat belts, and safety equipment. Both of them listened patiently, and Sandy looked rather impressed that their 'captain' took his duties so seriously, even on an aircraft this small. Michael found it very similar to the briefings he'd been taught to give, except that this plane carried a life raft and life jackets.

The briefing completed, Jake opened the pilot's door and slid his seat all the way forward to allow Sandy to climb into the back. Once she was seated, he slid it back and climbed in while Michael circled the plane and climbed in the passenger side. He couldn't hide the grin on his face as he settled into the seat, breathing in the familiar 'airplane smell' and checking to make sure he could reach all the controls and the rudder pedals, but careful not to move or disturb them. He noticed Jake nodding in approval, and felt he'd earned, well if not respect, at least an acknowledgement that he knew the basics of how to properly handle himself in a cockpit.

He watched intently as Jake went through the start-up procedures, let the engine warm up, and then did his run-up to ensure that the engine and controls were all working properly. It wasn't too much different from what he did in his 172, except for the constant speed propeller. To Michael the constant speed prop was an incredibly complex and mysterious piece of equipment that greatly improved performance, but was something that only the elite, inner circle of pilots could fully understand and master.

Remaining silent so Jake could concentrate on the run up, Michael waited until they began taxiing to the runway to start asking questions.

"I've never flown a constant speed prop; how does it work? I mean, I know the theory from ground school, but I've never seen it done."

"It's not that hard really. On your trainer you want to go faster you make the prop spin faster right?" Michael nodded. "Okay, so with a constant speed job you set the RPM and it stays set, you advance or retard the throttle and the blade angle changes. It's like changing gears, so you can go faster or slower without changing the RPM. It gives you more efficiency during each phase of the flight, like take off, approach, and cruise." Michael nodded, still not fully understanding, but deciding not to ask anything further before take-off, knowing Jake needed to concentrate on flying.

They were now taxiing to the end of the runway closest to the hills that you needed to fly between in order to land; they'd be taking off towards the ocean. "To keep it simple, the general rule is 'rev up and throttle back.'" Seeing Michael's puzzled expression, he went on, "It's not a hard and fast rule, there are exceptions on some planes, but it works most of the time. Always keep the RPM the same, or higher than, the manifold pressure. The prop control sets the RPM, the throttle controls manifold pressure." He pointed to the controls and the gauges as he spoke. "Let's say you want to run 2300 RPM, you push in the prop control until you reach 2300, then you advance the throttle to no more than 23 inches of manifold pressure. The operating handbook will tell you what settings to use depending on what performance you want, but the 182 is a pretty simple airplane so after a while you get to know where to set it without looking it up all the time."

Michael nodded in partial understanding. That wasn't so hard, but he disagreed with Jake's assessment that this was a pretty simple airplane.

"Let's say you want to reduce your power setting, what would you do?"

"Well, you'd 'throttle back', right? I guess you'd bring back the throttle, then pull back the prop control and make sure the RPM stayed higher than the manifold pressure."

"Exactly! Not so hard, is it?" Jake was scanning the area for traffic now but continued with his flying lesson. "As long as you remember that, you could treat this like a heavier, faster 172 and you could fly her yourself."

Michael grinned at that thought, that would sure impress his flight instructor!

Jake now spun the plane around and lined it up with the centre line of the runway. "Okay, feet on the brakes," he ordered, checking that Michael had done so and then letting go of the controls. Michael realized what was about to happen and felt his heart quicken in excitement, but he was also nervous, knowing he was about to be tested on something he'd never tried before. "The runway is only 2600 feet long, and it's a hot day, but at least we're at sea level and below maximum weight. Now, set the RPM at 2400." Michael looked down, hesitating a second to make sure he had the right control, then played with it gingerly until he had the proper setting.

"Keep the brakes set and advance the throttle." The plane rocked forward as the prop started tugging against the brakes, and Michael felt the thrill he always did when he was about to take off. "Okay, release the brakes, I'll watch your airspeed, you just keep us straight."

Compared to what he was used to flying, the Sky-lane accelerated very quickly, but the runway looked awful short and it was disappearing behind him at an alarming rate as they gathered speed. "Okay, rotate!"

Michael pulled back on the control wheel a bit too quickly, afraid that they were running out of room, but corrected before Jake had to say anything.

"Good," he acknowledged, raising the gear as Michael established a stable climb. "Now, ease the throttle back to 23 inches." Michael felt a mild stab of disappointment at not being allowed to raise the gear himself; that would have been another first, but he admittedly had his hands full already, having to jockey the throttle to get the right setting.

"Dmitri told me not to tell you where we were going until we got there, but I assume you know how to read a heading indicator?" Jake grinned mischievously at him, as if they were about to get away with something. Michael nodded without looking at him, concentrating on keeping the proper climb attitude. "Okay, so if I give you a heading to fly, you'll pretend not to notice it, right?"

* * *

Youlya had been fooling herself, she finally realized and chided herself harshly. She should have seen it much sooner. When she'd first been found, she'd held on to the hope that if Anton were to believe that he had all her money, plus some information as to Dmitri's location, that they would let her go. When that hadn't worked out, she'd been foolish enough to believe that once they'd found Dmitri and recovered all the money they could, that they would see she was on their side, so to speak, and then she would be set free. It was hard to think consciously about Dmitri falling into their hands, but she was by now far past caring what happened to him. Hadn't he got her into this in the first place? Wasn't it all his fault?

CHAPTER EIGHT

Of course it was!

She had never asked for untold wealth and a life of luxury in a foreign country, had she? Well, of course she'd dreamed of it now and then, who hadn't? But never had she actually believed it would ever happen. Besides, it wasn't at all as wonderful as she'd hoped it would be. She had been quite happy working for Yuri Stepanovich, she didn't need any more than what she'd had back then. True, he had been difficult to work for at times, and she had felt a healthy fear of him, but that had been much different than the fear she now had of Anton. She'd been paid a wage far above what most secretaries could expect in her country. Why had she fallen for Dmitri when there had been other suitors? She was refusing to remember that she hadn't really been free to date anyone that was not a part of the organization. Yuri wanted to ensure that she didn't divulge information that could have caused problems for his 'family'. Forgotten was the fact that, despite the duties he fulfilled for Yuri, there had always been an inner gentleness to Dmitri that was rarely, if ever, seen in such men.

There were any number of men working for Yuri that earned enough to live very comfortably here in Ukraine. Enough to enjoy trips abroad without having to give up their entire lives to do so. She should have chosen one of them instead, then she wouldn't be sitting here in this room, waiting for a fate that she was sure had already been decided by Anton. She sighed and sat up, looked around the room, and tried to come to grips with the fact that she might never leave it alive. The only reason she was still alive was that they did not yet have Dmitri, and they still needed her in case she might be able to provide more information. She'd co-operate, of course, or they'd torture her until she did. The problem was that they might assume she had information that she wasn't sharing, in which case they'd torture her anyway.

If only they'd turn off the light so that she could get some rest and think things through. They were keeping the light on precisely so that she'd lose track of time. No doubt the erratic meal schedules were for the same purpose. Though she had no way of knowing for certain, she was very sure that several times meals had been served to her less than an hour apart. Another time it had felt like more than a day had passed between meals. Just how long had she been here? It would almost be a relief if they did find Dmitri; it would put an end to her misery and she could comfort herself with the knowledge that Dmitri had not gotten away with it after all.

She glared at the door for what felt like an hour, half in fear and half in expectation, but nothing happened. She wasn't sure whether that should make her feel relieved or not. That's when it hit her. She knew what they were trying to do, but she hadn't realized until now just how well it was working. They'd worn her down. She hardly cared what happened to her as long as it all came to an end, one way or another. She'd do anything to end it. They'd won.

No! She wouldn't let that happen. Dmitri was always looking for his famous opportunities; well, she wasn't going to wait for one, she'd make one!

Rising from her seat she began searching the room. There wasn't much in it, but there had to be something, somewhere that she could use to create an opportunity.

* * *

Bogdan and Vasili had spent the late morning and most of the afternoon as tourists, enjoying the sights and delights of the island. Both men were still entranced by their exotic surroundings, never having dreamed that such a paradise really existed. Even though Ukraine was not completely land-locked, neither of them had ever seen the Black Sea, so the ocean alone was enough to enthrall them. Throw in sandy beaches, palm trees, and the island culture, and they both found themselves wishing that it would take them a long time to track down Dmitri. Anton had apparently called in a few favours and made a few promises, and had managed to recruit some American help just in case the other Ukrainians he had in the area weren't enough. His last message had been that they were on standby and could be there to assist them in bringing Dmitri in on a couple of hours' notice. Deep inside Vasili knew he should feel insulted that Anton felt he needed help, but he also knew how smart and slippery Dmitri could be. The help could very well be needed, but no matter what else happened he had to ensure that he would get credit for bringing in his former associate. He'd only call them in as a last resort.

Vasili gave a deep sigh and dug his toes deeper into the warm sand. He was sitting under a palm tree on the beach and gazing out to sea. There was something so peaceful about the way the waves washed against the shore, rolled out, and returned; it gave a timelessness to the setting, as if he could stay here forever and nothing happening anywhere else in the world mattered. But, unfortunately, other things did matter, and Anton was almost as relentless as Yuri had been when it came to updates and results.

"Dan!" Vasili called out, waving at Bogdan who was trying to start a conversation with a couple of young ladies sunbathing nearby. They'd decided that for the duration of their stay, he would be 'Dan' and Vasili would be 'Vince' when they spoke to each other in public. It didn't hide their accents, but they felt that they might draw less attention if they had more western-sounding names.

Bogdan's sunglasses hid what was likely exasperation or irritation in the look he gave Vasili, but he knew disobedience was not an option. He bid a reluctant farewell to the two ladies who, from where Vasili sat, looked rather relieved that he was leaving. He didn't even try to hide his laughter as Bogdan made his way back to the tree. Rising to his feet he nodded in the direction of their car.

"Time to go," he said softly, though there was no one nearby likely to care what they said, or what language they said it in.

"Da," Bogdan replied, trying to sound enthused about the job that they had to do. *How did anyone get any work done while living in such a place*, he wondered? Digging into the pockets of his recently purchased shorts he fished out the keys to the rental car and proudly pushed the button to unlock the doors. He never tired of doing that. While such devices were not unknown back home, he certainly couldn't afford a car with remote locks himself. *Well, he would some day* he promised himself.

They had already formulated a plan to try to flush Dmitri out of hiding which would, of course, once more require Bogdan to go in alone. Vasili would not risk being seen by their prey until they were ready to pounce, so Bogdan dropped him off at their hotel and made his way back to Dmitri's place where he was happy to see that the same man was still on duty at the front desk. "Good evening, I'm back," he announced with a friendly smile, in what he presumed was accent-free English.

"Ah, yes, welcome back, sir. Did you have some questions, or have you decided to book with us? I can make the reservations for you right now if you wish."

"No, we haven't decided yet, but I was hoping that the owner might be here. I may be bringing an even larger group than I thought and I hoped to talk to him about a discount on your price."

Hopefully the potential of a large booking would be enough to flush Dmitri out of hiding and into plain sight.

"I'm afraid he has not returned, sir, but perhaps I could get a message to him."

Juan was pretty much sticking to the script that Dmitri had laid out for him. With the exception of Michael and Youlya he knew more than anyone about Dmitri's past. Dmitri had rightly assumed that if he were to have someone he could completely rely upon, no matter what, that he'd have to trust that person with the whole story, treat him with respect, and reward him accordingly. Juan might have had misgivings about his employer's past if he hadn't known him so well. Never had he been given so much responsibility, nor been paid so well, and he wanted to be worthy of the way that Dmitri treated him. There was very little he would not to for 'Senor Dmitri'.

"Do you know when he will return?"

Bogdan tried to sound casual as he asked, wanting to sound as if it really didn't matter one way or another. If he couldn't speak to the boss then either he'd come back later, or maybe find another hotel that wanted his business more than Dmitri did.

"It's hard to say, really. Island time, you know." Juan smiled apologetically.

"Island time?"

Juan gave an apologetic smile, "We don't always stick to schedules the way people from the mainland do."

"Well, I was really hoping to talk to him. I will have to try later, I guess."

"I will see if I can get him on the phone," Juan said, picking up the phone and starting to dial. "Would you like to talk to him if I can reach him?" Before Bogdan could reply Dmitri had apparently picked up.

"Hello, sir, it's Juan," he was careful not to use Dmitri's name, fairly certain that this was one of the men he'd been warned about months ago. "Yes, I know you are busy, but there is a man here who wants a group discount. He would like to bring a large group down here." Juan pretended to listen for a few seconds. In truth he had not selected a line before dialing and was speaking into a dead phone.

"Would you like to speak to him, sir?"

Bogdan's eyes held a look of quiet panic. Suddenly he wasn't so sure his English was as accent-free as he hoped it was. If he actually spoke to Dmitri, he might scare him into hiding, or worse, fleeing to another island. "No, I don't want to disturb him."

Juan spoke back into the phone, "No, sir, he says he doesn't want to disturb you." Juan nodded as if listening intently to instructions being given to him by his boss. "Very well, sir, I'll let him know. Goodbye."

Hanging up the phone he turned his attention back to Bogdan. "He won't be back until tomorrow morning, but he would be most happy to meet with you then, and he's sure that he can offer you a very good deal on the rooms. We are, of course all-inclusive so that will include all your meals and full access to the beach and so on."

Bogdan nodded, but his mind was already racing, and the smile on his face had nothing to do with access to beaches or personal watercraft.

"I will come back then, thank you very much," he said, heading for the door even as he spoke.

Juan waited until he could see the man driving away and then picked up the phone for real.

"That man I told you about came back. Yes, the one with the same accent as you. Yes, sir, I told him you'd be back tomorrow morning, just like you told me to. All right, sir, good night."

* * *

CHAPTER EIGHT

Bogdan drove as fast as he dared back to the Bed and Breakfast where Vasili was waiting for him. They'd had little doubt that they had found the right place, and tomorrow morning they'd know for sure! He pulled into the parking lot and resisted the urge to run all the way to the room, but he did begin to mentally spend the reward money he was sure to receive. He wanted a shiny new car. One with a remote lock.

"Vasili!" he called out even before he'd closed the door behind himself, earning a dirty look that quickly faded as he continued. "The desk clerk spoke to him on the phone while I was standing there! He will be returning tomorrow morning!"

Vasili smiled and nodded. He was a bit more cautious in his optimism than Bogdan was, but not much.

"Then I guess we better call in the help Anton has arranged for us." As he picked up his phone and began dialing, he couldn't help but smile. Unfortunately, he would not be able to personally lead the group to capture Dmitri; all it would take would be one glimpse of him to flush Dmitri back into hiding. He'd been painfully close to capturing him more than once, only to have him somehow pull off one lucky escape after another. He couldn't risk that happening again. He'd have to stay in the background, but he'd still get full credit for returning him, and the money he'd stolen.

Yes, revenge would be sweet.

Chapter Nine

Dmitri hung up the phone, sat down in an armchair that gave him a view through the large front window, and began pondering what to do next. Ever since that first phone call with Mikhail, all his thoughts and energy had gone into making sure his Canadian friend would be safe no matter what else might happen. It was a shame that he'd brought his friend, Sandy, into the picture, but if the two of them would just stay where he'd sent them, they would be fine. The resort they were staying at was owned by an acquaintance of his, and they'd be completely anonymous there as long as they didn't do anything foolish. Now he could afford to turn his attention elsewhere.

No doubt Vasili and his accomplice had help nearby; they would not be working alone. If their roles were reversed, he would certainly have had a whole team with him, and they'd be kept somewhere very close by.

There were several ways this might play out. The worst case, of course, would be that they caught him; he wasn't so foolish as to think that he was invincible. He'd spent months planning his get away last summer and they'd still almost caught him more than once. Having Mikhail along had made things harder, and luck, he freely admitted to himself, had played a large part in his ultimate get away. If they were to catch him they would, of course, torture him until they recovered as much of the money as they could and then force him to turn all his property over to Yuri. Then they'd kill him.

Unless there was some hope of escape it might not be worthwhile to go through the torture. Vasili and Anton would enjoy it too much. It might be better just to give it to them and be done with it. As long as Mikhail and Sandy were looked after it didn't really matter, did it? He let out a long sigh as he wondered what would become of them if he were to be caught.

On the other hand, they could not kill him until they had what they wanted so badly, could they? That gave him an advantage; he could play rougher than they could. If they killed him they would never recover as much as if they could take him alive. But he didn't have to play by their rules. Then there was the second way things could work out: that he'd win.

That brought about yet another sigh, because he thought he'd left that part of his life-long behind. Everything he had done for over a year now had been an attempt to change his life for the better. To be the kind of person his mother had wanted him to be. But Yuri and his gang had proven that they would not give up pursuing him. They cared little about Mikhail; he was merely a tool that enabled them to find what they really wanted. They likely didn't know Sandy existed, though he wasn't willing to gamble her life on that. He could leave behind everything, even the resort, and start over somewhere else, but that would merely buy him time until they found him again. While running and hiding might be an option, it was a very poor one that would solve nothing in the long term. He would have to do something permanent.

Without conscious thought he rose to his feet and began pacing slowly around the room. He was going to have to go back in time, become someone he'd once been, someone he now hated. His fist clenched repeatedly until his fingernails had scratched his palms almost to the point of drawing blood. Mikhail didn't know, though he might have suspected, just how violent his past had been. Starting out as a petty thief he'd been groomed into a full-fledged Mafia enforcer by a string of ever more ruthless bosses who no longer used violence personally, but were in constant need of someone who would use it for them. He'd been more than willing to do it. He'd been paid to use his size to threaten and intimidate. When that wasn't enough, he'd used his muscles, beating and even torturing to get the results his superiors both insisted upon, and rewarded.

He stopped pacing and he looked out the window, searching for something, anything, to look at. Something so vibrant or important that it would draw his full attention. No matter what he looked at, he could only see the face that still haunted his dreams: it was supposed to be a beating, a severe one, but nothing more than that. Despite his best efforts the man had adamantly refused to pay the protection money that Yuri demanded, and so the beating had escalated until he went too far. The man had slumped from his chair to the floor and could not be revived. Dmitri swore to this day that he had still been breathing when he'd left, but his victim had been found dead the next morning. He blinked over and over, but the face remained as clearly before him as if he were actually looking at it. Bruises, cuts, blood, and all.

He had expected a severe reprimand for losing the money, but Yuri had laughed it off, actually congratulating him, saying that when others learned what had happened, they would be more willing to pay, and that Dmitri had actually made it possible for them to earn even more in the future. Dmitri's guilt and remorse had been transformed into confusion, then acceptance, and finally a perverted sense of pride upon being congratulated over and over again as word of what had happened spread to others. He'd been surprised to hear it referred to as his first murder, but they'd been right. There were others, too many others, but it was always that first face that returned to haunt him. If only he could remember the man's name, or if he had a family, but nothing would come to his memory other than the all-too-vivid image of that shattered face.

No, he didn't want to go back to being that person. He didn't want even more blood on his hands. But all the same, it was time to stop hesitating and take action. Yuri and his men had turned him into a person that he now despised, but if that's what it took to protect Mikhail and Sandy, he would become that Dmitri again. To destroy them.

* * *

Her stomach was telling her that it was long past time to eat, but Youlya knew by now that her meal times were dictated by the whims of Anton and her guards. It had nothing to do with her needs, or what the time of day might be. Was it breakfast or supper that was late? Though she had no idea what the answer to that question might be, she was sure of one thing: their tactics weren't working. Rather than sinking into a bottomless pit of despair, they were now strengthening her resolve to escape. To win. Not only was she going to survive, she was getting out of here with every single kopek she had left. The fact that she had betrayed Dmitri's location was long forgotten.

But how was she going to do that? Rising from the cot she walked around the room, searching for something she might have failed to notice earlier, but nothing new stood out in the sparsely furnished room. A small, empty garbage can sat alone in one corner, her cot in another, and the old desk was shoved against the wall beside the door. Aside from that, there was nothing else but a small pile of ash and cigarette butts on the floor.

Studying the desk, she tested the drawers one by one, half expecting that they might be locked. They slid open easily enough, but there was nothing inside them. Kneeling down she pulled out the bottom drawers on each side to see if anything useful might have fallen behind them, she only found a few scraps of paper and some paper clips. With a sigh, she sat down on the floor and picked up one of the drawers to slide it back into place. It stuck at first, so she gave a harder push but it still refused to slide back in. She glanced up at the door in a mild state of panic; she didn't want to get caught doing anything that might look suspicious. Wiggling it from side to side she felt it slide in just a bit further. Becoming more desperate she leaned into it with all her weight, and it suddenly slammed back into place with a crash that sounded loud enough to wake the entire neighbourhood. At least it might have if it were night time; and if they were in a neighbourhood.

Youlya held her breath and sat frozen on the floor, waiting for the guards to come crashing into the room. A minute passed, and then two, and she decided that either no one had heard the crash, or that they didn't care. Her breathing and heart rate returned to near normal and she rose to her feet and walked back to her cot. She could stop panicking now and return her thoughts to planning how she was going to get out of there. There had to be a way out. Dmitri was big enough to be able to use his size to overpower almost anyone, but she had a very petite frame. She was smaller than many teenagers, in fact. She stood no chance at all against Anton's guards.

As her eyes scanned the room yet again, she realized that the second drawer was still on the floor beside the desk. She glanced nervously at the door, but there was still no sign that she'd attracted any attention, so she darted quickly to the desk to put it back in place.

Kneeling once more she picked up the drawer and winced in renewed panic as it fell to pieces in her hands, the sides and bottom falling back to the floor with a loud clatter. She stuffed the pieces quickly back into the empty slot in the desk, but wasn't sure how to make the front stay in place since it was no longer attached to anything. Maybe she could just leave it on the floor and let them assume it had fallen apart on its own.

She pulled the pieces back out, hoping that perhaps she could somehow fit it back together so that it would at least stay in place, but a quick examination of the parts told her that would be impossible. She quickly shoved the broken pieces back into the desk, but just as she was about to prop the drawer front against the desk, she realized what she was holding. Though completely ignorant about what kind of wood it was, she could tell it was very heavy and sturdy; the other pieces had broken off from it, leaving it intact with a few shards of the sides still attached. If she were to hit someone with it with a good swing, it just might serve her purpose.

She picked it up and carried it back to her cot, stuffing it under the thin pillow that Anton had so thoughtfully provided for her. Now, if the guard would just come in with her next meal. She was half-starved, but eating could wait. Escaping was now her prime concern.

The longer she sat there the more nervous she became. There was usually only one guard, but what if there were two this time? Or a second one waiting out in the hallway? She patted the pillow to reassure herself that the piece of wood was indeed still there, and the solid feel of it under the pillow helped to strengthen her resolve. She was going to do it, she told herself. If there were two guards this time, so what? She'd wait till the next meal, or the next. She'd wait as long as it took because this might be her only chance.

There was no way to gauge the passing of time. It might have been ten minutes, it might have been half an hour, but there was no sound from the other side of the door, no click of the lock or turning of the handle. Her sleep-deprived body was telling her to just lay down and have a nap, but she couldn't do that. She had to be ready the moment the door was opened and guard's hands were filled with her meal tray. She needed the added element of surprise to make this work. If he saw her coming, even a split second before she got there, he'd drop the tray and ward off her blows. She grabbed the drawer front from beneath the pillow and went to stand beside the door, blinking away the sleep from her eyes as the minutes passed. By the way her stomach was growling, it couldn't be much longer, could it?

A barely audible noise from the other side of the door roused her, something told her that whatever it was, it was important for some reason. She was slumped against the wall, the heavy piece of wood still clutched in her hands, but it was as if she had fallen asleep standing there; time had passed without her being aware of it. More from instinct than planning she raised her hands as high as she could lift them and took a half step back from the door as the handle turned and it started to swing open. A tray appeared, seemingly floating in midair as it glided into the room. Then a pair of hands were visible holding the tray. Her arms rose higher.

An eternity seemed to pass before she could see the arms attached to the hands. She considered taking a vicious swing at the arms before deciding to wait a little longer, until a head had appeared.

Finally, the head did appear, the eyes blinking slowly in surprise when they didn't see her sitting on her cot. It started to turn but before it could swing far enough to see her, she brought her arms down with all the strength her weakened body could bring to bear. She put every gram of her weight behind the swing, and the board was almost torn from her grasp as it came down on the slowly turning head. A loud crash announced that the tray had been dropped, its contents clattering across the concrete floor as Youlya raised the drawer front again, and again, and then again.

She was breathing heavily and had sunk to her knees. The guard was laying face down on the floor, his head dripping streams of blood from numerous wounds. He might still be breathing; she didn't bother to check. Tossing the heavy piece of wood towards the cot, she rose quickly to her feet, peering cautiously out the door and down the hallway, waiting for the sound of running feet. There was nothing but silence.

Her lip curled derisively; they must have figured that they only needed one guard because she was 'just a woman.'

The meal he'd brought her was as meagre as all the previous ones had been, but she greedily grabbed a few slices of bread from the floor and wolfed them down. She'd need her strength.

Still moving cautiously, she slipped out the door, peeking around each corner before rounding it. When she came to a door she paused. Was it heavy enough that there were guards behind it who hadn't heard her earlier? Holding her breath, she pressed her ear to the door, but after a minute or more of listening, she had still heard nothing. She crouched beside it and tested the handle. As it turned easily in her hand, it made a loud 'click' that seemed to echo down the hallway. She paused again, waiting for shouts from the other side, or for one of Anton's men to burst through it; but again, nothing happened. She cracked the door open enough to peek through, but it was almost pitch black on the other side. She slipped through, closing the door as softy as possible behind her, waiting for her eyes to adjust to the dark.

She was in some sort of reception area with a small window and a glass door leading outside. There were no lights outside at all and she could now tell that it was very late at night. The light of a full moon streaming through the door provided enough ambient light for her to pick her way through the office without colliding with the desks and filing cabinets. The door was locked but she quickly found the knob and was able to unlock it from the inside. Now what?

She had over a million dollars in a bank account that she could not access from where she was, and not a single kopeck to pay for a taxi or a bus. For that matter, she didn't know where in, or out of, the city she was. It wouldn't be safe to go back to her apartment; that was the first place Anton would look for her. No, she needed to get somewhere else to access her money. But where? She couldn't even rent a hotel room without identification and a way to pay for it. Her grandmother had died a long time ago, and most of her friends had some idea, or at least some suspicion, about what she had done for a living. She could trust most of them to be quiet, but if Anton were to track them down, well, she knew how ruthless he could be. Then again, he'd likely question them all anyway.

Well, she had to do something. At any moment that guard might wake up; unlikely, but he might. Even if he didn't someone would eventually show up to relieve him. She spotted a phone on one of the desks.

Years of using her mobile phone had left her dependent on speed dial, and it took her several precious minutes to bring a number to mind. With a sigh of exasperation she picked up the phone on the desk and dialed. As she dialed, she wished she could remember some other number. This would not have been her first choice, but time was rapidly running out. It was late, which might have been why the phone rang several times before it was answered.

"Da?" The voice sounded dull and sleepy.

"Nastia? It's Youlya. No, really, it's me! I've been away for a while, but I'm back now. Yes, I'd like to get together sometime. In fact, I need a really big favour right now. Can you help me?"

* * *

Michael sighed loudly. Leaning against the patio door, he was staring out towards the open sea, but Sandy could tell by the look in his eyes that whatever he might be seeing, it wasn't anything that was visible through the glass. "So, you liked flying that plane, did you?" She forced a cheerful tone into her voice, hoping to draw his attention back to the here and now.

"Yeah, it was pretty neat!" He smiled a genuine smile and she could see that she'd succeeded. Besides, she knew enough about pilots to know that you could always distract them by turning the conversation to airplanes.

"You made a pretty decent landing too, considering you've never flown that type before. I ought to know; I've sat through enough of them."

"Thanks, Jake talked me all the way down to the ground." She thought his slight blush at her compliment was kind of cute, and she had meant it sincerely.

"Yeah, he did, but you were the one on the stick, right? Bet you could do it again without his help." If she could just get his mind far enough away from Dmitri, maybe she could talk him into hopping a flight back to the mainland. From there it would be a simple matter to get home on her own airline. Or was Dmitri right, would this Yuri guy track them down at home? She needed to think this through; and needed to focus Michael's attention so that he could help her make a decision.

Michael looked up at the ceiling as she spoke, still seemingly lost in thought.

"Yeah," he said slowly, "I think you're right, I could." The expression on his face changed, as if he were now thinking about something completely different than whatever he'd been pondering while gazing out to sea. Good, she'd shifted his thoughts to flying.

"So, uh, what do you want to do tomorrow?" She waited, but Michael was completely lost in thought. Sandy grinned and shook her head; she'd seen that look on pilots' faces before.

"Michael?"

"Huh? Sorry, what did you say?"

"We have full use of an all-inclusive resort. What would you like to do tomorrow?"

He shrugged and looked back out to sea. There were a lot of options, from paddle boards to deep-sea fishing, and under other conditions it would have been wonderful to turn this opportunity into something romantic with Sandy. "I don't know," he finally replied with forced cheerfulness. "What do you want to do?"

Left unspoken was the fact that he now knew exactly what he wanted to do tomorrow.

* * *

To Dmitri it was not something underhanded or shady. Nor was it something that he did consciously because of his past ties to organized crime. It was simply a way of life, something that he did all but unconsciously. In fact, he might have been mildly surprised to learn that very few other people did it. If someone were to have asked him to live his life without informants and contacts to let him know what was going on in places he could not always watch himself, he would have dismissed the suggestion out of hand.

So, almost as soon as he'd moved to the island, he'd set about to create a discrete network of resort owners and their employees, as well as taxi drivers and even the odd government official, to keep him apprised of the goings on in the area. Few of them knew, or even suspected, what purpose they were being used for, and in fact none of the information, at least so far, was particularly private or illegally shared. Even fewer ever actually contacted him directly since he preferred to keep as low a profile as possible. Juan was his chosen go-between to garner information from all over the island, often under the guise of insider gossip among the employees of the other resorts and hotels.

"Gracias," Juan said into the receiver as he jotted the information down on a piece of paper, then he hung up the phone and turned to his boss with a smile. "Jorge says they are staying there; he's sure of it."

Dmitri nodded, but did not smile, as he glanced at the paper. He was pleased to have the information, and more than willing to use it to his advantage, but this was business. Serious business. "Good work, Juan, thank you."

Juan nodded in reply. "Anything else you need, sir?"

"No," Dmitri replied absently, indicating his attention had already turned elsewhere. "That's all. Thank you." He stuffed the paper into his shirt pocket and retreated to his suite. Now that he knew where to find Vasili and his friend, he had to decide what to do about it. He could not assume that they were here alone. Even if they were, more help would surely be available somewhere nearby. They knew where to find him, and though he could hide out in a number of places on the island, he could not do that forever; it would be pointless. He needed to strike first, throw them off balance, scare them into doing something foolish. There was also the chilling possibility that they might find out where Mikhail was. Jake would never let anything slip. Dmitri trusted him fully, but no doubt there were records of the flight somewhere. If they were to find out who the pilot was, they were quite capable of forcing the information from him. He would not make the mistake of underestimating what Yuri's men were capable of, after all he'd once been one of them himself.

Retracing his thoughts, he started over with Vasili. To the best of his knowledge there were only two of them staying at the Bed and Breakfast where Jorge worked. So far. For now he would assume that they were a scouting party sent into the area to find him, at which they had succeeded. That meant they would soon be calling in more help. They knew where he lived and worked, but did not yet know where he was staying, and he didn't plan on spending the night. He took the paper from his pocket, studying the location jotted down on it as if somehow it would tell him what the next step should be. The problem was, he thought as he drew in a determined breath, that he already knew what their next step was. He needed to even the odds a bit before they became even longer.

Crumpling up the paper Dmitri shoved it in his pocket, then, grabbing a small duffel bag, began stuffing in the clothing and other items he thought he might need over the next few days. He was packing as if on autopilot, his mind busy with analyzing the problem and what to do about it. They knew where he lived, and might even be watching him now, so he needed to turn the tables. He knew the island well enough to know exactly where they were, so the obvious first step was to start watching them.

He walked back out through the lobby, offering an absent-minded farewell wave to Juan, threw his bag into the front seat of his truck, and headed for a stretch of beach adjacent to where Vasili was staying. He'd blend in with the locals and tourists if anyone but Vasili and his sidekick saw him, but even so he still parked a kilometre or so from his destination and went the rest of the way on foot.

There weren't many other people on the beach this time of night; most of them were in clubs or restaurants, and the few people he did pass paid him little or no attention. Soon he found himself along the stretch of beach in front of the Bed and Breakfast. He found a spot deep in the shadows of a cluster of palm trees and squatted down in the warm tropical night with the muted sound of music drifting out from a lounge somewhere in the distance. He was no longer trying to plan what to do next; he was already doing the next thing. His eyes swept back and forth over the structure, not only looking for Vasili, but also studying its layout and that of the surrounding buildings. He was waiting. Waiting for an opportunity.

Satisfied that he had the general layout of the place, he rose to his feet, fingering the slip of paper in his pocket. He didn't need to double check the room number; he had automatically committed it to memory. Just as he was about to make his way closer to the building, a man and woman stepped through the door, making their way to the beach for a romantic evening stroll in the light of the full moon. He was startled by their sudden appearance and checked his step, leaning instead against a palm tree and pretending to be looking out to sea. They passed him without so much as a sidelong glance and turned up the beach.

Dmitri waited until they were far enough away that they wouldn't be able to see him clearly in the dark, and then turned back towards the building. The door opened again and another of its guests came walking towards the beach. Diving for cover would only arouse suspicion, so he remained in place, leaning against the tree as a lone man approached.

The man paid no more attention to him than the couple had. As he drew near Dmitri, he paused and pulled a pack of cigarettes from his pocket. He smiled as he looked out towards the ocean. This was not unusual. Dmitri had seen that look on the faces of countless tourists. Indeed, he often smiled the same way. As the man flicked his lighter, it illuminated both the smoker and Dmitri. His startled look revealed that he hadn't noticed Dmitri standing there until that moment. The cigarette fell from his mouth as the lighter flickered off.

"Sorry, you scared me," the man said in heavily accented English as he stooped to retrieve the cigarette. The accent was Ukrainian.

Now it was Dmitri's turn to be startled, but he recovered quickly, knowing that the odds of having more than one set of Ukrainian guests at the same place was highly unlikely. This might not be Vasili, but it was his first *opportunity*.

Without conscious thought, the tone of his voice changed. He became once more the Mafia thug he'd once been. He spoke with an impatient authority, as if this man had already disappointed him.

"Where is Vasili? Do you know?" he demanded, reverting to his old, heavy Ukrainian accent. He was addressing an inferior, someone beneath his contempt, someone who should have volunteered the information without being asked because this idiot should obviously recognize him.

Bogdan furrowed his brow, squinting at his fellow countryman in the dark, panicking because he did not know who this was.

"Da," he responded out of shear self-preservation. The look of confusion became even deeper, visible even in the dim light. "Shto....kto...?"

"Speak English, you fool! What if someone hears you?" Dmitri barked, ignoring the man's questions. "You aren't here alone, are you. Vasili is with you, right?" His tone made it clear that a negative response would have consequences.

"I – yes, I am with Vasili – I am Bogdan. I –" He cleared his throat nervously. "We did not expect you until –"

"You better learn to expect everything!" Dmitri cut off his excuse, then glared into the darkness surrounding them, as if making sure it was safe to talk. Bogdan did the same, still confused and uncertain about who he was talking to. He had been brought along simply because he could speak English, and the tone of authority with which Dmitri spoke made it clear who was in charge just now.

As he turned to check behind him Dmitri landed a heavy blow on the back of his head.

"I told you expect everything," he hissed into Bogdan's ear as he dragged him into the shrubs behind the palm trees. He was stunned, but not unconscious, and Dmitri covered his mouth with one hand. "One word and you are dead!" he warned, shoving the man to his knees.

Bogdan nodded once; his eyes wide with fear. Dmitri glanced around again, for real this time. There was no one in sight, let alone within earshot, so he removed his hand from the Bogdan's mouth.

"Answer quietly. How many of you are here now? How many more is Yuri sending?"

"Yuri?" the man replied in obvious confusion. "Yuri is dead. He died the night you left." He'd finally figured out who he was talking with.

Dmitri started at the man's response, looking into his eyes as if to catch him in a lie, but he avoided the temptation to ask the man if this was really true.

"Who sent you then?"

"An ... Anton sent us."

Dmitri nodded, as if he'd known that all along and was satisfied with the response.

"Is it just you and Vasili here now?"

It was a threat, not a question, as if the fact that there were only two of them meant that Dmitri could easily dispatch both of them."

"Da," Bogdan answered, the panic in his voice obvious, then remembering Dmitri's earlier warning he blinked once, and with an effort that took all his concentration, he switched back to English. "Yes. Yes, just the two of us. But Vasili has called for more help; they will be here tomorrow morning."

Was the threat of more help arriving enough to scare Dmitri away? He prayed it would be.

"I will not tell anyone I saw you, not even Vasili!" The words gushed from his mouth in a desperate plea to be released. "I will say nothing. I promise."

"No, you won't tell anyone, because you will never have the chance," Dmitri growled back.

Chapter Ten

Anton was in an excellent mood. After more than a year they had finally located Dmitri. All the time, effort, and money spent tracking the movements of that troublesome Canadian had paid off as well, and soon he would have both of them, as well as Youlya. There would be no loose ends. That also meant he would soon have the money, or whatever part of it Dmitri had not yet spent. If Dmitri had planned for that money to last him the rest of his life then there should be a lot of it left. If he had invested it in something that would produce income, well, it might be worth hanging onto those assets, legitimate or otherwise.

The rest of his men would be joining Vasili and Bogdan shortly, perhaps later today, Ukraine time. From there it was a matter of being patient and putting together a plan to grab the two of them in a way that would not attract any more attention from the locals than was necessary. He scowled a bit at that thought. Hopefully Vasili would not move too quickly, or too slowly. Aside from his blunders the previous summer he had always proven himself reliable. If he screwed it up again it would be time to replace him.

He lit a cigarette and reclined in his chair; the smile having returned to his face. Capturing Dmitri would no doubt score him a few points with his bosses, which would be a nice bonus to add to the satisfaction of a job well done. He knew from the rumblings in the lower ranks that the effort poured into the search for Dmitri was having its desired effect with them, which was yet another bonus. His soldiers realized now that should any of them attempt anything like Dmitri had, they would be hunted, quite literally, to the ends of the earth. No one in his organization had any doubts as to what would happen to Dmitri once this matter was concluded. It might be too early to celebrate just yet, but it was certainly looking good, and it would benefit him in so many ways besides the boost in his bank balance.

The phone rang, breaking his train of thought. "Da?" First his face fell, then he sat upright in his chair as the caller broke the news of Youlya's escape to him. "I see," he said with an icy calmness in his voice. He could sense that the caller would have felt more comfortable if he had launched into a Yuri-like rage; so much the better.

"You do know that she has no money, no phone, and no one she dares to contact?" The caller confirmed that he was indeed aware of these facts. "And you have started looking for her. Watching her friends, and her flat, keeping an eye on all routes she may take out of the city." They were statements, orders really, not questions. According to the caller they were already being carried out.

"Find her," he said in a flat, toneless voice. The 'or else' was left unspoken but was still very clearly heard.

***

Dmitri looked down at Bogdan, his shirt looked rather worse for wear as one sleeve had been ripped off and was now stuffed firmly into his mouth. The long hem had also been ripped off and used to tie his hands tightly behind his back. A quick pat down revealed a mobile phone stuffed into one pocket, which Dmitri tossed casually into a nearby shrub.

"You are coming with me now, understand?"

Bogdan's wide-eyed gaze never wandered from Dmitri's eyes as he nodded in frantic agreement.

"If you make any attempt to run you will not see another of these beautiful sunrises."

Bogdan gave another frightened nod.

"When we get to my place you will tell me everything you know. You know what will happen if you lie to me."

This time a muted gurgle punctuated the nod.

Dmitri glanced around and, spotting no one, grabbed Bogdan roughly under his arms and pulled him to his feet with a lot more force than was necessary. His prisoner stumbled but caught his balance and continued along in the direction in which Dmitri had shoved him. They skirted the edge of the beach, sticking to the shadows and the cover offered by the lush vegetation along the shore line. Only once did anyone come into sight; a couple taking a stroll along the deserted beach. Dmitri spent a few seconds mentally scolding them for not being in some nice club or restaurant, but managed to direct Bogdan up a path running through the trees before they got close enough that he had to worry about having Bogdan's trussed arms and gagged mouth being noticed.

Once back at his truck he now had to decide exactly what to do with his captive. Obviously he needed to be questioned, but his plan for tonight had been to scope out Vasili's lair, not take a prisoner. He'd never been one to pass up an opportunity though, and since Vasili already knew he was here, he hadn't tipped his hand. In fact, this might work in his favour in more ways than one. In the first place, it meant that there would be one less adversary to worry about. In the second place, he knew how hot-headed Vasili could be when things didn't go his way. This just might provoke him into doing something very rash, something Dmitri could take advantage of.

Dmitri scowled as he looked at the truck. If he had a topper on it, he could shove Bogdan in the back, cover him up with something, then lock him in. But it would be no use trying to stuff him into an open truck box; even covered up he might be spotted. Worse yet, he might manage to jump out and escape. He'd have to put him in the cab, but he couldn't risk leaving him bound and gagged. What if he was spotted, or even stopped by a policeman? As remote as that chance was, it would be impossible to explain the situation, even to an officer he knew. Police here were just too honest; they couldn't be bought and bribed like many of the ones he'd known back home. Normally he figured that was a good thing, but not tonight.

"Get in the truck," he tried to make his voice sound as threatening as possible. Bogdan climbed submissively into the cab and simply sat there as Dmitri closed the door and circled around to the driver's side. "I'm going to untie you, now." The glare that accompanied his words made any threat completely unnecessary. In fact, if anything, his captive looked even more nervous than before. With Bogdan set free, Dmitri started the truck and pulled out onto the main road. Rather than head for his safe house, however, he turned in the opposite direction, making random turns back and forth and making use of every side road he came upon to fully confuse his passenger.

Once they had cleared the more built up area of the island, and the traffic had all but disappeared, Dmitri pulled to the side of the road. He took the fabric that had once bound Bogdan's wrists, using it to fashion a blindfold before continuing his round-about route to his destination. As he drove, he pondered what he should do with Bogdan once he was through questioning him. The obvious answer was to get rid of him permanently, and that was the easiest and most tempting option as well, but a sidelong glance at the man reminded him of how he'd started out himself. Was there hope for this man who, after all, wasn't the real enemy? With Yuri gone, his real concern was dealing with Vasili and Anton. Perhaps there was some other way of handling Bogdan.

CHAPTER TEN

No doubt the man would promise anything to survive the night, but how could he ensure that he had no chance to return to Vasili? He still had no idea. Not that Bogdan would be able to betray anything about Dmitri and his plans, or even the location of his safe house. Despite his circuitous route and the blindfold, he would not be returning to the beach house after tonight.

After deciding he'd thoroughly confused Bogdan, he headed for the house. Despite the long drive they weren't all that far from where they'd started, but hopefully Bogdan figured they were on the other side of the island by now. The turn off was to the right, but just for good measure, he cranked the wheel hard to the left and circled around in the middle of the road, completing a two hundred and seventy degree turn. As soon as the truck was out of sight of the road, he parked it and shoved his captive unceremoniously out the door. He followed him up the road, directing him along with wordless and overly rough shoves now and then, just to keep him off his balance both physically and mentally. Bogdan would be used to intimidating others, being in control and watching them squirm. Now that he was the helpless one, his own thoughts would become his biggest enemy as he began imagining how the night would end.

When they finally reached the house, Dmitri pushed Bogdan into a chair he placed in the middle of the living room, but left all the lights turned off. He took a seat on the couch, watching Bogdan silhouetted against the moonlight filtering through the large picture window. Leaning back comfortably he began speaking in Ukrainian.

"Now, there are some things we need to discuss. How many of you are there on Culebra right now?"

"Only – only Vasili and me."

"How many more are coming, and when?"

"Six more. I think. Tomorrow."

"You think?" His voice was low, and very threatening. "How many?" He barked out, and smiled inwardly as Bogdan flinched.

"Six!"

"What is Vasili planning?"

* * *

An hour later Dmitri concluded he'd drained his captive of any and all useful information. It wasn't much really, but then he hadn't expected much from him. Still, he'd seized the opportunity that Bogdan had presented him with, and now had much more information than he'd hoped to gain when he'd set out that evening. He also had only seven men to deal with rather than the eight Vasili had planned. That wasn't much of a shift in the odds numerically, but this was his island, his turf. The rules here were different than they were in Ukraine, and that gave him a big edge.

As he saw it, he still had one huge problem right now. What was he to do with Bogdan? The old Dmitri would not have hesitated. Were Bogdan to disappear forever Vasili would not dare to report it to the authorities. A shallow grave in the thicket behind the house. A few weights tied to his feet before he was thrown overboard. Those were easy options; quick and efficient. The old Dmitri was becoming stronger and stronger, but at the same time the new Dmitri knew this man was just a pawn. His disappearance would be nothing more than an inconvenience to Anton. He'd have a very brief temper tantrum over the fact that he was now short one man, maybe he would be a little bit angrier at Dmitri, but otherwise unfazed. Bogdan's life meant little to anyone, except to Dmitri. He didn't want to hurt anyone one but Vasili and Anton. It had been their decision to launch this vendetta against him, they alone should pay the price.

Rising from the couch he walked around Bogdan, who gave an involuntary shudder as Dmitri passed behind him, and stared out into the darkness of the ocean. The lights of a ship were gliding slowly from left to right. Too dark to be a cruise ship, it had to be a fishing boat, or a small freighter perhaps. Dmitri nodded to himself. That might work.

* * *

Youlya had not slept at all, but still remained in bed long after the sun had come up and Nastia had left for work. Nastia had no idea what she'd been through, and it would be easiest not to have to face her and explain it. She had thought briefly of Dmitri, wondering if they had found him yet. It was still the middle of the night back on Culebra. Was he still all right? Did he know they were coming for him if they weren't there already? She brushed the thought aside, assuring herself that he'd find one of his famous opportunities. She had her own problems to worry about. As far as she knew no one in Anton's circle knew about Nastia, but she wasn't about to risk her life betting on that assumption. She had to get out of Ukraine; as much as she'd wanted to come home, she'd learned that this wasn't home anymore. Even if it was, it was no longer safe to be here. She should have known that long ago. With the whole world to chose from this was the one place she should never have come. But where should she go now?

She, like many of her friends, had dreamed of living 'in the west' when they grew up. But her dreams had been somewhat vague. She didn't even know herself whether 'west' meant Europe or America. She'd tried life in what many might consider to be paradise, but it wasn't what she'd dreamed it would be. Wasn't that Dmitri's fault though? He'd refused to live like they could have with the money they had, choosing instead to live like a hermit on some back-water island in the middle of a hurricane belt. Well, she'd change that, but her first order of business was to get out of Ukraine. Should she go north, south, east or west? Belarus seemed the least likely place, so that's where she'd go. She could take a bus or a taxi out of the city, then take a train north to the border. Having learned a thing or two from Dmitri, she could then sneak across the border and obtain a counterfeit passport in Minsk. From there –well – she'd decide that later. With more than half her funds remaining, she hoped she'd have enough to set herself up somewhere suitable and finally live the life she deserved.

She'd leave tonight, under the cover of darkness, while Nastia was asleep.

* * *

It was still well before sunrise when Michael sat up on the couch he'd been sleeping on. Being the gentleman that he was, he'd insisted upon Sandy taking the bedroom. His eyes were still heavy with sleep and he rubbed them, shaking his head slowly while letting out a wide yawn. He really did need several more hours of sleep. If he didn't get up and get going soon though, he'd have to postpone his plan until the next day. If he did that, he might let the second thoughts plaguing his conscience win out. *Was he really seriously contemplating this* he wondered as he made his way to the bathroom? It wasn't really stealing if he didn't keep it, was it?

He closed the door as quietly as he could before flicking on the light and turning on the tap, splashing cold water on his face to help clear out the last of the cobwebs. He studied his reflection in the mirror, shaking his head at himself. Whether in disbelief or reproof he wasn't really sure. His clothes literally looked as if they'd been slept in, but this way he didn't have to risk making noise while getting dressed. It was best if he was gone before Sandy woke up.

He debated leaving her a note and concluded that he did owe her that much.

He switched off the light and slowly opened the door which, thankfully, swung noiselessly open. He fumbled on the dresser for the pen and pad of note paper that most hotels thoughtfully provide for their guests, then made his way back to the bathroom. Pen in hand, he wondered what exactly to say before jotting down a few words: 'Sandy, I'm sorry but I need to go help Dmitri. Please stay somewhere safe until this is all over.' He stopped short of signing it as he doubted she'd have any trouble figuring out who it was from. After further consideration, he jotted down his email address and left it at that.

Opening the door once more he set the note in the middle of the table on which they'd eaten supper the previous evening. It felt strange leaving a hotel room without a suitcase, but his bag was still aboard the cruise ship and he had no further use for the few articles Dmitri had sent along with him. With a guilty last look around the room he opened the deadbolt on the door that led out into the hallway and slipped out. It would have been a lot easier to leave through the patio door, but then he couldn't have locked it behind him. It was unlikely that anyone would try to break in that way, but he didn't want to compromise Sandy's safety. Besides, how unusual was it to see someone in the hallway of a hotel, even at this hour of the morning?

With the door closed silently behind him he took a deep breath, both in relief for having got this far undetected, and to steel his nerves for what he was about to do. As he made his way along the hallway to the exit door, he passed a row of vending machines. A chocolate bar, a bag of chips, and a Coke didn't exactly constitute a well-balanced breakfast, but there wasn't time for anything more, and he didn't think there would be any fast food places open between here and the airport.

He stepped out into the relatively cool air, it didn't really seem to ever cool off in this part of the world but at least there was no sun beating down on him yet. He drew another deep breath and glanced around to be sure of his bearings. It was that way, he told himself, looking to the left. Perhaps a fifteen or twenty-minute walk which should leave him enough time to find what he needed before the sun came up. If he lost the cover of darkness this would be far too risky to attempt.

"Just how do you plan to help him?" The voice sounded much too loud in the predawn darkness. It also sounded accusatory, sarcastic, and rather angry.

"Sandy!" He spun around, raising his hands as if in self-defence. His first instinct was to claim he couldn't sleep and had decided to take a walk. But she had obviously seen the note already. "I –" No, he thought to himself, this is the right thing to do. I have to do it. I'm the one that's right. His voice took on a new note of firmness and authority. "Dmitri saved my life; I'm not letting him face this alone. I owe him that much."

It wasn't the first time he'd expressed that thought, but Sandy heard the firmness in his voice this time and sighed, realizing there was no arguing with him this time. He had fully thought this through and was firmly convinced that his decision was right.

"What are you going to do, swim there? Charter a boat? Call Jake?" She was searching for a weakness in his plan.

He looked around; not nervously she noticed, just to make sure that no one was listening to them.

"No. I'm going to steal a plane." His voice was as casual as could be. He might have been telling her what he was ordering for breakfast.

"What?" She blurted out the word much too loudly, then lowered her voice to an angry whisper. "You really are crazy, aren't you? You're off to fight the Mafia and you're going to commit grand theft to do it?!"

Michael shrugged. "I'm not a good swimmer, I don't know how to navigate a boat, and Jake wouldn't fly me back for a million dollars. I could pay him that much you know! Flying is the best and fastest way to get there. Besides, I'm not keeping it. I'll even leave them some gas money." He patted the pocket where he had stashed his share of the cash Dmitri had given them.

"Have you really thought this through?" It was worth one more shot, wasn't it?

"Yes, many times, and yes, I do know what could happen, and yes, I've had second thoughts, and yes I'm still going to do it! I'll let you know when ..." When what, he wondered? How was this going to end? He had no idea, but it would end. One way or another.

"I'll let you know when it's over." He raised his hand before she could object again. "I need to go. Now." I have to be ready to take off before the sun comes up."

Sandy wanted to threaten him with something; who she'd tell, or that she'd call Dmitri, but deep down she knew she wouldn't. "Can I at least come with you to the airport?" Maybe some new argument would come to her mind in the time it would take to get there. She had long decided that she really liked Michael, as quiet and mysterious as he'd been on the plane, there was just something about him. Maybe his wanting to help Dmitri was part of what made him who he was, part of what attracted her to him, even if she was afraid of what it might do to him.

"Okay! But we need to go now!" The words came out in a sigh

of exasperation, but though he'd never admit it, he would be glad of her company. As long as she didn't try and talk him out of it along the way.

Michael set a brisk pace but Sandy, after a couple of quick steps to catch up, managed to match it. She saw the determined look on his face as they strode along the road and decided against any further attempts to dissuade him. It was obviously useless, so they made the entire walk in silence. They stuck to the road when they reached the terminal building, until they reached the turn off to the lot where the pilots of the smaller planes parked. The gate onto the ramp had a key pad that required the correct combination to open, but Michael was prepared for that. He knew that most airports had similar security set ups and was familiar with how it worked: the combination was posted on the inside of the gate so that arriving pilots would know how to get back out to their planes. Out of force of habit he'd made note of it when they'd arrived.

After punching in the combination, he swung the gate partly open, then turned to face Sandy. The look in his eyes was almost apologetic, she saw. "I have to do this," was all he could think to say. It was all there was to say.

"I know. Just ... just be careful okay?" Without even thinking about it she gripped Michael's arms and raised up on her toes to place a kiss on his cheek. "Come back in one piece."

Michael blinked in surprise. It happened too quickly to think or react, and it was over almost before he knew what had happened. He wished he had at least kissed her cheek in return, or hugged her, or something, but he just stood there with his mouth half open and nodded. "I'll try," he finally managed to mumble back.

As he turned to slip through the gate Sandy rolled her eyes. "I'm going to regret this," she muttered, and stopped the gate from swinging shut with her foot. Rather than step through it though, she held it just barely ajar, just enough that it didn't lock. She didn't know the combination.

The field was deserted, the only movement was the alternating light and shadow created by the rotating beacon on the small building that served as the airport's terminal. Michael dodged in and out of the parked planes. It had to be a Cessna, that went without saying, but thankfully those were in plentiful supply in most parts of the world. He picked a 172 first, but it was locked. As was the smaller 152 parked on the far side of the single-engine Piper next to it. The next plane was a 182 which was unlocked. He sighed to himself. One lone dual flight was hardly enough to qualify him for a solo flight in what he thought of as a high-performance airplane. At least not legally. But this flight was illegal on so many levels. He wasn't checked out in it, didn't have his student pilot permit with him, and he was stealing the plane no matter how he tried to justify or rationalize it. The fact that he wouldn't be filing a flight plan wasn't worth a passing thought.

He quickly checked the remaining aircraft, but only two others were unlocked, and both of them were Piper Cherokees that he'd only tried out of sheer desperation. He was rapidly running out of time. Okay, it would have to be the 182 then. Part of him was actually excited about the prospect of flying it now. Sure, its size, speed, and relative complexity intimidated him a bit, but he'd done it once already and if he could do it again, solo, it would prove he really was becoming a pilot! It was a good thing that Jake had given him such a thorough lesson on the way over here, it didn't seem quite as intimidating as it might have otherwise.

After a quick search of the cockpit, done as much by feel as by sight, he found a key stashed in the map compartment. Okay, this was really going to happen. *If it had enough fuel* he realized with a sinking feeling. What if the owner had left it empty? Could he handle a Piper? He flipped on the red master switch which activated the electrical system, then spent a few frantic moments locating the cockpit lighting control which allowed him to see that the tanks were a bit over three-quarters full. More than enough.

He then started a walk around inspection of the Cessna. There were no steps on the wing strut, and he didn't see a ladder nearby, so he couldn't get up to the wings to visually check the fuel. Hopefully the gauge was correct. There was another rule broken, but then it was still too dark to see anything without a flashlight anyway. He glanced eastward and saw the first hint of sunrise on the horizon. Okay, he was timing this almost right; he wanted to start the engine and do the pre-flight checks so he could take off just as the sun rose. He wasn't about to attempt flying over open water in the dark.

Circling the plane to check the control surfaces and other necessary items, he knew he was rushing, but he did his best to check everything from memory. He could see Sandy, still standing at the gate watching him, and gave her a cursory nod, not trusting himself to do any more than that. Maybe she was going to watch until he'd taken off safely, just to make sure he didn't manage to kill himself before getting that far. He finished the walk around and climbed into the cockpit, sliding the seat into position, checking that he could reach all the controls and the rudder pedals, then fastened his seat belt. He turned to give Sandy a wave goodbye and closed and latched the door.

Michael found the checklist stuffed into a pocket by his left foot, and with the cabin lights turned up just enough to read it, began going through the pre-start procedures. Brakes set, radios off, fuel selector on both tanks. It wasn't all that different from the 172.

The first ray of the rising sun shone through the window and he felt his heart quicken. It was time. So far, at the very worst, he was only trespassing, but now it was time to start the plane. He looked over towards the gate for one last look at Sandy and found himself wondering if he would ever see her again. For some reason he found that to be a very important question, but to his disappointment she was no longer there. Well, maybe she'd moved to get a better view of the runway, he thought.

Just as he was about to turn the key the passenger door opened and his heart stopped beating. He'd been caught before he could even start the engine! For one insane moment he had the urge to fight off whoever it was. He had to get to Dmitri! But he was helpless, strapped firmly in place by his seat belt.

"You can't leave without your cabin crew," Sandy informed him in a matter-of-fact tone as she climbed into the seat beside him and started to do up her seat belt.

"You can't come!" Michael blurted out as she closed the door.

"If you can be impulsive, stupid, and suicidal, so can I."

"You can't come!" He repeated, but the words sounded like those of a five-year-old child insisting on getting his own way. "You do know I'm not a licensed pilot, right? I'm a student pilot! The guys you fly with have thirty thousand hours in their log books. I barely have thirty!"

"Lady and gentleman, welcome aboard Illegal Air flight One with non-stop service to Culebra. If travelling unlawfully to Culebra is not in your travel plans this morning, please inform one of the cabin crew." She settled back into her seat as if waiting calmly for take off, pretending not to have heard a word he said. Michael just stared at her, not having the slightest idea what to do or say.

She looked over at him with feigned innocence and very real

impatience. "You're burning daylight, Captain Michael. You need to decide if we're going to spend the day here, or on Culebra, or in the local jail."

Muttering something unintelligible under his breath, Michael turned the key and cranked the engine.

Chapter Eleven

Vasili had been up all night, first angry, then apprehensive, and finally fearful. At first he thought that perhaps Bogdan had found a night club, or even a girl, and had gone so far as to search a few blocks in each direction looking for any sign of him. He then considered the possibility that he'd been attacked by a local mugger; but he was fairly certain now that Dmitri had become aware of their presence and had managed to make the opening move. If the element of surprise had been lost, then his job had just become much more difficult.

The men Anton had been holding in reserve would be here soon, so he'd have no shortage of help. Thankfully they were all Ukrainian, no Americans had yet been called in. But he now faced the task of having to explain Bogdan's disappearance to Anton, he fumed, kicking a nearby pebble in frustration. Why was it so hard to find competent help? That had been an ongoing problem since last summer. It was as if he and Dmitri were the only people in the whole organization with the ability to think. What had that idiot Bogdan done to tip his hand to Dmitri and allow himself to be caught?

Only now was he beginning to wonder what had actually become of Bogdan. Until this moment his anger had been directed towards the fool's actions before he'd been caught, and how it had inconvenienced him personally, but it was now beginning to dawn on him that Bogdan's permanent disappearance, and it was no doubt permanent, changed the game. Not that he really cared about the man, or what had happened to him, but until now Dmitri had focused on evading his pursuers. Bogdan's disappearance changed everything. Dmitri was on the offensive now and Vasili had to assume that he now knew everything Bogdan had known. That meant he was now in danger himself, and so was the rest of his team. Well, now he'd have to not only move to a new hotel, but likely start the search for Dmitri all over again. That story Bogdan had come back with last night about meeting Dmitri in the morning had all been a set up.

He spun around and began striding purposely back towards the hotel, pondering his next moves. Had Dmitri's attack on Bogdan been a random, chance act on Dmitri's part, a lucky break that had presented itself, or was it indeed a whole new tactic on his part? Was he actually planning on going on the attack and taking on the whole organization, or would he now go back into hiding? Had he already left the island?

He muttered a curse under his breath. Was he going to have to decide how to break up the team to start the search, not only here on Culebra, but also on other islands? Or had Dmitri already flown off to the other side of the world? For that matter, where was the Canadian? Had the two of them teamed up somehow? Michael Barrett had disappeared on a ship heading in this general direction.

He gave a violent kick at a pile of seaweed left behind by the retreating tide as he realized that he still hadn't answered the big question. What was he going to tell Anton? He snorted in disgust, not even noticing the curious look he drew from a woman jogging in the opposite direction. The answer was easy, really. For now, he would tell him absolutely nothing. He'd explain his absence to the rest of the men by hinting that Bogdan was busy keeping an eye out for Dmitri. When it became necessary, he'd then blame him for Dmitri's disappearance; it had been a stupid mistake made by Bogdan. Really, that is exactly what had happened, wasn't it?

Until then his own job would be to figure out the next move. It was time for a big cup of coffee.

* * *

"If you have any brains at all you will never come back here, or return to Ukraine. You will never make contact with Anton or Vasili or anyone else." Dmitri barked in Ukrainian.

Bogdan nodded in resignation. Not that he would have dared to give any other answer under the circumstances. Two burly deckhands, who spoke neither English nor Ukrainian, were stationed on either side of him, the expressions on their faces suggesting that they were eagerly awaiting a false move on his part so that they could use him as part of their morning work-out. Then there was the scruffy-looking captain with the toothless grin to whom Dmitri had just handed a large wad of American dollars. The dollars, Bogdan knew, were to make sure that he disappeared from the face of the earth.

An acquaintance of Dmitri's worked at the port and had put him in touch with the captain of a seedy-looking freighter who was more than eager to accept cash in exchange for taking on an unpaid deck hand. This old tub required more work than the present crew could keep up with in order to remain semi-seaworthy. The owners would never need to know about this particular volunteer, or the dollars he had just stuffed into his pocket. It served them right. This floating collection of rust should have been scrapped years ago, but the fact that it could still float and move under its own power meant they would continue to use it to make as much money as possible until the day it finally surrendered to the salt and rust that encrusted its hull. They'd collect their insurance money when it sank, and buy another rust bucket with the proceeds.

The money from this stranger was a moderate windfall to the

captain, and all he had to do in exchange was to keep this sorry-looking creature on board and out of sight of the officials for the next few ports of call. That would not be a difficult task.

Dmitri nodded to the captain, who then barked an order at his two deckhands, and Bogdan was escorted none too gently into the bowels of the ship. "Thank you." Dmitri said with a nod, pleased with himself that he had managed to find a way to dispose of Bogdan without having to resort to any unnecessary violence. The captain simply grunted in reply.

It would be weeks before Bogdan left the ship, and that would be on another continent. Perhaps Bogdan might find he enjoyed life at sea and stay on permanently. He shrugged to himself; anything was possible, wasn't it?

At any rate, he was safely out of the way for the foreseeable future as the captain was under strict instructions not to let him leave the ship or have any access to email or mobile phones. Even if he did get off the ship and run back to Vasili he would, hopefully, be too late to be of any use. Dmitri expected to have the whole matter dealt with long before that. He chuckled as he walked down the gang plank and onto the pier. If Bogdan did try running back here, it would be to face the wrath of Vasili and Anton. No doubt he was well aware of that himself, and simple self-preservation should be more than enough to dissuade him from attempting it.

He paused for a few minutes, watching as the ship made its final preparations for departure. The next order of business was to touch base with Juan and then try to track down Vasili. If his old friend had half a brain, he'd already figured out exactly what had happened to Bogdan and was likely in a new hotel by now. Juan just might be able to track his movements. Dmitri was too wrapped up in his own thoughts to pay any heed to the small plane that buzzed over the port.

* * *

Michael wiped the sweat from his brow, hoping that Sandy would think it had been caused by the sun beating through the windshield. In fact, a sidelong glance at his co-pilot-slash-cabin crew told him she was sweating a bit too. Hopefully it was because she was hot and not feeling as nervous about the upcoming landing as he was.

"We'll be on the ground in a couple of minutes now," he said with more confidence than he felt, leaving the rest of the sentence unspoken: 'one way or another.'"

"Aren't you supposed to say, 'Cabin crew prepare for landing?'"

"I've got an experienced crew, I figured they didn't need me to tell them what to do," he replied with a real smile.

"Oh, they do know, Captain Barrett, but it's always good to hear from the flight deck," Sandy smiled back before adding, "Cross check complete." She bit back the words 'you'll do fine,' figuring they'd sound like false encouragement. Truth be told, she was a bit nervous about the landing, but only because Michael seemed to be. Okay, so this wasn't the plane he was used to flying, but it wasn't that much different, was it? The aircraft he flew were very close in size and weight to this one and he'd done just fine on the last flight. The only difference now was that he had no one to back him up, but then he hadn't really needed it last time. She didn't understand that it wasn't the landing he was nervous about; it was the approach. He couldn't do a normal circuit and landing here, flying the normal squared-off pattern with a big white barn to mark his turning point and a long, straight final allowing him to judge and adjust the approach. Because of the terrain, this landing would require him to fly an approach that wouldn't even allow him to line up with the runway until the last moment. Michael had circled around the island, studying the area, gauging the winds, and purposely delaying the coming approach for a few extra minutes. More than once he'd considered flying to another island to land; one with a normal runway, but that would defeat the purpose of the whole exercise. He needed to be here. With Dmitri.

Finally acknowledging the fact that his piloting skill was not going to improve any before the fuel ran out, he headed out over the open ocean in the opposite direction from which he'd have to land. He'd lost sight of the runway now, but knew it was back there, behind those hills, and after checking for other air traffic he began a bank to the left, triple checking that he'd completed the pre-landing checklist. Nervously feeling for the unfamiliar prop control, he confirmed by touch that it was fully forward and told himself to just ignore it from now on. He then gripped throttle tightly, all the while eyeballing the turn.

He allowed a small smile as he saw that he'd called the turn about right, with the nose of the Cessna pointed straight down the middle of the valley. Lowering the flaps, he adjusted the trim and then jockeyed the throttle a bit. Without a clear view of the runway he wasn't sure how to set up the descent, but the plane he'd watched land here the other day had been below the tops of the hills as it flew between them, so he decided he couldn't go too far wrong doing the same thing.

It was a strange and unnerving feeling to look out the side windows and see solid, tree-covered ground on either side. The runway was off to his left now, but he was angled to the right. Keeping the plane in a right bank he adjusted the power slightly, feeling a bit more confident now that he knew he could control the altitude well enough to stay above the sinking terrain, while still maintaining a more or less constant descent. His knuckles were still white as he gripped the control wheel and the throttle. He didn't dare risk a glance to see how Sandy was doing. She hadn't spoken a word since he'd started this weaving approach.

Finally he cleared the hill to his left and reversed the turn, lining up with the runway with what felt like only seconds to spare. He was too low now he saw. Adding power to arrest the descent he over-corrected. He cut the throttle to idle just as he flared and the main gear hit the runway a bit too hard, causing the plane to bounce off the pavement. Okay, he'd done that more than once, no need to panic, just wait for it to start sinking again ... a touch of power ... ease back on the wheel a bit more.

The wheels made a soft chirping noise and the plane stayed on the ground this time, the weight now on the landing gear and not the wings. He pulled back a bit harder, raised the flaps, and braked as heavily as he could. He'd done it!

Letting out a long breath as the plane slowed to a crawl, he realized he'd been holding it for some time. Maybe since the bounce? He turned left off the runway and headed for the ramp.

"Ladies and, I mean lady, welcome to Culebra."

"That second landing was pretty good," she quipped, then perhaps feeling bad as she saw Michael blush heavily, she added, "I remember a pilot bouncing a 737 a lot worse than that with a full load of passengers on a trip into Toronto. You did okay. Really."

"Thanks," he replied absently, still concentrating on guiding the plane into the parking area, watching shadows of his wings. If his shadow didn't touch the shadow of the plane next to him, then the planes wouldn't touch either. Satisfied with his parking job, he shut down the radios and pulled the mixture to idle to kill the engine. "We made it," he said, with obvious relief in his voice. "It's just too bad I can't log that flight."

"Hey, the important thing is, you did do it. Even if it's not in your log book, you'll never forget it!"

"That's for sure." He finished securing the plane and unfastened his seat belt while Sandy followed suit. Then remembering his promise, he grabbed an air sickness bag and shoved a couple of hundred-dollar bills into it. That made him feel better, even generous, even if it was Dmitri's money. He jotted down the name of the airport they'd departed from on the bag as well, and left it on the seat. Remembering his airmanship, he set the park brake and installed the control lock before sliding out the door. Almost as an afterthought, he grabbed the rag normally used to wipe the dipstick and wiped down everything in the cockpit that he figured he and Sandy might have touched.

Walking to the front of the plane he gave the engine cowling an affectionate pat and grinned at the plane, proud of what he'd just accomplished, even if it was the most illegal thing he'd ever done in his life. Or was it? Which was more serious, grand theft airplane, or crossing a border without a passport? Well, in any case, this had been a lot more fun.

His thoughts turned more serious now as he remembered that when he'd crossed that border, he was getting further from danger. Making this flight had brought him closer to it.

Knowing how pilots could be, Sandy gave him his moment with the airplane. She'd once heard the comment that pilots were strange creatures that talked about airplanes when they were around women, and about women when they were around airplanes.

When she saw him turn serious, she knew the moment was over and broke the silence. "What do we do now?"

Michael paused to watch a commuter plane shoot between the

hills, make a perfect touchdown, then taxi smartly towards the terminal building. *That would be the life*, he thought, flying something like that from island to island all day long. The perfect job; and in a paradise like the Caribbean to boot.

"I guess I haven't thought that out quite yet. I suppose the first thing is to find Dmitri. I'm thinking that Juan should know where he is, or at least how to contact him." He hesitated for a moment; not sure just how involved Sandy wanted to be in whatever might happen next. Something had made her change her mind and come this far with him, so it was with some reluctance that he continued. "You know, we could go across to the terminal and get you a flight home. Or at least off the island. You might even be able to meet up with the cruise ship somewhere."

He saw hesitation in her eyes as she considered his offer. He really wanted her to stay, but on the other hand this was his fight, not hers, and there was no telling just how dangerous things might get. Or how it would end.

She looked at him, then took a long look around the airport, as if somehow she'd find the answer in the hills. "No, I'm curious now. I'll stick around and see what happens. Besides, if these guys really can track me down, I figure I'm safer with you and Dmitri."

Michael was sure he could hear some doubt in her voice, maybe even some regret, but he breathed a silent sigh of relief as she gave her answer.

* * *

Across the ramp from where Michael and Sandy were trying to figure out how to hail a taxi, the commuter plane was beginning to unload the passengers, most of whom were looking forward to a tropical holiday full of surf, sand, food, and a mix of relaxation and night life. Six of them, however, had an entirely different agenda.

Inside the terminal building an agitated Vasili was pacing back and forth, impatiently awaiting their arrival. Only two of them spoke English, and those two had been instructed to inform any fellow passengers who might become too inquisitive that they were business men from Europe attending a convention. Hopefully that would satisfy their curiosity, but most travellers were so wrapped up in their own plans that it was unlikely they'd be asked.

He ceased pacing when they began filing into the terminal building. As instructed, they had dressed as western tourists, and they were quite naturally acting the part as well. Some of them had never been out of Ukraine before and couldn't help but gawk at their exotic surroundings, excitedly pointing out to each other sights that they'd only dreamed of until this trip. Vasili caught their attention with a stern look and they managed, for the most part, to contain their excitement as they followed him out to the rented van.

Once he had his team loaded into the van, he started the engine and cranked up the air conditioning before turning to face them. For now, he'd decided, he would not mention Bogdan at all.

"As you know, I now know exactly where Dmitri lives, but he is being very cautious about being seen. You all have pictures of him?" He waited for their nods, several of them also waved their mobile phones in confirmation. "Good. Now we are going to go to a place I have rented as our headquarters. It is marked on this map." He handed each of them a map of the island with both their headquarters and Dmitri's resort circled and marked. "Study this so that you are familiar with the island by the time we get there. Once you are ready, we will set up a schedule to keep the resort under surveillance while the rest of you either sleep or patrol the island, in case they show up somewhere else."

Vasili paused, studying each face for any sign of disappointment or discontent. "You are not here for a holiday," he barked sharply, causing them to jump. "Find Dmitri and you will be rewarded with some extra time here. Waste just one minute playing tourist and you are gone." The tone of his voice implied that being 'gone' meant being permanently retired. Maybe 'permanently terminated' would be a more fitting term.

Having set the tone of the mission, he turned around and fastened his seat belt.

"All right. Let's get started."

* * *

So far, Michael's plan had gone no further than getting back to the island. His plan to 'borrow' an airplane to get back here might have been fueled as much by his desire to fly as his need to be here. He could have hired a boat instead, or he could have found a scheduled or charter flight flown by a real pilot. He found himself half-elated and half-horrified that he'd actually stolen an airplane, but he tipped the balance in favour of elation by reminding himself that it had been necessary to get here as secretly as possible. The fact that very few other pilots made their first solo cross-country flight over the ocean helped as well.

He now found himself in a taxi sitting beside a noticeably nervous Sandy. He debated asking her yet again if she was sure about her decision. He was being selfish, but having her here did make him feel better, if only because he had someone to talk to. Reality was setting in and he knew that his plan didn't include exactly how he was supposed to help Dmitri. Maybe Sandy was having the same doubts about helping him.

The first thing that he needed to do was to start thinking like Dmitri, who likely wouldn't take a taxi directly to his destination given the circumstances. He leaned across the seat and instructed their driver to drop them off short of their destination, at the resort next to Dmitri's. Sorry, but he had been mistaken in his earlier directions. As he sat back in his seat Sandy glanced at him with arched eyebrow before a look of understanding replaced her puzzled expression. She smiled weakly at him, a curt nod saying that she understood why he'd changed his mind and agreed with his plan. He reached over and squeezed her hand, smiling as she squeezed back.

The driver obligingly pulled up the driveway and parked in front of the lobby where Michael handed him the fare plus a moderate tip; he'd decided it shouldn't be too big or too small as the driver might be more likely to remember them if he went to either extreme. As he climbed out, he congratulated himself on thinking like Dmitri.

"Just act like we own the place," he said out the corner of his mouth to Sandy, and displaying a confidence he didn't feel, he led her in through the front door and through the lobby, nodding to several staff members as if he stayed there all the time and knew each one of them personally.

Making his way through the lobby he held open the door to the beach area for Sandy, and they strolled down the walkway to the beach itself. He paused a moment to get his bearings. "That way," he said with a nod to the left, as much to confirm it to himself as to inform Sandy.

He brushed her hand with his, and then clasped it softly.

"We should look like we're together, shouldn't we?" He saw her blush, but she gave his hand a soft squeeze in return.

They made their way as slowly as possible down onto the beach and then took a turn towards Dmitri's stretch of beach, just one of a score of couples strolling along the sand. When they reached the tree line at the edge of the beach Michael was relieved to see that a narrow foot path both provided a way through the brush to Dmitri's beach.

"This is it," Michael announced needlessly as they emerged back onto the beach. He caught up with Sandy and took her hand once again. She simply smiled up at him.

As they made their way across the open stretch of beach towards the path that led back to the resort; they both felt a sudden sense of unease at the thought that one of Yuri's men might be watching them. Until now the danger had been almost academic, but now it felt very real, even imminent. They both resisted the urge to look around, and managed to keep a slow, casual pace, but it was with a welcome wave of relief that they opened the door into the building itself.

Juan glanced up from his computer monitor and flashed them a welcoming smile; but as he rose from his chair to inquire if they had reservations, his smile momentarily froze. He didn't fully understand what was going on, but he knew enough to know that neither of them should be here.

He fought back his sense of dread, and the uneasy feeling that he'd somehow failed Mr. Dmitri, and forced a friendly smile back onto his face.

"Mr. Michael, Miss Sandy, what are you doing here?"

Michael blinked in surprise at the unexpected question, and felt Sandy give his hand a quick squeeze that conveyed a mild panic rather than any sort of reassurance. They'd both been hoping to be welcomed back, not challenged.

"Well, uh, is Dmitri here?"

"No, I'm sorry he's not in right now." The tone of his voice and the look in his eye conveyed the fact that not only was he not here, but that he wasn't expected any time in the foreseeable future.

"This was a really dumb idea," Michael murmured softy under his breath, and a glance at Sandy told him she was thinking exactly the same thing.

"Can you get a message to him?" Michael asked out loud.

Juan looked guiltily around the lobby, but no one was paying any attention to them. He weighed his options. This man was a friend, a good friend, of his boss, but he had a sense that Michael's presence here put all of them at risk. Still, his boss would not want him to turn the couple away; that might put them in even more danger.

Michael stood there, watching the hesitation in Juan's eyes. He told himself that it was right for him to be here, that Dmitri needed his help. Yes, it might have been a dumb idea to come, but that wasn't Juan's decision to make, was it? This man was coming between him and his friend. Just as he was about to speak, Juan broke the long, awkward silence. "Please come into the office," he said with a nod towards the door.

He opened the door and ushered the two of them inside, then with an audible sigh of resignation he picked up the phone and dialed a number. There was a pause that seemed much too long before he spoke. "It's Juan, I need you to call me immediately. There is a –," he glanced at Michael and Sandy, "There is a very urgent matter we must discuss."

Obviously the call had gone to voice mail and it was all Michael could do to keep from asking when Dmitri would call back. Juan had no way of knowing that, but Michael's frustration was growing by the second. Dmitri might be in desperate need of his help while all he could do was sit and wait. What if he couldn't call because Vasili or Anton had him? What if it was already too late to help him? It couldn't be, could it?

"I will let you know as soon as he calls back, but I think it's best to wait in here until he does." As he spoke Juan closed the blinds, blocking their view of the beach, then opened the door to the lobby, turned, and motioned towards a fridge in the corner of the office. "If you want something, please help yourself. If you need anything else, knock on the door and I will help you in any way I can." He stared at the floor, then glanced back up at Sandy before finally meeting Michael's eyes. "But please, both of you, stay in here."

They each nodded at him in response, then looked at each other with a mutual shrug. "I'm sure he'll call back soon," Michael offered.

"He will," Sandy responded, but neither of them sounded at all certain.

Michael opened the door to the fridge and pulled out a can of Coke for himself. "Do you want something?"

"Any orange juice?" she asked. Michael fished around in the fridge before finding what he was looking for, then handed the bottle to her.

They each opened their drinks, but just as Michael was about to take his first sip Sandy raised her bottle of orange juice in a toast. He couldn't help but crack a smile as his can clinked against her bottle. "To success –," she offered.

"To success," Michael responded firmly.

* * *

It was late afternoon, and many phone calls later, when Juan picked up the phone to hear Dmitri's voice on the other end. "What is it, Juan?" There was a nervous edge to his voice that Juan had never heard before, and it raised his level of apprehension several more notches. He took a deep breath before answering.

"One minute, sir, I need to step into your office." Dmitri didn't respond, but Juan could still feel the tension growing on Dmitri's end of the call. He opened the door and slipped into the office. Michael was watching a cricket match on TV, with no real idea of what was happening. Sandy was thumbing through a stack of magazines without actually reading anything. They both rose to their feet and looked at him expectantly. He nodded in response to their silent questions and returned his attention to the call. He really couldn't delay it any longer.

"Mr. Dmitri, sir, your friends are here."

"My friends? You mean the man that was looking for me earlier?" That couldn't be, could it? Bogdan and the freighter should be many miles out to sea by now. Was Juan trying to tell him that more Ukrainians had shown up?

"No, sir, your friends. The ones that stayed here the other night." He winced as he spoke.

"You mean the man and woman, the ones I brought there myself?" Dmitri waited for Juan to correct him and explain what was really going on. Obviously he couldn't speak freely and was trying to pass information on to him without actually having to say the words out loud.

"Yes, those ones," Juan dropped his voice as low as possible. "Mr. Michael and Miss Sandy."

That was exactly the answer that Dmitri had feared he would receive, but he still couldn't believe it. "They're back?" He asked the question so loudly that Michael could clearly hear him from across the room.

"Yes, sir, they are back, they arrived a few hours ago. I have them in your office right now."

"Put Mikhail on the phone! No! Just keep them in the office, don't let them leave that room!"

"Yes, sir, that is what I've already done."

There was a long silence during which Juan merely stood there, his eyes fixed on the cricket match while Dmitri decided what to do. "You did the right thing, Juan. Just keep them there. I'll be back as soon as I can."

"Of course, sir."

Why couldn't this have happened on his day off?

Chapter Twelve

Dmitri stormed into the room, removing a floppy hat that had been partially hiding his features, and uttering a single terse command without even looking at them. "Follow me!" He turned and walked from the office with Michael and Sandy in tow. His size and tone left Sandy feeling even more uneasy than she had been already. Michael claimed to know the man, but she couldn't help but feel a bit afraid of him; right now he looked angry enough to hurt someone. She looked to Michael for reassurance, but he didn't look back at her. He was glaring at Dmitri's back as they made their way to his residence, wearing a determined, defiant expression. If anything, he looked angrier than Dmitri did and it made her feel better that, on that score at least, the two men were on equal footing.

Michael took a seat on the couch with his arms crossed and his face set. Dmitri barely managed to keep himself from slamming the door before turning to glare at him. Michael simply glared back. Both of them ignored her.

"I told you I'd send for you when it was safe. Is my English so bad that you could not understand me?"

"I understood you perfectly. It was a dumb idea." Michael kept his voice even, in stark contrast with Dmitri's rising tone.

"It was dumb to keep you and your friend safe while I look after this? You don't know what you're dealing with here!"

"I think I know perfectly well what I'm dealing with here. Which one of us spent a couple of nights in Anton's basement last summer? I don't recall you getting worked over by those two thugs. They would have killed me if you hadn't come along, I know that," he sensed that Dmitri was about to bring that up and decided to end that argument before the point could be made. "But Yuri had his men follow me to Canada and if we don't deal with this here and now they'll keep following me until they have no more use for me. Then they'll kill me."

"Yuri is dead," Dmitri informed him, taking a bit of the wind from his sails. Michael paused as he absorbed this new information, then decided that it really didn't matter.

"Well then Anton, or Vasili, or some other Mafia kingpin had them follow me. It really doesn't matter, does it? I'm as involved in this as you are and I have been ever since you kidnapped me off that bus. This is my fight every bit as much as it is yours."

He took Dmitri's silence for agreement and continued. "I'm here to help you because I need to win this fight and I can't do that sitting in some resort pretending to be on vacation. I need to know what's going on and whether or not my life is going to come to a sudden end!"

Dmitri opened and closed his mouth several times, struggling to reign in his anger. "Mikhail, you have no experience dealing with these men," he held up his hand to silence his friend's objection. "Yes, they beat you up, but you never fought back. Have you ever really fought anyone?" The words 'to the death' were unspoken but hung in the air in the silence that followed the question.

"No, I haven't," the defiance was still in his voice, "But neither had Youlya when she went after that guy with a wrench."

"That should never have happened."

"But it did! What if you fail, what if they kill you, or drag you off somewhere to torture you? Who's going to look after me then? I won't even know they're coming until it's too late. If we stick together at least I'll know what's going on." He waited while Dmitri fumed in silence. "Tell me you can't use any help."

"If I need help it will be from someone that knows what they are doing, someone who can be as ruthless as needed."

"Is that why you used Youlya last summer? Is she that ruthless?"

"No! She was only supposed to drive me to Anton's. Nothing more."

"Michael stole an airplane to come here and help you," Sandy interjected, rising to stand between the two men. "You could at least show him a little gratitude!" She was glaring at Dmitri almost as hard as Michael was, though she had no idea what had possessed her to join in the fray.

"I am thankful for the offer," Dmitri replied, managing to bring his temper back in check, "But he has put you both in danger by bringing you here. I went to a lot of trouble to get you both somewhere safe. Are you ready to fight these men too?"

"Well, no, I mean, I just wanted to help Michael."

"You just helped him into a lot of trouble!"

Michael rose to his feet and stood toe-to-toe with Dmitri. "Look, we can spend all night arguing in circles. The fact is we're both in a lot of trouble and danger already. Instead of fighting each other, let's start fighting the Ukrainian Mafia. How's that for a plan? You want an opportunity? Well you've got one." He nodded towards Sandy. "In fact, you've got two opportunities. Now, do you want to take advantage of those opportunities or not? Do you have other people that can help you already? Do you have another source of help that fully understands what's happening and why? I told you to just let me go that first day in Ukraine," he continued, "But you wouldn't. None of this would be happening if you had listened to me back then. And now you've dragged Sandy into this too. It was your choice to bring her along; we could have left her on St. Thomas." Sandy nodded in agreement.

Dmitri sighed before answering, all the anger and frustration gone from his voice now, "Mikhail, I just don't want to see you hurt, I'm trying to keep you safe." Dmitri's sudden change of tone caught Michael short. He was being too hard on his friend. He should have been listening to himself when he had kept telling Sandy that Dmitri was only trying to protect her. He was taking out his frustration on the only person that could help him, instead of on the men behind this. It had been foolish to come down here expecting that Dmitri was going to offer up some kind of quick fix to a problem like Vasili. There was no quick fix, but together they would find a solution.

"I know, Dmitri, I know. I'm sorry for being so upset, I don't want to see you hurt either, but you've got a better chance of surviving this with some help, right?"

"Da," the word was spoken reluctantly, despite the sincerity it held.

"Okay then." Michael kept the surprise from his voice as he continued. "We all stand a better chance of surviving this if we work together, so why don't you bring us up to speed and let's make some plans. No unnecessary risks, I promise. We'll be smart about this and look after these guys once and for all."

Dmitri still wasn't sure Michael fully understood the words he'd just spoken, but he couldn't help but offer a proud smile at his friend. "Did you really steal an airplane to get back here?"

* * *

Vasili felt much better now. With a full team, not counting Bogdan who was obviously too inept to be part of the operation anyway, he could now concentrate on orchestrating things rather than taking an active role himself, at least until they were ready to make their move on Dmitri.

There were no trains or roads off the island, but there was an airport and so he had the various members of his team keeping the terminal building under constant surveillance. By altering sunglasses, hats, and the loud tropical shirts available in all the tourist shops, he figured that they could rotate off and on without anyone recognizing them. The docks were a bit harder to control, but he was doing his best there. Privately owned boats were an even bigger problem because they could come and go from any number of docks and beaches, but he felt certain that Dmitri was still on the island. He was certain that he could sense the presence of his old friend, now turned adversary. He needed to focus his effort on searching Culebra, not preventing Dmitri's escape from the island, which made the job just a bit easier. Fleeing Ukraine with the money had been one thing, but running was not Dmitri's usual behaviour; he should have thought of that sooner.

Bogdan's disappearance still gnawed at him. On the one had Dmitri had betrayed his presence to them; surely he understood that he'd tipped his hand and made his presence here undeniable. In so doing he had given his pursuers a slight advantage by narrowing their search area. But on the other hand, and there was always another hand, there was simply no way of knowing how much information Bogdan had given up. What critical piece of Vasili's plan might he now turn to his own advantage. He wasn't even sure if there was any such information, aside from that fact that they were closing in, and that alone was bad enough. It had, perhaps, been wishful thinking, but he had been hoping for complete surprise.

That brought him back to the thought that Dmitri was not at all likely to run this time. Yes, it did narrow the search area, but it also made their prey much more dangerous. He'd killed before, in Ukraine, on the orders of his superiors. He would be more than willing to kill again to save his own life and fortune. Vasili mentally cursed Bogdan once more for making the situation much more difficult and dangerous.

That was the biggest advantage that Dmitri now had; he could kill them, but they couldn't kill him, at least not until they knew where the rest of the money was. That was the problem these days, you didn't need to keep your cash in the local bank to have easy access to it. With online banking you could keep it in a bank in another country, even one on the other side of the world, and still access it twenty-four hours a day. All you need is a cheap, mobile phone and an internet connection. What did they have in their favour?

He sat back and took a long sip of coffee, then sampled the tray of fresh fruit sitting on his table. What was Dmitri's biggest weakness? The old Dmitri didn't have one, at least not one that he was aware of, but what about the new Dmitri? He needed something to use against him, something to take back the advantage he'd lost. Vasili took another sip of his coffee, his gaze fixed out the window towards a seascape that he wasn't seeing.

Of course! The Canadian!

He'd been seeing the Canadian only as a source of information, a way of finding out where Dmitri was, but he was potentially a much bigger asset than that. Hadn't Dmitri turned back from the border to rescue him last summer? Even back then they were only using him to find out what had happened to the money and what Dmitri's plans were; that had been very foolish. But then, the old Dmitri hadn't cared about anyone but himself. The new Dmitri cared enough not only to send him a sizable chunk of money, but also enough to protect him. That's why he'd sent for him, brought him down here and put him on that cruise ship.

Yes! If they had Michael Barrett they wouldn't have to look for

Dmitri, he would come to them. Not only that, but he was somewhere in the area, somewhere close by so that Dmitri could keep a protective eye on him. Maybe he should call Anton, have him send more men to search for the Canadian. The last information they had on him was that he was on that cruise ship, but they'd all but forgotten about him upon learning of Dmitri's location. It shouldn't be that hard to pick up his trail. Not that he'd stop looking for Dmitri, but Michael Barrett was too big an opportunity to let pass by.

* * *

"Okay. So, what's the plan?" Michael asked as the three of them sat around Dmitri's table sipping tea. Before Dmitri could answer he held up a hand to silence him. "I mean, besides waiting for an opportunity, what is the plan?"

"You have something against opportunities, Mikhail?" He looked so genuinely curious that Michael studied him for several seconds to see if he was being serious, then decided it didn't matter.

"I have nothing against opportunities, but sometimes you have to make your own. You already got rid of that one guy, the one you put on the boat. What do we do now?

There was no doubt now that Dmitri was serious, the look in his eyes made that very clear as he set down his cup and looked from Michael to Sandy and back again. "They will not give up. You understand that, don't you? Both of you?"

Michael and Sandy looked at each other with raised eyebrows, as if each was asking the other if coming back really was a good idea, before nodding in unison. "Yeah, I get that," Michael added, "They've been watching me ever since last summer, I think. They aren't giving up. I get that. What do we do about it?"

"I already told you about the man, Bogdan, that I put on the boat." His comment was met by two more nods.

"So that means one down and a few more to go." Sandy observed; the hope evident in her voice.

Dmitri shook his head. "No, it doesn't. Even if we get rid of every man that Vasili has on the island, all they will do is send more. If we get rid of the new ones they will send even more."

He let the sentence hang in the air, trying to impress upon his two guests just how serious the situation was. "I should have realized that before I left Ukraine. Maybe I should have left with nothing."

"Would they have let you go then?" Michael asked, knowing the answer and waiting for Dmitri to acknowledge it. Dmitri was regretting his decision and it was too late for that; they needed to focus on dealing with what was happening right now.

"No, they would still have looked for me, but they would have given up by now. Maybe." Even he wasn't fooled by his own response.

"Even if you give it back, they still won't leave you alone, will they? We've been over this before." It was more a comment than a question, and Dmitri ignored it, but it brought him back to the question at hand.

"It is Anton and Vasili that want the money back. It is also the two of them that want to make me pay for what I did. The only way to stop this is to get rid of them."

"You don't mean putting Anton and Vasili on a slow boat to nowhere, do you?" Michael thought back to that night last summer. The one that he hadn't expected to survive. Killing another human being wasn't something he'd ever even thought about seriously; it just wasn't anything he'd ever thought he'd need to do. But after what those men had threatened to do to him, after what they had done to him, he didn't think he'd have too many regrets if something happened to them. Still, he avoided looking at Sandy.

Dmitri ignored that question too, and the long silence that followed allowed both Sandy and Michael to think about the fact that by returning they were going to have to face a lot more than personal danger. They were committing themselves to a course of action that might have results that they didn't want to face.

"So, you still want to be here?" Dmitri looked at them as if urging them to reconsider.

"I'm in, Dmitri," replied Michael, "Like I keep telling you, these guys would have killed me last summer if you hadn't come back, and you just said yourself that they aren't going to give up. So as long as they're around I'm still in danger. I'd rather deal with this than run and hide again." He turned to face Sandy, "But this is my fight, Sandy, not yours. It's not too late for you to go somewhere safe until this is all over."

She took a deep breath as she considered all that they had been talking about. "Do you really think they'd kill you, Michael?"

"They already tried once," he nodded firmly. "I'm not going to let them get another chance at it without a fight."

"Then we're not going through this all over again." The tone of her voice told Michael that the question had been rhetorical, she had merely been setting him up for her answer. "If you two send me off then I'll be the one that has no way of knowing what's happening. Plus, you both told me back on the boat that there's a good chance they know about me too." She looked back and forth between the two men as if daring them to contradict what they'd told her previously. "I'm in as much danger as you two, so I'm sticking around too."

"So you're both staying." Dmitri's voice carried no emotion, it was merely an acknowledgement of what they had said. "I guess we need to make some plans."

"Good," Michael responded firmly, "It's about time. We've wasted enough of that already. What's our first step?"

"We need to find out where Vasili is staying now. I'm sure he's moved since I had that little talk with Bogdan. After that things should become more clear."

"How do we find that out?" Michael sounded ready to get his hands dirty with some real work.

"That's the easy part, Juan is already working on it. Once he finds out, well, that's when it gets dangerous."

"Then what do we do for now? Surely there must be something we can do to get ready?"

"There is not much we can do until we know where he is. Once we know that we will have to find out how many men he has and then figure out how to get to him without having to go through all of them first."

"So what, we just sit here and watch cricket?" Michael grumbled. His frustration was beginning to rise again.

Dmitri rose from the table without a word and disappeared into his bedroom, returning again after a minute or two. He sat back down and dropped a handgun onto the table in front of Michael. "No, if you want to do something, go look for Vasili, but maybe you better take this. I prefer to let Juan track him down by calling his friends at the other hotels and resorts, but if you want to do it yourself, go ahead."

Michael shrank back from the gun. It wasn't that he had anything against guns in general, but the fact that Dmitri had one, and that it could only have one purpose, shocked him. Yes, he'd wanted to help Dmitri and himself and Sandy by returning, but up until now getting rid of Vasili and Anton had been merely a wish. The presence of the gun made it all very real in a way he hadn't fully thought through.

"Go ahead, take it," Dmitri said, the words coming out almost like an order, displaying a side of him that Michael knew existed, but had never fully experienced. "What is the matter? You don't know how to use it? It's easy." Dmitri picked it up and worked the action, chambering a round, then he worked the safety back and forth, "See? Safety off, safety on, put it this way and it's ready to fire, put it this way and you won't shoot yourself in the foot."

"Okay," Michael sighed, "I get the point. We wait to find out where they are and make our plan from there. Just – just put that away until we really need it."

Dmitri allowed a self-satisfied smirk to cross his face as he unloaded the gun before shoving it into his belt.

"Good idea, Mikhail," he grunted as he resumed his seat. "Now we wait for Juan to learn where they are staying. If you don't want to watch cricket, we can always watch football."

Michael wasn't sure if soccer was an improvement over cricket or not.

* * *

"That will, of course, require more men." Anton was not as enthusiastic about Vasili's new plan as he'd hoped.

"How badly do you want the rest of the money?" Vasili asked rhetorically. "If you just want to play games, we will keep doing what we're doing. If you're serious, we need to use every advantage we have. You said you had some Americans willing to help; have them search the islands the cruise ship is visiting, then we can use our own men to concentrate on searching here."

"I've succeeded on my end already," Anton couldn't help but rub it in a bit as he'd long since transferred the funds from Youlya's account into his own. "You know where he lives and the island can't be all that big." He was looking at a map even as he spoke; the place was hardly a speck in the ocean. "Why do we need to waste time and money chasing after a boat that's only going to go back to where it started from?" It would be nice to keep tabs on the ship, but help from the Americans would come at a steep price, one he hoped to avoid having to pay.

"Dmitri managed to rescue the Canadian from your basement while your guards watched him." Vasili let just a little venom creep into his tone. "Dmitri's already proven that his weakness is Mr. Barrett's safety; if we have him, we can force Dmitri to come to us under our terms. This time," he added sarcastically, "My team and I will be ready for him."

"You want me to pay your men to enjoy a tropical vacation while taking even more men, who could be earning money instead of costing us money, to do the work for you?"

"That is not what I'm saying, Anton, and you know it. We will keep searching for him, but if we can capture the Canadian, I can get word to Dmitri through his employees, and then we will have them both. It could take days, maybe even weeks, to find him otherwise."

There was silence on the other end of the phone as Anton considered what Vasili was saying. True, they had followed the Canadian to Miami, which was in the right neighbourhood, but with Youlya's fortuitous reappearance he'd become unnecessary. However, the Canadian's trip to Dmitri's neighborhood so soon after his return from Greece was not a coincidence; there had to be a reason he was so close to Dmitri at this precise moment. Though he was reluctant to admit it, Vasili's plan had a lot of merit.

"Let me make some phone calls," he said before abruptly ending the call.

The cruise lines, from what he understood, were very large corporations with a lot of employees that didn't necessarily make much money. He could very easily use that to his advantage. He didn't necessarily need to send more men; he could use his contacts in America to look into a few things for him. Vasili might come up with some good ideas now and then, but he only knew how to work hard, not how to work smart. He checked the time and calculated the difference between Ukraine and the eastern United States. Then again, with what they would charge him for their services, who needed to worry about small inconveniences like waking someone in the middle of the night?

Chapter Thirteen

"Allo?" A groggy and somewhat disoriented Vasili mumbled into his mobile phone, a reflexive glance at the clock radio informed him that it was much too early to be awake, especially after the rum he'd enjoyed the previous evening. He heard a chuckle from the other end of the phone.

"Did I wake you, my friend?" Anton's voice sounded anything but apologetic.

"Da." Vasili began to shake his head to clear it, then realized that was a very big mistake and decided to try massaging his temple instead. "What is it?"

"You were right about the Canadian, I have learned something interesting." He paused and took a sip of his tea, more to keep his underling in suspense than anything, but Vasili wasn't feeling awake enough to rise to the bait; he used the pause to close his eyes and rest his head back on the pillow, offering only a grunt in response.

"It seems that Mr. Barrett isn't on the ship anymore. According to my sources at the cruise line he didn't return to the ship after one of their stops."

Vasili was by now alert enough to realize that this bit of information must have some significance, but he couldn't quite figure out just what that might be, so a question seemed a good way to cover his ignorance. "Which island? Do you think he's still there?"

"He might be, you could try looking there, I suppose. It wouldn't hurt." Anton sounded too smug and self-satisfied for that to be a real option.

"Which island?" Vasili repeated the question, allowing the irritation he was feeling from the hour of the call, as well as from the hangover, to creep into his voice.

Anton heard the tone and smirked at the knowledge that from half a world away he'd beaten Vasili to the punch. "He disappeared on the island of St. Thomas."

Vasili knew better than to ask how he'd managed to get that information, but he cursed silently knowing he'd recently been on that very island himself in hopes of spotting either Dmitri or the Canadian. He blinked to try and clear his head and managed to remember that he had two men keeping an eye on Dmitri's place through the night, and that the rest of them were currently sleeping in the room adjacent to his. It was time to regain some control of this conversation before Anton managed to make him sound like even more of a fool.

"Okay, it sounds like he's most likely here on Culebra with Dmitri, but I'm going to send two men to St. Thomas just in case. I should be able to get them there by later this morning." He sat back up and snapped on the bedside lamp, continuing to think out loud as he stumbled towards the dresser to grab some clothes. "I've got two men keeping an eye on Dmitri's place right now, and I'll get two more over there within the hour. I'll call you when we have Michael Barrett. Or Dmitri."

"Preferably you'll have both of them." Anton managed one last sarcastic dig before the call ended.

Vasili scowled at the phone before tossing it onto the bed as he pulled on a pair of shorts and one of his new shirts. If he had thought that life would be easier without Yuri Stepanovich, he couldn't have been more wrong. Anton was quickly becoming even worse than his predecessor and he pondered, not for the first time, how he might rid himself of his new boss. He deserved to be at the top of the ladder. Not because he'd treat his underlings any better than Yuri or Anton did. But life would be that much better when he called the shots and was able to reap the full reward of all his work. Not to mention reaping the rewards of the work of others.

Picking up the hotel phone on the end table he punched in the number of the room next door. The voice on the other end sounded as groggy as he himself had a few minutes ago. "Get over here. Now." He hung up without waiting for a response and turned on the room lights. The four men in the next room were sharing two double beds while he was enjoying a whole suite to himself. There would be plenty of room for the five of them around the dining room table.

While he waited, he pulled out a map of the Caribbean and unfolded it on the table, quickly locating both Culebra and St. Thomas. "Very smart, Dmitri, but you didn't cover your tracks well enough. You've got the Canadian hidden somewhere on this island, don't you? And he is your weak point, isn't he? Once we have him again, we'll have you too." He smiled to himself at that thought, contemplating all the things he couldn't wait to do to the two of them, and how the story would finally end. "Then we will get our money back. After that, my old friend, I will personally find a nice shady spot somewhere on this island so that the two of you can spend your eternities in paradise."

A knock at the door interrupted his day dream, and he rose to let his team in. They quickly seated themselves around the table where he explained his theory about where they might find Michael. "Boris and Andrei, you will find either a plane or a boat to St. Thomas. I need you there this morning. You have pictures of Dmitri and Michael?" They nodded in response but Vasili hardly even glanced at them. "Start asking around, check the hotels, resorts, Bed and Breakfasts. He won't likely go out in public, but tell them you are friends of theirs and you need to find them, or something like that." In dividing up his team he'd made sure that at least one of the men on each island could speak English.

"Fadyay and Victor, you join the others watching Dmitri's place, we need to watch along the beach as well as keep an eye on the road. They might try to come or go by boat as well, so watch the water too." With more men he'd be able to better keep watch on the whole place. This team would be stretched thinner than he'd like. "I know that he may not be at the resort himself, but we're pretty sure they are still here on this island. If they don't turn up soon we might have to detain some of his staff for questioning." That drew a few chuckles and grins from the men around the table; they were all eager for some real action. "I don't know when we'll be able to rest, but there will be a bonus for all of you when we recover the money." That drew some appreciative smiles as they rose to follow their new orders.

Vasili let them out, then found the remnants of last night's rum. After a healthy swig he turned the lights out and returned to bed. He remained fully dressed, just in case he was needed, but as team leader he needed his rest in order to be able to plan and think things through clearly.

* * *

Juan knocked on the door, then let himself in with his master key. The three of them were seated around the table when he wheeled the breakfast cart into the room. By the thankful looks on their faces, he judged that he was delivering it just in time. He uncovered the dishes, heaped high with fresh fruit, bacon, and scrambled eggs. He also had a carafe of Columbian coffee for Michael and Sandy, as well as hot water and a selection of teas for Dmitri. He'd added some yogurt and orange juice for good measure. Delivering breakfast wasn't part of his usual job description, but as Dmitri's most trusted employee, he'd taken over these duties to keep the presence of these guests as quiet as possible.

He waited for the three of them to serve themselves and begin their meals before delivering his morning report. "Mr. Dmitri, Julio says he thinks that there are at least three men watching the grounds now. He's not sure, but he says they don't seem to be doing anything other than walking around and watching. They are all spread out and aren't approaching each other, so they don't look like they are together, but they are all lingering around in about the same area. When you watch them long enough, they appear very suspicious." Julio was one of the groundskeepers and as such had the perfect excuse to wander the property and keep a close eye on everything and everyone.

Dmitri grunted through a mouthful of eggs and nodded in acknowledgement before swallowing. "Thank you, Juan, anything else?"

"No, sir."

"Very good. Let me know if he has anything else to report, and have him try to get a picture of them, if he can do it without being noticed. I want to see what they look like, if that's possible. That will be all."

"They know where we are." Sandy attempted to sound casual, but looked more than a little nervous as she poked at a piece of melon with her fork. Michael stopped eating to await Dmitri's response. Surely he must have a plan by now.

"No, I don't think so. At least, they are not sure. This is the only place they know to look right now. I think they are waiting to see if they can spot us coming or going, or pick up some clue about where we might be."

"What are we going to do then?" Michael and Sandy asked the question at almost the same time.

"I have a few more places where we can hide out that the two of you don't know about yet, and I think it would be best if we stayed in one of them. If we can figure out for sure how many men Vasili has watching us right now, and what they look like, I think we can avoid them and disappear while they keep looking for us here."

"That gives us some room to move, and more options," Michael said thoughtfully. Dmitri was about to agree when Sandy interrupted.

"You think we can avoid them?" She sounded as nervous as she looked. "What if we can't avoid them, or what if they decide to barge in here?"

"Vasili is smarter than that; he can't afford to let the authorities know he's here. He won't try and barge in." Dmitri shook his head decidedly.

"But what if we can't avoid them? How do we get out of here?"

"If it comes to that, if we really need to, well …" Dmitri left the sentence unfinished, reached behind his back, and patted the pistol, which he still wore tucked into his belt.

"Oh." Sandy sat back; her breakfast forgotten as she turned that possibility over in her mind. She wasn't sure she wanted it to come to that, but found strange comfort in the fact that Dimitri was not only armed, but was willing to pull the trigger if it became necessary.

"But you think we can slip by them and get to one of your safe houses, right?" Michael asked the question more to comfort Sandy than anything. He gave Dmitri a furtive look, asking him to agree.

"Of course we can, Mikhail," Dmitri not only understood the look, but had every confidence in his ability to get them to safety.

He'd get all the information he could from Julio and Juan, and go from there.

They finished their breakfast in silence and then the men channel surfed while Sandy poked around the room looking for something to read. She found a few local papers and after gleaning everything semi-interesting from them, settled down with a pen to tackle the crossword puzzle. None of them were really paying much attention to what they were doing, their minds were too preoccupied with what Vasili might be planning and what they could do about it.

Sandy sat back in her chair and cast a glance at Michael, who was alternating between watching the TV and looking at the window. With the curtains drawn there wasn't much to be seen, but he looked anyway. At one point he glanced in her direction and they made eye contact, each looking away, embarrassed to have been caught looking at the other. Michael, his gaze fixed artificially on the TV, couldn't help but wonder what had made Sandy decide to come along with him on the plane ride, but was thankful she had. He just wasn't sure what to do about it right now. Would Dmitri consider this an opportunity?

Sandy, for her part, had to bite her lip to hide a smile at their mutual embarrassment. There was something about him, she thought to herself once more, his bashfulness was kind of cute, and she was even more certain than ever that he was worth tagging along with. When this was all over, she wanted to be there with him. His red cheeks told he felt the same way.

Their boredom was broken a few hours later by a discrete knock at the door. Sandy was roused from a nap, while Michael almost jumped from his chair. Dmitri merely watched the door as it slowly swung open to reveal Juan's face.

"Mr. Dmitri, Julio has been watching very carefully and we think there are four of them. One is watching the main road and one is keeping an eye on the front door from the parking lot. The other two are at either end of the beach. He sent me their pictures."

Dmitri took in the new information with a nod as he studied the pictures on Juan's phone. He formed a mental picture of where each of them was and was now forming his get-away plan. Finally, he nodded at his faithful employee, "Thank you, Juan, it might be best if both of you disappear from their sight for a while. We don't want them getting suspicious. I'll let you know if I need anything else." Juan left the room with a nod and a polite, but somewhat concerned, smile.

Dmitri grabbed a piece of paper and a pen from his desk and called the others to gather round the table with him. He made a rough sketch of the resort and the surrounding area, then placed an X at the entrance to the lobby, then another where his driveway met the main road. "Okay, going out the front door is out. I wouldn't have tried that anyways, so Vasili wasted those two men." He chuckled as if he'd pulled one over on Vasili, but they all knew that there was no way Vasili could have left the main entrance unguarded. "Now, if he really has only one man at each end of the beach," he marked two more X's at each property line, "Then we have them outnumbered. Four to one makes good odds for us."

"Four?" Sandy interrupted him. "Do you mean that Juan is going to help us escape?"

"No, it's Vasili's man against the four of us." Dmitri winked at her as he patted his gun, and despite herself she had to laugh.

"It's even better odds if you count all the bullets," Michael added, earning chuckles from both Dmitri and Sandy. They all seemed to be on the same page now, and were celebrating the fact that they actually had a plan. "But can't the two guys on the beach see each other? That kind of evens things out a bit."

"They are very far apart. Too far apart to get to each other fast enough to do anything." Dmitri countered.

"But close enough to raise an alarm," Michael persisted.

"Yes, but not if we can distract one of them, or get them out of each other's sight. By now they will be getting bored. It shouldn't be too hard to do that."

"We need to distract them both, right? It will have to be long enough for us to get past the one without the other seeing us," Sandy mused, trying to think along with Dmitri, or even ahead of him. What might work to force their attention elsewhere?

"We could do that," Dmitri allowed, though his attention was now as much on formulating a plan as it was on explaining what he was thinking.

"What else would we do?" Michael didn't want to be left out of the loop at this point. They were now so close to finally figuring out what was going to happen that he was impatient for his friend to share his thoughts with them.

"I think it might be a good idea if we take one of them with us."

"What?" Michael and Sandy chorused.

"Vasili will have come up with a new plan now that he has lost Bogdan and gained a few new men. We might be able to get some valuable information from him."

"But won't that just prove to Vasili that we were here?" Michael objected.

"It will," Dmitri acknowledged, "But that will work in our favour too. Think about it, Mikhail, if we prove that we were still here, he will have to keep watching the resort, and with one less man to do it. If he figures out that we have left, then it's even better for us because he will still have to watch the resort, but will have to cover the rest of the island as well."

"But you said he'd just call in more and more men if we got rid of the ones he has."

"True, but that will take time. Time for us to come up with a plan after we learn what he's up to."

"What if the guy just clams up and refuses to talk?" Sandy wanted to know. "Don't you guys have some kind of code of silence or something?"

Dmitri's face took on a darker look. It wasn't anger, it was more like determination, Michael thought. Though even that word failed to fully describe the look on Dmitri's face as he answered with three simple words. "He will talk."

* * *

It was now early afternoon and their plan was in place and ready to be executed. Both Michael and Sandy had an ominous, heavy weight in the pits of their stomachs which seemed to be growing by the minute. After all the talk and planning it was finally time for action, but now the thought of actually putting it into motion didn't make them feel as eager and excited as they'd expected it would.

"Couldn't we just wait until it's dark and slip away unnoticed?" Sandy thought that sounded like a very reasonable plan. Besides, it would buy them a few more hours of relative safety before they did anything stupid, like trying to kidnap a member of the Ukrainian Mafia, for example.

Michael was just as nervous, but then with Dmitri's help he'd already been hijacked, kidnapped, wrecked a stolen car, and crossed a border illegally. Now he could add stealing an airplane and aiding and abetting in the commission of a kidnapping. Would he be adding accessory to murder before the day was through? Or would the Mafia finally succeed in finishing him off? How on earth had it ever got to this point?

He took a deep breath and resigned himself to the fact that the chain of events which had begun with being assigned to an aisle seat on last summer's flight to Athens had now come to the point of 'me or them'. However it had come about; he was here now and this had to be done if he was ever to get his life back again. It was time to act.

Why couldn't he have been assigned the window seat he'd wanted?

* * *

Juan was in the room with them, as was one of the maids. She was wearing a colorful wrap over a swimsuit in place of her usual uniform. Dmitri was once again going over their part in the plan while they nodded in understanding. Michael and Sandy listened along with them, and watched their faces, hoping that they understood just how vital a role they were playing, and how important it was to do exactly what Dmitri was saying. What might happen if they failed was something they didn't want to consider; but they considered it anyway.

At last everyone seemed sure of what they were to supposed to do, and Dmitri was satisfied that they fully understood the plan, or at least their part in it. The maid, neither Michael nor Sandy had caught her name, was to leave via the beach door, followed shortly thereafter by Juan. Since there was a possibility that he might be recognized by the men watching them they didn't want it to appear that the two of them were together. She was to walk up and down the beach without wearing the wrap, as if she was looking for something, making a bit of a scene by approaching and talking to a few of the guests on the beach. Once she had attracted enough attention, Juan would step out onto the beach to keep an eye on her.

After a few minutes of an apparently fruitless search, and looking very agitated, she would approach the observer on the right-hand side of the beach and tell him that she had lost her purse. Hopefully he would be willing to help a damsel in distress to look for it. She would suddenly remember that she'd had it with her while strolling on the next beach over; could he please help her search over there, and along the pathway? All her cash and her credit cards were in it and she didn't know what to do.

Meanwhile, Juan had called ahead to the neighbouring hotel and they were more than willing to let their neighbour have the use of one of their vans. After all, he'd helped them out on several occasions. Once Juan was satisfied that the maid had succeeded, he'd send Dmitri a text that it was safe to move out. That would leave the three of them to deal with the man on the left-hand side of the beach.

Dmitri was intent upon his phone, awaiting the message. Michael and Sandy looked at each other uncertainly and Michael reached over to give her hand a reassuring squeeze just as Juan's text came in. He looked up at the two of them and nodded, "Time to go."

Still clasping Sandy's hand in his, partly to reassure her, partly to reassure himself, but mostly because it just felt right, Michael led her from the room. Dmitri followed close behind them, but lagged behind as they stepped through the door that led to the beach. He let the two of them get well ahead of him before following them out the door, and then tried to stay more or less hidden among the small knots of people moving about the beach while Michael and Sandy headed straight for the path on the left side of the beach.

Since she was the least likely of the three to be recognized, Sandy was the one that deliberately made eye contact with the lookout man. She smiled and gave him a friendly nod. The man glanced about in surprise, mixed with a bit of unease. He was supposed to be watching other people, they weren't supposed to be paying attention to him. They weren't even supposed to notice him. But the pretty girl seemed so friendly that he couldn't help but return the smile, his attention focused on her while Dmitri, who had managed to make his way to the treeline and was now working his way along it, made his approach. Sandy had him fully distracted, which is exactly what they wanted.

Michael deliberately pulled up short of their target and he and Sandy turned to look out to sea as he pointed out something on the horizon. The man followed their gaze and tried to figure out just what it was they were looking at.

"Beautiful view, isn't it?" Sandy asked him.

"Da. Yes, beautiful view," he agreed in his thick accent. He could barely speak English at all. Though he had a pretty good idea of what she was saying, he could do little more than agree and mimic her words.

"Are you staying here at the resort?" Sandy asked, managing to keep her eyes on his, rather than on Dmitri, who had almost caught up with them. Michael figured his sunglasses would hide where his own gaze was directed, but he still forced himself to look at Sandy as she spoke, keeping an eye on Dmitri with his peripheral vision.

"I sorry, I no speak English good," the man offered them a friendly, apologetic smile. He didn't notice Dmitri until it was too late. He was holding the gun in his left hand, and at the distance they were from the other guests, it was all but hidden from view. To the man that had it levelled at his stomach, it was the most clearly visible object on the beach. Michael almost thought the guy was going to faint, and it seemed to take forever for him to raise his gaze from the barrel to Dmitri's face. Surely, he must have known who was holding the gun, but his eyes grew even wider when he recognized his former prey.

He cast a sideways glance at the couple that had been speaking to him, desperate for some help. That was when he recognized that it was Michael Barrett behind the sunglasses and concluded that his last hope of rescue had just evaporated. Sensing recognition in the man's eyes, Michael removed his glasses and couldn't resist a smile. "Zdtrastwitya, dude," he said in his friendliest voice, just to rub it in a bit.

Dmitri motioned with the barrel of the gun and their captive obediently turned in the direction indicated by the wordless instructions. Apparently the language of a loaded gun was universal. A few steps and they were out of sight of most of the crowd on the beach. That's when Dmitri grabbed him roughly and gave him a quick, rough pat down, removing his phone, but not finding anything else to worry about. "What is your name?" he demanded in Ukrainian.

"Fadyay," came the response, which sounded almost as frustrated as it did frightened.

"Walk. That way." Again he let the motion of the gun indicate the direction Dmitri wanted him to go, which was to continue along the path. "Make sure you walk, don't run, not unless you think you can run faster than my bullets. Don't turn around, just walk." Neither Sandy nor Michael could understand the words, but the even, threatening tone Dmitri used left no doubt as to the nature of the threats he was issuing.

As Fadyay obediently turned and began walking, Dmitri reached behind his back, tugged the loose tropical shirt he wore aside, and stowed the handgun back in the waistband of his khaki trousers.

They let Fadyay lead the way, Dmitri a few steps behind him, and Michael and Sandy bringing up the rear. Michael cast a nervous glance behind them to make sure that no one else was following them, but they seemed to be alone. As he turned back, he caught a look from Sandy that seemed to be saying, 'Are we really doing this?' Michael made a grimace as if to reply, 'I can't believe it either.'

They emerged from the path and found themselves back on an open stretch of beach. Dmitri grunted a few more words in Ukrainian at Fadyay, who nodded without turning around and bore to his left, heading towards the parking lot.

A few more terse phrases guided their captive towards a white van parked near the main entrance to the hotel. The parking lot was deserted, and Dmitri took advantage of that fact to manhandle Fadyay roughly into the back seat so that he was laying face down on the floor behind the driver's seat.

"Mikhail, you will drive," Dmitri said, his Ukrainian accent thicker now. Maybe speaking in his native tongue had brought it back, or maybe he was going back in time himself. Back to a time when he'd done things like this on a more or less regular basis.

Sandy hopped up into the front passenger seat while Michael circled the vehicle and climbed in behind the wheel. He turned back in time to see Dmitri fastening Fadyay's wrists together with a pair of zip ties. "Keys?" he asked, glancing about nervously to see if anyone was paying them any attention.

"Under your seat." Dmitri responded as he pulled the ties extra tight.

"Which way do I go?"

"Back to main road. Turn right. Keep going and I will tell you when to turn."

Michael's heart was still beating wildly as he turned the key and then headed down the drive way. "Keep an eye out for police cars," he muttered to Sandy.

* * *

"What do you mean he's gone?" Vasili roared into the phone.

"I mean he's gone; he's disappeared. I tried to call him and he didn't answer. We can't find him anywhere." There was as long pause before Victor added somewhat hopefully, "Maybe he decided to defect, like Dmitri did." The noise that Vasili made caused him to think better of offering any further ideas.

Andrei and Boris had yet to give him anything useful from St. Thomas and he was thinking that he'd now have to bring them back before he ran out of help completely. It was unlikely that the Canadian was there anyways. He must be with Dmitri who had obviously been at his own hotel very recently. He'd have to find a way to blame this on Anton; after all, he'd selected the men sent along for this job.

"I thought you told me you could see each other from where you were standing." It was an accusation, not a comment, and the tone of his voice should have warned Victor to think carefully about his answer.

"We could see each other most of the time, but a lady asked me to help her look for her purse. I was only gone a few minutes."

"By some strange coincidence it was at that very moment that Fadyay disappeared." There was no response at all, just a dead silence as Victor was forced to put together the pieces of the story that he'd been, so far, forcing himself to ignore.

"Dmitri planned it all, can't you see that, you fool?' Once again the only response was silence, which was the only acknowledgement he needed in order to continue his rant. "The next time you are asked to do something by anyone but me, you will say 'no'. Do you understand?" This time he waited for a response and got a very humiliated-sounding 'yes', which was satisfying more in tone than in content.

Vasili continued to fume silently for a while, knowing full well how much discomfort it was causing Victor. The problem was that he was now out of things to say because he didn't know what to do himself. He'd proven that Dmitri was there, or at least had been. He was likely long gone by now, no doubt down the very path that Fadyay had been assigned to watch. It had cost him yet another member of his team, but perhaps it wasn't a total loss. Dmitri was definitely on the island and most likely the Canadian was as well. He was pretty sure there was no point in leaving two men on St. Thomas with nothing to do but waste time. He'd call them back to Culebra. He'd also have to find yet another place to stay.

"Switch places with one of the other men. They know who you are now so do your best to keep out of sight. And whatever you do, don't let anyone distract you again!"

* * *

Michael had been driving around the island for several hours now. Sometimes he'd been following Dmitri's directions, while at others he'd been driving aimlessly; circling around and retracing his route. Dmitri had managed to find a beach towel in the back of the van and covered Fadyay's head to prevent him from using the sun to keep track of the direction they were going. Since the sun had now set that was no longer a problem. He'd also been keeping an eye out to make ensure that no one was following them. He didn't think they would be, but he wasn't about to take that for granted.

Sandy, meanwhile, had found nothing to occupy her time other than to watch the passing scenery. Neither she nor Michael felt much like making small talk while they could be overheard by their passenger, even if he didn't speak much English, so she was relieved when Dmitri tapped Michael on the shoulder and motioned him to turn into a driveway to their left. The road wound gently back and forth until it ended in front of a small building which was little more than a shack. As he put the van in park and shut off the engine, he couldn't help but wonder if Dmitri had bought up half the real estate on the island to set up safe houses. Then again, maybe he just had some friends he was borrowing them from. Now wasn't the time to ask though.

None of them spoke as Dmitri pulled open the side door of the van and yanked Fadyay, his head still covered by the towel, from the vehicle. Taking a firm grip on the man's shirt, he shoved him in the direction of the front door. Maintaining his hold, he guided his captive towards the front door, not bothering to mention that he needed to step up onto the porch. Fadyay stumbled over the step, but Dmitri's grip yanked him roughly back upright before he could fall.

Sandy and Michael waited for Dmitri to open the door and push their captive inside, flicking on a light switch as he stepped into the house. Michael motioned Sandy inside first and by the time he'd closed the door Dmitri had Fadyay sitting in an arm chair, his hands still fastened painfully behind his back, his head still covered by the towel. Motioning them to follow, the three of them made their way to the kitchen where the fridge held an assortment of drinks. "Anything to eat?" he asked.

"There is food in the cupboards, help yourself." He'd pre-stocked the shelves with an assortment of food that didn't need much in the way of preparation, and the three of them had what might best be described as a good snack rather than a proper supper.

"Anything for our friend?" Sandy asked, gesturing towards the living room.

"I think we should talk with him first," Dmitri responded. The three of them made their way back to the living room where Michael and Sandy took seats on the couch, while Dmitri stood over Fadyay.

"You are here with Vasili. How many of you are there?"

"Six of us came in to join Vasili and Bogdan," he answered hesitantly, as if gathering his thoughts. "Eight."

"Seven," Dmitri corrected him. "I already got rid of Bogdan." Dmitri almost wished he could have seen the expression on the man's face at that bit of information. All he could see was a startled jerk beneath the towel.

"Where are they now?"

There was a long silence as if he were weighing the danger of incurring Vasili's wrath against the possibility that he might not leave this building alive. To speed his answer, and remind him who was in charge now, Dmitri gave him a slap through the towel. It likely didn't hurt all that much, but it did help Fadyay to make up his mind. "Two ... two are on St. Thomas, four of us are watching your place."

Vasili is no doubt enjoying the hospitality of a resort somewhere, Dmitri concluded. "Why are the other two on St. Thomas?"

"They are supposed to be looking for the Canadian."

"Then they are wasting their time. Too bad for you that you weren't one of those sent there. But why are they looking for him? It's me you want"

"I don't know."

His response was a bit too defiant to suit Dmitri, who gripped his shoulder with all the force his large, muscular hands could exert, and gave him several hard shakes. "Would you like to join Bogdan." He let the words hang for a moment, then shouted, "Why are they looking for the Canadian?"

"Because you came to rescue him last summer. Vasili said if we could not find you, and we had the Canadian, that you could come for him, and that he'd be ready for you when you did."

The information didn't surprise Dmitri, but it did make him angrier than ever. He practically picked the man up and carried him down the hallway, shoving him into an empty room, a rough kick speeding his way through the doorway. They heard him stumble to the floor before Dmitri slammed the door shut.

When he was back in the living room, he claimed the chair Fadyay had recently occupied.

"Don't we need to keep an eye on him?" Michael asked.

"He's not going anywhere with his hands tied behind his back," Dmitri dismissed his concern and spent a few minutes translating the gist of the conversation. "I told you that you should have stayed where I sent you! They are looking on the wrong island and would never have found you."

"We covered that already," Michael countered. "We're here now and we'll deal with it, let's not waste time covering possibilities, we need to deal with what's happening now."

Dmitri opened his mouth and closed it. He still wished that his friend had stayed put, but he was right, they needed to decide how to proceed from here.

Chapter Fourteen

Anton gazed at his computer screen with a very satisfied smile. He'd known pretty much what his bank balance had been before he'd logged in, but he enjoyed seeing the numbers; so much so that he often looked at them several times a day. Youlya's contribution had given them a rather large boost.

His personal bank accounts, already very healthy while Yuri had still been in charge, had been growing at a very impressive rate over the past year. Not that he was able to keep everything that passed through his hands; a sizable portion of it had to be passed on up the line, but he had every intention of making it higher up the chain of command himself very soon. As nice as it was to see all those regular deposits, what he'd recently retrieved from Youlya had made those regular amounts seem rather pale in comparison. It made him hungry for even more.

Not even a small fraction of that amount would be passed along. Yuri's estate had more than settled the debt caused by Dmitri's disappearance. Since Yuri himself wasn't around to lay claim to it, it would stay right there in his account. There was no reason to share any of it with Vasili either, since it had come into his possession with no assistance or effort from him whatsoever. No, this was his. All his. But what should he use it for? As long as he was alive there should be a steady flow of funds into that account, so there was no need to worry about a retirement plan. Still, it was nice to see so much there and, unlike others he knew, he didn't want to waste it on unneeded luxuries. He had no need for a new car, but a dacha would be nice. A nice vacation house somewhere warm and pleasant, like The Crimea. Yes, that would be very nice, wouldn't it?

He took one last, fond look at the balance and did a mental calculation of how much interest it might earn each month as he logged off. He really did need to think about how best to launder it so that he could put it to good use, but for now it was safely in an unnumbered, offshore account that wasn't likely to cause him any problems. It was nice of Dmitri and Youlya to have deposited it there in the first place and save him that hassle. A few taps of a computer keyboard and what had been theirs was now his. Safe and secure in the Caribbean, ironically enough.

Speaking of the Caribbean, what was he to do with Vasili? The man was too short-sighted, too sure of himself; no wonder he'd had no success in bringing Dmitri back in. Yuri had entrusted him with bringing in Dmitri right from the beginning and for that reason alone he'd left him in charge, but he'd proven repeatedly that he was not up to that task. What else could he do with the man? For that matter, did he have any abilities at all that justified keeping him around? True, he'd had some success in the past, but he'd long since been promoted beyond his ability to produce anything worthwhile.

He pushed his chair back from the desk and stared out the window. From here he could see his backyard. The trees through which Dmitri had approached the house a year ago, and the road down which they'd made their escape with Michael Barrett. It was hard to believe that a year had passed already. Thankfully Yuri had been in charge back then, and he was the one officially held responsible for the fiasco. The only reason they had brought him here was because his house was conveniently located and he had the ability to question the Canadian in English. Even those two guards had been picked by Yuri. None of the blame could be laid at his feet, which is why he was in the position he now occupied.

So, what should he do with Vasili? The man's biggest flaw, now that he thought about it, was that he had no real ambition. Vasili actually believed if he could rise as high as Yuri had risen that he would have it made. He could see nothing beyond that, nowhere to go from there. Simply sit there, pass out orders to others, and reap the rewards. The fool thought he was all but there already and as a result had stopped trying. He wanted the position, make that *the benefits of the position*, but wasn't willing to work at achieving it. It was as if he expected to be handed Yuri's rank as a gift and then be set up for life. Not at all like himself. He knew there was more beyond what he had, and he was willing to work and pay the price to earn it.

When it came right down to it there really was no room in the organization for someone like Vasili, he concluded. No one quit this job, but you could be fired. Of course, it wasn't as simple as that, not for someone who had managed to rise as high as Vasili had. He'd have to clear it first with someone that had more clout than he did. Yet another reason to rise higher than this, he told himself as he spun the chair back to face his desk. Yes, he would have to make that call and have it all arranged. But should he allow Vasili to keep working this job for now, or find someone more capable to take over immediately?

Somewhere deep inside himself, in a place he hardly acknowledged existed, he felt a twinge of conscience at what he was plotting against a man who had risen through the ranks alongside him, but his only response was to mentally shrug it off. His only real conscious thought was that it had to be done for the good of the organization. And the good of his bank accounts.

He had just picked up his phone to make a call when it rang in his hand. It was Vasili. "Allo?"

"Anton, Dmitri is still at his hotel. At least he was an hour ago, so we can be certain he's still here. I'm thinking that I should call the other two back from St. Thomas so that we can focus our search here."

"How do you know he's still there?" Anton cut him off.

"One of my men saw him," Vasili hedged, quickly brushing the question aside. "You know how dangerous Dmitri can be, so I think it's best I get the team back together. I don't want to take any chances that he'll get away from us again."

"No, we wouldn't want that to happen, would we?" Anton replied, not bothering to hide the icy sarcasm in his voice. There was silence on the other end, Vasili was either waiting for approval, or didn't know how to respond. "It is your operation to run. Do whatever you think is best," he finally replied. *Why not give him the leeway to screw things up on his own?* It would make his part of the job that much easier

"Ok, I'll have them return immediately." Vasili acknowledged, and Anton had to assume that the enthusiasm in his voice was genuine.

"Let me know when you have something to report," Anton answered dismissively before ending the call. He had another much more important call to make.

* * *

Vasili pocketed his phone. The call had gone much better than he thought it might; at least he hadn't had to admit to Anton that he was now short two men thanks to Dmitri. Still, he had a vague feeling of unease. There was something about that call, something he couldn't quite put his finger on, that felt wrong. There had been nothing in Anton's tone of voice that he'd not heard before, nor was it the words he had spoken. It was just an impression. Well, he assured himself, once he had Dmitri, and of course the money, none of that would matter. Dmitri had been making a fool of him for the last year. No, that wasn't quite right, he'd been made to look like a fool because of the real fools: the men assigned to help him. If it weren't for them, and men like those two guards who'd let Dmitri break in and out of Anton's house aided by a woman armed with a wrench, he'd have had Dmitri last year, long before he'd been able to get out of the country. He'd succeeded in catching the Canadian and that should have led to Dmitri's capture. If anything, that was the fault of Yuri himself. This time would be different and he'd get the credit he deserved.

Anton had been promoted only because Yuri had screwed up and Anton had been the only one not officially involved when everything had gone so wrong. This time he'd show them all that he deserved far more recognition than some second-rate bootlicker who'd never accomplished anything more than making himself look good. He never made a mistake because he never did anything. Last summer he'd known that Yuri needed to go; now he could see that Anton needed to go as well. Then there would be no one left in his way.

That is when his phone rang. One of the team checking in, he figured. Hopefully it would be good news for once. His heart almost stopped when he saw who it was. Fadyay! He must have followed Dmitri or Michael somewhere and hadn't been able to call until now.

He practically stabbed the button to accept the call. "Allo!"

"Hello, Vasili. I heard you were here, but I haven't had a chance to greet you in person yet." It took him a moment to recognize the voice. Dmitri!

"Hello, Dmitri, you've caused us a lot of trouble. It's time to end all this. Let's meet and talk about how we can resolve this. I'm sure we can work out something reasonable."

"Should I bring the money too? You want that just as much as you want me."

"Make arrangements to return the rest of the money to us, and perhaps I can arrange to let you go free. That's the best deal I can offer you, and you know it. This will not end until we get it back. We already have what Youlya took." Whatever reaction he had hoped to elicit with the news of Youlya's capture, he was disappointed. Dmitri's tone betrayed nothing.

"You cannot even make me that offer, Vasili. We both know that, and there are other ways we can end this. This was Yuri's fight, not yours, and he is no longer around to carry through with it. Stop this foolishness while you can. You have already lost two men."

"I can replace them!" Vasili snapped, he hadn't meant to sound that angry; he needed to sound calm, in control.

"Yes, you can, can't you? You can go on replacing them as long as you need to. But, my friend, ask yourself one thing. Can you replace yourself?"

* * *

"Well?" Michael looked at Dmitri, who had said nothing since ending his call to Vasili. "Did it work?"

Dmitri had wanted to make the call to goad Vasili, hoping to force him into doing something stupid.

"They have Youlya," Dmitri responded flatly.

"Oh," Michael answered slowly as he thought about what that could mean. "I'm sorry. I know you two sort of ended badly, but I liked her. She did help save my life after all."

Dmitri nodded, acknowledging his words without expressing any emotion whatsoever. "She made her decision," he finally said after a long pause, and Michael figured it was best not to pursue the matter any further.

"What about our guest?" Sandy finally asked, as much to break the silence as anything. She didn't know Youlya at all, and though she could sympathize with any woman that fell into the clutches of an angry mob boss, she couldn't understand why she hadn't covered her tracks better once she'd decided to leave Dmitri. But if they had captured Youlya, maybe it was a good thing that Sandy hadn't run for home herself when she'd had the chance.

"What about him?" Dmitri shot back, though she was thankful to see Michael nod in agreement with her question.

"What are we going to do with him? If you think I'm gonna stay here and babysit him while you two go traipsing around the Caribbean you've, got another thing coming." She pondered the possible answers to her own question, and then added weakly, "You're not going to, well, you know, you're not going to – rub him out, are you?" She didn't think he'd make her help, or even watch, but she didn't like the idea of adding murder to kidnapping. Her rap sheet was getting longer by the day.

"He tried to break into my hotel and rob me," Dmitri responded, as if it were an actual fact. "The police will arrest him, question him, and when they find he has no papers and cannot tell them where he was staying, they just might keep him for a very long time. He won't be a problem."

"Why won't he be able to tell them where he was staying?"

"Because," Michael was able to answer that one, "If he does tell them, Vasili will rub him out for us." That earned him a 'very good' nod from Dmitri.

"You're going to call the cops on him?" she persisted. "How do you explain that he broke into your hotel but you're holding him in a shack miles away from where it happened?" She was puzzled rather than angry.

"Juan will look after it. We will meet him somewhere and he will turn him over to the police for us. I'll call them later and give them a statement. He'll be their problem and we can concentrate on Vasili and the rest of them.

"Gee, if only they'd all tried to break into your hotel at the same time," Michael commented ruefully. "So, we dump our friend on the local cops, then what do we do?"

"This has been going on for over a year," Dmitri said, thinking aloud. "My phone call didn't help him any, he's angry and frustrated and doesn't know what to do."

"Tell him to join the club!" Michael grunted.

"What club?" Dmitri was genuinely puzzled.

"It means I feel the same way," Michael explained as Sandy stifled a laugh.

"Oh," he responded, still sounding a bit confused. "He's angry and frustrated," he repeated thoughtfully, "I think maybe we can use that to our advantage."

* * *

There was a long silence on the other end of the phone as Arkady Vladovich considered what Anton had just discussed with him. It's not that such action had never been necessary in the past, nor that it wouldn't be again in the future. It was just that one did not rush such a big decision.

"I will need some time to think about this, Anton. Vasili has been with us a long time."

"Of course," Anton replied respectively. "I only suggest it for the good of our organization. Vasili is a bad example to those under him. He is rash, careless, and isn't producing any real results. For someone who has been with us for so long, he is not showing the maturity and leadership he should be. He has made a mess of this whole situation with Dmitri, and is so obsessed with finding him that he is ignoring everything else. I honestly feel that he has outlived his usefulness to us. He still seems to think he's entitled to much while producing nothing."

"You may be right. If you were to proceed how would you handle it?"

"I hadn't thought that far ahead," the lie slipped easily from his lips. "Although, with him being out of the country right now it would be a good opportunity for him to have an 'accident'. We could even blame it on Dmitri."

"Aren't the men with him right now too loyal to him to carry out an order like that?"

"Perhaps," he allowed, pausing as if he hadn't already considered that detail either. "It might be best for me to do it myself. I could go over there under the guise of checking up on him."

There was another long silence, and finally, "I will think about it, Anton."

He'd expected no more of an answer than that from this phone call. All he'd wanted to do was to plant the seed and get Arkady thinking. It was not an outright 'no' and in a case like this, that was a good sign. For now, he'd content himself with planning it out, and that would start with figuring out how on earth to get himself to Culebra. He'd bring along at least one man as a body guard; he didn't dare travel alone anymore. The biggest question he had was whether or not to tell Vasili that he was coming ahead of time. Would he be on his guard if he knew he was going to have company, or would he be even more suspicious if he were to show up unannounced?

* * *

"So how do we use Vasili's temper to our advantage?" Dmitri had been silent for quite some time now and Michael was growing impatient.

"We force him to do something before he can think about it. We get him somewhere that we can ambush him."

"Are you going to have Juan try to track him down again? Maybe we shouldn't have taken that guy," Michael jerked his thumb in the direction of the bedroom. "We gave ourselves away and now he's probably moved, like you said. We'll have to start looking for him all over again."

Dmitri shook his head. "No, he is scared now. He's good enough at what he does, but he does not like it when things don't go the way he planned, and we've upset him very much. What we did will work in our favour. As for finding him, Juan has already contacted many of his contacts to let them know who he is looking for. If he shows up at a hotel he's already called, they will call him back to let him know."

"When you find him, what will you do?" Sandy had been gazing vacantly out the window but had been listening intently to the conversation. She wanted to ask Dmitri again if he was really planning to kill Bogdan, but had come to realize that even Dmitri didn't know the answer that question. Yet.

"That is up to him," Dmitri replied gruffly, understanding the question behind the question. Then his tone softened as he turned to face her. "I don't want to kill him, I really don't," he said, his tone pleading with her to believe him. "I left Ukraine to start a new life, one without this kind of violence. But these men won't let me do that. I will do no more than I have to," a steely hardness filled his eyes as he paused, "But I will do anything that I need to do."

"Even if I had not taken the money, if I had left Ukraine without a single kopeck, they would still be looking for me because I know too much. I could put many men in prison." He was trying to justify the position they were now in. "I had to leave. You understand that, don't you?"

"Maybe you should have put them in prison," Sandy suggested softly. There was no accusation in her words or tone, nothing more than the suggestion that it might have been the right thing to do.

Dmitri was about to object, but then thought better of it. He'd never even considered that possibility, and perhaps she was right. But then again, he could never have put enough of them in jail to keep himself safe. Then another thought occurred to him. "Even if I had done that, there are hundreds, no thousands, of men willing to take their place. It would not have made a difference." He decided to continue his explanation before he got side tracked again. "I do not want to kill anyone. Ever. But I am not going to let them kill me. Or Mikhail. Or you." His voice was becoming more emphatic with each word. "If there is a way to get rid of them without killing them, I will do it, but there is nowhere you or I can hide where they will not look for us. There is probably no other way to end this."

Michael shot Sandy a pained look, as if to say, 'I don't like this any more than you do, but he just might be right.'

"We are all in this together, now that you two have decided to return." He couldn't resist reminding them that they could have sat this out in relative safety.

"If that's what it takes, that's what it takes," Sandy replied softly. "Like Michael already said, with things as bad as they are, we'd rather know what's going on that sit somewhere and wonder."

Dmitri couldn't do anything more than look at her. He'd been expecting more of a fight. They were both finally beginning to understand what was at stake, he decided; maybe she'd just been thinking out loud. "I'll call Juan and arrange to have Fadyay arrested." A small smile came to his lips at that thought, "Once we know where Vasili is staying, we should maybe pay him a visit." He rose from his chair, "But for now I'm going to have a nap. Fadyay shouldn't be any trouble, but one of you should watch him until I wake up, just in case."

"Yeah, no problem, I can do that," Michael volunteered. "If you want to take a nap, Sandy, go ahead, I think I can handle one Mafia thug on my own."

"I'm sure you can. Keeping a hired thug in check is child's play compared to stealing airplanes and pulling off a kidnapping in broad daylight."

"You mean especially when someone else has already cuffed him?" They shared a laugh that helped relieve the stress they'd both been feeling ever since the minutes leading up to the text from Juan which had set the plan in motion.

"A nap sounds good. It's been a long day. Are you sure you don't need one yourself?"

"I'll be okay," Michael assured her, although it would be nice to close his eyes for a while. "I'll get some rest when Dmitri gets up."

"Okay." Though she sounded as tired as she looked, she made no move to get up, seemingly intent on something outside the window.

"Something out there?" Michael turned to take a look himself, fearful for a moment that Vasili might have somehow tracked them here.

"No," she replied with an embarrassed laugh. "I was just thinking."

"About what?"

"About what's going to happen when this is all over. Kind of a life-changing holiday we're having here."

"Yeah, I've thought about that a few times too. I just kind of assumed I'd go back to work. That's what I did last year, and in some ways last year was way worse than this is. Thing is, I'm not sure I'll have a job when I get home."

"What, you didn't schedule this holiday?"

"No, I figured I needed more excitement than I get at work so I flew down here to see if I could mix it up with the Mafia again. Work can get pretty boring, you know."

"Wow, I guess I just assumed that you and Dmitri had planned all this out ahead of time. Maybe because that's what you told me when we met on the plane." She shot him an angry glare that had him worried for a moment, but then he saw the teasing glint in her eyes. "Don't worry, Michael, I don't blame you for not giving me the whole story up front. I wouldn't have told me either. How does it feel to be a millionaire though? It would be nice to be able to go home to that much money."

Michael grimaced as she mentioned the money. "I don't know, I guess I'm not really sure I am a millionaire. That's Dmitri's money. Mob money. I'm worried that if I try to keep it I might get arrested or something."

"Good point. What will you do with it, do you think?"

"Don't know," he responded with a heavy sigh. "At least you get to go back to an exciting job, travelling all over the world. New cities and countries every day. I wish I could fly for a living."

"It's not a bad job, but it's not as exciting as you might think. After a while all the airports start looking the same, and living out of a suitcase isn't really all that glamorous."

"No, I guess not, but I'd enjoy the flying. I've always thought that it was, well, magic." He felt himself blush at this admission and hurried to explain. "I mean, here you are sitting in this big, heavy metal contraption, and yet it can defy gravity, you know? Every time I take off, I watch the wheels leave the runway, watch the ground sink away until everything is so tiny and distant, and there I am, floating with the clouds. It's like riding a magic carpet."

She smiled back at him, as much at the look in his eyes as at his words. "I guess I never thought about how romantic it is to be able to fly."

"It's like that old poem, about 'slipping the surly bonds of earth.'" He was beyond feeling embarrassed about his feelings now, seeing as how she seemed to understand.

"Then why don't you fly for a living? Quit your job and go be a pilot?"

"Or retire and buy a plane with my million dollars?" he chuckled. It sounded like a wonderful idea when she said it, but he knew deep down that it wasn't practical.

"Why not?"

"I guess it depends how you get the money. I mean, I appreciate what Dmitri did and all, but – well, I don't think it's a good idea to try and keep it." The tone of his voice made it evident that he wished he could though.

"It'll all work out somehow," she reached over to cover his hand with hers and gave it a squeeze. He felt himself blushing again and turned his hand over to hold hers. She smiled back.

Michael's smile widened. "Maybe I should just quit my job, if I still have one, and move down here. I could handle this weather year round I think. Maybe Dmitri can give me a job."

"Anything else besides your job keeping you up there?"

"Not really, besides family. You know, my Mom and Dad. Nothing else. What about you? He tried to make the question sound as casual as she had, but he felt that his tone sounded a bit too hopeful.

Sandy just smiled and shook her head, so he gave her hand another squeeze.

Chapter Fifteen

Anton adjusted his sunglasses as he waited for his driver to circle around to his side of the car and open the door for him. The engine had been left running, and the air conditioning left on full, to spare him the full brunt of the late afternoon heat until the last possible second, but as his door was opened, he could no longer avoid it and he stepped out into its fierceness. The weather forecast had promised an afternoon high approaching forty degrees Celsius and it certainly felt like that estimate had been on the low side. He wondered briefly if it could possibly be any hotter than this in the Caribbean before giving a nod to his driver, who followed a step behind him as he made his way across the driveway and into the factory. They looked completely out of place, their neatly pressed suits contrasting sharply with the dingy reception area.

"Can I help you?" asked a receptionist who looked as drab as her surroundings, and was openly surprised at the appearance of two such important-looking men. Was she supposed to have known that they were coming today?

"I am here to see Sasha," Anton replied brusquely.

"Do you have an appointment?" She appeared to be in a mild state of panic. These two men were here to see the boss and she didn't know anything about it, or even who they were. Who would be more upset with her, her boss, or these men?

"No, but he will see us. Immediately." Anton kept his voice icily calm, yet still managed to convey an additional two words without actually using them: 'or else'.

"Yes, sir, I'll have to page him, I believe he's out on the factory floor."

CHAPTER FIFTEEN

"I'll wait in his office," Anton replied, and walked past her desk and into the manager's office without further discussion. He didn't ask for directions or permission, and she didn't dare challenge him.

When Sasha stepped into his office a few minutes later, after a short discussion with a rather flustered secretary who had no idea who was waiting in there for him, it was to see a man in a well-tailored suit sitting in his chair behind his desk. Before he could identify the intruder, he was startled as the door closed behind him and he turned to see a large, unpleasant looking man, also in a suit, standing beside the door as if to guard it.

"Sit down, Sasha," Anton gestured hospitably towards a chair, the chair usually reserved for Sasha's own visitors and employees. That's when he finally recognized the man claiming his office.

"Anton, I know why you're here and –"

"Then you also know that this visit should not have been necessary." Anton dropped his friendly tone, cutting off the rest of Sasha's sentence. The force of his voice shoved Sasha abruptly into the well-worn chair.

"I wanted to send you the payment, but with the economy the way it is I do not have the cash I need to pay my bills. I barely had enough to pay the workers last month, and my suppliers..."

"Sasha!" The way his name sounded coming from this man's lips was almost enough to stop his heart. He barely glanced at the man by the door who took a step towards him, only to have his advance halted by Anton's raised hand. Then the voice become calm, almost friendly again. "I thought you understood how this worked. My payments are the most important expense you have. If they are not made, there will be no factory, no workers, no business. Surely you understand this?"

He waited for a frightened, mumbled confirmation that his

point was properly understood. "Good, then you will have the payment to me within two days." A surprised sound that could almost have been taken for an objection was stifled, and instead out came a choked, "Of course, I will get it to you by then. Somehow."

Without another word Anton rose from the man's chair and started towards the door. It was opened by his driver who fell into trail behind him, following his boss down the dingy hallway, past the receptionist who offered them an unanswered farewell, and back out into the scorching heat of the afternoon.

As he waited for his door to be opened, he was well aware of the fact that he might soon force this company into bankruptcy, but that was nothing to be concerned about. He'd bleed it dry, and then find another company to pay him protection money. He might even buy the business at a huge discount and use it to launder funds from other sources. Or sell it to other men who, like himself, were always looking for ways to appear legitimate. Of course, he'd then take a cut of their action for himself. The only thing he could not do was ease up his pressure on Sasha. If word got around that he was growing soft, well, it would be very bad for business.

Giving a satisfied sigh as the cold blast of the air conditioning washed over him, easing the discomfort of the suit, he settled into his seat. "Take me back home," he instructed his driver, only to have his relaxation shattered as his phone rang. The call display informed him that it was not Vasili this time, with another report of his so-called progress, but this call might well have far reaching consequences for him.

"Da?"

"Your request is approved."

"Thank you."

With those few words the decision was made. He'd have to call his secretary and have her book two tickets to Culebra.

* * *

The next morning a rather pleased looking Dmitri brought Fadyay down the hallway and into the living room where Michael and Sandy stood watching them. Dmitri had spent some time convincing their captive that confessing to a crime he had not committed was a far better option than being tried for his real intentions: kidnapping and murder. He'd also pointed out that the police chief was a personal friend of his and that there was no way he would take Fadyay's word over that of a friend. To seal the deal, he'd also mentioned that confessing to being a thief was much, much better than suffering the same fate as Bogdan. Though truth be told, he'd been rather vague about what had happened to Bogdan

"I'll drop him off with Juan; he has some groceries for us. If no one follows me I should be back in a couple of hours," he informed them. "Juan said he as some news to pass on, so I think he may have found them." He patted Michael heartily on the shoulder and gave Sandy a reassuring smile. "This will all be over soon, I think, and then you can both go home."

They both smiled back weakly, hoping he was right, but not yet quite ready to believe it was going to work out that well and that easily. If Dmitri noticed their lack of enthusiasm, he didn't let on as he gave Fadyay a push towards the door and barked something at him in Ukrainian. Michael couldn't help but wonder if there wasn't just a trace of relief on Fadyay's face. Maybe he was starting to believe they really were going to turn him over to the police rather than slit his throat and leave him to be eaten by insects and lizards in the jungle.

As they watched the van disappear into the trees, Michael realized that he and Sandy were holding hands. He couldn't remember just when they'd slipped their hands together, but somehow it felt right. She smiled up at him as he turned to face her.

"Sandy?" His voice hesitated, wanting to speak, yet nervous about how to start.

"What?" Her response came almost before he'd finished speaking her name, as if she'd been waiting for him to say something.

"I ... I'm glad we met, I really am. But, well, I wish we'd met when all this wasn't going on."

"I'm glad we met too," her smile seemed brighter than the tropical sun streaming through the window. "If this is what it took for us to meet, then I'm glad it happened. You wouldn't have been on that cruise if it hadn't."

"So, you're okay that I helped kidnap you?" he asked with an awkward grin.

"Well, not quite." She was smiling too.

He turned to fully face her and took both her hands in his. "When this is all over, do you think, somehow, we could, you know, still see each other?"

"I think we could," she said, her smile widening as she slipped into his embrace, and their lips met.

* * *

Dmitri returned a couple of hours later; without Fadyay, they were both relieved to see. He looked from Michael to Sandy, and then back at Michael with a somewhat puzzled look on his face, opened his mouth as if he were going to ask a question, then seemed to change his mind. He gave a knowing chuckle and motioned them to join him at the table where he set down the bags of groceries he'd brought in with him.

"Fadyay will not be a problem anymore," he began.

"That shifts the odds a little more in our favour," Sandy allowed.

"That was a great way to get rid of him, Dmitri. Thanks for not killing him."

"I won't hurt anyone unless I have to," Dmitri reminded her. "The rest of them seem to be busy watching my place, and Juan and a few of the other staff are keeping watch on them. That's the advantage of working there; you can watch everyone on the property, even ask questions, and never worry about being spotted yourself. Even better, Juan was able to learn from his cousin where Vasili is staying."

"Aren't your staff curious about why you have them watching these guys?" Michael wanted to know, worried about what might happen to Dmitri if too many of his staff found out about his old Mafia connections.

Dmitri waived his hand dismissively, "All they need to know is that it's a security matter. For all they know they might be thieves planning to rob the guests. I will know almost right away if anything changes." He waived his cell phone to punctuate the point. "In the meantime, and unless Vasili receives more help, that leaves us free to watch him." The grin on his face widened.

"What if he does call in more men, then what?"

Dmitri gave another dismissive wave, "He is a long way from Ukraine, Mikhail. More will come, but it is not that easy to get them here; it will take time. But, if we are watching him, we will know if he does, right?"

"I guess." The previous summer there seemed to have been an unending stream of goons and thugs at Vasili's disposal, and if anything, he was more determined than ever to catch them. He now had a good chunk of their money himself and they were sure to want that back. Last summer he could honestly claim innocence when he'd been caught and captured. This year he'd have to lie if he was caught.

"This could be the opportunity we've been waiting for," Dmitri added with a grin.

In the silence that followed Michael pondered just how they could turn this into an opportunity and began thinking out loud. "So Vasili is all alone right now –"

"Yes, at least most of the time," Dmitri answered slowly, realizing that Michael was not making an idle comment.

"And he wants all three of us, right, or at least two of us? I'm not sure if he knows about you or not," he nodded to Sandy. "Would he still keep your place under surveillance if he only needed you, Dmitri?"

"Yes, I'm sure he would," Dmitri responded, still not sure where Michael was going with this line of thought.

"Then he'd keep his guys at your place, or at least some of them, if he had me." It was a statement, not a question.

"What?" Sandy and Dmitri asked in unison, both of them shocked at the sudden, unexpected turn of Michael's thoughts.

"Fadyay said Vasili wanted me. He figures that if he catches me then he can use me to get to you." Michael held up his hand, cutting off their objections. "Let me finish. If we can get me inside his place, maybe with a cell phone or something so you can find me, then he'll be worried about getting information out of me, and he might drop his guard a bit. That would give you a chance to get in there and do whatever you need to do."

Sandy sat in shocked silence at the idea of Michael walking willingly into the lion's den, while Dmitri began to object verbally. "Mikhail, do you have any idea what they will do to you?"

"Yeah, I do," Michael answered calmly. "In fact, they already did it, remember? The only reason Anton didn't kill me last summer was because they thought they could get some information out of me. This time they will know they can, so they won't dare do anything permanent to me until they have you."

"Except maybe beat you to within an inch of your life!" Sandy didn't seem to be the least bit proud of him for volunteering himself in this way. Dmitri nodded in agreement.

"They beat me last summer, and I survived. Besides, the only reason they beat me is that I wouldn't talk. This time I will."

Dmitri gave a slow nod, grasping what Michael was thinking, though he still didn't like it.

"I could give them some false information to make him spread his men even thinner. Maybe even give them the location of that first place you took us. You could leave a few things around to prove we really had been there. Then they'd have to keep an eye on your place, and the safe house too. The further apart we can spread them, the easier it will be for you to get to Vasili."

"Michael! You can't do that!" Sandy looked as if she was ready to either cry, or attack him herself; Michael wasn't sure which.

"Vasili would be very suspicious if you just showed up at his door offering to give me up."

"He might believe me if I tell him the truth about why I'm doing it."

"Why are you doing it? What is the truth?" Dmitri sat back, squinting in concentration as he tried to follow Michael's thoughts.

"The truth is I want my life back. I'm tired of running and hiding from these guys. I'm tired of being followed and feeling like my life might end anytime in the next ten minutes. I don't blame you, Dmitri, it was a fluke we wound up in the same plane. If the situation had been reversed, I likely would have done the same thing you did; but I've had enough." Michael paused for a moment, before continuing. "If you really don't think he'll buy that, I could make sure he saw me somewhere and let him 'catch' me."

Dmitri pursed his lips and nodded in acknowledgement. "It is my fault, Mikhail, and that's why we are going to fix this. Permanently." He looked directly into his friend's eyes. "Here is what we will do. We will go, all of us," he paused and nodded at Sandy, "We will all go and stake out the place Vasili is staying. When we are sure he is there, I will check with Juan and make sure that the others are all accounted for. Then, we will decide what to do." He could see that Michael was considering this compromise. "Maybe your idea will work, but let's have a look first, okay? There is no guarantee I can get you out again if you do decide to go to Vasili."

"What guarantee do we have that anything will work?" Michael let out a deep sigh, partially in frustration and partially in relief. Then he rolled his eyes. Dmitri would never change, always seeming to wait until the stars aligned perfectly before taking any action. As little as he wanted to hand himself over to the Mafia, at least it was a plan. It was a chance for him to finally take some action. He paused, looking from Dmitri to Sandy, and then out the window at the paradise he couldn't enjoy until this was all over. "Okay we'll go have a look first."

* * *

It was late the following morning when Dmitri eased the van to a stop in the parking lot of the resort where, according to Juan, Vasili was staying. There was total silence in the van as he shut it down. The three of them sat looking at each other, each with their own thoughts about what they were about to do. Dmitri and Michael were both eager to get on with it, but Dmitri with an eye to figuring out what to do, while Michael was nervously hoping that before the day was over they might finally end this. Sandy was at least as nervous as Michael was, though she was having serious second thoughts about the whole plan. Make that first thoughts, she'd never been willing to even consider it. Both men had offered to let her stay at the house, but she'd insisted, almost against her own will, on coming along with them out of concern for Michael. If he actually decided to hand himself over to the Mafia, she wanted to be there to talk him out of it.

"Okay, let's do this." Michael finally broke the silence, opened his door, and stepped out into the heat. The others quickly followed him and they huddled together in front of the van. They had already donned loose, baggy tropical wear: hats and caps that hid their eyes and faces, and sunglasses to complete their disguises.

"We will go and check the beach first," Dmitri said, handing each of them a beach towel. He'd brought several along to help complete their charade. "We will stick together for now, Vasili likely won't be looking for us here, but we'll look less suspicious as a group." The other two nodded, more because his pause seemed to request a response than because they were in agreement with him. The butterflies in their stomachs were more pronounced now that they were standing out in the open, outside the relative safety of the van. Maybe butterflies didn't really do their feelings justice, they were more like hummingbirds. Or seagulls.

With a deep breath, and feeling as if he were dragging a heavy weight behind him, Michael took Sandy's hand in his and they followed Dmitri around the hotel to the beach. There was a patio with a cluster of small tables sheltered from the sun by large umbrellas. They used them as partial cover, Michael's eyes scanning the beach for a familiar face while Dmitri spoke. "He may be in his room, or he might even be at my place. But knowing him, he will want to be 'managing' the operation rather than doing any work himself, so he just might be on the beach. Look for a man all by himself, Sandy. Michael, you know what he looks like so I'm sure you'll recognize him if you see him." Michael nodded, certain that he would recognize Vasili anywhere. How could you forget the face of a man who'd once captured you and may very well have killed you given the chance? He'd never thought he'd get out of that basement alive.

"What do we do if we do find him?" Sandy was really beginning to hope that they wouldn't, and knew there was no answer to her question.

"We watch him." Dmitri replied sharply, with stern gaze at Michael. "Don't talk to him, don't let him see you. Don't even react if you see him. For now, we watch and wait."

"Wait for what?" Michaels asked. "Hey, maybe he'll wander off into the woods so we can take him out while no one's looking!"

"Maybe." Dmitri's voice had a cold edge to it, colder than either of them had yet heard in him. Yes, that had been a possibility, they knew. They'd been aware of that ever since Dmitri had first flashed his gun. But now they were possibly standing only a few metres from their target and the possibility that they might witness or even be party to a murder was chillingly real. The tropical sun felt suddenly dim and weak. Michael felt Sandy give his hand a very tight squeeze.

Draping their towels over their shoulders, they began wandering among the tourists scattered along the beach as if in search of a good spot. It was rather crowded so it really was necessary to look for a good place to enjoy the day. For appearances sake, Sandy kept up a running but meaningless conversation with Michael as he scanned the beach for Vasili. Dmitri walked beside them, scanning the beach also. They'd only walked a few paces when Sandy gave Michael's arm tug to get his attention. She used her chin to point in the direction of a man lying in the sun. He shook his head, wrong build and hair colour, that wasn't their target. Or was Vasili their hunter? Michael decided he was both.

As crowded as the beach was, it was a slow process to weed all the non-Mafia members out of the crowd. Whenever possible they mixed themselves in with other small knots of people wandering the area. As conspicuous as they felt themselves to be, no one really paid them any attention. Except when they paused and inadvertently blocked the rays of the sun from shining on a sunbather trying to work up a good tan before having to return home to a more northern clime.

Michael spotted one of the resort's waiters picking his way through the crowd with a tray of drinks and stepped aside, drawing Sandy with him to make room for him to pass. "Thank you, sir," the man smiled at him politely.

"You're welcome," Michael responded with a nod. Then he froze. The waiter was making his way towards a man sitting under one of the scores of identical beach umbrellas. It was Vasili. He took a deep breath, trying to calm himself and slow the pounding in his chest.

"What?" Sandy demanded. She'd felt him freeze and though she was almost certain what had caused it, she was praying it would be something else.

Her question drew Dmitri's attention to Michael, his eyebrow arched in an unspoken question to which Michael responded with a nod. "Watch the waiter," he said, his voice barely a whisper though there was no way he could have been heard by Vasili from that distance.

He turned his back to Vasili, partially blocking the big Ukrainian from Vasili's view in case he turned towards them. Vasili's attention, which had been focused on his phone, was now fully directed towards the waiter delivering his drink. The waiter didn't have any problem understanding the accents of the North Americans who made up the bulk of his customers, but this man hadn't been able to speak English at all and he was really hoping that he had the order correct.

Apparently he did. Vasili nodded as he accepted the drink, and after a sip turned his attention back to his phone.

Dmitri guided the three of them to an open spot in the sand behind and to one side of Vasili so they could keep an eye on him without being noticed themselves. The umbrella sheltering him from the sun's rays meant that all they could see of him was the bottom half of his legs, but in turn he wouldn't see them unless he stood up and turned around. They arranged themselves so that even if he did just that, only Sandy would be facing him. Even if he did know she was with them, it was unlikely that he knew what she looked like. Or so they hoped.

"What do we do now?" Michael asked in a hoarse whisper.

"I told you, we watch for now. Then we'll figure out what to do." Dmitri could not help but chuckle at the look on Michael's face. "Unless ..." he cocked his head and stared into the sky, obviously contemplating something very seriously.

"Unless what?" Michael's voice was a mixture of excitement and impatience.

"Unless you have a clear shot at him. I have my gun; do you want it?" Michael wasn't sure how to respond to that, but then joined in with Sandy and Dmitri as they chuckled softly. "Okay, I get it, we do nothing on a beach full of witnesses."

"If he leaves, we'll follow him, okay, Mikhail? If we can get him alone, we will decide what to do then."

"What if he's not alone when he leaves?" Sandy interrupted, but it didn't sound like a casual question and both men had to resist the temptation to turn around and see why she was asking. Both of them had visions of half a dozen Mafia thugs congregating around Vasili and, crowded beach or not, being outnumbered like that sent a chill up both their spines. They glared at Sandy, waiting for her to explain her question. "A guy just walked up to him and he sure doesn't look like a tourist." She paused a moment before continuing. "Okay, they're talking, and they both look pretty intense about whatever they're discussing. I think you can risk a look."

Michael had the better angle and after checking that his sunglasses were in place, and tugging the brim of his hat down as low as he could over his eyes, turned just enough to see Vasili and his visitor. He instantly recognized the new arrival and had to stifle a surprised gasp.

Dmitri saw his shocked reaction, but resisted the urge to look himself. "What is it, Mikhail?" he asked urgently.

Michael turned back to his two companions but focused his gaze on Dmitri as he responded. "It's Anton!"

Dmitri pursed his lips and nodded, and Michael was disappointed that he didn't get a stronger reaction from him. "Are you sure?"

Michael's answer was dripping with sarcasm. "You really don't think I'd recognize the guy that ordered two goons to beat me up, and threatened to have me killed after interrogating me? What is he doing here? I thought he was some kind of big boss, the kind of guy that's above getting his hands dirty out in the field."

"He is," Dmitri responded thoughtfully, wondering himself what Anton was doing here. "Is there anyone else with him?"

"No," Sandy responded.

"Not that I can see," Michael added.

"Well, he didn't likely come all the way from Ukraine alone ..."

Dmitri began.

"They're getting up," Sandy interrupted him before he could continue his thoughts verbally.

"Which way are they headed? Back into the hotel?" Michael adjusted his position to face even further away from the two men.

"No, it looks like they are headed for the far side of the beach." They waited, watching the expression on her face as her eyes followed them. She craned her neck to see around Michael, "Okay, it looks like they took a path into the trees, I can't see them anymore."

"Let's follow them!" Dmitri rose as casually as he could to his feet and motioned for the other two to follow him.

As eager as Michael had been for action, having the odds somewhat evened out to three to two instead of three to one caused his desire to flag somewhat. "You can stay here, if you want," he offered to Sandy, somewhat upset with himself for debating what he wanted her to do: remain safely on the beach or come along with him.

She weighed that option for a moment, "I'm coming to. No way I want to be left alone if more of these guys show up."

Chapter Sixteen

"Vasili!"

Vasili started at the sound of his name being called out in such a familiar way. For a single heartbeat he actually thought that Dmitri had turned the tables on him and found him while he was defenceless, without a team of bodyguards to protect him. Looking into the shadow that fell across his legs he felt his heart race in anger when he recognized Anton towering over him. Having to look up at him made him feel strangely vulnerable, so he rose to his feet, forcing Anton to look up at him.

Quickly covering his shock, he adopted an annoyed tone in his reply. "What are you doing here?" He was angry at Anton for showing up, obviously because he didn't trust him to do this job alone. There was even more anger directed against himself, for being afraid of this man. Until Anton's promotion, which Vasilis still felt should have been his, he'd never had any cause to fear him. Only that promotion, and the power that came with it, gave Vasili any reason to fear. In a fair fight he had no doubt that he would come out on top. Anton had always been more comfortable behind a desk, playing his political games rather than getting his hands dirty. But then Anton didn't need to fight fair anymore, did he? He could simply dictate what he wanted done and it was carried out. This man could make decisions that could affect his career, his advancement in the organization, even his life, should it come to that. Once he was finally finished with this Dmitri business, he'd have to deal with that somehow.

Anton laughed in a way that sounded friendly. Too friendly. Vasili was immediately on his guard. "I decided that I could not let you enjoy this paradise all by yourself," he gestured around them at the palm trees and the ocean view, "So I thought I would come down and experience it for myself."

Vasili nodded, thankful for the dark sunglasses which, he hoped, would mask his disbelief. "It is very beautiful and, I think, ripe for the picking. We could make a fortune down here and it would give us access to a lot of hard, western currency."

"You could be right," Anton's casual response indicated that he wasn't really listening; he had his own agenda for this conversation. "I wanted a full update on how things are going. You seem to be working very hard." He raised his hand as Vasili started to reply. "But not here, let's take a walk. Someone nearby might be able to understand Ukrainian."

Vasili nodded and warily followed Anton as he made for a pathway through the trees that hemmed the beach. As they walked Anton brought him up to date on some of the happenings back home, making small talk to fill the time until they reached the shelter of the trees.

* * *

The trio halted at the entrance to the pathway into which the two Ukrainians had disappeared. Michael and Sandy hesitated for a moment, unsure whether to continue down the path, but when Dmitri spoke his tone left no room for argument. "I'm going to follow them."

Both Sandy and Michael wanted to object, or at least ask why, but they knew that any questioning of his decision would be fruitless. They both watched helplessly as he stepped into the path. As uncomfortable as the beach had been, at least they'd been in a public place. No one else would be able to see them if they wandered into that tangled jungle of trees and shrubs.

CHAPTER SIXTEEN

Michael shook his head, and then looked helplessly at Sandy, "I'm gonna go with him, he must figure something's up."

"Well I'm not staying here alone! Some of those thugs might show up while you two are playing detective. Besides, someone has to keep you from doing something incredibly stupid." Michael was about to object, but instead took her hand and together they entered the pathway, quickening their step until they caught up with Dmitri.

"What do you think they're up to? And why is Anton here?" Michael's voice was hardly a whisper. He didn't expect to get an answer, in fact all he got from Dmitri was a shrug. He didn't even turn to face him.

Fortunately, the path wound back and forth among bushes and it afforded a great deal of cover for them. Once or twice they caught glimpses of the two men, who were deep enough in conversation that they weren't watching to see if they were being followed. Each time they caught sight of them they'd pause and wait a few seconds until they once more disappeared from view before continuing their slow pursuit.

Finally, the two men stopped in a small clearing, and the three fugitives, now turned spies, knelt down behind some bushes that allowed them glimpses of the two men without being seen themselves.

* * *

Once they were out of sight and earshot of the beach, Anton got straight to the point. "You've had no success yet." It wasn't a question.

"We know where he lives, we're watching it, and we know that the Canadian is here," Vasili began.

Anton waived his hand dismissively. "Youlya told us where he lived. For all you know he could be on the other side of the world by now."

"He is still here," Vasili snapped back.

"You've seen him?"

"No," Vasili answered, trying not to sound defensive.

"Then how do you know he is here?"

"We have ..." Vasili hesitated, he had no wish to admit to his boss that he knew Dmitri was nearby because he had managed to capture and dispose of two members of his team, and they'd spoken on the phone. "We have clear evidence he is still on the island, and it is a very small island."

"I see," Anton replied. "Then I guess you have everything well in hand." He didn't sound concerned, or even sarcastic, as he reached into his back pocket and withdrew a handkerchief that he used to mop the sweat from his forehead. Vasili's eyes narrowed suspiciously. He sounded much too calm, even for Anton.

"I guess I can just go home then, or perhaps find a nice resort somewhere and enjoy a vacation myself." He reached for his back pocket again as if to replace the handkerchief, but once his hand was out of sight, he used the handkerchief to grip the handle of a fishing knife he'd secreted beneath the shirt he'd worn to the beach.

Vasili was already on his guard or he would have missed the sudden movement as Anton's hand shot from behind his back and swung viciously towards him. Instinctively he reached for the man's forearm, thwarting the slash that would have ripped open his belly, at the same time stepping back to distance himself from the blade.

Anton had hoped to use the element of surprise to carry out his mission, but that opportunity was now lost, and he was now dealing with a man much stronger than himself. For a few seconds he was more annoyed than scared, chiding himself for somehow having telegraphed what he was about to do. He should have stabbed him in the back while they'd been walking along the trail, but his pride had demanded that he be able to see the look in Vasili's eyes when he realized he was about to die. His annoyance didn't last long, though, it was quickly replaced by fear as Vasili grabbed the arm holding the knife just below his elbow and began twisting it painfully. Anton took a step back to try and gain some distance between himself and his adversary, but Vasili took two steps into him and swept his leg behind Anton's, knocking him off balance but not quite enough to trip him.

Holding the knife with the handkerchief had been meant to ensure that there were no fingerprints left behind, but now it was working against him; it made the knife too slippery to hold on to, and as Vasili squeezed harder he felt his tenuous grip loosening. He couldn't let Vasili get the knife.

* * *

Sandy gave a barely stifled gasp as she saw the knife flash and the two men began struggling. Dmitri shot her a look which fairly screamed 'keep quiet!' so she grabbed Michael who grabbed her back. They were both certain they were about to witness a murder and Sandy gave him a pleading look as if to say, 'what should we do?' Michael didn't know either, so they both looked at Dmitri, who tore his eyes from the struggle long enough to give them an annoyed shake of his head as he hissed, "Just shut up!"

* * *

Both men knew that the knife was the key to the fight, if either gained control of it the fight was over. Only one of them would walk away from this spot. In desperation Anton pulled his arm as hard as he could against the force of Vasili's grip and, naturally Vasili pulled back. As he did, Anton relaxed his arm, letting Vasili's tug propel his arm forward. He released his grip on the knife and let it fly from his fingers and into the bushes, safely out of Vasili's reach.

Vasili actually smiled when he saw the knife fly from Anton's hand; the knife had been the only thing giving Anton any sort of real chance, now the advantage was his! He released his grip on Anton's arm and smirked at his boss as he took a step back. He'd soon wipe that relieved look from his face.

The two men began circling and feinting, each searching for an advantage until Vasili stepped into Anton, swinging first his left fist, then his right. Anton blocked the first, but barely deflected the second. He wasn't at all prepared when Vasili stepped into him, wrapping him up with both arms and using his weight to knock him onto his back. From there the fight was all but over as Vasili pinned Anton's arms to the ground with his knees and began raining heavy, aimed blows at his head, not stopping till long after Anton was unconscious, his face and Vasili's hands bruised and bloodied.

With all his rage and frustration vented, Vasili finally stopped, his arms hanging limply at his sides, his chest heaving as he fought to get his breath back. He looked contemptuously down at the man he blamed for holding him back from his rightful place, the man who'd been about to kill him with no warning at all while pretending to be his friend. "Coward," he spat on the limp form.

* * *

Sandy shuddered and gave a sigh of relief; she'd expected much worse. Michael gave her hand a soft squeeze, both to comfort her, and to warn her to keep quiet. He was half hoping that Dmitri might confront Vasili right then and there, when he didn't have half a dozen goons standing around to protect him. A glance at Dmitri, however, showed that, so far, he planned to stay hidden as he continued to watch. It was almost as if he expected something more to happen.

Just as Michael's impatience reached a peak, Vasili rose to his feet. For a moment the three observers were afraid that he was about to head back up the path and as silently as possible they edged further back into cover, but Vasili didn't head back towards them.

* * *

Vasili had tried to follow the knife with his eyes as it had flown from Anton's hand, but all he knew for sure was the general direction in which it had gone. He was sure it could not have gone far though. Anton hadn't really thrown it so much as released it, letting momentum launch it out of his hand. He began sweeping his foot back and forth beneath the scrubby brush and was soon rewarded as his foot struck the handle of the knife. He bent down and scooped it up before walking back towards Anton, pausing only because he was considering letting the man regain consciousness before finishing him off. But no, he wasn't worth the wait. Without a second thought he knelt down and drove the knife into Anton's stomach, twisting it as he did so to cause as much damage as possible.

He didn't hear the startled feminine gasp in the bushes behind him, it was drowned out by the gasp from Anton. The intense pain of the knife wound had brought him back to consciousness. His eyes flew open in pain and shock, but Vasili's work was already finished. He rose back to his feet, taking the knife with him, and continued down the path, wanting to put as much distance as he could between himself and the beach he'd just left. The first thing he needed to do was to get rid of the knife; then he needed to wash up.

A short walk brought him to a deserted stretch of beach. First, he wiped the knife off as best he could. Only the blade itself had any blood on it and that was easily rinsed off by wiping it in the damp sand along the shoreline. After making sure there was no blood left, he wiped off the handle using his shirt; he didn't want any prints left on it. A quick look around told him that he was still alone, so he held the handle with the first joints of his fingers, drew back his arm, and threw the knife as far as he could into the surf. There was a small splash, barely noticeable in the waves, and it was gone.

He gave a satisfied sigh and knelt back down, using sand to scrub his hands and forearms as thoroughly as he could to remove the last traces of Anton's blood, but his knuckles were still bleeding. Well, it wouldn't be safe to go back to his hotel before dark looking like this, would it? He'd find a sheltered spot to sit and wait until dark.

* * *

Only when he was satisfied that Vasili was not going to return did Dmitri cautiously rise to his feet and walk over to where Anton lay, his shirt was soaked in blood which trickled down onto the ground to stain the sand. Michael and Sandy had followed closely behind him. Not wanting to get too close to the body, but at the same time feeling that only by staying close to Dmitri were they safe.

"Is he..."

Michael's question was answered by Anton as he turned to face them, his eyes glazed over, and though he obviously saw them, his gaze seemed to be fixed on a far distant place. He finally managed to fix his gaze weakly on Dmitri, his eyes seeming to plead for help as he tried to speak his name, but all he could do was mouth the word 'Dmitri'. Nothing else but a wheezing gasp escaped his lips.

"He will be soon," Dmitri replied, his voice void of any emotion or feeling. Then he looked Anton straight in the eye. "Goodbye," he said in Ukrainian.

The three of them stood watching the prone figure struggling to draw each breath, two of them wishing there was something they could do to help him, or at least ease his pain. Almost before they could ask themselves what to do though, there was one last, loud gasp and then silence. Anton's gaze was fixed straight into a sun that was far too bright to look at with living eyes.

Sandy gave a muted sob and turned to Michael who hugged her tightly and tried to turn her so that she didn't have to look at Anton's body, but just as he did, he heard her cry out, "What are you doing?"

He released her from his arms and spun around to see Dmitri rolling the body over with his foot, "What are you doing?" His voice echoed Sandy's.

"Quiet! Unless you want everyone on the beach to join us here."

The body slumped over, now lying face down, and Dmitri knelt beside it. Michael felt himself shudder, he didn't think he could bring himself to touch a dead body, not so soon after such a messy, violent death, but Dmitri seemed unaffected by such squeamish thoughts. Carefully, using only the backs of his fingers, he brushed the shirt up above Anton's waist. Then, just as carefully, he slid his thumb and index finger into the back pocket of his pants. He took extra care not to touch the wallet with his fingertips, gripping it instead with the fist joint of each finger, slid it out, then cast it to one side of the body, letting it land a few feet down the trail as his companions watched with a growing mixture of indignation and curiosity.

He flipped the wallet open, again with the backs of his fingers, and deftly drew out a wad of bills, both American and Ukrainian, shoving them into his pocket.

"As if you need that money!" Sandy spat out angrily, though managing to keep her voice down.

"I don't. Do you want it?" Dmitri answered calmly as he went after the credit cards, adding them to the bills in his shirt pocket."

"It's okay, Sandy, I see what he's doing," Michael interjected. "He's trying to make this look like a robbery."

"It will keep the police occupied and looking for someone local," Dmitri added.

"Oh," she replied, "That makes sense. I guess."

"Tourists usually don't come here to rob each other," he continued, "But they might come here to kill each other. It's enough dealing with Vasili and his men, we don't need t police mixed up in this too." He looked back at the body and actually smiled, "This might come in useful!" He slid his hand into the other pocket and drew out Anton's mobile phone, then he rose and surveyed the scene carefully, ensuring he hadn't missed anything. Seemingly satisfied, he turned and took a step back up the trail. "Let's go," he ordered.

Dmitri led them on a roundabout route back to the van, managing to avoid the beach and its crowd altogether. Michael and Sandy trudged silently behind him. Even though they understood Dmitri's actions, the were both disturbed by the fact that they weren't reporting the murder to the police, and even more disturbed that they were party to Dmitri disturbing the crime scene and, in fact, forcing the police to follow a false trail in their investigation. It didn't cross either of their minds how traumatic it might be for whoever finally found the body.

None of them were any more talkative after climbing into the van, and the drive back to the house was made in a complete, tense silence. Only after they were back in the house, and the relatively familiar setting made Michael feel somewhat disconnected from what he'd just witnessed, did he turn to address to Dmitri, who seemed to be waiting for him to speak.

"Why..." Michael started to ask.

"Anton started it," Dmitri answered, prepared for what he thought he was about to hear, "Vasili killed him in self-defence. It was between the two of them, I had nothing to do with this." Mikhail, knowing Anton and Vasili that fight was over who was going to run things. That battle has been coming for many years and it would have come to this no matter what I did or didn't do."

"It might sound terrible, but I have no problem with what just happened. Actually, now that I think about it, I wish that they'd killed each other. Then this would all be over and we could go home. What I want to know is why didn't you do something? You had a gun. That might have been your opportunity to end this."

"A gun is not a magic solution to all problems, Mikhail, and do you know for sure that neither of them had a gun? Do you know for a fact that Vasili doesn't have one?"

"Well, no." Michael confessed.

"Think about it. What would have happened if I'd used my gun to kill Vasili back there?"

"The whole resort would have heard the shot. They would have called the cops and we'd have had to explain a double murder."

"Or he might have pulled a gun and shot us," Sandy added.

"It was not the right time to do anything so drastic. Vasili has now done us a favour and evened out the odds a little bit. We now know that when we have dealt with him, there will be no Anton to worry about, right?"

Both Michael and Sandy nodded in agreement.

"I do not like what happened any more than you do, but you need to understand that in the end it is us or them, right? If they are willing to kill each other, they won't hesitate to kill us." He took their silence for agreement. "If they want to do the dirty work, then so much the better for us. I didn't know Anton was here, but now we know he will never be a problem again. Let's concentrate on dealing with Vasili, okay?"

"Okay." Michael agreed with a nod, and there was fresh determination in his voice.

* * *

Vasili had spent the rest of the afternoon biding his time just inside the treeline of the secluded stretch of beach where he'd washed up after his altercation with Anton, awaiting the safety of evening twilight. Now that the sun had begun to set, he slowly worked his way back towards the resort, managing to bypass the clearing in which, he assumed, the body still lay.

By the time he made it back to the resort it was completely dark and there were few guests in sight on the beach side of the building. Most of them would be eating supper or getting ready to go out for the evening. He shoved his hands into his pockets to hide his raw knuckles, and the few people he passed in the hallway paid him no undue attention.

Once inside his room he stripped off his clothes and threw then into the bottom of the bathtub, turned on the water, and took a long, hot shower, making sure to thoroughly scrub and wash himself down and, in the process, thoroughly soaping and soaking the clothes which he'd worn. Finally satisfying himself that he was as clean as he was going to get, he towelled off and dressed in fresh clothing. Using the mirror, he studied himself from head to toe and decided that he looked presentable. Aside from some scraped knuckles he'd left no visible trace of Anton, or of their encounter.

His next task was to commandeer the garbage bag from the container next to his dresser, and stuff his wet clothes into it. For good measure he also added the towel which he'd used to dry off. He'd watched enough western TV shows and movies to know that the police were capable of solving crimes from the smallest of clues, and he didn't plan to give them anything to work with. It was a pity that he didn't know any policemen down here that he could buy off; surely there were some of them, even here, that could use the extra money.

The garbage bag was then stuffed into a beach bag which had been thoughtfully provided by the resort. Next he went back outside and slowly walked around the area, trying to look as casual as possible, until he found a bank of dumpsters into which he placed his bundle. Only then did he breathe a sigh of relief and make his way back to his room, a sneering smile on his lips.

He considered ordering room service for supper, until he remembered that he wouldn't be able to make himself understood over the phone. He'd have to go to the dining room for the evening buffet, where following the waiter to his table would be the only human contact he would have to have. As he reached for the doorknob, he noticed that his hand was visibly shaking.

Sitting back down on the couch, he realized it wasn't just his hands that were shaking, his whole body was trembling, which both confused and angered him. He'd seen death before, even caused it, why was it affecting him so much now? Was it because he'd almost been killed himself this time? If he hadn't been on his guard, if he hadn't reacted so quickly to Anton's failed attack, he could very well be the one lying dead and forgotten on a foreign beach thousands of kilometres from home.

No, it couldn't be that, he was alive and well and in the best position he'd ever been in. Anton was not in his way anymore; it was his turn to take the lead now. He was finally able to take the place he deserved, to make some real money and wield some real power. That was what was making him shake, it was excitement.

Steeling his nerves, he forced himself to stop shaking, or at least to slow it down. A little outward show of excitement was okay on a night like this, wasn't it? He'd have some supper and a drink to celebrate. A big drink.

* * *

The three of them were sitting around the table discussing the day's developments. "Look, Dmitri, I know you like your opportunities, to wait and see what presents itself, but our lives are on hold, not to mention in danger. We need to do something to force the situation. We have to take the initiative from Vasili and put ourselves in control." Now that the shock of witnessing a murder was starting to wear off, Michael figured that the time to act was now. One down, and one to go.

Dmitri recognized the look in Michael's eyes, it was the same look he'd had when he'd been thinking about giving himself up to Vasili. Hopefully this would be a better idea.

"You have another idea, Mikhail, what is it?"

"We need to isolate Vasili, get him away from his team, somewhere that they can't get to him, somewhere that we can be waiting for him." Michael waited for nods from his companions and then continued. "It has to be somewhere that we can be in control and know if he's armed or not. Somewhere that he will be completely helpless."

"Where? How?"

"I don't know the where. You're the native here, you know the island. There must be some spot where we aren't likely to be interrupted by someone passing by."

Dmitri thought for a moment. "Yes, there are many places." He thought for a few more moments. "There is such a spot not too far from where he is staying."

"We need to make sure he wants to be there, and that he thinks it was his idea to be there, right?" He received two more nods. "Maybe even somewhere that he thinks he is in control when really we are."

"Yes, that would be helpful," Dmitri agreed.

"Okay, and we need to make sure he's there alone." Dmitri and Sandy nodded yet again, wishing he'd get to the point. Michael now seemed to be speaking to himself more than to them, lost in the thoughts churning in his mind. Neither of them pointed out that he was repeating himself; he seemed to be replaying some idea over and over in his mind and trying to make sure he was covering all the bases.

Dmitri squinted at his Canadian friend. There was something in Michael's expression, and the tone of his voice, that was starting to make him feel excited as well, even though he still had no clue as to what Michael was planning.

"And," Michael concluded, "We need to make sure that he can't call for help from the goon squad." He paused, wondering if he had missed any angles, then a smile came to his face.

"What?" Sandy demanded as his smile grew.

"Go on, Mikhail," Dmitri urged.

"Okay, here's what we do." Michael outlined his plan, pleased to see from Dmitri's smile that he thought it might work.

"Before we do that, let's throw him off balance again," Michael suggested.

* * *

Vasili was just starting on his second helping of dessert when his phone rang. He smiled, knowing that he'd told his men not to bother him unless they had something worth reporting. Today might bring good news on several fronts. It was almost a shame Anton had not lived long enough to see that his plan had worked.

He looked down at the call display to confirm it was one of his team calling, and dropped his fork with a clatter that attracted several curious looks from his fellow dinners. Anton's number! His fingers were shaking again, this time uncontrollably. How could that be? He answered the call, then immediately hung up without speaking or listening to whoever was on the other end.

Any desire for more cake was gone now and he rose from his seat, striding down the hall to his room. Could Anton have possibly survived? Had someone found him and saved his life? Impossible! He'd ripped open the man's abdomen; he'd have bled out within minutes.

Someone had found the phone, that was it! They were going through his previous calls, or his phone book, and trying to advise someone of his death. Okay, he thought to himself, steadying his nerves, he'd answer it if they called back. If it was the police it was best to answer them, even if he couldn't talk to them. Refusing to answer might make them suspicious.

The phone rang again just as he reached his room and he stepped inside before answering. "Allo?" He expected the voice on the other end to be speaking English, or whatever it was they spoke on this island. He was wrong.

"Vasili, my friend, how are you?" This time he recognized the voice immediately.

"Dmitri?" He couldn't hide the astonishment in his voice. He could understand that Dmitri would call him on Fadyay's phone, but how on earth did he get Anton's phone?

"Yes, it is me. How have you been?" Dmitri paused, allowing Vasili to hear him chuckling on the other end of the phone. "It was good to see you today. I'm sorry we didn't have a chance to talk."

"You saw me? How –" Vasili's voice trailed off as he realized he might be playing into some kind of trap. Silence was the best policy.

"Yes, I saw you, you are looking very good. This tropical climate suits you as well as it does me. Though it does not seem to agree with Anton, does it?" Dmitri could sense Vasili's growing anger and confusion, and took a moment to thoroughly enjoy it before continuing. "I wanted to talk to you, but you and Anton seemed to be having a bit of a disagreement. I thought it was best to wait until you two worked things out."

Vasili almost blurted out, 'you saw what happened?' but managed to bite off the words before he spoke. If Dmitri knew what had happened, or worse yet witnessed it, he needed to act quickly, before Dmitri went to the police.

"Good bye for now, my friend, I will be watching for you. I hope we get an opportunity to speak again, very soon. A pity that we will not be able to pay our respects to Anton at his funeral, but it seems that our current situation makes that impossible. Until later."

Vasili collapsed into the closest chair, his head in his hands. What was happening? How and when had he lost control?

* * *

Later that evening, a call was made to the local police station that would spare some poor vacationing tourist the shock of stumbling upon a dead body. A woman, who refused to identify herself, claimed to have seen the body and gave them the location where she said they could find it. No, she hadn't seen what happened, or seen anyone else in the area. No, she couldn't answer any of their questions, but could they please hurry and do something before some poor, innocent child stumbled upon it? They tried to call her back only to learn that the phone had an eastern European area code.

Chapter Seventeen

The men drifted into the room singly and in pairs, nervously taking seats around Vasili's table. They had known the moment they'd received his summons that he was very upset about something, but then Vasili was rarely in a good mood. They should have known his recent good mood would not have lasted long. Their boss circled the table impatiently, glancing repeatedly at his watch as he waited for the last of them to arrive.

The last man to enter the room earned an extra sharp glare from Vasili, who didn't even wait for him to sit down before lacing into them. "So not one of you has seen Dmitri or the Canadian?" They shook their heads, bracing for what they felt was sure to come. They weren't wrong. "Then how is it that he is watching us and knows everything we are doing?"

He didn't even bother to watch their puzzled expressions or listen to their excuses. "Anton has come here," he announced, knowing that would get their attention. He smiled inwardly at the frightened looks he saw in their eyes, but outwardly managed to keep his annoyed scowl. "He won't have anything to say to you about your failure to find Dmitri, because Dmitri found him first!"

They looked at each other nervously, wondering what Vasili meant by that. He let the question stew in their minds as he paced around the table, asking himself one last time if this was the right way to proceed before deciding to go ahead. "Dmitri has killed Anton."

He let them exchange shocked looks and gasps, certain now that he could use this to his advantage. "I am in complete charge of this operation now, and I will not tolerate any further lack of results!

Dmitri knows exactly what we are doing and how to find us. He even has my phone number because he has Anton's mobile." He preferred not to mention the call he'd received from Fadyay's phone. "We cannot kill him or there will be no way to recover the money he stole from us." Left unspoken was the fact that he was now first in line when it came to who had first claim on anything that they did manage to recover. "Why is it that with all of you looking for two men, you can't find them but they can find us?" His tone both mocked and threatened them. "Which of you will be the next one that Dmitri kills?"

"It's not just two men we are up against," one of them protested. "He lives here, he knows how to get around unnoticed, and he has his whole staff, plus who knows how many other informants here. Anyone who sees us might be working for him and reporting back to him."

"Then I suggest you come up with a new plan." No one dared to point out to Vasili that they were already following his orders, and that this whole operation had been his plan. "We must find these men before more of us turn up dead or missing. "You, you, and you," he pointed out three of his men at random. I want you to start watching the other resorts and anywhere else on the island where he might be staying, and watch for anyone following you. If you see or suspect anything, you will let me know at once. The rest of you keep watching Dmitri's place. He's most likely staying somewhere else because he already knows you're watching, but he just may try to return there for some reason. Pay special attention to the staff or anyone else that seems to be watching you."

"What about Anton?" It was the same man that had tried to excuse their failure just moments before.

"What about him?" Vasili shot back.

"Well, aren't we going to claim the body? Have him sent back home?"

"Good idea! Why don't you go to the police and tell them that you are a friend of the man who was just murdered? I'm sure they will hand over the body to you with no questions at all and let you send it back home. Can you look after that for me?"

The man shrank visibly back into his chair. "I just thought that his family would want ..."

"We will worry about it later. The police will see to it once they have identified him." He waved dismissively, "For now you all have more important things to worry about. Go."

He waited as the men left the room, then began pacing the floor again. Were these fools really the best team that Anton could assemble? Well, if so, he deserved what had happened to him. He had surrounded himself with incompetent help while keeping such a tight rein on Vasili that he couldn't do his job properly. Well, that would not be an issue anymore, he was now free to do things his way with no one to report to. He could start over with a clean slate and do this properly. Yuri had tried to interfere last summer and he was dead. Then Anton had done the same thing and had met the same fate. That said something about their methods, didn't it?

He got out his map of the island, more to help him think than because he thought it held any answers. He took out a pencil and circled Dmitri's resort, then the place where he was now staying. He almost put a dot on the map at the approximate location of where Anton now lay, but then thought better of it. The wrong person might see the map, and that mark would be hard to explain.

He was drumming on the table with the pencil when the phone rang. Not his cell phone, but the room phone. Who would be using that number, and what was he going to say? Whoever it was might expect him to answer in English, and he had no one to translate.

The ringing finally ceased and he went back to studying the map, but after a few minutes it began ringing again. Almost against his better judgment he picked it up and did his best to speak English, "Hello?" The word felt strange in his mouth.

"Hello, is this Vasili?" The voice was speaking Ukrainian, but he wouldn't let that surprise him enough to throw him off his guard. Was this another ruse by Dmitri? It wasn't his voice, but was it someone that worked for him? Were they standing outside the door even now?

He paused far too long and the voice on the other end of the phone began speaking again, still in Ukrainian, "Hello? Hello? Is anyone there? Hello?"

"Who is this?" he demanded.

"This is Maxim."

"Maxim?"

"I came here with Anton, and I cannot find him. Is he with you?"

Of course, Maxim, Anton's bodyguard! Well, he hadn't done a very good job, had he? When it came time to hire his own bodyguard, he'd be sure to look elsewhere. "Ah, yes, Maxim, how are you enjoying the tropics?" He asked the question to stall for time, he needed to be careful how he answered, because Maxim was fiercely loyal to Anton.

"It is nice enough," Maxim seemed annoyed at the question and his response was simply to brush aside Vasili's banter and return to the reason for his call. "I dropped him off at your hotel yesterday. He said he needed to speak with you in private and that I was to return to our hotel. Did you see him?"

It was always best to mix some truth into the lie. "Yes, we spoke briefly on the beach, then I got a call from one of my men. He thought he had spotted Dmitri and I had to deal with him. It turns out it was a false alarm, I'm afraid."

"What about Anton?"

"He told me to see to the mission and that he would talk to me later. Maybe he decided to see some sights. It is a beautiful island."

"But he didn't come back to the hotel last night." Maxim was now sounding very worried.

"Maybe he met a woman," Vasili offered, knowing very well that such an occurrence would not be uncommon for his former boss.

"But he would have checked in with me; I'm sure he would have."

"Well, did he make sure his mobile had service down here? I've found that mine does not work everywhere on the island. If he comes back, I will tell him to call you, and you need to have him call me when you find him. I have some information he will want to hear."

"Okay, thank you. I will do that." Maxim didn't sound at all relieved, but as Vasili had nothing more to offer him he decided that the best idea would be to go out and start looking himself.

Vasili sat down on the bed after hanging up the phone. With Maxim around he'd have to be very careful; he was big, powerful, hot-tempered, and regarded Anton as his father. Maxim had grown up as a homeless orphan and had come to see Anton's organization as his only real family. Because of his loyalty, not to mention his size, Anton had shown him special favour and he'd eventually become his personal bodyguard. It was rumoured that Maxim had once killed a man just for taking Anton's parking spot. Vasili doubted that it had really happened that way, but he hated to think what Maxim might to do the man that had killed his 'father.'

* * *

Dmitri was placing a grocery order over the phone with Juan, who was to pick up what they needed or raid it from the resort's kitchen, and then the two of them would meet at a location somewhere between the safe house and the resort. Michael, meanwhile, was finishing off the last of the cookies in the pantry while he and Sandy poured over a map.

"Okay, I think I've got the route down now, test me on it," he said, pushing the map over to Sandy.

Sandy turned it around and studied it for a moment to orient herself. "All right, you've just left Vasili's resort, where are you going?"

"I head out of the parking lot and turn right," he began.

"You're not lost yet, Sandy teased. Michael gave a dramatic sigh, then continued with his recitation, his eyes closed in concentration as he read out to her the various twists and turns of the route they'd worked out to the location Dmitri had suggested.

"Very good, you got it completely right this time." Michael smiled at the way she scrunched up her nose as she backtracked to the midpoint of the route. "What if you miss that second turn, what then?"

Michael closed his eyes again, picturing the exact spot she meant. "Okay, then I have to go past the second road to the left ..." He paused another moment and then described an alternate route that would take him to the same spot.

"Very good, you passed your navigation test!" She smiled at him a bit more proudly than memorizing the way from point A to point B merited, Dmitri thought with a chuckle. He was enjoying watching the two of them and couldn't help but think how much the chemistry between them had changed since they had, in her words, kidnapped her.

"It's a whole lot easier navigating in the air than on foreign roads," Michael commented as he pulled the map back from Sandy and gave it another look. Part of him could not believe they were actually going to try this. It was as if it was a scheme they'd cooked up just for fun. But they were really going to do it, and likely very soon. Most of it had been his idea, with some input from Sandy and a lot from Dmitri since he knew the island best. Since he wasn't sure if he should feel excited or terrified, he felt a little of both. There were also a few other feelings he couldn't identify thrown into the mix.

"I have to go get the groceries now, you two better behave while I'm gone." They both blushed slightly at the comment, but the grocery run gave Michael an idea.

"Why don't we go along with him," he said to Sandy, then turned to Dmitri. "We could get the groceries and then make a dry run. It's one thing to plan it out on a map, but I think it would be best to see it for real, just in case there's something the map isn't showing us."

"That is a good idea, Mikhail," Dmitri said after a short pause. He wasn't weighing the merits of the idea, he'd already planned to have Michael drive the route a few times, but why not let him think it was his idea? "Let's go." He tossed the keys to Michael and the three of them headed for the van.

"You know," Michael mused as he climbed into the driver's seat, "this all depends on us being able to find Vasili. Do you think he might have moved to a new resort? I mean, after the body was discovered, and now that he knows we know where he's staying, he might decide to go hide somewhere else."

"He might," Dmitri allowed from the back seat, "But moving might draw some attention from the police if they are investigating the murder. Besides, we can always get in touch with him if we need to." He pulled Anton's cell phone from his pocket and waved it at

Michael. "Remember, he wants to find us at least as much as we want to find him. We will find him when the time comes."

* * *

Vasili did, in fact, want to move to a new resort. The thought of arousing suspicion with the police by such a move hadn't yet crossed his mind; he just wanted to put a bit of distance between himself and Dmitri. He couldn't allow his prey the advantage of knowing where he was staying. The problem was he needed someone to speak English for him in order to make a new booking. He had tried to have one of his men call a few other resorts, but they hadn't had any available rooms and he'd finally decided in his frustration that their time was better spent hunting for Dmitri, not running from him.

Instead, he'd decided to spend as little time as possible at the resort, using the days to cruise the island in his rented car. He planned to have at least one of the team spend the night in his room to act as a body guard. Thankfully none of them had accused him of cowardice, at least not to his face; and to him the precaution was justified. After all, with Anton out of the way he had gained a new status, though for the time being he was pretty much ignoring Maxim, the only man there with any real experience as a bodyguard.

So far, his driving had consisted of meandering aimlessly around the nearby streets and roads as he'd familiarized himself with the immediate area before attempting to drive too far from his base. He was also a bit nervous about being stopped by the local police since he couldn't speak the language. At least on this island they drove on the proper side of the road; he'd heard that on some nearby islands they drove on the left, like they did in England. Thankfully the car and the roads weren't too different from what he was used to, except that he enjoyed the scenery a lot more here.

He'd now been cruising long enough that he felt he could risk getting a bit farther from home. Since he was already headed back in the direction of his hotel, he figured he might as well drive on past it and keep going for a while.

* * *

"I hope you two don't think that just because I'm a woman I'm going to do all the cooking," Sandy quipped good-naturedly as they stowed the last box in the back of the van.

"No worries there," Michael shot back, "Dmitri's a better cook anyways." Sandy scowled and threw a playful punch at him.

"Ouch!" Michael let his arm sag and rubbed his shoulder tenderly. I think I'm in too much pain to unload the groceries when we get home. I'm not even sure I can drive."

"You better be able to drive, buddy, this is your first dry run, remember?"

"I'll try, but I don't know, it's pretty sore."

"Oh, come on, that wasn't even a real punch, it was more of a love tap." They both blushed as she realized what she had just said, and while Dmitri did his best to ignore their exchange, he was chuckling as they climbed back into the van.

"Now which way to Vasili's resort again?" Michael asked to break the tension between himself and Sandy. He swung the van out of the parking lot in which they'd met Juan. "I think I'm lost. It's a good thing you didn't punch me in the head or I'd really be messed up."

Sandy shot him another mock scowl but said nothing as he turned the correct way and cruised along with the flow of traffic down the road which led them to the resort where, they hoped, Vasili was still staying. Michael was mumbling to himself as they drove, calling out the various landmarks along the way ahead of time, feeling pleased as he passed each of them in the order in which he called them out. His two passengers remained silent to allow him to concentrate on the task at hand.

"Okay, this is the place," Michael said as he swung into the parking lot. "Now, I'm going to park as close to the exit as I can," he said, mostly to himself, but the others listened along. He swung into a spot facing the main road and put the van in neutral. "The next order of business is to get Vasili's attention and then get back to the van before he can catch me."

"That would end our plan pretty quickly," Sandy mused.

"Might end my life pretty quickly too, if he catches up with me."

Dmitri didn't catch the irony. "If he catches you, he'll keep you alive until you help him find me, but it won't be pleasant for you."

"Thanks for the reminder, I'd forgotten what these guys are capable of when they really want something. Guess their mothers never taught them to ask nicely. Now, assuming it all goes according to plan to this point, I just have to get myself to the right place without having a car accident, or having Vasili run me off the road."

He put the van back into gear and headed for the exit. "First turn is to the right," he reminded himself as he rolled to a stop. There was a small stream of traffic coming towards him from his left, but as he waited for them to pass he realized that the van had a much shorter hood than his car did, and that he'd stopped well short of the stop line. He rolled forward a few more feet as he waited for the stream of traffic to pass.

* * *

Vasili was stuck at the tail end of a line of cars bunched up behind a large truck, and while it would usually bother him that someone was in his way and slowing him down, he really didn't mind this time. He was in no hurry and the slower pace meant he had more time to pay attention to his surroundings. As he passed his own resort he quite naturally glanced towards it. A van was waiting its turn to pull onto the road and he watched a bit apprehensively as it began to roll forward again after stopping. Was it going to pull out in front of him? The last thing he needed was an accident, he'd have to call in a translator to deal with the police, so he took his foot off the gas and was about to hit the brake when the van stopped again and he decided it was safe to keep going.

As he rolled past the driveway, he glared angrily at the driver who, unfortunately was not looking at him. He was still looking to his left to see if it was safe to proceed. He did a double take. The driver was Michael Barrett! The Canadian! The passenger wasn't Dmitri though, it was a woman he didn't recognize.

* * *

Michael waited until the last vehicle had passed, then pulled in behind the last car in line, the little red one, and followed it at a careful distance. He saw it, but his mind was on the turn he'd have to make a few kilometres down the road.

* * *

Vasili could not believe his good fortune and was already thinking of how he could boast about his success in front of his men. He'd found Michael, and hopefully Michael was about to lead him to Dmitri. If not, well, it should be a simple matter to capture him and the woman. From what he remembered of the man from the previous summer there was not very much fight in him. Once he had captured Michael and the woman, Dmitri was as good as his. That meant he'd soon have Dmitri's millions.

But following another vehicle is usually best done from behind, not from ahead. He backed off from the vehicles ahead of him to allow himself more time to keep an eye on the white van behind him. At least it was large enough that it stood out from the other vehicles, which where were mostly compact cars. So far so good, but he had to find a way to get behind the Canadian. He was now dividing his attention between the vehicles in front of him, the van behind him, and watching the road for some point at which he could pull off to let Michael pass him. He slowed down a bit more.

* * *

"This guy in front of us must be lost or something, he keeps slowing down." Michael commented, the words were not quite a complaint, but he was impatient to get this dry run out of the way.

"Gosh, imagine someone on this island that isn't familiar with the roads. Couldn't possibly be a tourist in this part of the world, could it?"

"Nah, couldn't be, who'd want to come here for a holiday?" Michael countered with a chuckle, "I mean, what is there to see or do?" Dmitri peered around Sandy's seat to see what they were talking about, and was considering a response of his own.

"Oh, okay he's pulling over. Maybe he's checking his map or something." Michael checked to make sure there was no oncoming traffic and pulled slightly across the centre line to give the red car a wider berth.

* * *

Vasili was getting a bit frustrated with the lack of shoulders on this road. He didn't want the van to get too close to him, even though he was sure Michael wouldn't recognize him from behind. He was considering other options when the road suddenly widened a bit, some thoughtful person had constructed a roadside turnoff. Flipping on the signal light he braked and pulled over. He fought the urge to look at the van as it accelerated past him, but decided it was safe enough since the woman on his side of the van wouldn't recognize him even if she did look at him, which she didn't. He couldn't see into the rear seats of the van as the windows were all heavily tinted.

* * *

Technically speaking Dmitri was a native, and a resort owner to boot, so he had a vested interest in any tourists that might be in need of help. It was the most natural thing in the world for him to take a close look at the vehicle at the side of the road as they passed it. If they were lost, or looked in need of help, he was planning on having Michael pull over so he could offer assistance.

At first glance nothing seemed wrong with the vehicle. Did the driver just need directions? He looked down into the passenger window and sat bolt upright as he recognized the driver. Vasili!

"Mikhail, turn left!"

"But the next turn is to the right, isn't it? And it's not for a few more kilometres or so." Michael couldn't believe he had messed up that badly already.

"He's right, it is a right turn," Sandy waved the map at Dmitri as evidence.

"Michael, take the next left turn!" Michael blinked upon hearing Dmitri pronounce his name correctly for the first time since they'd met. "Just do it, no questions."

Michael, his heart pounding, looked into the rear-view mirror and saw that Dmitri had twisted around in his seat and was staring out the back window. His mirror told him that the red car had pulled back onto the road and was behind them. "What is it, Dmitri, is that guy following us?"

"It's Vasili, and yes, he's following us. No! Don't speed up or he'll know we spotted him." Michael eased his foot back off the accelerator. "Just turn left and go where I tell you to go."

"We're going to lose him," Michael gave Sandy a reassuring look.

"We could," Dmitri said from the back seat, his eyes still on the red car behind them. "But that might not be the best idea."

"Then what are we doing?" Michael demanded; the fear obvious in his voice. So much for reassuring Sandy. "If I'm driving, I need to know what to do."

"I just told you what to do," Dmitri answered in a matter of fact tone. "For now, turn left and go the speed limit."

"And wait for an opportunity," Michael finished the sentence under his breath, tightening his grip on the steering wheel. The turn was coming up so he flipped on the signal light and braked for the turn. "We're turning this way, Vasili," he called out. "Are you watching? Make sure you follow us!" His mirror assured him that Vasili was signalling also. "Good boy, don't lose sight of us until our opportunity knocks."

He rolled his eyes when he heard Dmitri laugh out loud in the back seat.

* * *

Vasili kept as far back from the van as he dared and was thankful for the fact that there was enough traffic that he wasn't likely to stand out as he followed them. After Michael made his turn, Vasili let an oncoming motorcycle go by and then followed him. This was a much quieter road that wound back almost in the direction from which they'd just come. So, Michael and his new accomplice must have been trying to spy on him back at his resort and now, hopefully, they were returning to wherever he and Dmitri were hiding out. He contemplated calling in his men as back-up but decided against it. He didn't yet know exactly where they were going and the last thing he needed was a parade of vehicles that might tip off the Canadian to the fact that he was being followed.

Chapter Eighteen

Michael drummed the steering wheel nervously as he navigated the narrow, winding road. His thoughts had returned to the wild car chase the night he'd met Dmitri and they'd torn up the back roads of Ukraine in that beat-up wreck of a stolen car. His instincts were telling him to drive the way Dmitri had driven that night. Instead he was poking along at the posted speed limit and allowing a murderer to keep him in sight. This was insane! One glance at Sandy was all he needed to see that she felt the same way, but Dmitri seemed quite pleased with the way things were going.

"Is your plan to let him catch us on some lonely stretch of road where the odds are three-to-one in our favour?" He knew their original plan was now impossible to carry out, but what was Dmitri thinking?

"No, but if it comes to that, we need to be ready."

"Good plan so far," Michael muttered.

"We're going to try and lose him, but without letting him know it."

"Okay, and how are we going to do that? Hypnotize him?"

"Just keep driving. I think he will stop following us all by himself."

"If you say so," Michael sounded dubious and saw his own feelings reflected in Sandy's eyes. "Then we need to find something different to drive so he doesn't find us again."

"No," Dmitri countered. "We keep driving this; it will make it even easier later."

"Either easier or impossible." The whole thing had been his idea, but he'd been counting on an element of surprise. Now he wasn't so sure about the whole thing. "So you just want me to keep driving for now?"

"Yes, stay on this road," he ordered in a distracted tone, his full attention was on the little red car behind them.

* * *

Vasili made sure to keep a respectable distance between the van and himself. So far Michael had made no sudden or abrupt changes in his driving, so for the time being he would assume that he had not been spotted. The only thing that would make it just a little bit better would be to have another vehicle between himself and the Canadian. That van really stood out on the road and would be easy to follow, even with a vehicle or two between them, and it would give him better cover. For now, he'd rely on keeping a good separation between the two vehicles, and the fact that most people watched cars, not drivers. As long as he did nothing to draw attention to his driving, he should be fine. He'd just need to stay alert for any sudden turns or stops.

* * *

"He's still back there," Michael muttered, more to himself than to his passengers. Dmitri was sitting sideways in his seat, the better to keep an eye on Vasili, while Sandy was scrunched down in her seat so that she could watch through the side view mirror.

"Yes, he is," Dmitri agreed. "If he loses us, we will go back to the safe house and try again tomorrow."

"What if he doesn't lose us?"

"Then we keep going." Dmitri turned to take a look through the windshield. "Keep going straight for now, but in a few minutes we will turn off this road, I think, depending on what our friend decides to do."

"What if he decides to run us off the road and slit our throats?"

"Then you won't need to make any turns," Dmitri deadpanned, earning him nasty looks from both Michael and Sandy. "But right now, he is behaving, so I don't think you need to worry about that. Plus, he needs information from us first, so no throat-slitting, I think. Not today."

"That's a comforting thought," said Sandy, in a tone that left little doubt that she took no comfort from it at all.

"Sorry I got you into this," Michael said, taking his eyes from the road for a moment to look at her.

"You keep saying that, but you didn't get me into this. I came of my own free will this time for some reason that I may figure out someday in the far distant future. By then I may have decided I don't even regret it."

"There's a stop sign up ahead, what do I do now?"

Dmitri turned to peer through the windshield again. "If I was driving, I would stop."

"I was planning on that! What do I do after I stop? And please don't say 'go.'"

Dmitri took just a moment to orient himself before making his decision, then he began directing them through the more built-up area they had arrived in. Michael now had to pay more attention to the streets and corners, not to mention the other traffic. "Is he still there?" he asked as he followed Dmitri's orders.

"So far, yes, there's a few cars between us and him now, but he's still there," Sandy answered since both Michael and Dmitri were occupied in navigating the route to wherever Dmitri had in mind. They were now doubling back to the left, around a bay that jutted into the island.

"Just stay on this road for now; it will take us where we need to go." Dmitri seemed very calm now, as if he were sure how this was going to all play out in their favour.

"Where's that, a dead end?"

"No, I'm going to drop in and see some friends of mine," was all Dmitri would reveal. The road led them along the coastline with the sea to their left, until they reached a bridge. "After you cross the bridge, go left," Dmitri instructed.

Michael did as he was directed and found himself once more driving parallel with the coastline. All that driving through town had given him something to concentrate on, but now that he didn't need to worry about navigation, he had time to feel edgy again.

"Ahead on the right," Dmitri finally said, pointing through the windshield at their destination, "Pull in at that building right there." Michael almost laughed out loud when he realized where he was parking.

* * *

Vasili smiled as he saw the van pull over and park, congratulating himself on successfully following the van without giving himself away. Now, he'd just drive a bit further down the street and find a place to park where he could keep an eye on them. They obviously weren't staying here, so Mr. Barrett must be running an errand, he decided. Then he saw where they had parked and a wave of panic swept over him.

He may not be able to speak English, or read it either, but like many Ukrainians he did know enough of the English alphabet to sound out the odd word, and the letters on the building spelled out a word he didn't need to interpret. They'd parked in front a police station!

As a general rule, the idea of a policeman didn't scare him that much. He dealt with them back home, and most of the ones he'd dealt with had either been bribed or blackmailed, but he knew that most of the ones in the west were much more honest. What scared him now was the knowledge that if Dmitri knew what had happened between himself and Anton, that Michael Barrett likely did as well, and if Michael was at the police station to report what had happened, he could very well be in a lot of trouble. Even though it had been a clear case of self-defence, he wanted to do all he could to avoid any contact with the police. At best it would cause unnecessary complications that would slow down his mission. At worst it could lead to, well, it wouldn't come to that would it? He would not allow it. It was best not to be seen anywhere near the Canadian while he was with the police.

He jotted down the licence plate number of the van, which he'd already committed to memory anyways, and decided that the best plan was to go back to the hotel. The desire to change hotels came to him once again. If Dmitri knew where he was, it might not be safe to stay there, but if he moved it might look bad in the eyes of the police. How many people came here for a holiday and changed resorts? Twice. Not many, he figured. No, he'd stay put for now, but perhaps he'd come up with a good excuse to have Maxim stay with him. Surely it wouldn't be too hard to convince him that Dmitri was responsible for what had happened to Anton, should it come out, and having a bit of muscle to back him up wouldn't hurt. He wasn't so sure that he could handle Dmitri by himself, so why risk it? Besides, shouldn't a man of his position have others to do that kind of work for him?

* * *

"What are we doing here?" Sandy asked as Michael turned off the engine. Almost as soon as the engine shut down, and the air conditioner along with it, they all sensed the heat of the tropical sun pouring through the windows.

"I think Dmitri's idea was to scare him off," Michael replied, congratulating himself for finally understanding what the plan had been all along. Dmitri had said that Vasili would stop following them all by himself, and he'd been right. He had forced himself not to look at the red car as it passed them, seemed to hesitate, then accelerated and proceeded down the street and out of sight.

"That was the plan," Dmitri agreed. "But I was planning on coming here anyways, this just saves us some time. Let's go inside."

Michael figured that it didn't really save them any time at all, since they'd have to start all over again with another practice run to their chosen sight, but he dropped that for now.

"Why are we going inside? Are you going to tell them what really happened to Anton?"

"No, if they figure it out themselves, fine, but we're going to deal with Vasili one way or another, so it really doesn't matter. I'm just going in to gather some intelligence." He gave Michael a friendly, but rather heavy, pat on the shoulder and winked at Sandy. "We're going on a spy mission!"

Michael and Sandy looked at each other, both rolling their eyes at his words, then Michael shrugged, "Guess his plans are working so far. Might as well go along with them." They stepped out of the van into the hottest temperatures they'd yet experienced on this trip. Michael locked the doors, wondering if anyone would actually dare to steal such a conspicuous vehicle in front of a police station. He took Sandy's hand as they followed Dmitri inside.

"Mr. Dmitri, how are you, sir?" The friendly officer smiled a greeting at their host as they entered. "These are friends of yours, are they?"

"Yes, this is Michael and his friend Sandy," Michael kind of liked how that introduction sounded, it made them sound kind of official. "Michael is an old friend of mine who is down here visiting me." The words sounded so casual and, well, honest, as Dmitri spoke them. Michael and Sandy shared a glance and an implied shrug as if to say, 'might as well play along.'

"This is Domingo," he informed them, gesturing towards the man standing behind the counter. "He is going to be a very famous detective someday. A very fine officer."

"Just call me Hercule," Domingo laughed. "A pleasure to meet you," the smiling officer said, pumping each of their hands in turn. "I hope you are enjoying your stay here on Culebra? it is the most beautiful island in the Caribbean, is it not?"

Michael hoped that his agreement with this man's assessment of his home island sounded sincere; he hardly dared tell the officer that he hadn't known he was coming here, or that Sandy was only here because she had been kidnapped. Or that their second arrival on the island had been in a stolen airplane. Their time here was, quite literally, no holiday.

"Dmitri's resort is wonderful," Sandy added. "I'm so thankful that he's allowing us to stay there." She gave Dmitri a sarcastic smile, though there was enough of a real one to let him know that she was teasing him.

Dmitri's face took on a serious look as he leaned closer to Domingo, "I'm afraid I'm not here to visit today."

"Nothing serious, I hope," Domingo became more concerned as he reached for a notepad. "Another attempted robbery at your place?"

Dmitri shook his head, "No, no more robberies, thankfully. Did that man you caught tell you anything?" Michael had to cough to keep from laughing. It struck him as rather funny that Dmitri was crediting him with Bogdan's arrest.

"No, I'm afraid we have learned nothing from him. He confessed to the robbery, but we have no idea who he is or where he came from, though his accent does sound a lot like yours."

"Maybe he figured a fellow countryman would make an easy target. But I'm not really here to talk about that. You see, there has been a lot of talk about …" Dmitri glanced around as if to make sure no one could overhear them, causing the rest of them to look over their shoulders as well. "There has been a lot of talk about that murder." Dmitri continued. "It is always upsetting to the staff and the guests when something like that happens, and you know how the staff can be. They talk too much, rumors get started, and everyone gets even more frightened."

Domingo nodded and set his notepad aside, "I understand. Sometimes the rumours can upset people almost as much as the crime itself."

"What can you tell me. Should we be concerned?"

"We don't have a lot to go on, I'm afraid. We haven't been able to recover the murder weapon yet. It appears that it was nothing more than a robbery gone bad. We don't usually see such terrible crimes here on Culebra."

His last comment was directed towards Michael and Sandy.

"It happened in a secluded place to a man who was there alone. A crime of opportunity, and if no opportunity is given, none can be taken." He spread his hands apologetically. "If you two stay together, and in public places, you will be perfectly safe here. I'm sorry if you feel threatened in any way, but that is really all I can say to you about it right now."

"Is there anything or anyone we should be watching for?" Dmitri's voice sounded suitably concerned.

"I wish there was something more I could tell you, but I really can't. It is still an ongoing investigation. If you see anyone suspicious, though, let us know." Domingo seemed genuinely sorry that he could offer nothing more.

"Okay, thank you, I will do that," Dmitri raised his voice, signalling that he needed nothing further. He smiled at Domingo. "I know that you will do your usual fine job. Whoever did this will be brought to justice. I have no doubt about that."

They returned to the van in silence, which Michael broke as he pulled back into the flow of traffic. "Is this guy really a friend of yours?"

"Mikhail," Dmitri's voice took on a condescending but teasing tone, "A man in my position must always have friends in the police department. Domingo was one of the first men that I got to know when I moved here. "Now I know what they know, or what they suspect, and by coming to him as a concerned resort ..."

"You remove suspicion from yourself," Sandy finished with a knowing nod.

"Exactly! Now, Mikhail, let's go back to Vasili's resort and try this again."

* * *

Vasili waited impatiently as the entire team filed back into his suite, but this time his impatience was not fueled by anger. It was a pleasant and unexpected change, but it also set them on edge and made them wonder when his mood would shift yet again.

"Sit down, sit down," he gestured at them to take their seats. "I found Michael Barrett!" he smiled broadly, not attempting in the least to hide his pleasure and pride."

"Where?" several voices asked warily, wondering if they were going to get a lecture or a tongue-lashing for failing in their searches while their boss had succeeded.

"I do not know where he is now, but I spotted him driving a white van this afternoon. I followed him for a while, but he parked in front of a police station and I thought it was best not to stay." Heads nodded at the wisdom of his decision, whether or not they actually agreed with it. "There was a young lady with him. I did not get a good look at her, but she has light brown hair and is about his age."

"Was Dmitri with him?" one of them dared to ask.

"He might have been in the back seat; I could not tell. The windows were tinted so he may have been there," he waved his hand as if the question was unimportant. "What we do know is that Michael is here, and if he is, Dmitri is too. If not, as I've told you already, if we find the Canadian then we will get Dmitri too. The girl will make a good bargaining chip as well. Dmitri has grown soft and I don't think he will just stand by and let any harm come to his new friends." They all nodded in agreement, as was expected of them.

Vasili gave them as complete a description of the van as he could, as well as the plate number. "This is the best lead we have had since we started so I want you all to concentrate on finding that van. Check every parking lot, every street, every resort. Watch for it driving around on the streets. Find it. If you find it parked and no one is inside, then stay out of sight and watch it. If it's moving, follow it. Let the whole team know the moment you spot it."

Vasili looked slowly around the table, making eye contact with each man there in an attempt to convey to them know how serious this was. "We are close, very close. Now, get going. Finish the job," he concluded brusquely.

He waited as they filed from the room with more energy and enthusiasm than they had shown since their arrival. Vasili understood why they might be feeling that way, the thought of driving around looking for something tangible was much less tedious than maintaining surveillance on one location as most of them had been doing for the past few days. Hopefully they would find that van again soon.

His next order of business was to call Maxim. He hadn't yet been informed of Vasili's version of the facts as the rest of the team had been, and that might have been a mistake. He was going to have to tell him something if he wanted his help now. As he dialed Maxim's number, he realized he'd have to isolate him from the other men to make sure he didn't find out that the others had known long before he had.

Maxim answered on the first ring. Good, he was tense and waiting for information. That made him vulnerable. "Maxim? Vasili. I need you to come to my hotel right away."

"What is it?" his voice was thick with worry. "Do you have some news?"

"Yes, I do"

"Is Anton with you? What has happened?"

"Not over the phone," he insisted over Maxim's pleas. "I'm in room 126. Come right away."

Silence was the only answer he received as Maxim hung up. Vasili allowed himself to smile, and even to laugh for a short time, but then forced himself to turn serious. Or at least to appear that way. Not knowing how soon Maxim would arrive, he hurried to the front desk with the room service menu in hand. Fortunately, it had pictures and he was able to let his finger do the talking to the desk clerk on duty, pointing at a bottle and using a word that was pretty much identical to its English equivalent. Vodka.

After bringing it back to his room he promptly poured a glass-worth or so of the clear liquid down the sink, and then filled a glass about half full, setting it on the table in front of him. He mussed up his hair a bit to make himself appear disheveled and worn out, then waited for his guest to arrive. Less than twenty-five minutes passed between his call and Maxim's knock at his door.

He put on his best 'in mourning' face and swung the door open. "Maxim, my friend, please come in." He avoided making eye contact with Maxim as they shook hands, his gaze fixed on the floor.

Maxim looked at Vasili, then glanced around the room, noting the glass in his host's hand, as well as the open bottle on the table. "What news do you have, Vasili? What has happened?"

"Sit down, Maxim, let me pour you a drink."

Maxim's heart was pounding even as it sank in his chest; it must be bad news. He took a seat and waited for Vasili to pour him a glass. Vasili raised his half-empty glass in a half-hearted toast and took a sip. Maxim simply looked at him, his glass gripped tightly in his hand but still untouched.

"Vasili, please, what is it?" As tough as the man was, he looked almost on the verge of tears.

"Maxim, I am sorry. There is no easy way to say this. Anton is dead."

"What?" They were the words he had been afraid he would hear, but it was still shocking to actually hear them. He'd known it from the moment Vasili had called, but he'd still held out hope that Vasili had something else to say. Anything else. He hadn't just been hoping, for the first time in his adult life he'd actually been praying. "No! It cannot be! What happened, an accident, or ... or something else?"

"Have a drink first." Maxim nodded and swallowed half the glass in one gulp. Vasili managed to maintain his serious look as he refilled the glass, pushing his own aside as Maxim took another long pull.

"Vasili, please I must know. He insisted I drop him off and return to our hotel. He would not say where he was going or what he was doing. I should have been there."

"I wish he had told me as well, but he didn't. He told me he would be in touch when he left, but nothing more. I only found out what happened through a local contact. If only he'd told me I might have been able to prevent it." He looked out the window, a forlorn expression on his face. "I guess if he told you to stay behind then you cannot be blamed."

Vasili gave Maxim a reassuring pat on the shoulder before playing his next card.

"Did you know that Anton had found Dmitri?"

"No, I had no idea. He said nothing."

"Then perhaps it wasn't planned. Perhaps it was a chance encounter."

Vasili nodded thoughtfully, as if trying to figure out how the events had transpired. He gave his head a single shake, as if to say that wondering was a waste of time and that the fact must simply be accepted. He leaned forward, lowering his voice, causing Maxim to lean in closer. "He met with Dmitri, maybe to confront him, maybe they met by accident, I do not know. Maxim, I am sorry, I know how much Anton meant to you, that you feel responsible for him, but Dmitri killed him. Stabbed him. He bled to death. Slowly. The pain –" he shook his head sadly. "– It must have been excruciating."

"If only you had been with him, Maxim." Vasili looked back out the window, allowing the words to hang in the air between them.

"I would have been, Vasili, I would have been there, but he told me to stay at the hotel. He insisted. He said he would not be long. I thought maybe it was a woman." He took another long drink, draining the glass, his voice trembling, sounding even more defensive. "He told me to stay at the hotel."

"I know, Maxim, I know. It was not your fault." They were the proper words to say at such a time, but they lacked any force or conviction, a fact not lost on Maxim who was desperate for some form of comfort after failing so badly. He eyed first the bottle, then his empty glass. Vasili refilled it.

"It is too late to do anything about it now." Were his words a statement of fact, or an accusation Maxim wondered? "But perhaps there is something you can do now."

"What? I will do anything!"

"If Anton knew where to find Dmitri, he did not share that information with me, but I did spot his Canadian friend today while trying to find them. My team is trying to locate them again. Will you work with me, Maxim? We can find Dmitri and his friend and recover the money he stole from us."

"Of course I will help you," Maxim nodded firmly. "I want revenge. Dmitri will pay for what he did."

"Yes, he will pay. But we must find the money first, Maxim, do you understand? We cannot kill him until we have it. We can hurt him, but we cannot kill him until we have the money."

Maxim blinked. On one level he understood, but his pride and his grief were demanding blood.

"It's what Anton would have wanted, Maxim. That is why he sent me here. That is why Anton came here. We cannot let Anton's last wish be in vain. We must recover what Dmitri took from Anton." Technically he'd taken it from Yuri Stepanovich, of course, but at this point, Maxim wasn't worried about technicalities.

"I understand, Vasili. I will not let you down." The way his voice trailed off, it was as if he was about to add, 'like I let Anton down.'

Yet his words still carried the conviction of a vow.

Vasili reached across and gave Maxim a hearty pat on the shoulder.

"Good, Maxim, good. I know you won't."

* * *

Michael had refused to run the route again until they'd secured another vehicle, a compact car this time, and hidden the van back at the safe house. It would be fine to be recognized when the time came, in fact it would help just like Dmitri had said, but he didn't want any more accidental encounters until they were completely ready.

The first dry run had gone flawlessly, and the second one had been nothing more than a pleasant afternoon drive. He had it memorized and felt confident that he knew the surrounding area well enough that he was ready should they need to alter the route for any reason.

He was ready, both Sandy and Dmitri said so, and he'd agreed with a confident smile as they'd driven back to the shelter of the safe house. As he waited his turn at a stop sign, however, he changed his mind. He was prepared, but he wasn't sure he'd ever be ready.

Chapter Nineteen

"Huh? What?" Michael sat up groggily in his bed. Something had disturbed his sleep, but he wasn't sure what. Had it been something real, or something in a dream? He rubbed his eyes but that didn't help him to see any better in the complete darkness of the room. Then he heard it again; a very soft knock on his bedroom door.

"Michael? Can I come in?" Sandy's muted voice was barely audible through the door.

"Yeah, come in Sandy. I'm awake." He tried and failed to make himself sound fully alert.

"Sorry, I know you were asleep, but I wanted to talk to you."

"That's okay, come on in," he sat up in the single bed, switched on the reading light, and slid over a bit to make room for her to sit down on the edge of the mattress.

"Thanks," she smiled, relieved to find him willing to talk, though as far as Michael was concerned, any time was a good time to talk with her.

"What's up?" he asked as she perched on the edge of the bed, but Sandy hesitated at first, as if unsure of how to start.

"Well, when we met on the ship, I kinda figured you'd be a great guy to get to know."

"I wanted to get to know you when we were still on the airplane."

Sandy smiled and reached to take his hand in hers. "But when the two of you kidnapped me, well, I was ready to let you have it!"

"Hey," Michael protested, "I didn't kidnap you. I knew what Dmitri was trying to do and tried to stop him. I tried to talk you out of coming, remember?"

"It didn't work, did it?" she teased.

"No," he admitted, "But now I'm kinda glad it didn't"

"Just kinda?"

"Very glad? Overjoyed? Ecstatic?"

She laughed, and then turned serious again. "I can't wait for this to be over, I really can't."

"Sandy, Dmitri has this all figured out, all we have to do is get Vasili to follow us. Dmitri knows what he's doing, I saw him take out two guys bigger than Vasili last summer. There's nothing to worry about." He hoped he sounded convincing.

"I know, I'm sure he can, but that's not what I wanted to talk about." She paused again. "That's not what I'm worried about."

"What is it then?" He leaned closer to her, a look of genuine concern on his face.

"Remember when you asked if we could keep seeing each other when this was all over and I said we could?"

Michael felt suddenly very empty, as if he'd been completely deflated, nothing remained inside him but a lead weight in the pit of his stomach. "Have you've changed your mind?" He couldn't keep the disappointment from his voice.

"I haven't changed my mind that you're a great guy."

"Then what is it?" Michael felt his heart start beating again. Whatever she was worried about couldn't possibly be as bad as what he had been afraid she was about to say.

"Well, how do we see each other? I mean, we live hundreds of miles apart and I have to go back to work when this is over." She sensed what he was about to say and cut him off before he could say it. "No, I'm not going home before we get through this. There's no way I could work, or even sit at home and wonder what had happened and whether you two were still okay. I'm staying here!"

"Well, how often do you fly out my way?"

"That's not going to be enough, Michael. A few hours, or a few days once a month, if even that often? No, that won't work. Long distance relationships don't survive. Trust me, I've worked with a few girls that tried it, there's just too many things that can go wrong."

"Sandy, I'm not going to start seeing anyone else, honest."

"You say that now, but when we only see each other once or twice a month, well, what if you change your mind? What if I change my mind? What if we just grow apart and forget each other? Do you really think it will work?" She saw the hurt in his eyes and quickly added, "I want it to work. But I don't see how it can."

Michael felt a twinge of guilt at her words. The truth was that as much as he liked Sandy, and as much as he wanted to be with her, most of his mental energy had been directed to freeing himself from Vasili and his Mafia buddies. The fact that he and Sandy would be together when it was all over had been a given in his mind and heart, but he'd put no thought at all into how to make it work.

He reached over and gave her a tight hug. "Sandy, I really don't know. I don't know what's going to happen to me." With a million dollars in his bank account, did he really need to go home to his job? It had been a while since he'd even thought about the money, and for the first time he began to seriously consider keeping it. Sure he'd been tempted with the thought a time or two, but that had only been a daydream. But Dmitri had been very insistent that it was his. At his age, a million dollars wasn't likely enough to last him the rest of his life if he never worked again, but maybe it would be more than enough to help him get a new start, to make a new life possible. A life somewhere else, doing something else, with Sandy.

He drew back from her a bit, enough to be able to look into her eyes as he caressed her cheek. "Sandy, we'll make it work. I'll make it work. I promise."

She smiled and kissed him.

* * *

Vasili was having a sleepless night, but he wasn't worried about it in the least. In fact, he was enjoying it as he lay there in bed. He had turned on the TV when he couldn't fall asleep and found a movie that he'd already seen with a Ukrainian soundtrack dubbed in to replace the original English one. There was enough action in it to justify him watching it again, even in English, but it only held half his attention. The rest of it was absorbed with the events of the evening and the possibilities of the future.

Maxim had slowly worked away at the vodka, Vasili recalled, until the bottle was empty, then had continued to eye it wistfully as he'd talked. His thoughts, which Vasili had not bothered to interrupt, kept wandering back and forth. At times he would go on about not being there when Anton needed him most, at others pathetic pleas for Vasili to understand that Anton had wanted to go alone. It was not his fault, was it? Vasili had assured him that it was not, though Maxim had not seemed to hear his words of agreement; he was awash in a sea of vodka-influenced thoughts.

Finally, when the bottle had been long since drained, he had sat back and vowed to avenge Anton's death, his fist repeatedly pounding the table as he raved about all the ways in which he would inflict unbearable pain upon Dmitri until he had fully paid for what he had done and coughed up every single kopek of what he had taken. He would be begging to return the money by the time Maxim was done with him. He'd do the same to the Canadian as well, they were in this together after all, weren't they? Yes, they would pay for everything they had done, and Maxim would be the one to collect the debt.

"Vasili," he had said as his tirade had ended. "I want to be the one to kill them; both of them."

"There is a woman involved too, I think," Vasili informed him. "I saw her with the Canadian, but I do not know what part she is playing in all this."

"Then I will kill her too. I will kill everyone involved. They must all pay. Vasili, it must be me that kills them, no one else." Vasili managed to keep from smiling and to appear somewhat hesitant as he'd promised the forlorn bodyguard that he would indeed be the one to kill them all.

Upon securing that promise from Vasili he'd stumbled to the couch and passed out. He was still sleeping there and was emitting a steady stream of incredibly loud snores. Having the door to his bedroom closed and the TV turned on drowned out all but the loudest of them.

It had been a good day all round for Vasili. He knew for a fact that they were still on the island, and he knew what they were driving, as did the rest of his team. He had some new and very useful muscle, not to mention some personal protection in the form of Maxim. He had been a bit hasty to judge the man, hadn't he? If Anton had been foolish enough to try to kill him without bringing some extra help along, well, he deserved what Vasili had done to him. Now, Maxim's loyalty had been transferred to his new boss. As a bonus, Maxim wanted to be the one to get his hands dirty by torturing and killing Dmitri, Michael, and the woman; such acts really should be beneath Vasili now; they were best left to others.

As he thought about it, he decided that it might be a good idea to start with the woman first. He could have her tortured in front of the two men, give them the false impression that she would be spared if they returned the money. Even if she knew nothing, the two men would be willing to do anything to protect her from harm, and that would make the whole process much faster and easier. Yes, things were coming together. The breaks were starting to go his way now that he had finally assumed his rightful position and could call all the shots himself.

He got out of bed and went to the mini-bar, gathering a handful of snacks to bring back to bed. The best part of the movie was coming up.

* * *

Despite spending much of the night watching movies in English, Vasili woke early, eager to renew his search for Dmitri and his friends. Now that he knew what vehicle they were driving, and possibly the areas of the island that they frequented, he was full of hope that they would be in his custody very soon. He had to rouse the sleeping Maxim, who struggled to sit upright, rubbing first his eyes, then very gingerly, his temples.

"It is time for us to get going, Maxim," Vasili informed him in a voice that was much too loud and cheerful for the ailing Maxim. "This may be the day we finally catch Dimitri and avenge Anton," he added, totally oblivious to his companion's discomfort.

Maxim, unable to respond with words, nodded his head gently, but even that small movement brought a fresh wave of pain and nausea. Raiding Vasili's well-stocked mini-bar when he'd awakened in the wee hours of the morning was not as good an idea as it had seemed at the time. "But before we go, we will have breakfast," Vasili informed him as he opened the door, "They feed you like kings here."

Maxim raised himself unsteadily from the couch with a low groan, blinking rapidly from the exertion, and managed to follow Vasili to the dining room. Vasili walked along the serving tables, picking and choosing from an assortment of hot and cold food, piling his plate high with food both familiar and strange to him. Maxim shuffled sullenly behind him, eyeing the food wistfully, but knowing what a mistake it would be to attempt such a feast after the night he'd just had. He finally selected a glass of tomato juice and joined Vasili, who was already digging happily into what would be only his first plateful of the morning. As he savoured each mouthful, he hummed happily to himself. His earlier fears that Dmitri or Michael might have reported him to the police were forgotten; this was a new day, and one that held great promise.

"I think," he said, taking a sip of his coffee, "that after breakfast we will take a drive. You need to learn the layout of the island, and we may get lucky and spot that white van again. We don't know yet where Dmitri is hiding out, but if we can spot the van and follow it to where he's staying, I think we just might be able to get to them when they are not out somewhere in public." It was too bad that before his death Anton had not provided him with some proper weapons. It would have been impossible to bring them in on the plane, and he had no contacts in this part of the world, as Anton apparently had. But they would make do. They'd stop at a store somewhere and pick up some fishing gear, including a couple of knives. He might not be able to speak English, but he could read a price tag and store owners rarely had any trouble understanding the language of cash.

Maxim grunted in acknowledgement of his instructions, and for the first time Vasili understood just how much discomfort he was in. He wasn't likely to be of much use as a driver for a while, but no matter. Vasili would drive himself, they'd enjoy the sights, get to better know the lay of the land, and maybe, just maybe, catch up with Dmitri's gang. He gave Maxim yet another hearty clap on the back.

"Let's go, it is time to finish this job." Together they headed for the parking lot and climbed into Vasili's little red car. He'd start by retracing the route Michael had led him on the previous day. The odds were small he'd see them again, but it was a starting point.

* * *

"You have the phone all set, right?"

"Yep, it's all set and fully charged."

Michael felt a bit foolish asking yet again, but the butterflies in his stomach wouldn't let him relax. This had to go off perfectly and so he was double and triple checking everything. He didn't want to take any more of a risk than they already were. "You've got both Dmitri and Vasili programmed in, right?"

Sandy held up the phone and waved it at him. "Yep, still there!"

She found it a bit creepy to be carrying the phone of a murdered man, as if it was somehow tainted, or even haunted, by the violence that had ended its owner's life. She still saw the entire fight in vivid detail every time she thought about it, and she doubted she'd ever forget the sounds of Anton's last few laboured breaths. She also wondered if it was possible that someone might be able to track her position through the phone. The whole point of today's operation was to be spotted, but on their terms

"I still wish Vasili hadn't seen us in the van, if he recognizes us too soon, we might lose some valuable time." Michael wasn't trying to make the mission sound doomed from the start, but this is not the way he'd originally planned for it to go. He wondered if it was time to let Sandy in on one more part of the plan that he hadn't mentioned yet, the fact that he wanted to drop her off somewhere if they did find Vasili. He didn't want to put her in any more danger, so it would be best if she wasn't there when Dmitri and Vasili finally met. He had no doubt she'd object to that part of the plan, so he decided to wait for later to mention it.

"We'll have to make sure he doesn't see us until Dmitri is at the clearing," Sandy agreed.

He and Sandy were planning to hang out at Vasili's hotel, hoping to catch sight of him. Once they did, they were to let Dmitri know so that they could head for the clearing he'd selected. Once he was in place, they would allow Vasili to spot them, hoping he'd chase them into an ambush. The fact that he knew about the van meant he would have an easy time following them. Dmitri thought that would work in their favour. The problem was if Vasili saw the van in the parking lot before they could locate him then he'd know they were there. If he called the rest of his team in, Michael and Sandy would be facing all of them alone.

Dmitri was insistent that Michael and Sandy be in the van while being chased as it would be much easier for Vasili to follow it, so it had been decided that he would wait nearby with the van while they took his truck to the hotel. When they'd located Vasili, they'd call him and he'd drive there in the van, then take the truck to the clearing leaving them the van.

Michael agreed that they could not leave the van unattended right under Vasili's nose, he had no wish to risk being spotted too soon, but had argued that they should just use the truck and not bother swapping out the vehicles. Vasili might see Dmitri making the swap, Michael had argued. But Dmitri had been insistent. Vasili might become suspicious if he were to spot them driving two different vehicles. Besides, if everything went according to plan, they'd have Vasili under surveillance the whole time and could warn Dmitri off if they thought there was any chance of him being spotted as he switched vehicles. That was just too big an 'if' for Michael's liking. So far nothing seemed to have gone according to plan. Not since last summer.

"Okay, here we are." Michael announced as he turned into the parking lot. Sandy caught his tone and didn't bother responding. It would have been easy to either agree or make some snappy comment about how obvious his observation was, but what he was really saying was, 'There's no turning back now.'

He found a spot that he wouldn't have to back out of, as close to the exit as he could. That should make for a fast get away, he hoped. He rolled up the window and pocketed the keys. He was tempted to leave the doors unlocked to make it an even quicker getaway, but then remembered that he wouldn't be leaving in it anyways.

"Text Dmitri," he told Sandy, "tell him to park facing the road, and to leave the doors unlocked."

He reached back into his pocket and made sure that he had keys for both the van and the truck as Sandy typed out the message. She was much better and faster at texting than Dmitri was, and they had to wait a while for his reply to come back.

After a minute or two the phone emitted a soft buzzing noise. "He says he's ready and he'll leave the van in a good place for a quick getaway."

"Okay," Michael said as he reached for the door latch. "Here goes everything."

"Don't worry," Sandy announced, hoping her voice conveyed more confidence than she felt, "I've got your back."

"Thanks." Michael's smile was weak but genuine.

He didn't think to look for Vasili's red car in the lot, and had no way of knowing that they'd missed Vasili and Maxim by less than five minutes.

* * *

CHAPTER NINETEEN

As Michael and Sandy unpacked a few items from the back of the truck to make themselves appear as much like tourists as possible, Youlya was staring at the screen of her new laptop and sighing. She'd managed to access her remaining funds and was now staying at one of the finest hotels in Minsk. The sigh was because she was looking once again at her bank balance. Had she stopped to consider it, she'd have realized that she still had much more money than she had ever dreamed she'd have when she'd worked as Yuri Stepanovich's secretary, but it was only about half of what she'd brought with her from Culebra. She had thought, back then, that she'd be fair to Dmitri, but maybe she should have just taken all of it. He was likely dead by now anyways, and Anton now had all his money in addition to what he'd taken from her. If Dmitri was still alive then he had his silly little resort and could earn all the money he'd ever need running that.

She gazed about the room, thinking that she really did deserve this kind of life. If Dmitri had not given away so much of their money, she'd have that much more to enjoy. Oh well, it just meant she'd have to be careful with what she had, or maybe find someone to help her with investing it wisely so it would last her that much longer. The idea of buying a business was absolutely out of the question; she would never work another day in her life!

With yet another deep sigh she switched off the laptop and stowed it carefully back in its case. She still had no idea of where she would go yet, but then her new passport would not be ready for a few days anyway. She'd been assured it would pass the scrutiny of even the best border guards, so it should be able to take her anywhere.

In her mind's eye she studied a map of her immediate surroundings. She could speak Russian, Ukrainian, and English, but English would likely be the most useful of the three. She had no desire to go to Russia, and returning to Ukraine was absolutely out of the question as long as Anton, Vasili, and the rest of them were alive.

Returning to Dmitri was also out of the question. She had no desire to live the way he wanted to live. What a shame that he had changed so much. If only he'd kept his own desire for a wealthy and carefree life. One free of the Mafia to be sure, but which allowed them to fully enjoy what he had brought with him.

She shook her head as she considered Great Britain. It had never really appealed to her, but then there were enough English speakers scattered throughout western Europe that she could surely find somewhere suitable. Perhaps even someone suitable. A rich playboy in the south of France? That was a possibility. Well, she'd figure that all out once she had her passport. It was time for bed.

* * *

The setting was ideal, and the weather was perfect, but neither of them could enjoy the beautiful stretch of tropical shoreline. On the odd occasion when they bothered to pay attention to the surroundings, they could readily acknowledge its beauty, and they hadn't been here long enough to grow accustomed to the palm trees and the warmth of the sun, but there were other things on their minds. So, while they might look like any other couple on the beach, they were anything but relaxed.

"I don't see him," Sandy grumped, "I don't even see anyone that looks vaguely Ukrainian."

"What about anyone that looks like a member of an organized crime gang?" Michael asked. Sandy flicked a handful of sand in his direction. "Hey, watch it!" he grinned back, "That sand will block the sun. You're gonna ruin my tan."

"More like keep you from getting sunburned," she laughed.

"No, I think this umbrella will prevent either of those things from happening," Michael replied, glancing up at the bright red umbrella that was sheltering them from the full force of the sun. "I just wish it would block the heat too. I'd kill for a few minutes in the water."

"Poor choice of words," Sandy said, as her thoughts returned to the reason they were here. "But, yeah, a swim would be nice. Just our luck though, Vasili would show up the minute we decided to go in."

"Half of me can't wait till he shows up ..." Michael started to say.

"Let me guess, the other half hopes he doesn't." Michael nodded as she finished his sentence.

They were both silent for a few minutes, scanning the crowds and watching the path that led up to the doors of the hotel. "I wish we knew which room he was staying in," Michael lamented in frustration.

"They don't give out room numbers anymore, at least not at most hotels."

"No, but I bet Juan could find out. I think he's related to everyone who works at every resort on the island."

"He probably could," she agreed. "But then what would you do? Go and knock on his door so he can chase you down the hallway?"

"It might beat sitting out here in the sun all day. Sandy, I am sorry I ruined your holiday like this. You could be off somewhere having fun right now."

"Stop apologizing, I'm where I want to be," she replied, and Michael wished she wasn't wearing the sunglasses. He wanted to be able to read the look in her eyes as she spoke those words. "Why don't you go get us something to eat? It's way past lunch time. I'll make sure to stay out of sight if he shows up."

***

At that moment Vasili and Maxim were enjoying lunch at a restaurant not all that far from the police station. It was a seafood place, which Vasili was enjoying immensely. He'd never enjoyed fish so fresh before. Maxim on the other hand, never a big fan of seafood, found the smell almost too much too take. He managed to make do with a salad, as well as some fish and chips. Without the fish.

"When we find them, we follow them to where they are staying right?"

Vasili nodded at Maxim's question. "I'm sure wherever they are staying it will be somewhere secluded, so we shouldn't have to worry about witnesses."

"We can deal with witnesses," Maxim grunted back.

"Not here, Maxim, we are not back home. That could cause too many questions. If there is anyone else around we will have to be careful. But I don't think we will need to worry about that." Maxim shrugged as if he didn't care one way or the other. All he wanted was vengeance. They'd deal with the consequences later.

"We haven't had much luck yet," Vasili thought out loud as he explored the morsels on his plate with a fork, trying to decide what to sample next. "I think this afternoon we should try some of the side roads, see if we can spot the van in some secluded spot. It was luck that I saw them the first time. I don't think we're likely to just stumble on them again, but it is a small island. They're here somewhere."

Maxim gave a grunt of agreement, resisting the urge to tell Vasili to hurry up and finish his meal. It was time to get back to work.

***

Sandy gathered up the remnants and wrappers from their lunch and tossed them into a nearby garbage can before settling back under the umbrella with Michael. "This is getting boring, and we might be missing him somewhere in the crowd." She surveyed the crowded beach once more. "Let's take a walk around the place. You go that way and I'll go this way; we'll meet back here."

"But we've got a direct line back to the parking lot from here. If we spot him while we're walking around, he might end up between us and the van."

"We're supposed to let Dmitri know if we spot him first, not make a beeline for the parking lot."

"If he sees us before we see him, we're leaving that very second. We can let Dmitri know later. He loves planning on the fly. Besides, this whole vehicle swap will slow us down too much. We should just stick with the truck."

"We'll do that if we have to," she brushed it aside as unimportant. "Besides, what's he gonna do right here on the beach with this many witnesses?"

"He murdered a guy just a few hundred meters down that path."

Sandy shuddered as the whole fight replayed itself in her memory yet again. "Look, that was pretty gruesome, but it's not like Vasili started it. It was self-defence."

"Okay, but only once around the beach, then we meet back here. Don't do anything to let him know you recognize him if you do see him, and if he tries anything, yell at the top of your lungs."

"Okay, I promise."

They both made a slow patrol around the beach, pretending to admire the scenery, but when they met back under the umbrella neither of them had anything to report. The lack of results was both reassuring and disappointing.

* * *

As the sun began to set, Vasili and Maxim decided to head back to the resort. Maxim had been keeping track of the areas throughout the day's search, marking them carefully on Vasili's map. They had checked in with the other teams several times and had even managed to coordinate a revolving search pattern so that no two teams were in the same area at the same time. There had been several false alarms, but the vans they'd spotted had all been delivery or commercial vehicles from various island businesses. No plain white vans.

The lack of results was disappointing, but not discouraging. With the number of men he had scouring the island for the white van, Vasili knew that his three targets could not remain hidden forever. They pulled into the parking lot about half an hour after Sandy and Michael had given up for the day and returned to the safe house.

Dmitri too had returned to the safe house. After parking and concealing the van, he'd removed the magnetic signs he'd 'borrowed' from a local delivery company. He'd return them, at night of course, when he was done with them. It was amazing how a couple of large stickers advertising a local seafood joint could make it look like an entirely different vehicle.

Chapter Twenty

Michael awoke to the same mix of dread and anticipation that had hung over him the previous day while keeping watch on the beach with Sandy. He stretched and rolled out of bed with the vague feeling that something wasn't quite right. At first, he wrote it off to a case of nerves and scolded himself, this whole plan had been his idea after all. He was just nervous about putting the plan into action. But something still felt wrong.

He was still trying to figure it out when a loud explosion rocked the house. He had a sock half on and the sound shook him so badly he tripped and tumbled back onto the bed, expecting a wave of Vasili's men to burst into his room with drawn weapons. The second clap of thunder reigned in his imagination. That was what had been bothering him, the sound of rain against the roof and sides of the house. The volume of the rain doubled as the peals of thunder echoed back at him from every direction.

Drawing back the blinds, he could see that the sky was a uniform dull grey, and a driving rain was hammering against the glass. A third, and almost immediately a fourth, bolt of lightning flashed across the sky and he knew that their plan was on hold for the day. The storm looked as if it was here to stay. He finished dressing and headed for the kitchen where Dmitri already had water boiling to make their morning tea.

"'Mornin'" Michael mumbled, grabbing a mug and selecting a teabag from Dmitri's collection. "Looks like the mission's off for today."

Dmitri was about to reply when a sleepy-looking Sandy emerged from her room, nodding a wordless greeting to each of them while making her own selection of tea. She was almost getting used to starting her day without coffee. Dmitri added hot water to the mugs and they settled around the table where this morning's breakfast would be cold cereal and fruit.

"Operation's on hold today," Michael said, repeating his assessment of the day to Sandy as he selected a mango.

"Yes," Dmitri agreed looking out the window. "Best to wait for better weather." He didn't seem at all concerned about it one way or the other, which frustrated Michael. He wanted everyone else to feel as upset about it as he did.

* * *

Vasili, on the other hand, was greeting the new day with almost gleeful anticipation. True, yesterday's search had been fruitless, but once he'd manage to coordinate his team's search they had, as far as he was concerned, narrowed down their search area. He'd had the entire team meet with him earlier that morning, pouring over maps and assigning each pair of men specific areas to search.

"Look everywhere," had been his final order. "Check every side street, every country road, every parking lot and every resort. If you're asked what you're doing on private property, then tell them you are lost. Search every centimetre of this island and call me the second you find them!" Today was the day. He could feel it.

After the team had been dispatched, he and Maxim went to the dining room to enjoy a leisurely breakfast before setting out to cover their assigned portion of the island. This time Maxim was feeling much better and easily managed to out-do Vasili in quantity, making several visits back to the buffet tables, though he simply could not understand how his boss could stand to drink coffee. Maybe it was because the tea in this part of the world was not as good as it was back home? Still, poor tea was better than good coffee, in his opinion.

"This is miserable weather for paradise," Maxim stated as he settled back in his chair, already wondering if he was going to regret that last plateful.

"I think it could work in our favour," Vasili countered. "They might just decide to stay inside for the day. If they do, they won't be moving around and that might make it easier to find them.

Maxim shrugged, Vasili might be right, he just hoped they'd find them soon. He had a personal score to settle quite apart from the money Vasili was obsessed with. The sooner he got his hands on Dmitri and his gang, the better.

* * *

Dmitri's calm demeanor helped to settle Michael and Sandy down somewhat. From all appearances he was simply an average working man enjoying an unexpected day off. All his cares and concerns had been left at the office, not to be picked up again until the next day. After finishing a leisurely and relaxed breakfast, he'd led them in cleaning up the kitchen and then turned on the television.

"Great, more cricket!" Michael commented with a roll of his eyes that only Sandy caught. It was all she could do to keep from laughing, and only refrained from doing so out of respect for Dmitri's love of the game.

The two of them scoured the house for anything that might keep them occupied but found nothing other than a badly out of date magazine that wasn't worth more than a few minutes of perusing. There were no games, newspapers with crossword puzzles, not even a deck of cards. Dmitri had been too thorough in his housekeeping.

The time they'd spent in their search didn't put too much of a dent in the day, and they finally decided to sit out on the covered porch and watch the storm. They were sheltered from the worst of the wind on that side of the house, and the cooler air was actually a relief after the heat of the past few days. Michael doubted he could ever get used to it.

They dragged two chairs together and sat there, holding hands, and talking about their lives back home, their hopes for the future, and what they were going to do once they had their lives back. Michael found the thunderstorm strangely relaxing and was enjoying it, along with Sandy's company.

"You know," he said after a particularly violent clap of thunder that they had felt as well as heard, "For once I'm glad I'm not up there flying."

Sandy nodded, "I've been up in some pretty bad storms. It's not often that I wish I was on the ground when I'm working, but there have been a couple of times."

Michael turned to her. "Want to tell me about some of those times?"

"Sure," she said with a bright smile. They swapped flying stories until Dmitri stuck his head out to announce that it was lunch time.

After lunch they decided that they'd had enough of sitting out in the rain and joined Dmitri at the television set. Much to Michael's surprise not only was he still watching cricket, but apparently it was the same game. Dmitri's explanation that it was a test match that could go on for three days or more only made matters worse; but with nothing better to do he sat down and did his best to try to comprehend what was going on.

* * *

Vasili's enthusiasm had held out all morning as he and Maxim explored every street and alley, they could find in their search area. He'd congratulated himself on being able to order lunch at the finest restaurant he could find. Even if he couldn't speak English, he'd still managed to make himself understood by the waiter. He'd savoured every succulent mouthful, oblivious to Maxim's growing resentment at how he was enjoying all the finer things in life while, in Maxim's opinion, the priority should be to avenge Anton. True, Anton had lived the same way, but he had earned it by way of his status in the organization. Vasili, on the other hand, seemed to be taking advantage of the fact that he was the ranking member here and had no immediate superior to answer to. If Anton were still here, he would have kept Vasili in his place.

Unfortunately for Vasili, lunch had been the high point of the day. The storm continued unabated and if anything increased in fury. That, coupled with a total lack of success by the whole team, took the edge off his anticipation. He didn't really notice that the afternoon was about to turn into evening as they'd seen no trace of the sun all day. The sky just turned a darker and darker shade of grey until it became too dark to see much of anything.

Finally, the two of them decided to give up for the day and return to the hotel.

'Maybe tomorrow' was the sentiment in both camps.

* * *

A full day of inactivity had left Michael tired and ready to turn in early, but then he'd been unable to find sleep. He'd spent most of the night tossing and turning, reliving the whole nightmare from the moment he'd boarded that ill-fated flight to Athens. When he'd reached the present, he spent the rest of the night wondering if he was making the right decision, and how things would play out when they found Vasili, which might well be tomorrow. Make that later today, he thought with a glance at the alarm clock and a deep sigh. Then there was Sandy. Why did he have to meet her at this point in his life? Then again, she had stayed of her own free will, so maybe it would work out, somehow. If they came through this alive. Maybe he should just take her and fly her somewhere safe in the morning. Dmitri wouldn't mind if they did; he'd even be glad to get rid of them, or at least he'd say that he would be. Yeah, he'd just fly off somewhere. Why risk his future for a fight that wasn't his?

He rolled over and kicked the covers off his feet. He was too hot. No, he couldn't just fly home because this was his fight, or at least there were people like Vasili who thought that it was his fight; they'd never stop chasing him until this was settled. Then there was the reason he'd come back to Culebra in the first place. Dmitri was his friend and he shouldn't have to face this alone. It had nothing to do with the fact that Dmitri had tried to give him a million dollars, he was a friend, and that's what friends did for each other. Why was he still rehashing this when he'd settled it all long ago?

The whole time he lay there tossing and turning and debating, the rain beat incessantly on the roof and walls.

* * *

The seemingly eternal rain storm was not what had Vasili upset and bothered, and he still managed to enjoy the breakfast buffet, but the brief glimpse of the Canadian and the girl had given him hope that his quest was all but completed. Yesterday's fruitless search had drained that hope and now he felt just like he had last summer when time after time the two men had eluded him. He should not have let himself be scared off by the fact that they had parked at a police station. What had happened between himself and Anton was self-defence after all. He should have parked nearby and followed them when they left. Or he could have called in the others to follow them. Well, it was too late to second guess his decision now, but the next time he found them nothing would stop him. In addition to his pride, there were several million reasons to succeed.

"They can't hide forever," he said aloud, not sure if it was for his benefit, or for Maxim's.

* * *

Dmitri once again had the kettle boiling when Sandy and Michael emerged from their rooms, and once again Dmitri's lack of anxiety irked Michael in a way he could not quite understand. If their forced inactivity frustrated him and made him anxious and nervous, and made Sandy anxious and nervous, why couldn't Dmitri respect and validate their emotions by feeling the same way too? The peace Dmitri seemed to exude made him feel guilty for being anxious to get on with things, and that made him even angrier. What was he supposed to do, just sit and wait for the right opportunity?

He toyed sullenly with his food, poking and shoving the remaining pile of scrambled eggs around his plate. He gave an inward shrug. Maybe Dmitri was onto something, the trials and problems weren't obstacles to get past so you could live life, those events were life, and you were supposed to just live patiently in the moment. What was that old saying? Seize the day? But how do you seize a day when there are people out there that don't want to let you have a day? That didn't want to let you have any more days at all, for that matter. That was almost too deep a thought for a rainy morning, but maybe he should give it a shot. He scooped up the pile of eggs and finished them off.

"Well, what are we going to do today?" He did his best to make his voice neutral since he didn't feel at all enthusiastic about the day, but didn't want to sound like he was complaining either.

"The cricket match is starting up," Dmitri said with a glance at his watch, "It could even end today, and I want to see who wins." He pushed back from the table and took his tea cup with him to the couch where he turned on the television and settled in to watch the game.

"Let's do the dishes," Sandy said. "That way we can let our host enjoy his game."

Michael found himself readily agreeing and wondered if wanting to do the dishes with her meant something. Spending any time at all with her, no matter what they were doing, appealed to him. Even doing the dishes. "Afterwards we can sit out on the porch again," he suggested. "It is kind of peaceful watching the rain out there, even without the thunder storm to go along with it.

"Okay," she agreed, testing the temperature of the water. "If we get tired of that we can come back inside and watch the game with Dmitri."

"I don't know about that. If I spend any more time watching cricket, I might actually start to understand it!"

Though Vasili and his gang never really left his thoughts, he was able to enjoy the day, or at least enjoy it more than he had the previous day. That night, when he turned in to bed, he fell asleep almost immediately.

* * *

The next morning Michael woke early to the sun streaming in around the blinds, which were just a little to small for the window, this time he had to rebuke himself for wishing it was still raining. A day spent with Sandy and Dmitri was something to enjoy. No, he couldn't think that way, not yet. They had work to do today, work that had to be done before he could spend another day like yesterday.

He dressed and found that Sandy was already working on the breakfast Dmitri had prepared for them. He slid in beside her and peeled a banana as Dmitri dished up his plate at the stove. As the three of them worked on their breakfasts, they discussed their plan once more, making sure they had every detail worked out, or at least every detail they could control. Once they were face-to-face with Vasili, there was no telling how it would go, but Michael figured that there were three ways this might end. Either they would up in his custody, which would ultimately be a death sentence, or Vasili ended up dead. He really didn't like that idea either, not as much as he once had, but it was a real possibility. The third way, which he desperately hoped would work, was that they could throw enough of a scare into him that he'd leave and never come back. But was that just wishful thinking on his part? Even if they did scare him off, wouldn't he just return with an even larger force? If so, he could very well end up spending the rest of his life on the run. Yuri was dead and so was Anton. Was Vasili the last person left that still cared enough about the money to carry on the fight? His stomach told him that his breakfast wasn't sitting too well.

This time they left the dirty dishes on the table and headed out into a beautiful morning. Dmitri double checked that the magnetic signs were in place on the van, then asked Sandy to make sure that Anton's phone was fully charged. She was still a bit creeped out at the thought of using a dead man's phone, but knew it was part of the plan, maybe even an essential part of it.

When they were all satisfied that every detail they could possibly foresee had been covered, they stood together, looking at each other awkwardly. Though none of them were superstitious, it didn't feel right to wish each other good luck. It was Michael that finally gave a decisive nod. "Let's do it."

Dmitri boarded the van and pulled out first. Michael and Sandy climbed into the truck where Sandy leaned across and gave him a kiss on the cheek, but said nothing as he shifted into gear and followed the van out to the main road.

* * *

"Now I know what they mean when they say that something is no day at the beach," Sandy quipped as they approached the resort. Michael grunted an agreement but neither of them so much as smiled. Were they imagining it, or did the resort have a sinister aura about it? Though there wasn't a cloud in the sky, the sun seemed dimmer and weaker than it had back at the house.

Michael wheeled in and parked the truck facing the main road where Dmitri could easily see it when he drove in. It wasn't hard to find a suitable spot since everyone else parked as close to the entrance as possible. Just as he was about to shut off the engine Sandy poked his arm. "Michael, isn't that the same car that Vasili was driving when he followed us?" She was pointing at a small red car a few rows over.

"Could be," Michael said after studying it for a few seconds. "Most of these cars are rentals, there could be dozens of them." He wasn't trying to discount her observation; it did look the same. "If it is, he's still here. If he is still here, I just hope he doesn't hide in his room all day."

"It is the same car, I'm sure of it."

"Okay, then let's be very careful, we don't want him seeing us till we can let Dmitri know we've found him." Suddenly he found himself agreeing with Dmitri. It was a good thing they weren't in the van right now. If Vasili came out he'd spot them instantly.

Sandy turned to look through the back window, scanning the parking lot which seemed to be deserted at the moment. "I can't see anyone at all, I think ..." Her heart skipped a beat and her mouth suddenly went dry. There he was, the man she'd seen commit murder! "Michael! I see him, he just walked out the front door!"

"Where's he headed?" It took all his will power not to turn and look for himself.

"He's headed for his car, I think, and he's not alone!"

"How many men are with him?"

"Just one, but he's huge."

Michael hesitated, wondering what to do now. The plan had been to see him first, when he was alone, and when they had time to coordinate everything with Dmitri. Should they slink down in their seats and hide?

"Are they carrying suitcases?"

"No."

Okay, so that means they're coming back. They could just find a spot on the beach, or even in the outdoor restaurant, and wait for them to return. Maybe he was going to drop the other guy off somewhere and come back alone.

"Michael, what do we do?"

Sandy's question needed an answer, and in a split second he made up his mind. "We grab the opportunity. Call Dmitri and tell him to forget the swap, he needs to get to the clearing now!"

As she punched Dmitri's number on Anton's phone, Michael shifted the still idling truck into gear and swung around in a big loop, squealing the tires to make sure he got their attention. He slowed down as he passed a few metres in front of Vasili and his companion. With a wave he yelled through his open window, "Hey! Vasili! Great day for a drive!"

Chapter Twenty-One

Even as Michael was yelling at Vasili, Sandy had Dmitri on the phone. "Dmitri, we found him, but he's not alone, there's someone else with him. Forget coming here, they're already chasing us, we'll meet you there!"

"What is happening?" He demanded.

"No time to explain, we'll see you there!" She hung up, fingers fumbling as she dialed Vasili. She felt the truck moving again and glanced back to see that Michael had pulled up to the parking lot exit, but he wasn't going anywhere just yet. Both of them had to fight the urge to get out of there as soon as possible; the whole point was to make sure that they brought Vasili with them. They wanted him to follow them, but just him, so that part of the plan was blown already. Well, she'd do her best to make sure that he didn't call in any more help.

As she looked back, she could see Vasili and Goliath sprinting towards their car and as she heard the call connect, she saw Vasili grabbing at his pocket to pull out his phone. He didn't break stride, as he took the call. "Da?" she heard.

"Zdrastwitya, Vasili," she said in as cheerful a voice as she could muster, "Kak deela?" She knew that she'd slaughtered the words and had just exhausted every word that Dmitri had taught her. She wondered if Vasili could even understand her, but that wasn't the point, was it?

* * *

"Hello, Vasili, how are you?" Vasili heard over the phone, but he couldn't recognize the voice and the heavy accent made the words almost impossible to understand. He'd expected it to be one of his men and was about to order whoever it was to head back to his hotel immediately, and to contact the rest of them. He reached into his pocket and clicked the button on the key fob to unlock the doors, climbing into the driver's seat and starting the engine. Maxim was barely inside and hadn't closed his door when Vasili hit the gas and sped off after the truck. He had them! But what was the phone call about?

"Who is this?" he demanded sharply.

* * *

"Kto eta?" came back the harsh reply.

"They're coming, let's go, let's go!" Michael hit the gas, peeling out of the parking lot, but turning left instead of right, cutting off several vehicles in the process and earning himself several angry blasts from the horns of the offended drivers.

"Where are you going?" You were supposed to go right!" Sandy was afraid that the plan was completely blown now and her phone call was momentarily forgotten.

"I have to give Dmitri time to get ahead of us. If we go straight there, he won't get there till after we do. Stay on that phone!"

"Right," she said in acknowledgment of both comments, and brought the phone back up to her ear.

"Kto eta?" Vasili demanded again. She didn't understand the words, but the tone made the question obvious enough.

"This is Sandy, nice to meet you, Vasili. We're going on a drive today, care to join us?" *That was a stupid thing to say*, she thought. *How do you carry on a conversation with someone in another language?* The phone went dead and she immediately hit redial.

* * *

Vasili didn't understand a single word spoken by whoever it was that had called him, and in frustration ended the call. He had to get hold of the rest of his team. He kept the phone in his hand as he wheeled onto the main road. "Don't lose sight of that truck," he barked at Maxim. There were several vehicles between himself and the Canadian and while it was unlikely they could turn off without him noticing it, he didn't dare take that chance. He was too close to blow it now.

As he accelerated, he kept one eye on the road and the other on his phone as he tried to scroll to his contact list, but the phone rang again. This time he looked at the call display. Anton!

"Dmitri!" he shouted angrily, but he answered it again, only to once more hear the lady's voice talking gibberish in his ear. He angrily stabbed the button to disconnect the call yet again.

* * *

"He keeps hanging up on me!" Sandy grumbled in mock agitation, hitting redial as soon as she heard the call disconnect.

"Told you he wasn't a very polite guy. You should have seen how he treated me last summer." He could almost feel the boots kicking at his back and stomach as he lay on that dusty Ukrainian street. It was payback time.

"There goes Dmitri." He saw the white van speed by in the opposite direction and hoped that Vasili was fixated on the truck. If he recognized the van and went after Dmitri it would really mess things up. He kept one eye on his rear-view mirror and felt a grim pleasure when Vasili shot past the van without even slowing down.

"Okay we got him. I'll go up to that next road and then turn around. Keep him on the phone, Sandy, we don't want any more company." He tried to sound more encouraging than commanding.

"I'm trying, but I don't think he likes talking to me."

* * *

Maxim had his eyes glued to the truck but wanted desperately

CHAPTER TWENTY-ONE

to know what was going on with Vasili and his phone calls. Every time his new boss hung-up, the phone rang again. "Someone keeps phoning me from Anton's phone," he finally blurted out in frustration. It had to be that woman in the truck with the Canadian, he'd finally concluded. Who else could possibly have that phone? He was about to give the phone to Maxim and tell him to call the team so that he could concentrate on following the truck. It was odd, though, they were making no attempt to lose him. It was almost like they wanted to be followed. For that matter, why had Michael Barrett yelled at him in the parking lot? Something was wrong here.

"But who would have his phone, and why?" Maxim demanded, eager for anything that might tell him exactly what had happened to his old boss.

"Dmitri would," he blurted out before realizing that he was on very dangerous ground. He could not have Maxim asking too many questions about Anton's death. If whoever did have the phone was able to tell Maxim anything about what had really happened that day, he could find himself suddenly outnumbered. Nor could he have Maxim learning that everyone else had known of Anton's death long before he had. He couldn't take that chance. Rather than ending the call and giving him the phone, he cursed and tossed the phone into the back seat.

"This Canadian is a coward; you should have seen him last summer in Anton's basement, he was practically in tears before we touched him. It is just him and Dmitri, and this girl. We can handle them ourselves."

"I get Dmitri" Maxim growled, which was just fine with Vasili.

* * *

"He didn't hang up this time," Sandy informed Michael. "The call is still active, but there's nothing but background noise."

"Stay on the line, make sure you call him back the second he hangs up!"

"Don't worry, I will. I think this is going to work." "I hope so, hang on." Michael cranked the wheel at the last possible second and with tires squealing in protest, swerved left into the entrance of a parking lot.

* * *

"He turned in there!" Maxim yelled, blocking Vasili's view with his arm as he pointed out Michael's vehicle.

"I see him!" Vasili yelled back, swatting his arm out of the way and pushing the brake pedal all the way to the floor, the steering wheel chattering as the anti-lock brakes kicked in. He just barely managed to swing into the lot behind them.

So, he was trying to shake them off after all. Was he just trying to lure him away from his hotel? Why? He didn't have time to think this through and that bothered him. But he couldn't lose them.

Michael kept the turn going to the left, then shot across the parking lot and back out onto the main road through another approach, completely ignoring the stop sign. Vasili raced after them as they reversed direction.

* * *

"He's still behind us, and he's still on the line."

Michael wondered for a moment if he should have her call Dmitri again and let him know they were headed his way, but no, they needed to keep that phone tied up to keep the odds as close to even as possible. Dmitri was the only one worth anything in a fight, there was no way Michael could handle Vasili, let alone that guy he had with him. Maybe this wasn't such a good idea after all. "Okay," he said after taking a moment to sort through his thoughts. "He's right behind us now, I can see him in the mirror. Good boy, Vasili, follow me."

"You sound like you're calling a dog," Sandy laughed despite herself.

"More like a wolf," Michael replied with a grimace, his knuckles white as he gripped the steering wheel. The traffic was thankfully very light. The last thing he wanted was to have to start weaving in and out of traffic on this narrow road, and he had to keep ahead of Vasili.

"What does he honestly think he's going to gain by chasing us? I mean, does he plan to run us off the road and kidnap us in full view of everyone?"

"I don't know what he's planning. He probably doesn't have a plan. He just saw us and he's going for it. I sure hope that works in our favour." He glanced in the mirror again; he was catching up to some slower traffic now and wondered if Vasili would try something, then he saw where they were and a grim smile crossed his lips. Vasili wasn't going to get that chance. "Here's our turn off. Hang on!" He jerked the wheel to the right as he down shifted, then accelerated again as he pulled onto the side road. There was no one ahead of them now.

"He's right with us," Sandy said, feeling both elation and fear that this part of the plan was working.

* * *

Dmitri arrived in the clearing at the end of the road and wheeled the van around to face the only road back out. Hopefully they wouldn't need to make a quick getaway, but he wanted to be prepared, just in case. He knew that Mikhail hoped for a happy ending, that they'd have a little talk with Vasili and explain that they just wanted to be left alone; but he knew better. There was only one possible way for this to end. Well, two really, but he didn't want to contemplate the second. He desperately wished that he knew what had changed. Who was with Vasili and why? Had Mikhail, in his haste to end things, jeopardized everything? He'd know soon enough; already he could hear revving engines in the distance as the two vehicles raced up the hill towards him.

* * *

Vasili was doing his best to stay as close to the truck as possible, but its suspension was much better suited to this road, which had deteriorated into two ruts as it wound through the trees and brush. Several times he lost sight of it and forced himself to push his foot closer to the floor to keep it in sight. There hadn't been any side roads branching off from this one yet, and it couldn't go on forever. He'd catch them eventually.

The trail ended without warning and he jammed on the brakes as he popped into a clearing to see the truck coming to an abrupt stop next to the van he'd just spent several days searching for. Beside it stood Dmitri.

* * *

"They're right behind us," Sandy announced in a shaky voice as Michael jerked to a stop beside Dmitri and the van.

"Here's where it gets interesting," he muttered, turning off the ignition and shoving the key into his pocket. His heart was racing and from the look on her face, Sandy's was too. He looked over at Dmitri who stood calmly, arms folded across his chest, his eyes locked on the little red car. He considered telling Sandy to stay in the truck, but depending on how this went down, she might be safer outside where she could make a run for it if things started going bad. He'd had to abandon his plan of trying to drop her off somewhere en route. The two of them got out of the truck and stood slightly behind Dmitri, as if he could somehow shield them from what was about to happen. They watched as Vasili and Goliath slowly emerged from the car, eyeing the trio warily.

"Good job, Vasili, you found us at last!" Dmitri said in Ukrainian, as if sincerely congratulating his foe on a job well done. Sandy looked at Michael, her expression clearly asking 'what is he saying?' All he could do was shrug. He had no idea either.

"I think you wanted to be found, my friend," Vasili answered back, standing beside the car door as he waited for Maxim to circle around and join him.

"I did. It is time to end this. I took nothing from you, Vasili, I owe you nothing. Two of your men are gone, Yuri is dead, Anton is dead ..."

"Dead at your hand, Dmitri!" Maxim cut him off angrily. "You will pay for his murder!"

"I did not kill Anton. Vasili killed him. I watched it happen."

"That's not true!" Maxim spat out the words, "You lie!" But he didn't sound quite so sure of himself now, and looked over at Vasili, waiting for him to confirm that Dmitri was indeed responsible for Anton's death.

"Why would I kill Anton? I had nothing to gain from it," Vasili tried to sound confident, more confident than he felt, hopefully the heat could explain away the sweat suddenly appearing on his brow. He couldn't afford to have Maxim turn against him now.

"You had everything to gain. You're no different than the rest of us, Vasili. We all tried to claw our way to the top, not caring who we hurt along the way. You stood to gain power and money. Anton was going to take that from you, wasn't he? He was going to take your life and you took his; with his own knife."

Maxim was listening to Dmitri's words, and looked at Vasili in confusion. One of these men had killed his boss and if he had to, he'd kill them both to avenge Anton.

"He's lying, Maxim." Vasili's voice had its hard, confident edge back, and Maxim felt a bit more sure of the situation. "Get him!"

The decision made for him, Maxim pulled out his knife, took a step toward Dmitri, and then froze in his tracks. Dmitri had pulled the gun from the waistband of his slacks and was pointing it casually at Maxim. "Get back in the car, drive to the airport, and go home. Never come back. I don't want to hurt you. You don't need to die for Vasili too. I just want to be left alone. That's all I ever wanted."

"Do you have the courage to fight me without that gun?" Maxim shot back angrily, throwing his knife to the ground and raising his fists.

"What's going on?" Michael demanded, unable to wait any longer.

"He thinks I killed Anton. Now he wants to kill me."

"Tell him you didn't!" Maxim was yelling something else now, his scowling face growing redder by the second.

"I did, he doesn't believe me."

"Well, do something!"

"Shall I shoot him? Shoot both of them?" Or maybe we should have a nice, long talk and work everything out."

"Well ..."

"There is only one way this can end, and I won't shoot an unarmed man, not even this one," Dmitri said to Michael as he hesitated. Then he handed him the gun. "Safety's on," he muttered softly.

Michael held the gun at arm's length, as if it were a living animal that had every intention of biting him. He watched in disbelief as Dmitri took a step towards Maxim, who now wore a broad smile. This wasn't how the plan was supposed to work!

"Don't kill him!" Vasili barked.

"I won't, I will just hurt him. Very badly!" Maxim closed the distance between the two men and launched a vicious punch that might have ended the fight had it connected. He'd always relied upon his size and strength to either end the fight quickly, or scare his opponents into submission. Dmitri was different, he was a street fighter, and as big as he was, he had learned early to fight smart. He easily avoided Maxim's well-telegraphed blow, wrapped the man up in his arms, and in seconds the two men were rolling around on the ground, which was exactly what Dmitri wanted. Beating this man certainly wasn't a given, but he had two advantages, he reminded himself as they wrestled, rolled and traded punches. Maxim's orders were not to kill him, but Dmitri had no such restrictions. Even if he did lose, though, Mikhail had the gun, should worst come to worst.

Michael and Sandy circled the two men as they fought, completely forgetting about Vasili as they watched the struggle. As far as Michael could tell neither of them seemed to have an advantage and he was now seriously regretting forcing this confrontation. It was supposed to be the three of them, and the gun, against Vasili; and the gun was supposed to be in Dmitri's hands, not his. He held it gingerly, being careful not to put his finger on the trigger. The last thing he needed was for it to go off accidentally and shoot one of his friends. Or himself. He couldn't even consider taking a shot at Maxim, not the way he and Dmitri kept trading places. Even if he could have risked it, he wasn't sure he had it in himself to pull the trigger.

Sandy circled with him, silently urging Dmitri on. What would happen if Dmitri lost? Michael had the gun, he could protect the two of them, couldn't he? He'd 'borrowed' an airplane and come up with the plan to force the confrontation with Vasili. He had what it took to finish it.

Maxim and Dmitri had all but forgotten about everyone else

during their desperate struggle. The observers heard the noise and could see the motion of arms and legs. They couldn't really tell who was getting the worst of it, but the two men now knew. Dmitri was breathing heavily, and sweat had soaked through his clothing, but he could tell that Maxim's strength was ebbing faster than his. His punches were too weak, and they were too close together for him to get the full advantage of his weight behind them. He had no idea how to fight like this. Another minute, perhaps two, and Maxim would be weak enough that he could get a better grip on him. He just needed an opening, the wrong reaction to one of his moves, and he'd be in position to choke him out, or break an arm or a leg. He could do this. He was going to win. All he needed was one more minute.

Maxim was beginning to fear that the struggle would end in Dmitri's favour as well. His strength and anger had failed him. He could feel his punches weakening and it was becoming more and more difficult to throw them. His frustration only made it worse.

In the heat of battle, everyone had forgotten Vasili, who couldn't understand why the much larger Maxim was struggling to finish off Dmitri. He'd expected the two men to trade no more than a few blows before Dmitri went down. He needed to turn this meeting to his advantage, and suddenly he saw his chance.

Michael and the girl were right next to him now, their full attention on the fight as they circled the struggling pair. He took a step back and waited for Michael to pass in front of him. A moment later the girl was in front of him. He gripped the knife firmly in his right hand as his left arm shot around her neck.

"Michael!" Sandy's scream caused his heart to skip a beat as he swung around, the fight forgotten the moment he saw her in Vasili's grip. He was so much taller than she was that her feet were kicking desperately several inches above the ground. Though she was beginning to have trouble breathing, the knife held to her throat was her biggest fear.

"Let her go!" Michael screamed, knowing that the man couldn't understand him, but maybe the gun he was holding in his trembling hands would translate for him. Even as he pointed it towards Vasili's head he knew that he had no idea where the bullet would go, he didn't dare pull the trigger.

"Drop the gun or I will kill her!" Vasili knew he couldn't really kill the girl; he'd lose his shield and his only bargaining chip. In fact, he realized, his best bet might be to leave now. With the girl. He smiled a twisted smile as he saw the gun wavering in the Canadian's grip before he dropped his arm to his side. He was saying something in what he recognized as a pleading tone. Good. This girl meant something to him, he'd be willing to bargain for her. Maybe the money. Maybe Dmitri. Maxim would just have to understand that this was for the best, the mission had to come first. Besides, they'd likely keep him alive to bargain for the girl.

A sudden yell of pain brought him back to the moment. The two men were on their knees now. Dmitri was behind Maxim and had his arms locked tightly about Maxim's neck. Only now did Dmitri have the luxury of turning to see why Sandy had screamed, and seeing her in Vasili's grip caused his face to turn as purple as Maxim's.

"Let her go!" He barked in Ukrainian, but his words had no more effect than Michael's had.

"I'm taking her with me," Vasili said, a nasty smirk on his face as he edged closer to his car. "I'm sure she and I can get very well acquainted. Unless you give me back the money. You have my phone number. Call me this afternoon and we will arrange a trade."

Michael looked desperately back and forth between the two

men as they spoke. He didn't need to understand the words, the sinking feeling deep in his gut told him what was happening. The knife was pressed so tightly to Sandy's throat that it had pierced her skin, blood was trickling down her neck. Why didn't Dmitri do something?

"Let her go!" Dmitri roared the words again, his eyes blazing in pure rage. As he shouted, he released his grip on Maxim's throat with his right arm and grabbed his head instead. With a single, swift movement he twisted the man's head sharply. There was a sickening crunching sound, Maxim's eyes went wide and then something inside them seemed to fade. Dmitri released his grip on the man and his body slumped forward.

Vasili nodded towards the body, his grip on Sandy and the knife as firm as ever, "Now you have nothing to bargain with except the money, Dmitri. Maxim was nothing. I can replace him today. Can you replace the girl?"

Dmitri was standing now, his eyes still blazing in helpless fury. Michael was trying to keep both men in his sight, the gun hanging forgotten in his right hand. Why wasn't Dmitri doing something, he asked himself again? He always had a plan, always found an opportunity just in time.

"I'm going now," Vasili said firmly. "Both of you back off. I won't hurt her if you do what I say. Call me in two hours." He lowered Sandy enough that her feet met the ground and began dragging her towards the car.

"What's he doing?" Michael demanded of Dmitri.

"He won't hurt her, Mikhail, he doesn't dare. We will get her back, I promise." He would get her back, he promised himself. Even if it took every cent he had left. Even if it took his own life.

"What do you mean get her back? He can't take her!" Michael

blinked back the tears in his eyes. Tears of rage, he told himself. "Do something, Dmitri!"

Vasili dropped his right hand, the one with the knife, towards the door handle, groping for it as he wondered how he was going to get the girl into the car without exposing himself. He'd set her in the driver's seat between himself and the window, he decided. He'd drive far enough to get out of sight and then worry about what to do with her. "Neither of you move," he warned. "Tell him not to move, Dmitri. If he twitches a finger, she is dead."

"Don't move, Mikhail," Dmitri repeated in English. He cursed himself for giving the gun away. The only way this could have ended well was with the death of both Maxim and Vasili. It had been foolish to try and end it with a fair fight, not against men that had never fought fair in their lives. Even if Mikhail had never spoken to him again, he should have shot them both the instant they stepped from the car.

Vasili turned slightly to find the door handle and as he did, Sandy felt his grip relax. She hadn't understood Vasili's words, and wouldn't have believed his promise even if she had. This man wanted to take her with him, and she wasn't going to let that happen. Not without a fight. As his attention was turned to the handle and the knife was lowered, she found her chance. Lashing back with her foot she dealt Vasili a sharp blow to the shin, but even before he could react to the kick she twisted in his grip and bit down as hard as she could on his forearm, hard enough to draw blood.

With a howl of pain, he dropped the knife and grabbed at his arm. Sandy's foot lashed at him again as she rolled out of his grasp, and she felt it connect with his knee as she fell to the ground. Unable to find her footing she started rolling and kept rolling.

The loss of his prisoner scared Vasili enough that he momentarily forgot his pain, kneeling to scoop up the knife he took a step towards Sandy, who'd already rolled past the rear bumper.

Michael watched in slow motion as if it were a scene in a movie. He'd remember every detail of it for the rest of his life: every blade of grass, the blood dripping from Vasili's arm, the anger in his eyes as he retrieved the knife and turned toward Sandy, and her screams as she rolled away. Even the glint of the sun and the reflection of the trees in the sideview mirror were burned into his memory.

The only thing he'd never remember would be raising the gun and bracing it with his left hand. He'd never remember pulling the trigger only to have nothing happen, but then somewhere in the back of his consciousness he recalled Dmitri's words. 'Safety's on.' He somehow found the lever and flicked it off.

He'd never remember any of that, but he'd never forget the explosion erupting from his hands as the gun discharged and everything flashed out of slow motion and into fast forward.

Vasili froze at the sound of the shot, certain for an instant that he'd been shot, but the bullet had gone wild, over the roof of the car. "Drop the gun! I will kill her," he barked at the Canadian, more angry than afraid now, and brandishing the knife threateningly. *This man didn't know the first thing about a gun, he had no idea how to aim*. Most people had no idea how hard it was to hit a target with a handgun.

But Michael moved slowly with careful, calculated movements, bringing the barrel of the gun back down and aiming it once more. It fired a second time. This time the rear passenger window exploded. The next shot ripped a hole in the door.

"Give me the money back," Vasili screamed defiantly. He'd had them! He'd won. He deserved it! He didn't realize he'd lost until the next shot rang out. The bullet caught him in the chest and knocked him back against the car. Michael had found the range now and two more shots rang out almost before the pain could register in Vasili's brain, both bullets finding their mark.

Michael kept pulling the trigger until the sharp, reassuring barks stopped and all he heard was an empty, disappointing click. He looked at the gun in confusion, but before he could figure out what had gone wrong, he felt Dmitri beside him, gingerly taking it from his grasp. He didn't see him flicking the safety back on before removing the clip and ensuring it was empty, then tucking it back into his waistband, because the realization of what he'd done was beginning to sink in.

He stared mutely at Vasili's body which had tumbled sideways as it slid down the side of the car. The man's eyes seemed to be fixed on his accusingly. He tried to look away but couldn't. He'd killed a man.

He started shaking, but still couldn't tear his eyes away from the lifeless form. Even when Sandy wrapped him tightly in her arms, even when she kissed him fiercely, he never blinked, he just looked into those eyes.

He felt Dmitri's heavy hand on his shoulder and heard him speak two words. "It's over." Only then did he blink, and leave his eyes closed. He gripped Sandy tightly and felt her sobbing. Then he started sobbing with her, feeling so many emotions wash over him that he didn't know which one to feel. Relief, regret, elation, fear of having to explain it all to the police.

"We need to leave. Now," Dmitri told them as gently as possible, but still managing to convey the urgency of his words to Sandy.

"I killed him," Michael said in a dull, far off voice.

"Yes, you did, Mikhail. You saved us all. It's over now."

"It's over?"

"Yes, Mikhail, this is the only way it could have ended, and you ended it. But we need to go, before anyone else comes."

"What are we going to tell the police?" There was a hint of panic in his voice. "It was self-defence, right?"

"We will tell them nothing."

"But ..." Michael started to object. This was against everything he'd been brought up to believe, but he could not find the words to explain to Dmitri that they had to tell the police everything.

"Can you drive?" Dmitri asked, shifting his gaze to Sandy. She was shaken, but not as badly as Michael, and he could see from her eyes that she understood what his question implied.

"I think so." She reached for her neck, there was a trickle of blood, but the cut wasn't deep enough to have caused any real harm. "Yes. Yes, I can drive." She blinked aside her thoughts and feelings, knowing she had to drive.

"Good, let's get Mikhail into the van. Follow me." He retrieved the keys from Michael's pocket, then the two of them helped steady him as they guided him towards the van, easing him gently into the passenger seat. Dmitri's mind was already working out everything he needed to do, including borrowing the boat again. He'd take the gun on a final cruise, a few miles off shore should more than suffice. There was much to do.

Vasili's team would disappear once word of his death became public. All those Ukrainian 'tourists' staying together while three murdered Ukrainians lay in the morgue? No, they wouldn't be wise to hang around any longer than the next available boat or plane off the island. Would anyone else be sent to look for them? He doubted it, but he'd be on his guard for months to come.

He returned to Vasili's body and pocketed his mobile phone. Once he'd seen to his friend's safety, he'd call up the rest of the men on the island and let them know what had happened. He doubted they'd still be here come nightfall.

"Are you sure you're okay to drive?"

"Yes, I'm fine," Sandy said in a firm, determined voice that convinced Dmitri that she really was.

Dmitri took a final look at his friend, who sat trembling and struggling to hold back his sobs.

"Good. Let's go."

Epilogue: Two Years Later

Michael took a moment to enjoy a long, luxurious stretch. There was a light breeze wafting through the open bedroom window bringing with it the intoxicating scent of bougainvillea. He swung his legs to the side of the bed and sat up, enjoying another stretch. As long as he might live here, he knew he'd never stop enjoying waking up like this. Sandy was still asleep, so he left her in bed while he took a quick shower and then went to start breakfast.

"Good morning, Captain Barrett," Sandy called from the bedroom as he began setting the table. "I'll be right out."

She smiled happily as she dressed. Her husband had slept peacefully through the night again. It had been weeks – no, come to think of it, more than two months now, since he'd last thrashed about in his sleep. The mumbled words were almost always unintelligible, but she knew exactly what was going on in his dreams. It still troubled her some nights too, but in a different way. All she could ever do was hold him, tell him that it was okay, that what he had done had been necessary. He'd had no other choice. He pretended to agree with her; maybe somewhere deep down he really did.

It struck her that it was a good thing that it bothered him. He wasn't a cold-blooded killer. If it didn't bother him, that would mean there really was something wrong. Maybe it bothered Dmitri too, but she was sure he'd never let on if it did. Besides, he had a different background and as nice a guy as he might be now, he looked at the events of that day in a completely different light.

As happy as she was over the peaceful nights he'd been enjoying for the past several months, she really doubted he was completely over it. Perhaps neither of them would ever be completely over it.

CHAPTER TWENTY-ONE

It was a part of them, a part of their shared history, and it always would be. The one good thing was that it had brought them together. Maybe all things really did work together for good.

Breakfast was waiting for her when she stepped into the kitchen. Michael stood by the counter wearing his black dress slacks and a crisp white shirt. As he turned, she could see the letters 'I.A.' and a stylized airplane emblazoned on the breast pocket.

"Today's the big day, isn't it?"

"Oh? It is? I didn't forget something did I? Is it our anniversary?" Michael looked at her in mock panic.

"You're not fooling me, honey," she smirked. "As if you'd forget your first flight as captain on a scheduled run in the Twin Otter."

"Well, it's only to San Juan and back, then I have a couple of scenic flights in the 206. You know, the other guys don't like those local flights in the small planes, but I really love them."

"That's because you love flying no matter what you're in." She smiled and gave him a kiss, then they sat down together at the table.

"Yep, I've got my dream job, that's for sure. In fact," he smiled at her, "I'd have to say I've got my dream life." Sandy beamed at him and they shared another kiss before digging into their breakfasts. He really did love flying and it didn't matter to him if he was flying a two-seater on a training flight, captaining a plane full of passengers to another island, or even flying as co-pilot or passenger. To him every flight was a thrill. She smiled as she recalled the first time he'd told her it was as if he was riding a magic carpet, openly defying the law of gravity. It was pure magic to him.

"Don't forget we're supposed to go to Dmitri and Carol's for that BBQ tonight. Dmitri's pretty good on that grill for a European."

"You mean for an ex-Mafia enforcer?" he grinned. "Don't worry, I'll be done in plenty of time to pick you up and get you to the party on time. Besides, Dmitri and I are gonna watch the cricket match during the BBQ; don't wanna miss that!"

Sandy smiled that conspiratorial grin that let him know he was either in for something really good, or was about to be asked for something really big. She was also chewing her bottom lip, so this must really be something.

"Oh-oh, what is it? What do you want me to do?"

"Well, I know we said we'd wait so we could tell everyone at once, but really, I don't think I can wait anymore. Can we tell them? Tonight?"

"Just Dmitri and Carol, right? No one else?"

"Of course, just them." But her sly grin told him that it might be leaked to a few other people before the night was through.

"Well, I guess we can tell them. But just them."

"Cross my heart!" She said with a look that was just too sincere to be believed.

He reached across and gently rubbed her stomach. "Then sure. Besides, a few more weeks and you won't have to tell anyone; they'll know anyways."

"I know," she was beaming again. "Before long you'll have your very own co-pilot." He was beaming too now, and didn't care if he looked like a fool for doing so. "I kinda miss being on active flight status, but I think I'm going to enjoy motherhood."

"You'll be great at it too. But you know, Jake's talking about a bigger twin. If he decides to go for it, we might need a few flight attendants. Do you think we could hire you away from the big airline?"

"Hmph," Sandy grunted in mock disgust. "If you start flying around the tropics with attractive young women, you'd better behave yourself, honey!"

"Don't worry, hon, only room for one stewardess in my personal life."

She swatted them for using what she called the 'S-word', but couldn't hide a smile.

Michael polished off the rest of his breakfast and took a few moments to savour the last of his coffee before pushing back from the table. "Okay, better not keep those passengers waiting or they might figure I'm not coming and fly off in the Twin Otter themselves."

"Well, we can't have that, can we?" She rose with him and followed him to the front door where he grabbed a flight bag full of maps, charts, and approach plates on his way out the door. As he stuffed the bag into the back of his Jeep, she spotted a few weeds in the lush flowerbed that ran along the driveway and bent over to pluck them.

"Okay," he said giving her a last kiss, "Wish me luck!"

"You don't need luck," she said. "You're the best pilot on the island."

"Don't tell my boss that," he retorted, but just then her phone rang.

"Hi Carol. No, we won't forget, we'll be there tonight. Can we bring anything?"

"See you tonight, Mrs. Barrett," he waved and climbed into the Jeep as she stood there watching him prepare to drive away, already deep into her conversation with Carol.

He settled into his seat, which was almost too hot to sit on, and started the engine. He rarely put the top up unless rain was in the forecast. Or if he and Sandy were going somewhere fancy and she didn't want a wind-blown effect. After suffering through enough brutal Canadian winters, and cool summers for that matter, he craved all the sun and fresh air he could get. Some days he joked that he needed oven mitts to hold onto the steering wheel, but he much preferred a natural breeze to air conditioning. though the house was also air-conditioned, he and Sandy both preferred open windows and a natural breeze on all but the hottest of days. Though as her pregnancy progressed, she might need the added chill of air conditioning, or so her mother warned. Both sets of parents had come for their wedding just over a year ago, and now both mothers were insisting on being there for the birth of the baby. They might need to look at a bigger place.

Well, it's not like they couldn't afford one. Dmitri had insisted that Michael keep the money he'd been wired. Much of it had been used to buy into Jake's flying business even before he'd been licensed commercially, but there was still a sizeable chunk left. On top of that he was making decent money as a pilot, thanks again to Dmitri. He'd insisted that he needed something to invest in and his sizeable capital injection had allowed *Island Air* to buy newer and bigger aircraft than Jake had ever dreamed of operating.

Even though Michael had bought his way into the business, it had been mutually agreed that he would work his way up the ladder just like any other line pilot. Of course, having Jake tutor him privately on all the intricacies of flying in a tropical environment, along with his keen desire to learn everything he could from a more experienced pilot, meant that his promotions had come rapidly.

Today's promotion was a big one. He was going to make his first flight as a captain on what he considered a big plane, the Twin Otter. He'd be taking a load of tourists back to San Juan on the first leg of their journey home to North America; a place he no longer considered home. The plane was big and shiny and worth much more than his personal investment in the company had been. He couldn't wait.

Business had improved so much that he and Jake were talking

about the possibilities of a bigger twin. That would allow them to expand operations and fly larger loads of passengers all over the Caribbean. He could end up being a real airline pilot for his own airline someday.

He wheeled the Jeep into his parking spot and walked into the office. A quick but thorough check of the weather showed there was nothing to worry about for this morning's flight, but there was the seemingly ever-present threat of showers and thundershowers for the afternoon flight. It would be a shame to have to cancel, but who wanted a plane full of scared and air-sick passengers? He'd keep an eye on the reports and make a final decision at the time, which was typical for pilots everywhere.

A few more minutes on the computer and his flight plan was filed. The next step was a discussion with the dispatcher and a double-check of the weight and balance calculations based on the passenger load he'd be carrying. After that came a step he always enjoyed, his chance to give the gleaming aircraft a thorough pre-flight inspection. After two years he still felt a thrill whenever he walked up to any airplane he was about to fly.

Satisfied that it was fully airworthy he walked into the passenger lounge, flight bag in hand to make himself look official.

"Good morning, folks, I'm Michael and I'll be your pilot on the flight to San Juan this morning. I've got the aircraft all ready to go and we'll be boarding in a few minutes." He gave them a huge reassuring, and very genuine smile. "It's going to be a great day to fly!"

ABOUT THE AUTHOR

Doug Morrison has made many trips to Ukraine, doing volunteer work with children and young adults. This book grew out of his love for the country and its people. He is a voracious reader but when the weather is good he can often be found cruising in his vintage muscle car. He lives with his family in central Alberta. This is his second book.